## 100 Reasons to Celebrate

We invite you to join us in celebrating Mills & Boon's centenary. Gerald Mills and Charles Boon founded Mills & Boon Limited in 1908 and opened offices in London's Covent Garden. Since then, Mills & Boon has become a hallmark for romantic fiction, recognised around the world.

We're proud of our 100 years of publishing excellence, which wouldn't have been achieved without the loyalty and enthusiasm of our authors and readers.

Each month there will be something new and exciting to mark the centenary, so watch for your favourite authors, captivating new stories, special limited edition collections...and more!

# Available in January 2008
# from Mills & Boon® Intrigue

## "I enjoyed your company."

Tony hadn't expected to say that when he'd opened his mouth. This was much too personal and revealing.

"So did I."

Whatever else Sasha might have said was interrupted by the insistent buzz emitted by his pager.

"You thought right, Henderson. Now call for backup." Tony closed his phone. His expression was sober. "They found another body."

She stared at him, her eyes widening in horror. "I'm coming with you."

"This isn't exactly according to the rules," Tony said.

"Neither is death," she answered softly.

She had him there, Tony thought. As he glanced in her direction, he wondered why he was really letting the doctor talk her way into coming along.

# Her Lawman on Call

## MARIE FERRARELLA

MILLS & BOON

*Pure reading pleasure*

*First published in Great Britain 2008*
*by Harlequin Mills & Boon Limited,*
*Eton House, 18-24 Paradise Road, Richmond, Surrey TW9 1SR*

© Marie Rydzynski-Ferrarella 2007

*ISBN: 978 0 263 85924 9*

46-0108

*Harlequin Mills & Boon policy is to use papers that are natural, renewable and recyclable products and made from wood grown in sustainable forests. The logging and manufacturing processes conform to the legal environmental regulations of the country of origin.*

*Printed and bound in Spain*
*by Litografia Rosés S.A., Barcelona*

## MARIE FERRARELLA

This *USA TODAY* bestselling and RITA®
Award-winning author has written over one
hundred and seventy-five books, some under
the name Marie Nicole. Her romances are
beloved by fans worldwide. Check out her
website at www.marieferrarella.com.

To Dr Tonia Marralle,
who delivered my children and gave me
an idea to work with.

# Chapter 1

There was something about a parking structure that always made her feel vulnerable. In broad daylight, she found them somewhat confusing. Most of the time she had too many things on her mind. Squeezing in that extra piece of information which identified where she had left her vehicle was usually one piece too many. Finding her car when that happened turned into an ordeal that lasted for what felt like an eternity.

At night, when there were fewer vehicles housed within this particular parking structure, she felt exposed, helpless.

And déjà vu haunted her.

It was a completely irrational reaction, she was the first to acknowledge it as such. But it changed nothing.

She wanted to run, but chose to move slowly, re-tracing steps she'd taken thirteen hours ago, when her day at Patience Memorial Hospital had begun. The lighting down on this level was poor. One of the bulbs was out, leaving the resulting shadows to threaten one another.

The air felt heavy and clammy, much like the day had been. Typical New York City autumn, Sasha thought. She picked up her pace, making her way toward where she thought she remembered leaving her car, a small vintage Toyota that had seen more than a handful of design changes come and go.

Dr. Sasha Pulaski stripped off her sweater and slung it over her arm, stifling a yawn. She felt ex-hausted. By rights, she should have left for the apart-ment she shared with her two younger sisters more than two hours ago. She'd actually been on her way to the elevator when Angela had called out to her. Angela Rico was a nurse on the floor, but more than that, she was a friend. Angela told her that the young woman who'd given birth less than two hours ago had suddenly started hemorrhaging. Sasha doubled back quickly. It had taken her less time to cauterize the tiny broken vein than it had to calm down her patient, who was convinced she was going to die.

But eventually, she'd managed to get the situation under control. By the time she left, her patient was doing much better and was arguing with her husband about the name they had chosen for the baby. A name, Sasha gathered, her patient no longer liked.

She eased out of the room before her patient or her husband could ask her to weigh in on the matter. As she passed the nurses' station, she saw that Angela had left for the night. Probably in a hurry to see her little girl before she fell asleep, Sasha mused.

Once upon a time, she'd thought that was going to be her life, too. Until the unspeakable had happened.

She forced herself to think of something else. Anything else before the loneliness took her prisoner.

God, but she felt drained. If she was lucky, she could be sound asleep in less than an hour. Never mind food, she thought. The urge for food had come and gone without being satisfied, fading away as if it had never existed. Now all she wanted was just to commune with her pillow and a flat surface—any flat surface—for about six hours.

Not too much to ask, she thought. Unless you were an intern. Those days, mercifully, were behind her. And still in front of her two youngest sisters. Five doctors and soon-to-be-doctors in one family. Not bad for the offspring of immigrants who had come into this country with nothing more than the clothes on their backs, Sasha thought. She knew that her parents were both proud enough to burst.

A strange popping noise sounded in the distance, breaking her train of thought. Instantly, Sasha stiffened, listening. Holding her breath. Memories suddenly began assaulting her.

One hand was clenched at her side, the other held tightly onto the purse strap slung over her shoulder.

She willed herself to relax. More than likely, it was just someone from the hospital getting their car and going home.

Or maybe it was one of the security guards, accidentally stepping on something on the ground.

Several people had been robbed in and around the structure in the last six months and the hospital had beefed up security. There was supposed to be at least one guard, if not two, making the rounds in the structure at all times.

That still didn't make her feel all that safe. The hairs at the back of her neck felt as if they were standing at attention.

As she rounded the corner, heading toward where she hoped she had left her vehicle, Sasha dug into her purse. Not for her keys, but for the comforting shape of the small can of Mace her father, Josef Pulaski, a retired NYPD police officer, insisted that she and her sisters carry with them at all times. Josef fiercely loved his adopted country, but he had no illusions about the safety of the streets, not where his girls were concerned.

Her fingers tightened around the small dispenser just as she saw a short, squat man up ahead. He had a mop of white hair, a kindly face and, even in his uniform, looked as if he could be a stand-in for a mall Santa Claus.

The security guard, she realized, her fingers growing lax. She'd seen him around and even exchanged a few words with him on occasion. He was retired, with no family. Being a guard gave him something to do, a reason to get up each day he had said.

The next moment, her relief began to slip away. The guard was looking down at something on the ground. There was a deep frown on his face and his body was rigid, as if frozen in place.

Sasha picked up her pace. "Mr. Stevens?" she called out. "Is something wrong?"

His head jerked in her direction. He looked startled to see her. Or was that horror on his face?

Before she could ask him any more questions, Sasha saw what had robbed him of his speech. The body of a woman lay beside a car. Blood was pooling beneath her head, straying toward her frayed tan trench coat. A look of surprise was forever frozen on her pretty bronze features.

Recognition was immediate. A scream, wide and thick, lodged itself in Sasha's throat as she struggled not to release it.

Angela.

Horror vibrated through Sasha's very being.

How?

Why?

She wasn't sure if she'd only thought the questions or if she'd actually said them out loud until Walter Stevens answered her.

"I don't know. I just found her like this. I think she's dead," he added hoarsely. Walter's watery eyes looked at her helplessly, as if he was waiting for her to do something about that.

Sasha dropped to her knees, pressing her fingertips against Angela's neck, frantically searching for a pulse.

There was none.

"Call the police!" she ordered the hapless guard.

Tossing her sweater and her purse aside, Sasha began a round of CPR that she already knew in her heart was useless. But she had to try because, despite everything she had been through, despite Adam's death, she still believed in miracles.

But there were no miracles for Angela Rico tonight.

By the time Sasha rocked back on her heels, finally giving up her efforts to bring the maternity-ward nurse around, more than a few of the people who worked at the hospital had gathered around her, drawn by the sounds of approaching sirens and the security guard's frantic call for help.

The murmur of voices went in and out of her head. Everyone was horrified. Angela had been one of their own. Everyone had always liked her.

In a daze, hating that it had already been too late to help Angela before she'd even got there, Sasha looked down at her hands. They were covered in blood.

Just as they had been once before.

With almost superhuman effort, Sasha fought hard to keep the dark shadows of the past from smothering her. Exhausted, she made no such effort to curtail the tears that came to her eyes.

Detective Anthony Santini was not very happy about getting the call that roused him from a sound sleep upon the sofa where'd he'd collapsed earlier. Today was supposed to be his day off.

On days off, a man could do what he wanted and what Tony had wanted to do was court oblivion. Especially today of all days.

Because today was his third anniversary.

*Would* have been his third anniversary, he corrected tersely in his head. If Annie were alive.

But she wasn't.

Annie hadn't been numbered among the living for the last ten months and nineteen days and the hole her death had created in his life just kept on getting deeper and deeper instead of closing up the way that know-nothing police shrink had told him it would when their paths had crossed. Involuntarily on his part. He placed no faith in shrinks. No faith in anything now that Annie was gone. All he had left was his work.

On days alone, he needed something to dull the pain and nothing seemed to work except a few hard drinks.

But tonight, his attempts to trample down his memories had been shattered by the phone.

Tony'd initially cursed at it, but it wouldn't stop ringing. Not until he'd finally answered it. Captain Holloway was on the other end, asking him to check out the homicide at Patience Memorial Hospital. The captain'd had the good grace to apologize, saying that everyone else was either busy tonight, or out sick.

Tony had felt like calling in sick himself, given the way his head was throbbing. But now that his sleep had been summarily disrupted, he knew that he wouldn't be able to get back to it. The best he could hope for was tossing and turning the remainder of the night away. So he might as well lose himself in his work. It didn't ease the pain that haunted him night and day, but it did give him a reason to go on.

Sometimes.

Pulling into the parking structure from the street entrance, he drove down the winding path until he saw the crowd of people clustering together and staring at something on the ground. Tony parked his car to one side and got out.

The crowd, judging by the uniforms and lab coats, were all from the hospital. He hoped that they knew better than to trample the crime scene. Holloway wasn't here, but he'd sent in several patrolmen as well as Bart Henderson, a tall, strapping man with fading red hair and a handlebar moustache straight out of another era. The man should have retired years ago.

There were times, like now, that Tony saw himself in the man's ruddy face. It didn't improve his mood.

Moving forward, Tony saw the body on the ground first. And the pale woman with blood on her clothing second.

Something about the woman brought to mind a line from an old fairy tale. For a second, it eluded him, and then he remembered. It was the description of Snow White. Skin pale as snow, hair black as night.

It went on, but he couldn't remember the rest of the description. However, from what he could remember, the woman who was standing beside the body could have posed for the fairy-tale princess.

Tony took out his badge and held it up as he approached. The crowd parted, letting him through, some asking him questions he didn't bother answering.

"Detective Anthony Santini," he told the pale woman. "You were with her when she was killed?"

His tone indicated that he made no final assumptions, waiting for her to answer one way or another. His dark gray eyes took precise measure of her, looking for some kind of sign, a "tell" as the poker players called it, to show him whether she was lying.

The woman's voice was low, soft, but strong as she replied, "No. She was already shot when I saw her. Mr. Stevens was standing over her—he was the one who found her." She took a breath, as if trying to put that between herself and the memory. "I tried to revive her. I'm a doctor," she added belatedly.

Tony nodded, keeping his eyes on her face. "Then she was still alive when you came?" It didn't seem likely, given that the victim was shot in the middle of her forehead, but he played along, waiting to see what the woman would say. "Did she try to say anything?"

Sasha moved her head from side to side, still trying to come to terms with what had happened.

"There was no pulse," she told him, her voice devoid of emotion, as numb as she felt.

"But you still tried to revive her."

She couldn't tell if he was being sarcastic, or just pressing her for information. "Sometimes, you can bring them back," she replied quietly.

The hurt was beginning to burrow its way into her. Death was a terrible, terrible thing. In her head, she could still hear Angela's voice.

*I'll see you Friday,* Angela had said.

Except now, she wouldn't, Sasha thought. Who was going to tell Angela's little girl her mother wasn't going to be coming home anymore?

"But this wasn't one of those times," she heard the detective saying.

Sasha looked at him sharply. But there was no humor, no sarcastic twist to his mouth. After a moment, she shook her head.

"No," she whispered more to herself than to the tall, dark-haired detective with the attitude, "this wasn't one of those times."

The woman looked, he thought, genuinely shaken up and he wondered why. Was she close to the victim? Did she know more than she was saying? Like the popular cult icon from a few years ago, Fox Mulder from *The X Files,* Tony's initial approach to a case was always the same: "Trust no one." Every word needed to be verified or supported before it became a viable piece of the puzzle.

Tony looked at the small, heavyset man in the

dark navy-blue uniform standing beside Dr. Snow White. A quick glance would have had someone labeling the older man a policeman. Only closer scrutiny would have taken note of the differences in uniforms. But there was one unsettling similarity.

"You have a gun," Tony observed.

One ham-like hand immediately covered the gun butt as if to acknowledge the weapon's existence.

"I've got a license," Stevens said quickly. "The agency pays more per hour for guards who have gun permits. And there've been muggings…" With a sigh that seemed to come from his very toes, Stevens's voice trailed off as he looked down again at the slain nurse.

Tony was aware that there'd been reports of people being accosted late at night in the hospital's parking facility.

"But none of them were fatal," he pointed out to the security guard.

"No. Not until now," Walter Stevens agreed heavily. Looking at the police detective, he blew out a shaky breath. "It's my fault."

Tony's eyes narrowed. Confessions didn't usually come this early in the game and in his experience, never without some sort of prodding and usually in trade for a lessening of the ultimate sentence. Taking that into account, he truly doubted that the guard was about to make life easy for him.

Drawing on his rather limited supply of patience, Tony asked, "How's that?"

Scrubbing a hand over his stubbled chin, Stevens
rendered his confession. "I usually make my rounds
earlier. If I'd been here five, ten minutes sooner, who
knows? The nurse might still be alive." He looked
down at the prone figure. "I might have been able to
stop whoever did this."

Moved, Sasha placed her arm around the man's
shoulders. At five-seven, she was approximately an
inch taller than he was. "You don't know that," she
said in a comforting tone. "Whoever it was might
have shot you, too."

One of those, Tony thought, scrutinizing the
woman again. A perpetual spreader of sunshine.
Someone who felt called upon to lift burdens and
cheer people up.

They had their place, he supposed, but preferably
not in his investigations. Frowning, Tony focused on
what was important.

"Why were you late in making your rounds?"
The question was sharply asked, pinning the security
guard to the proverbial wall.

If the attack had actually been planned, someone
would have gone to a lot of trouble learning the
guard's rounds and when he passed areas of the
complex. For the nurse to have been slain when she
was, it had to have been an unexpected attack,
without any previous knowledge of the security
guard's route. Maybe this was just a crime of opportunity and the young nurse had been in the wrong
place at the wrong time. Or someone could have

followed her without giving the guard any thought at all, which meant that he or she was unfamiliar with the hospital's policy.

There were a great many things to consider before they could feel that they were on the right path to solving the crime.

He looked at the guard expectantly.

"Something I ate," Stevens told him, pressing his wide hand to his less-than-flat midsection. "Been to the men's room three, four times so far tonight." He offered a sheepish smile. "Throws off my timing."

"I'll bet." Tony cut him off before the man could get more graphic. He glanced toward the doctor. "I didn't get your name, Doctor."

"Sasha Pulaski."

"Sasha," he repeated. "Is that Russian?"

"Polish," she corrected. "My parents are Polish."

He noticed, even though she still looked shaken, that there was a touch of pride in her voice. He wondered what that was like, to be proud of who you were, where you came from.

His eyes swept over the doctor and the guard. "I'd like to take you both down to the precinct for a formal statement."

Stevens looked a little uncertain about the turn of events. "If I go, there's no one down here to cover for me," he protested, concerned. "I'll lose my job and I can't afford to have that happen. I have bills—"

The guard sounded as if he was just getting

wound up. Tony put his hand up to stop the flow of words before they started.

"Henderson," he called over to his partner. The older man was consulting with one of the forensic investigators. "See if we can get one of the patrolmen to fill in for the security guard here until I get him back from the precinct."

"Why don't you just take a statement from Mr. Stevens right here for the time being? It might save you both a lot of time and effort," Sasha quietly suggested.

That caught him off guard. Tony thought about the solution she'd offered, or pretended to. He didn't like having anyone poke around in his investigation unless he asked them to, but the truth of it was, she was right. The patrolman could be put to better use canvassing the immediate area instead of taking the guard's place. And unless the guard had something significant to offer, such as having seen someone fleeing the scene just before the body was discovered, taking him down to the precinct would be a waste of time.

Mainly a waste of *his* time. In his experience, most security guards with night beats were not overly observant and spent most of their working hours just struggling to stay awake.

"Does that go for you, too, Doctor?" Tony asked, shifting his attention to her. "Do you want to just give your statement here and then go?"

There was something abrasive and off-putting

about the detective, Sasha thought. And he was doing it on purpose. Why? she wondered. Was he trying to create distance between himself and the people he considered suspects, or was he just trying to keep everyone at arms' length, in which case, again, why?

Had he seen too many dead bodies and had that hardened him, or had he started out that way?

She thought of her father. All the years that Josef Pulaski had been on the job, he never once allowed it to affect him, to influence him once he was home. She knew that her father had made a conscious decision to draw a line between what he did in order to put food on the table and the time he spent with the family he did it for. When he walked across that threshold and into their house, it was as if that other world where he spent so much time each day didn't even exist.

She supposed not all policemen could be like her father. And that, she knew, was a real pity because her father was a great cop and an even greater father, the kind who sacrificed his own comforts for his children.

"That's up to you," she told the detective, her eyes meeting his. She sensed that Detective Anthony Santini had no respect for the people he could successfully intimidate. "If you want to question me about what I saw just now, you'll find yourself on the receiving end of a very short interview because I didn't see anyone or anything—until I came up to Angela's car."

She'd set up an obvious question and he obliged

her by asking it. "And why did you come up to the victim's car?"

"Because mine is parked right over there." Sasha pointed toward the light-blue vintage Toyota.

He nodded. There was more and she'd left it unsaid. "And what would make for a longer interview?" he wanted to know.

"If you want to ask me what I know about Angela."

The way she said it, Tony thought, indicated that the doctor knew something. Whether or not that "something" was what had gotten the nurse killed had yet to be discerned. But then, that was his job, separating the fool's gold from the genuine article.

"All right." He looked at the security guard, making up his mind. "You can give me your statement here—for now," he qualified, then turned to look at the tall, willowy physician. "As for you, I think you had better come down to the precinct with me for that longer statement." The crime scene investigator stepped away, finally having gotten enough photographs of the dead woman. Tony immediately stepped forward. "But first I want to take a closer look at the body."

"Angela," Sasha told him. There was tension vibrating in her voice as he turned to her. "Her name is— was," she corrected herself, "Angela. Angela Rico."

Tony nodded, allowing the doctor her feelings even if he couldn't allow himself to have any of his own. Not that in his present state he even thought that he was capable of having any of his own. They'd all been burnt out of him the day he had to view what was left of Annie's mangled body.

"Angela," he repeated with a slight incline of his head.

Squatting down beside the inert body, careful not to disturb the pool of already drying blood, Tony noted that the young nurse's right hand was fisted. Had she been trying to punch her assailant when she'd been shot? It didn't seem very likely.

Tony narrowed his eyes, focusing. As he examined more closely, he saw that there was just the tiniest hint of some sort of piece of paper peeking out between the second and third knuckle of her hand.

"Peter," he beckoned to the investigator with the camera, "come here."

"Perry," the man corrected as he came forward.

Impatient, Tony ignored the correction. He tended not to remember names, only faces. "She's got something in her hand. Take a picture," he instructed.

The investigator aimed his camera. The shutter clicked twice.

Very carefully, using the tweezers he kept in his pocket, Tony extracted the paper from Angela's hand. When he unfolded it, he found four words printed on it: First Do No Harm.

# *Chapter 2*

**T**he frown on Tony's lips deepened. He turned his head slightly in Sasha's direction so that his voice would carry to her.

"I thought you said that she was a nurse."

"She was."

*Was.*

The single word vibrated in her brain. God, it felt so strange, using the past tense about a person who, only two hours ago, still had a future ahead of her. Angela had told her that she wanted to make something more of herself, to continue up the ladder, so that her daughter would be proud of her. Now, she wouldn't have the opportunity. And, at three, her daughter was too young even to have any decent memories of Angela. It just wasn't fair.

Tony continued looking at the note he held with his tweezers. Something didn't add up. "Then it looks as if our killer's confused. Correct me if I'm wrong, Doctor, but isn't this the first line of the Hippocratic Oath?"

Sasha looked over his shoulder at the paper the detective held up. Her knees bumped against his back, and something self-conscious shimmied through her. She took half a step back. "It is."

"Then why would the killer shove that into her hand?" Tony thought out loud.

"Maybe he didn't. Maybe it was something Angela shoved at the killer before he shot her." Sasha thought it over for a second. It made about as much sense as anything, she supposed. "Maybe that's why he killed her."

Tony rose slowly to his feet and turned around to look at the woman who'd been standing behind him with interest. "Do you know something, Doctor?"

She could almost *feel* his eyes penetrating her skin. As if he was expecting some sort of a confession.

She met his gaze head-on, refusing to give in to the urge to look away. "I know a lot of things. But nothing that'll do any good here." And that made her feel frustrated and helpless.

She had guts, he'd give her that. Most people looked away when he looked at them. "Maybe I should be the judge of that," he told her.

He glanced over to where the other detective was standing. The man had over twenty years on him, but the Captain had placed Henderson under him, a situation anyone else but Henderson would have been annoyed at. Not very much ever bothered Henderson. The older detective was talking to the hospital staff members who were clustered over to one side. Henderson didn't have much use for the crime scene investigators—said all the lab work got in the way of his gut instincts.

"You okay here, Henderson?" Tony asked.

Watery green eyes looked at him from beneath bushy eyebrows. "Haven't I always been?"

Sasha half turned her body so that the other detective couldn't see her lips. "He doesn't sound as if he likes you very much," she observed.

Turning the paper over to one of the forensic technicians for evaluation, Tony indicated to the doctor where his car was parked.

"Nobody does," he said as she fell into step beside him.

Sasha looked at the unsmiling detective, wondering if Santini was putting her on or if he was serious. His expression made her lean toward the latter, but she found it hard to believe that he would be so unaffected by what he'd just volunteered.

"Doesn't it bother you?" she asked, grateful to turn her attention to something other than Angela's body on the garage floor.

"No." Sparing her a glance, he raised one eyebrow in silent query. "Should it?"

On second thought, he didn't seem like the type to stay up nights losing sleep because he thought someone disliked him. "Most people like being liked," she pointed out.

"Most people *need* to be liked," he corrected. "It's an overt manifestation of insecurity."

"And you're not insecure." It wasn't really a question so much as an observation on her part. The man was the picture of confidence, and yet, there was no conceit evident. She would have said that was hard to pull off—until she'd met Santini.

"Nope." He opened the passenger-side door for her. "Watch your head," he instructed.

The words made her smile. It was something she knew that policemen said to the suspects they usher-ed into the back of their vehicles. Her father must have said the same phrase hundreds of times.

"Force of habit?" she asked.

He realized what she was referring to and shook his head. "Small car."

She was surprised that the department let him drive this little sports car. She waited for Santini to get in behind the wheel. "Regular car in the shop?" she guessed.

Starting the engine, Tony glanced at her waist, to see if she had buckled the seatbelt. Annie had never liked using it. Always said it wrinkled her clothes. In the end, it was her undoing. The first officer on the scene had told him if she'd used her seatbelt, there was a good chance she would have survived the crash.

God, but he wished he could see her just one more time, clothes wrinkled all to hell.

Tony banked down the ache and shoved it away into the darkness. He couldn't let himself think about Annie.

"This was my wife's car." She'd used his car that day, because hers was in the shop. He'd caught a ride to work from his partner. He should have insisted he needed the car and made her stay home.

Married. The man was married. Sasha tried to picture that and couldn't. Couldn't envision the man sharing himself with anyone. And, obviously, since he'd used the past tense, he was no longer doing it.

"Let me guess, you got this in the settlement." The moment the words were out, she regretted them.

A muscle twitched just above his jawline. "I got this at the funeral."

She'd never heard a tone so devoid of emotion. Or sound so incredibly empty. Beneath that emptiness, she had a feeling there was an endless abyss filled with pain. Guilt tightened her stomach.

"I'm sorry," she apologized. "I didn't mean to sound so flippant." Sasha spread her hands, feeling restless. "I do that when I get nervous."

She saw him slant a glance at her and it took everything she had not to shift in her seat. "Do I make you nervous?"

Sasha knew he was asking not as a man, but as a cop. She supposed he had to rule out everyone.

"No. But seeing Angela like that did. Does," she amended, since she was still fidgeting inwardly. "Everybody loved Angela."

"Obviously not everybody," he pointed out. "Someone killed her."

She couldn't bring herself to believe it was on purpose. Angela had never hurt anyone. But her purse was still beside her body, so robbery hadn't been a motive. If the killer *had* stolen Angela's purse, Sasha thought, he would have found very little in it. A single mother who doted on her daughter, Angela was always struggling to make ends meet. That was why she was hoping to become a nurse practitioner.

Sasha pressed her lips together as they emerged out of the structure. There was no moon out tonight, but the streetlights made up for it. "Maybe it was just an accident."

There was something in her voice that caught his attention. "You *do* know something, don't you?" He looked at her as he turned right at the end of the next block. "Was there an ex-boyfriend in the picture?"

"An ex-husband," Sasha corrected. Alex was his name. Angela didn't have time for a boyfriend. Her daughter and the hospital took up all her time. And then, because she knew the detective would find out, she added, "Angela had a restraining order against him."

"Why?" He fired the question at her before she was even finished.

Angela had confided in her and telling the detective felt as if she was breaking a trust. But death had changed the guidelines.

"Because he couldn't see his way clear to letting her leave him, even after the divorce papers went through. But he'd never hurt her," she added quickly. "Not like that." If you loved someone, you couldn't just put a bullet in the center of their forehead, she argued silently.

The light turned red. Tony looked at her, his voice steely. "What way would he hurt her?"

She remembered the black eye, the bruises that Angela had tried to pass off as clumsiness until she'd finally been convinced that she was setting a bad example for her daughter by remaining. "He hit her a couple of times. That's why she left him."

Tony nodded, doing a little math in his head. "Doesn't take much for abuse to escalate into something lethal."

Something in his voice sent a chill down her spine. "You speaking from experience?" she heard herself asking even though it was none of her business. She fully expected him to say as much.

He didn't.

"Yes." And then he looked at her as they came to another red light. "I'm supposed to be the one asking questions," he informed her mildly. "Not you."

She couldn't help herself. Ever since she'd been

a little girl, she had always pushed the envelope a little further than it was supposed to go, always wanted to know everything about everything. And to help if she could. It was in her nature. In her genes. Nothing had changed with age.

"Who did you abuse, Detective?"

"I didn't," he told her tersely.

And he never would. Not after growing up in a house where abuse was as regular as the seasons. Not after having his father beat his mother. He'd jumped to her defense, hitting his father over the head with a frying pan, then calling 911.

After his mother's death a few days later from the severity of the abuse, he and his brothers were propelled into the quagmire that was the state's foster-care system, moved around from house to house like unwanted pieces of furniture until his mother's Aunt Tess came forward to take them in.

"Your father—?" Sasha guessed, only to have him cut her off. More with his expression than with anything he actually said.

"I'm not one of your patients, Doc."

There was a warning note in his voice, a warning that told her if she continued to cross the line he'd drawn in the sand, there would be consequences to pay.

Instead of retreating, she flashed a smile. The first she'd felt capable of mustering since she'd seen Angela lying on the ground, dead. "You couldn't be. I'm an OB-GYN. You're the wrong gender."

"First time anyone's ever said that to me," he quipped.

Sasha glanced at Santini's rugged profile as he signaled for another turn. That, she thought, she could well believe.

Sasha sighed as she let herself into her small three-bedroom apartment. It was just a few minutes after one o'clock in the morning and she was beyond exhausted at this point. A second wind had come and gone and so had a third. At the moment, her energy was totally depleted, leaving her feeling barely human and incredibly sad.

The handsome detective with the permanent scowl on his face had wound up asking her more questions on their way down to the precinct than he actually did once he was at his desk and typing out her responses. In reality, there wasn't all that much more she could tell Santini beyond what she'd already said. What that amounted to was that as far as she knew, Angela Rico had no known enemies. Yet someone had deliberately killed her. Executed her, she thought, numbed by the thought.

Dutifully, she had given the detective the name and address of Angela's mother. Selena Cruz watched Rita, Angela's three-year-old, while Angela worked at the hospital. She assumed that Angela's mother might be able to give the detective information about Angela's ex, although she still didn't think Alex Rico could have killed his wife. If he had, he would have killed himself as well, because he maintained that he couldn't live without Angela.

Walking across the threshold, Sasha closed the door behind her. The single twenty-five-watt bulb they always left on for one another in the hallway cast dim pools of light on the floor beneath it. She yawned and sighed, debating just falling on her face on the sofa. Her bedroom seemed to be too far away.

A click vaguely registered in the back of her mind and suddenly, the apartment was flooded with light.

Sasha covered her eyes, blinking several times until she got them acclimated to the brightness. "You're blinding me," she accused whichever sister had turned the light on.

"My God, are you operating in the middle of the night now?" Natalya wanted to know.

Dropping her hand, Sasha saw Natalya coming into the living room, frowning at her. She and Natalya, eleven months her junior, shared high cheekbones and a passion for healing. Beyond that, they were as different as night and day. Natalya was shorter, with more curves and medium-brown hair that brushed against her shoulders. Her sister's eyes were brown, not blue, and right now, they were fixed on Sasha's clothing and filled with confusion and concern.

"Sasha, you're covered in blood," she cried. "What happened?"

She'd forgotten about that, Sasha thought. But before she could answer, another light went on, this time from the bedroom on the right. Leokadia, barefoot, her eyes half closed, stumbled into the room. The oversized T-shirt she had on indicated that of the three, she'd been the only one who had actually made it to bed tonight.

She didn't look any the more cheerful for it. "You two want to hold it down? Some of us are actually trying to get some sleep around here. You do remember sleep, don't you?" Kady looked accusingly at her sisters. "It's—oh my God, what happened?" Her mouth dropped open as she stared at her oldest sister. "Are you all right?" she cried, rushing toward Sasha. "Are you hurt? Whose blood is that? Sash, sit down," the petite blonde ordered, pointing to the sofa. "Can I get you something? Do you want—?"

In an effort to get her own word in edgewise, Natalya put her hand over her younger sister's mouth. She looked at Sasha, who everyone else had always regarded as the rock of the family. "Whose blood is that, Sasha?"

"Angela's. Angela Rico's."

Pressing her lips together, Sasha paused for a moment, struggling with her emotions as the reality of the situation finally sank in. The next moment, she offered her sisters a halfhearted smile of apology. At times it was hard to remember that although they all worked at the same hospital, Patience Memorial, or PM as everyone who worked there affectionately referred to it, they all had different areas of expertise. That meant that their spheres didn't always cross, which, in turn, meant that they didn't always know the same people.

She cleared her throat and tried again. "She was a nurse on the maternity ward."

Natalya nodded. "I've heard you mention her." Her voice was soft, gentle. It was unnerving for them to see Sasha like this. Except for when her fiancé had been mugged and fatally stabbed, it was generally believed that Sasha had nerves of steel.

Coming up on her other side, Kady placed her hand on Sasha's arm. "What happened to her, Sash?" she asked softly.

"Someone killed her in the parking structure."

Very slowly, her hand now on Sasha's wrist, Kady was drawing her over to the sofa. "Do the police have any idea who?"

Numbly, Sasha shook her head. Her legs seemed to give out from beneath her just as she came to the sofa. "I was just at the precinct."

"Precinct?" Natalya echoed. "You? Why?" she wanted to know. She was quick to become defensive and protective of her family.

"Because I found her," Sasha answered, her voice hardly above a whisper. The entire time she'd spent with the detective, she'd done her best to be clear-headed, sharp. But here, with her sisters, she let herself grieve. And it felt awful. "Actually, the guard did. Walter Stevens," she added. Neither of her two sisters probably knew who she was talking about.

She was the one who always stopped to talk to people. "But he looked so upset and confused…" Sasha slid her tongue along her lips, but they continued to feel like two pieces of dry sandpaper. Just like her insides felt. "I tried giving Angela CPR, but…"

Natalya took her hand. "You can't save everyone, Sash," she said compassionately. "Mama always says there's a time for everything, remember? A time to be born and a time to die."

A semismile curved her lips. "You start singing, 'Turn, Turn, Turn' and I'm leaving."

"I won't sing," Natalya promised. "Not tonight."

"You want me to draw you a hot bath?" Kady offered. When things got to her, she always sought refuge in a hot bath.

Not waiting for an answer, Kady was on her feet and halfway across the room, heading toward the bathroom before Sasha could open her mouth.

"Wait," Sasha cried. "Stop. Stop." Kady skidded to an impatient halt and turned around to look at her, waiting for further instructions. Sasha shook her head. "The way I feel right now, Kady, I'd probably drown in the tub. I'm too tired for a bath. I just want to get these clothes off and fall into bed."

"That can be arranged," Natalya said as she took her sister's hand and helped Sasha to her feet again.

Sasha felt a laugh bubbling up in her throat. It was a welcome sensation, even though there was such a thing as too much help.

"Thanks, but I can still undress myself, Nat. I'm not that out of it." She sighed. "It's just that…" Sasha's voice trailed off as her sisters looked at her, waiting, not wanting to interrupt. She dragged her hand through her hair, loosening pins. A few rained down on the light-gray rug. "God, what a waste."

Her sisters both nodded, even though neither one of them had actually known the dead woman. But each had already seen death, been touched by death's sharp talons, and knew instinctively what Sasha was going through right now.

Or thought they did, Sasha amended silently.

Right now she was just incredibly sad. And tomorrow, Sasha promised herself, or rather today, she amended, glancing at the digital clock on the coffee table, she was going to get up early and go to Angela's mother. She should have gone tonight, with that detective, but she couldn't face the woman with Angela's blood on her. But tomorrow, she was going to offer to do anything she could.

As if that could somehow help, she thought sadly. She felt powerless, and hated that feeling. Hated being imprisoned by it.

"If you need to talk, Sash," Natalya was saying as she began to leave the room, "you know where to find me."

"Me, too," Kady added.

They both meant it. They were both willing to give up their night to sit up with her, holding her hand both physically and emotionally, until she no longer needed comforting. Until the shock had passed and the pain was manageable.

Sasha could only think, not for the first time, how very grateful she was that she was not one of those poor souls who walked the earth alone. How grateful she was that she had her family to fall back on. Not just Nat and Kady, but Marja and Tatania as well.

And, of course, her parents.

Her wonderful, loving parents who always gave and never took. What would she have done if they hadn't been there for her when Adam had been slain eighteen months ago? She doubted very much if she would have been here today if not for them. They thought of her as the strong one, but they were her strength.

She looked from one sister to the other. "It's not that big an apartment. I'll find you."

# Chapter 3

Tony leaned back in his chair. The frown on his lips deepened. Nothing. Granted, he'd expected as much, but he had still held out a smattering of hope.

The trouble these days was that anyone with half a brain now knew how to cover up their trail, thanks to all the different forensic programs on the airwaves. With everything but an intense, flash-of-anger crime of passion, perpetrators knew how to make reasonably sure that their prints didn't turn up on the things they'd handled while committing the crime.

And even with crimes of passion, if the suspect took a moment to think about his actions telltale prints would be wiped off.

Sighing, Tony stared at the crime lab report the tech had just delivered to him. The note extracted from Angela Rico's hand had only Angela's prints on it. To compound the disappointment, the note had come from a printer that had nothing remarkable about it to set it apart, no quirky imprint to separate it from the thousands of other printers he would find in the area if he were to look. The note had been produced by a standard color printer, not a laser, not the old dot matrix, which might have made things easier if the suspect had access to it.

And that was another thing, Tony thought, his annoyance growing. Their only viable suspect in Angela Rico's murder had an alibi. A substantiated alibi. At the time of his ex-wife's murder, Alex Rico was in Atlantic City, hoping he would have better luck at the blackjack tables than he had in love.

As it turned out, Angela's ex was a loser in both but no longer a murder suspect.

"Not unless he hired somebody to do it," Henderson volunteered wearily, ending a discussion that had been halfheartedly under way between the two of them.

They were the only ones in the immediate area. Everyone else, including Captain Holloway, had gone home for the night.

Tony glanced in his partner's direction. Together a little over two years, he and Henderson hadn't hit it off all that well. But then, to be fair, he hadn't hit it off with too many people. He preferred working alone.

Preferred everything alone, actually. Alone, there was no one else to disappoint you but you, he thought.

The notion brought a cynical half smile to his lips.

"If he hired somebody, what's the note about?" Tony asked.

The note bothered him. A lot. He felt as if it was pointing to something, but to what, he hadn't a clue.

Henderson shrugged his wide shoulders haplessly, the unironed shirt moving stiffly with the gesture. Without thinking, he scratched his neck.

"To throw us off?" he guessed.

Tony's half smile looked a bit sarcastic. "Alex Rico strike you as particularly clever?" Tony asked.

It was a rhetorical question. Still, Henderson considered it. "No, just grief-stricken. And mad. Very mad."

Tony thought of the victim's ex, and the rage that he'd viewed in the man's eyes, just behind the grief. "If Rico's innocent, we might have some trouble from him when we catch who did this."

"You meant *if,*" Henderson pointed out.

"No, I mean *when,*" Tony repeated.

Although he regarded the rest of his life with a jaded, negative eye, it never occurred to Tony that he wouldn't catch his quarry. Otherwise, there was no point in going through the motions. He'd taken the job, the badge, to make a difference. You didn't make a difference by not catching the bad guy.

Henderson nodded, backing away from a con-

frontation. "Cross that bridge when we come to it."
With that, he switched off his computer and pushed
his chair back. The legs scraped along the scarred
vinyl floor that had long since needed replacing.
The current budget couldn't handle it. "I'm calling
it a night," he said needlessly. "Maybe something'll
turn up fresh in the morning."

"Maybe," Tony murmured under his breath.

He scrubbed his hand over his face and tried to
recenter his thinking. The pretty doctor had been right.
Everyone had loved the victim. At least, everyone he
and Henderson had talked to in the last week.

Pushing back his own chair, he began to rise when
the phone on his desk rang.

"Looks like it might not be a night yet," he said
to Henderson as he reached for the receiver.

Déjà vu.

It had never been one of Sasha's favorite words
or sensations. As far as that went, it was way down
on the list.

At the very least, it encompassed a teasing sensation that tormented her until she could finally
recall what, where and when she'd done "this"
before, whatever "this" might be. Most of the time,
the answers to the questions that occurred to her
never materialized as she struggled to recall an
elusive memory that would put things in perspective
for her.

This time, she didn't have to try to recall. The

memory that had sent the sensation rippling through her was still sickeningly fresh in her mind.

Angela, lying in a pool of her own blood on the concrete floor beside her car.

Since the discovery, Sasha hadn't stopped parking in the structure. It was either that or resort to taking a cab or some mode of public transportation. Although the city had probably the best public transportation system in the world, Sasha was possessed of an independent streak that fairly demanded she be in charge of deciding how she came and went. Subways and buses left you depending on others.

Besides, she loved that little ten-year-old Toyota. The vehicle had been her parents' gift to her when she'd graduated medical school. They could hardly afford to splurge the way they did, even though they'd bought it used. And, since they did buy it for her, not to use it would be tantamount to insulting them.

Entering the level where she'd parked this morning, Sasha realized she was holding her breath as she made her way down a deserted row.

She was too old to be afraid of the dark, she scolded herself.

It wasn't so much the dark that frightened her, actually, as it was who might be hiding in that dark.

Sasha glanced around to see if Walter Stevens was around somewhere. But if the security guard was on duty, he was making rounds on another level of the structure. There was no sound of anyone walking around here. No sound at all, really.

And then she heard it.

Every nerve ending in her body tightened as she listened.

A moan? A gasp? She couldn't make it out.

Sasha looked over her shoulder toward the elevator doors. For a second, she thought about running back. And then she became annoyed with herself. There were still cars here. Probably just someone going home for the night. Or coming on for the night shift.

"Hello? Is anyone there?" Sasha called. But even as she asked, she was hurrying over toward where she'd parked her car this morning before making her rounds.

There was a prickly sensation traveling along the back of her neck. It refused to go away, refused to be blocked.

And then she saw it.

Her breath caught in her throat, threatening to suffocate her. A scream escaped her, vibrating amid the trapped air. There was a figure on the ground, sprawled out like a mutilated doll. Like Angela, there was a pool of blood beneath her. Like Angela, there was a bullet hole in the center of her forehead. Her eyes were wide open, unseeing as they stared at the ceiling.

This couldn't be happening. Not twice. She was having some kind of hysterical hallucination, Sasha silently argued. Any second now, the figure would disappear.

But it didn't.

Legs no longer made of lead, Sasha broke into a run. But it was too late. The figure on the ground was not moving. The gray-haired woman had surrendered to death the moment the bullet had found her.

And then another sound came. The sound of screaming. Sasha did not immediately realize that it was coming from her.

She was never going to get warm again.

The iciness that surrounded her went clear down to her soul, despite the blanket that someone had draped over her shoulders.

Sasha was sitting in her car, on the driver's side, her feet planted outside the vehicle on the concrete floor as she faced the activity that was going on just a few feet away.

What were the odds? she wondered. What were the odds of this kind of thing happening twice? Two women, nurses, both shot execution style. And both times her car was parked close enough to the scene of the crime to be touched by the killer.

She shivered and took another long sip from the hot container of coffee the detective had shoved into her hands. It was half-consumed. Only belatedly did it register that he must have drunk out of it before he'd given it to her.

Whether it was meant to warm her hands or her insides, she didn't know. The no-frills coffee—black no sugar—failed to do either. But the jolt of super-strength caffeine did help her focus. Did help her hear his questions rather than just drift numbly away from the scene in a desperate act of self-preservation.

Her lashes felt moist. Was it the steam from the coffee, or was she crying? Sasha didn't know. She couldn't tell. Everything seemed so surreal.

"The hospital has signs up in the staff lounge advising women to go into the parking structure in pairs," she said hoarsely, more to the container in her hands than to the detective she knew was staring down at her.

"So why didn't you?" he asked her quietly.

The question surprised her. She had been referring to the dead woman, to the fact that if the grandmother of two had heeded the advice, maybe she would have escaped being the center of another homicide investigation.

Another homicide at PM.

It seemed absurd. They had above average success in keeping their patients from dying within their walls, whether they were brought here for surgery or because of some extensive illness.

*But it's not the patients who are getting killed, it's the staff,* a voice in her head whispered.

Why?

Sasha looked up blankly. The detective—Santini, wasn't it?—was looking down at her. There was a frown on his lips. It seemed like there was always a frown on his lips, she thought.

But then, murders were nothing to smile about.

"What?" she finally asked him.

"Why didn't you?" Tony repeated patiently, aware that she could be going into some kind of shock. "Why didn't you take someone with you? Why did you go into the parking structure alone?"

She shrugged. One side of the blanket slid down her shoulder. Tony moved it back into place, his fingers brushing against the side of her neck. They felt rough, as if he worked with his hands when he wasn't being a cop.

"It was late," Sasha replied.

"All the more reason," he pointed out. When he'd taken the call that brought him back to the location where he'd been just two weeks ago, canvassing the area, he hadn't expected to find the doctor at the center of the scene again.

The sensation that had shimmied through him was a surprise as well.

Sasha thought for a second. She supposed, to the detective, it must have appeared stupid. In hindsight, she had to agree. But she'd been going alone to the parking structure every night since they'd found Angela's body. Besides, she didn't think of herself in terms of mortality.

Sasha's hands tightened around the container. "No one else was leaving when I left and I don't like inconveniencing people."

His eyes met hers. "Murder is the ultimate inconvenience," he commented. Satisfied that the woman could understand him and process his questions now, he began by asking the obvious one. "Did you know the victim?"

Sasha bit back a sigh. She nodded. "Her name's

Rachel Wells. She's a nurse. And a grandmother."
Sasha suddenly realized where he was going with
this. "I didn't know her well. Just to nod to, that kind
of thing. She once showed me a photograph of her
grandchildren. It was a Christmas-card photo," she
added.

Santini gave no indication that he was pleased or
displeased with her answer. She didn't like faces she
couldn't read. Everything that any of her family felt
was right out there for everyone to see.

"Did the other victim know her?" he wanted to
know.

The feeling of helplessness swaddled her. She
hated being useless, but there wasn't anything useful
she could tell him.

"They were both nurses. I suppose they knew
each other, but I really couldn't say for sure." Did he
think there was a serial killer out there, focusing on
PM's nurses? She narrowed her eyes. "Why?"

"I don't know yet," he told her simply, even
though as a rule he didn't like having questions about
his methods being put to him. "I figure if we ask
enough questions, we might wind up finding an
answer that'll tell us something."

That made sense. Right now, it was difficult to
pull her thoughts together coherently. "Do you think
this is some kind of a serial killer, going around
murdering nurses for some twisted reason?"

He didn't answer at first. "What do you think?"

Sasha looked at the detective sharply, her mind

kicking in for the first time since she'd looked down to see her second victim in a little more than two weeks. Was he toying with her? Baiting her? She raised her chin slightly.

"I don't know what to think."

Tony inclined his head, as if in agreement. "Neither do I," he admitted mildly.

That was a crock. She didn't buy it for a minute. Detective Anthony Santini looked like the kind of man who knew *exactly* what he thought at all times. Moreover, he looked like a man who was on top of everything, be it situations or people, and he undoubtedly made it a point to remain that way.

And then she saw a spark enter his eyes. His interest seemed to sharpen, as if a new idea had just occurred to him. Sasha wasn't sure if she wanted to know what it was.

The next moment, she decided that she *had* to know what it was. If she didn't find out, she knew she would have no peace.

"What?"

Tony pointed out the obvious, straddling a fence, as if to see which side he was going to climb down on. "You found both bodies and both victims were holding the same note."

For the first time, she felt something other than grief for the victims and the family members who were left behind. Was he actually saying he suspected her of being the one who'd killed both women? How could he possibly even *think* something so stupid?

"The guard found Angela," she reminded him. "But technically, I guess you could say that, yes," she allowed. Her stomach felt as if it was on its way to meet her throat. Dear God, she hoped she wouldn't wind up doing something stupid, letting her nerves get the better of her. "Why?"

This doctor might or might not be the common thread here, he thought, since they had no other viable lead. It seemed an incredible coincidence that she was in the same vicinity as both of the victims.

"Do you know anyone who might be doing this to get your attention?"

It took her a second to absorb the question.

"My attention?" she repeated incredulously.

"You know, like a cat coming into the house and laying whatever they've killed down by your feet." He saw the revulsion enter her eyes. He'd thought doctors didn't become grossed out. "To them, it's a flattering gesture, not a sickening one."

Sasha pressed her lips together. Someone was killing their nurses and this man was talking nonsense. "No, I don't know anyone who would bring me dead bodies as a gift."

The ghostly pallor was receding from her cheeks, he noted. He was getting her angry. Righteously, or was that bravado? "You said you were a female doctor?"

How archaic did that sound? "I'm an OB-GYN," she corrected.

His eyes never left her face. "Lose any mothers or babies lately?"

Did he think some deranged husband or parent was killing innocent people because they were trying to get back at her?

"You *are* crazy," she told him, taking umbrage for her patients and their families.

He never batted an eye. "Part of the job, ma'am."

Tony glanced over toward the yellow taped-off area. As he'd instructed at the first homicide, one of the crime scene investigators was scanning the area with a video camera. He wanted to compare tapes, see if anyone who had come to the first homicide turned up at the second. Besides the good doctor here.

He turned his attention back to her. "I'm afraid I'm going to need you to give me a statement again."

She'd expected as much when she'd placed the 911 call to report the murder.

And then something suddenly dawned on her. "Do you think I did it?"

"I think everyone did it," he answered. "Until I can weed the non-suspects out, one at a time."

This seemed just too fantastic for her to absorb. That someone would think she was a murderer boggled her mind.

"Why would I kill Angela and Rachel?"

His eyes met hers. She'd never seen such serious eyes in her life. "If I had the answer to that, this would be easy."

"Then I'll give you an answer," she told him heatedly. He was wasting his time with this line of thinking and the sooner he moved on, the closer he would get to catching Angela and Rachel's killer. And maybe preventing another murder as well. "I didn't kill them. I didn't kill anyone. I don't even step on bugs."

There was just the barest hint of amusement evident. "Maybe you should. Their population is really exploding these days. Had to move out of my last apartment because the roaches reclaimed the building."

Sasha shook her head. "You're insane."

"So you already pointed out," he told her, unruffled. He took the empty cup from her and saw her stiffen indignantly.

"If you want my prints," she told him tersely, "you just have to ask. My DNA, too."

He laughed softly, humorlessly. "Everybody's a CSI wannabe." Glancing around, he beckoned over a policeman. "Sergeant, take the doctor down to the precinct. We need to get her statement."

"I can do it," Henderson volunteered, pocketing the small notebook he always used to take down information that came his way.

"I need you here," Tony told him. "I'll have a patrolman drive her in." He spared a glance at Sasha. "I'll see you at the station."

"Doesn't matter where you'll see me," she informed him, "the answers will still be the same."

He merely nodded, walking away to speak to one of the patrolman. "Good, means you're not lying."

Sasha felt a flash of temper. She opened her mouth and then closed it again, feeling it more prudent not to say anything until she had more control over what could come out. All she knew right now was that the detective was getting under her skin at an amazing speed and rubbing her completely the wrong way.

# Chapter 4

"Can I get you anything?"

The voice came from behind her. Sasha twisted around in the hardback chair to see Tony approaching her in the squad room. She'd been sitting beside his desk for the last fifteen minutes, waiting for him to make an appearance. She couldn't help wondering if he was making her wait on purpose.

"A time machine," she quipped, turning back around to face him as he moved his chair out.

Tony sat down and turned on his computer. A low grinding noise began to hum through the office as it went through its paces.

"Why?" he asked. "How far back would you go?"

"Two weeks."

He looked at her. Two weeks was the amount of time separating the two murders. Was she making a backhanded confession?

"And maybe I'd start taking the bus to work," Sasha added, thinking out loud. "Coming across one victim was bad enough. Two…" Her voice trailed off as she shook her head.

Then she raised her eyes to his and Tony found himself thinking that he'd never seen eyes quite that shade of blue before. Intense. Beautiful. And pretty damn hypnotic if he allowed them to be. Mentally, he pulled himself back.

"I know you're overworked here and under-staffed," she said, edging closer on her chair, "but you must have some kind of a lead, a clue, a hunch—"

Tony regarded her with mild interest. People didn't usually attribute human frailties to the police department. They expected tireless, around-the-clock vigilance. And crimes to be solved in a timely fashion—as in yesterday. All the best crime dramas on television made it seem easy.

If only.

"How do you know we're overworked and under-staffed?" he wanted to know.

Was the man born antagonistic, or had he just acquired the habit along the way? She was trying to be nice here.

"Well, aren't you? Why should you be any differ-ent from the rest of the world? Besides," she sighed, sitting back again, "that's the way it always was when my father was with the two-six in Queens."

She'd succeeded in getting his attention, Sasha thought. The look in his eyes changed. "Your father was on the job?"

Tony noted the way she smiled before she answered. Pride mingled with memories. A family girl, he thought. He should have realized that. Because of his own situation, he had a tendency to think of people simply as detached individuals. He wasn't close to either one of his brothers, even though they both lived in the city and worked for it, Joe as a detective in Brooklyn and Tim as a firefighter in Staten Island. But for all the contact they'd had in the last five years, they could have just as well have been spread out all over the country.

"Twenty-six years," she told him. Definitely pride there, he thought. It was audible in her voice. "Josef Pulaski. He made detective before he retired."

Just like his father had been, he thought. Except that he was willing to bet that was where the similarity ended. If he'd ever been proud of his father, that had changed a long time ago—by the time he could understand what was going on behind his parents' closed door.

He nodded in response to her words. "So that makes you more aware of procedure than most of the people who've sat in that chair."

She couldn't tell if he was attempting to extend an olive branch or not. "If you mean do I know that you have to rule me out as a potential suspect before you can move on, yes."

Maybe she wasn't going to give him trouble after all, he thought. The computer sat, ready, its grinding noise reduced to a soft, constant hum. Time to get started.

"No run-ins with—" Tony paused, referring to his notes. The victim's name had momentarily escaped him.

"Rachel," Sasha supplied before he could flip to another page. He raised his eyes to hers. "No, no run-ins. I don't know all that much about her, actually," she warned him. She and the older woman hadn't been friends by any stretch of the imagination, although their paths had crossed a number of times. "Only that she was past retirement age."

The woman had looked it, Tony thought. "Then why didn't she retire?" In his experience, retirement was the carrot people coveted. "She love the job that much?"

Sasha thought of the couple of times she'd overheard the slain nurse complaining about conditions at the hospital, or about a supervisor who was riding her. "I think it was more of a case of her tolerating the job."

"Then why—?" Tony left it to her to fill in the rest.

"The same reason a lot of people stay at a job they don't like. Money. She needed the money," Sasha

emphasized. "Rachel had two grandchildren to raise.
Her son's sons. Eight and ten I think."

She was making his job easier for him.

He raised his eyes to hers for a second. "Where's
the son?" he asked, tapping slowly on the computer
keyboard. He typed like someone who had no
knowledge of where the letters were arranged.

Sasha shrugged. "Ran off somewhere." She tried
to remember what the hospital gossip had been. "I
don't think she knew where."

He stopped searching for keys. "So this son took
a powder, leaving his kids high and dry, and Rachel
stepped in?"

Sasha nodded in response to his question. "According to what I heard, he left the boys with her for
the weekend two years ago. Mailed her a letter a
month later, said he couldn't handle being a father.
Rachel complained about it." To anyone who would
listen, she recalled. "But she said she couldn't just
let the county raise the boys."

Her words struck a chord. Aunt Tess had said
something similar once. Tony shut down the momentary flashback.

Staring at the keyboard, he hunted and pecked in
the new information. "Anyone else in the picture?"

He typed so slowly, she had the urge to push him
aside and take over. Sasha knotted her hands in her
lap. "Her husband. He's a handyman. I think he does
work for the apartment complex where they live."
She stopped trying to remember bits and pieces and

looked at the detective who was engaged in a hopeless duel with the keyboard. "Why are you asking me this? Wouldn't you get more information from PM's Human Resources Department?" They all had forms they'd had to fill out when coming to work for the hospital. PM was extremely careful about who they ultimately hired.

"You're doing just fine." Hitting the period that brought the last sentence to an end, he sat back and regarded her for a second. "For someone who didn't know the victim, you have a lot of information at your disposal."

Was it her imagination, or was that a veiled accusation of some sort? Sasha could feel herself growing defensive. "I pay attention when people talk."

The look he gave her was very pointed. "So do I."

Except, she thought, in his case, what he listened to was probably all related to his work. Detective Santini didn't seem the type to be concerned about people as people, the way she was. Concern was what had brought her into medicine in the first place. It was her overwhelming desire to heal, to fix, to make things right if she could that had made her decide to become a doctor. She'd gone into obstetrics because there she also had the added thrill of seeing new life coming into the world.

It helped balance out the times when she *couldn't* fix things or make them right again.

"A man who listens. Your wife must be a lucky

woman." It was a flippant, sarcastic thing to say, but she was edgy and wired and heartsick all at the same time. She'd forgotten that he'd told her he was widowed.

Santini looked at her sharply. Had she been standing, Sasha thought, she would have reflexively taken a step back, like someone on the receiving end of a physical blow. Obviously, the wound was still very fresh. It wasn't like her to have forgotten something like that, even if he was a stranger. She attributed it to the fact that she was very shaken.

"Sorry," she offered.

His voice was completely dead when he responded. "Nothing to be sorry about."

The silence hung between them, thick, uncomfortable. At least, it felt that way to her. Sasha took another stab at making amends. "I got personal and I shouldn't have. It's a habit I have."

His eyes met hers again. "Talking first and thinking second?" he guessed.

That stung. "Your turn to apologize," Sasha said after a beat.

A small, faint smile played along his lips before retreating. She had guts, he thought again. Brains, beauty and guts. On a good day, she was probably a very dangerous lady to tangle with. "I guess that makes us a couple of sorry people."

She didn't know if he meant it as a joke, but she gave him the benefit of the doubt and smiled anyway.

Tony asked her a few more questions, including inquiring about her immediate whereabouts around the time of the murder and if there was anything further she could tell him about the victim.

She noticed that he used the word *victim* rather than Rachel's name. It made it sound so impersonal, so detached. But, she supposed that was probably a defense mechanism on his part. Otherwise, after all the horrible things he'd undoubtedly encountered as a homicide detective, he would have become completely paralyzed emotionally.

She wasn't completely certain that he wasn't now.

Taking a breath, Sasha told him everything she could remember.

"Rachel didn't stay after hours and socialize," she told him. "At least, not that I know of. She came, did her work, and went home." Rachel never tried to get away with anything, but neither did she feel the need to give more than she was being paid for. She wasn't one to go the extra foot, much less the proverbial mile.

Tony looked thoughtfully at what he'd typed. "Except for tonight."

"Except for tonight," Sasha repeated softly. And then she looked at him as a fresh thought struck her. "Who's going to tell her husband? Who's going to tell Arthur?"

Arthur. That had to be the handyman husband, Tony thought. "I am." He'd done it more times than he cared to remember, and he hated it each and every time, but someone had to and he was not one to shirk responsibilities. He rose from his chair. They were done here for the night. "As soon as I take you home."

She got to her feet as well. "To the hospital," Sasha corrected. "My car's still in the parking structure."

"Okay," he agreed, mentally changing his route, "I'll take you to the hospital. There are still patrolmen there." Dropping her off would be safe.

"Look, why don't you take me to Rachel's place first?" she suggested suddenly. Tony looked at her quizzically. Now what? "This is going to be a huge shock for her husband when you tell him. He's not in the best of health. He had a heart attack just before the children came to live with them. You don't want to chance that happening again." She gave a half shrug. "Maybe I can help soften the blow."

Tony searched her face, looking for signs of logic, trying to understand her reasoning. "How do you do that, Doc? How do you soften death?"

Was he insulting her? Sasha looked at him. "Are you always this abrasive, or do I just bring it out in you?"

He didn't answer. Not directly. "Actually, this is one of my better days."

Sasha rolled her eyes and shook her head. "God help the world."

"My thought exactly." It was a droll remark at his own expense, she thought. Except that he was looking at her when he said it. "Okay, you want to come,

come." She was surprised he didn't offer more of a resistance. "You can help with the kids if they're up."

Sasha walked toward the doorway. "We seem to be on the same page, Detective."

"I wouldn't get used to that if I were you."

She looked at Santini a second before she preceded him into the corridor. "I wouldn't dream of it, Detective."

As it turned out, Rachel's grandsons were not up and neither was her husband. It took a great deal of knocking and ringing before the sound of any sort of rustling was heard from within the first-floor apartment.

Opening the door a crack, leaving the chain securely fastened and in place, Arthur Wells looked like a man who'd been pulled out of the arms of a very deep sleep. His eyes at half-mast, he resisted taking the chain off even after Tony held up his badge for inspection. It was only after he heard Sasha introduce herself and say that this was about his wife that he finally opened the door for them.

"Rachel's mentioned you, Doctor," Arthur told her, gesturing toward his living room. "She worked with you in the ER once," he recalled for her benefit, in case she didn't remember. "Said you were something to watch under pressure. My Rachel doesn't usually give favorable comments." A smile quirked across his lips nervously, as if he was instinctively attempting to forestall something he knew he didn't want to hear. He looked from her to the detective. "Can I get you something?" Arthur began to edge away toward the small kitchen. "Coffee? Water? I've got some soda in the refrigerator, but—"

"Mr. Wells," Tony began, his tone serious, his expression more so.

Frightened, nervous brown eyes darted toward the detective, then toward her, silently imploring her not to allow any words to be said that couldn't be taken back. Words that would ultimately shatter and destroy his small world.

Sasha stepped in between the detective and Mr. Wells. Barefoot, he was shorter than she was, but almost as wide as he was tall. At the moment, he looked completely devoid of strength, as if every one of his years weighed heavily on his shoulders. She took the man's hands in hers. They were large, capable and rough, reminding her of her father's hands. There was nothing that her father couldn't repair or build if he set his mind to it. She had a feeling Arthur was the same way.

Her heart went out to the man. "Mr. Wells," she began softly, "I am very, very sorry—"

"No," he moaned, tears springing to his eyes, "No, no, no."

The burly man began to sway. Sasha threw her arms around him and was just barely able to keep him from sinking to the floor. She looked over her shoulder at the detective. "A little help here."

Tony stepped in quickly, assuming the bulk of the

sagging weight. Between them, they managed to get Arthur to the sofa.

"Not the best bedside technique," Tony commented, stepping back from the man.

Obviously a case of the pot calling the kettle black, she thought. For the sake of the grieving man on the sofa, she bit back a more terse retort and merely replied, "Like you said, there's really no way to soften a blow like this."

Arthur's wide, florid face looked drained. He took two quick breaths to sustain himself before trying to speak.

"Is she—is she—?" But he couldn't bring himself to finish the question, to say the words that would acknowledge his final separation from the wife he'd loved and fought with for forty-three years.

Tony delivered the news swiftly. To him, it was like removing a Band-Aid. You tore it off quickly. Anything else only prolonged the agony. "Someone killed her in the parking garage at PM."

Arthur's eyes widened in confusion. "The parking garage?" he echoed, shaking his head as if there had to be some sort of mistake, some sort of mix-up. "We don't even have a car."

"Then someone must have lured her there," Tony concluded.

Under what pretext? he wondered. Another piece of the puzzle that didn't seem to fit anywhere. *Yet.* And instead of a single murder, or two, it looked as if they had a serial killer on their hands. Targeting nurses? All nurses, or just those from that particular hospital? Or was there something else entirely going on?

"Who? Why?" Arthur cried, his voice cracking with each word.

"That's what we're trying to find out, Mr. Wells," Tony told him. He began to ask the man a question, but Sasha cut him off.

"Do you have anyone we could call for you? Someone who could stay with you?" Sasha asked. She could feel Tony glaring at her, but right now, this was more important, making certain that the man didn't remain alone in the first few hours of his grief.

Arthur looked at her blankly, as if thinking was far too hard a process for him to cope with. And then, just as she was about to repeat the question, he nodded. "Rachel's brother. Her younger brother." The words were tumbling out, disjointed. He was struggling not to cry. "Jerry. I can call Jerry."

Sasha was already taking out her cell phone. "Give me his telephone number, Mr. Wells. I'll call him for you."

Arthur swallowed, nodding his head. It took him a few minutes before he could remember the numbers in the right order. But before she could begin pressing the proper buttons on the cell phone keypad, he caught her wrist.

"Could you stay with me until Jerry gets here?" he asked brokenly. "If the boys wake up—oh God, what am I going to tell the boys?" He looked at her, stricken. "Their father and mother already walked out on them. How are they going to deal with this?"

"Kids are more resilient than you think," Tony told him before she had a chance to reply.

Sasha looked at the tall detective, wondering what he had gone through in his own life that would make him say something like that. He didn't strike her as the kind of man who would offer up empty platitudes in order to comfort anyone. She doubted if he knew how.

"I'll stay with you," she promised, then pressed the keys that connected her to Rachel Wells's brother. She braced herself for the ordeal.

His hands shoved into his pockets, Tony waited until she finished talking to the victim's brother. When she terminated the call, he took her aside.

"Why are you doing this?"

The blunt question caught her off guard. Didn't this man have a clue about what people felt? "Because I hate to see anyone in pain," she said simply. And that was it, the long and the short of it. The sum total of what motivated her.

He glanced over toward Arthur, then back at her. "Look, I can't—"

She anticipated his words. "You don't have to stay here with me. I can catch a cab back to the hospital and get my car after his brother-in-law gets here." She paused for a second, trying to conquer the kernel of fear that threatened to erupt, then asked,

"You've got patrolmen posted there, don't you? I mean, it's still a new crime scene, right?"

"Right."

She was trying to mask it, but she was afraid. Fear was a good thing, it kept civilians from doing reckless things—something he didn't put entirely past her. Tony blew out a breath. He didn't like the idea of her going back to the parking structure alone. His men had swept through all the levels, but there were no guarantees in life about anything.

"Hang on," he finally said. "Let me make a call."

Before she could ask why he was even bothering to mention making a call to her, Tony had turned away, connecting to someone with a single press of a button. With a shrug of her shoulders, Sasha turned her attention to the broken man sitting on the sagging sofa.

He looked, she thought as she came over to him, as if someone had stolen his soul.

Sitting down beside him, she placed her hand over his. "You need to stay strong, Mr. Wells. For your grandsons' sake. They're going to need you more than ever."

"What about me?" Arthur wanted to know, his voice breaking. "What about what I need?"

"That comes later," she said softly. "You do what you have to to get through a day, and then two days and then a week. A month…until there's enough time between you and the pain for you to be able to attempt to handle it."

Arthur shook his head. A tear slid down, hitting the top of her hand. "I don't think I can."

"You can." Her voice was firm beneath the soft tone. "We're all stronger than we think we are."

Numbly, Arthur nodded his head, staring straight ahead at the framed candid shot of his wife on the coffee table. She was laughing. He looked as if he never would again.

Sasha could sense the detective's eyes on her before she looked up to see him standing there. Santini was less than a foot away, looking at her with an expression she couldn't begin to read.

He flipped the phone closed. "I'll stay with you until his brother-in-law comes."

There was no room for selfless protests so she didn't bother making any. She welcomed the company.

# Chapter 5

Bart Henderson hung up the phone with such force the resulting contact sounded as if something was being thrown. It caught Tony's attention. He raised an inquiring eyebrow and looked in his partner's direction. Of the two of them, the burly Henderson was the one who could be accused of being sunny, despite the fact that each morning, Tony could overhear him reviewing a litany of complaints about what offending part of his body hurt the most that day. He was usually exchanging the information with the other "old-timer" in the squad room, Harold Lincoln.

Henderson usually didn't display any evidence of a shortness of temper. As far as Tony knew, his partner's temper had no end.

Unlike his own.

Henderson sighed, leaning back in his chair. The resulting breeze ruffled a few papers on his desk, bringing them precariously close to the edge. He moved them back where they belonged and narrowed his small eyes even further. They nearly disappeared beneath the tufts of fading red eyebrows as he looked at his partner.

"That was the hospital administrator at Our Lady of Patience Memorial Hospital. Again," he growled. "She wants to know if we've made any headway in our investigations." The man glanced in his direction hopefully. "Have we?"

Tony thought of the cool, tall blonde he'd interviewed the morning after the first body had been discovered, and then again when the second was found. In her late forties and slender, Lauren James had a chin that seemed to be permanently raised, giving her the appearance of looking down on everyone she dealt with. Her manner did nothing to change that impression.

Tony shook his head. "Not unless there's been a break in the case in the last five minutes that I don't know about."

They'd been at this for three weeks now, fielding calls from well-meaning people that always led nowhere, interviewing everyone remotely associated with the two women and relentlessly going over the data that the crime labs sent up. So far, they were no further along than when they'd started.

"Dunno why she's calling me. You're the one she talked to before." Henderson looked at him over the top of his rimless glasses. "I guess maybe I look friendlier to her."

"Maybe," Tony agreed, already retreating back into the file he'd been reviewing when Henderson had intentionally dropped the receiver.

Restless, Henderson rocked in his chair. "She says the murders are bad publicity for the hospital."

"Murders generally are," Tony commented, trying to block out the annoying sound made by Henderson's chair. Certain sounds had a tendency to distract him.

Just like certain thoughts did. And ever since he'd taken this case, he'd found that doctor, the one who'd been the first one on the scene both times, intruding into his thoughts at very odd, unforeseeable times. He didn't know what to make of it yet.

Maybe his mind trying to tell him something he'd missed. And then again, maybe not.

Tony turned his chair and looked back at the bulletin board on the wall behind him. The actual board had a multitude of tiny holes, evidence of all the thumbtacks that had been driven into it over time, securing bits and pieces of other murders he'd solved. Or that had temporarily been left unsolved.

The puzzles gave him no peace until he either solved them or something larger took their place. But once that was done, once the current case was put to bed, the old, unsolved cases would resurface to haunt him until he finally had all the pieces in the right place. Until he found the killer.

Because of his junkyard-dog tendency never to let go, Tony had an unprecedented record for solved homicides within the precinct. Probably, he'd been told, within the country.

Right now, the board had the photographs of both nurses and every scrap of information he and Henderson had gathered that stood out. The rest of the information existed within his notebook and the hard drive of his computer. A great deal of that overlapped.

There wasn't much to go on. Both victims were females, both were nurses, both worked at PM, but then the similarities ended. The two women had moved in different circles. One had been in her twenties, the other in her sixties, one was a single mother, the other a grandmother raising two grandchildren. They were both struggling to get by, but he didn't see that as a strong connecting factor.

At least, Tony amended, looking from one photograph to the other, not yet.

And what did the note that they'd both been clutching mean? Obviously, it was from the killer. Was it someone who hated nurses in general and wasn't educated enough to know that the phrase he'd typed referred to physicians and not nurses?

Or was it more personal than that? More devious than that? Was there a clue within a clue that he wasn't seeing?

"You know," he theorized out loud, "one of the

murders could have been committed to cover the other."

Henderson pushed away from his desk and turned his chair to face him. "Come again?"

Tony stood up and went to the board. "Someone had it in for either Angela or Rachel and kills the other one to make it look like some dumb serial killer is on the loose."

Henderson wrinkled his brow, trying to follow the reasoning. "Why dumb?"

Tony glanced at the data beneath each photograph, summarizing the last few hours of each victim's life. Nothing remarkable sprang out. "'First do no harm' is the beginning of the Hippocratic Oath, not a pledge a nurse makes."

"Maybe they should have." When Tony looked at his partner, Henderson shrugged his wide shoulders beneath the hound's-tooth jacket he always wore. "Maybe one of them—or both—did some harm."

Tony slowly nodded his head. It was a possibility. But only one of many. It carried no extra weight at the moment.

For the time being, he mentally filed it away.

"Nothing stands out, yet," he told Henderson. And he could only sit at his desk, playing with papers, pecking his way along on the keyboard, for so long. He needed to be hands-on, to be out in the field. "I'm going back to the hospital to nose around. Talk to the security guard who found the first one."

Henderson was already shutting down his machine. "Don't forget that doctor," he said when Tony gave him a quizzical look. "She was around for both murders. Seems like an odd coincidence," he commented affably.

Tony shook his head. "I told you, I've already ruled her out."

Henderson walked down the corridor. A knowing smile moved the ends of his handlebar moustache. "That kind of woman does cloud the mind."

Tony shot the other man an annoyed look. "There's nothing cloudy about my mind. According to the M.E.'s time frame, Dr. Pulaski was five stories away from the scene of both crimes. During the first, she was dealing with a hemorrhaging patient and during the second, she was making her rounds. In each case, a lot of people saw her."

Henderson looked willing to be convinced, but still slightly skeptical. "Making rounds that late in the day?"

Tony's careless shrug indicated that he didn't care what Henderson thought doctors did. He was only interested in one. And only so far as the case went. "Woman's dedicated, I guess."

Reaching the elevator, Henderson pressed the down button. "Nice to know there's someone else out there other than us." And then he laughed. "'Course, she probably makes a hell of a lot more money than either one of us."

Tony laughed shortly. As far as salaries went,

cops were on the low end of the scale. But it had never been about the money for him.

Getting into the elevator, he looked at his partner. "I didn't picture you being in it for the money."

"Not me. I'm strictly in it for the glamour," Henderson deadpanned, then laughed. "And to get material for my book."

The elevator doors closed noisily. A grinding noise accompanied their descent to the ground floor. Henderson had a book? This was the first he'd heard on the subject, Tony thought. But then, he didn't exactly leave himself opened to exchanges that went beyond the cases they were handling.

"What book?"

A faraway look entered Henderson's faded green eyes. "The book I intend to write once I finally retire from this job."

For the first time that morning, Tony smiled. Henderson could no more retire than he could grow another set of arms. This was where he felt he belonged and they were going to have to surgically remove him from his desk to get him to leave permanently.

The elevator came to a stop and the doors drew open. Tony got out. "You keep telling yourself that, Henderson," he tossed over his shoulder. "You keep telling yourself that."

He hadn't planned on revisiting the doctor he'd silently dubbed Snow White. The one Henderson seemed still to be suspicious of. He and Henderson had parted company at the hospital elevators, each intent on their own line of questioning. Henderson had gone to the place where Rachel had reported for the last six months of her life, the surgical floor, while he had gone to the nurses' station on the maternity ward where Angela Rico had worked for over two years.

Had the dark-haired obstetrician not been on the floor, he wouldn't have gone out of his way to see her. But he didn't have to. She was right there.

He'd stopped at the nurses' station where Angela Rico had sat, making notes on patients' charts and talking to the people she worked with. A couple of minutes later, Dr. Sasha Pulaski came walking out of one of the rooms, looking tired and harried.

It was too early in the day to look like that, he thought. But then, maybe the day had come on the heels of a hard night. He supposed that gave them something in common. Both of them could be summoned out of bed at a moment's notice. And there was no saying no once the call came.

Their eyes met as the doctor was passing the nurses' station. Tony rose from what had unofficially been Angela's desk, moving into the corridor. Blocking her way.

"Doctor," he said, nodding at her.

"Detective," she returned. He noticed that the woman drew in her breath, as if she expected him to ask her something.

But just for a split second, as he glanced down at

the button that was coming undone on its own just at the point he assumed was the top of her bra, he'd lost his train of thought. And every other thought as well. But only for a moment.

"Have you thought of anything to add to your statement?" he finally asked.

She'd gone over the events of those two evenings a thousand times in her mind. There was nothing new to add, nothing she'd forgotten to tell him.

Sasha shook her head. "You don't have any suspects?" She knew if he did, he couldn't elaborate, but it was worth a shot. Besides, she was feeling strangely awkward and very aware that the two nurses in the glass-enclosed station were staring at her. At them. And taking in every word that was being said.

"No one who crosses over into both areas," Tony replied after a moment.

They'd found out that Rachel's husband owed a local bookie almost five hundred dollars, but Tony couldn't see his way clear to the bookie killing Arthur's wife because of a payment default, or even as a warning for others. Besides, Angela's background was clean and so was her ex-husband's. Neither was even remotely connected to the bookie so there was no common ground on that score.

Tony's stomach growled, reminding him that breakfast had been half a muffin and lunch hadn't happened for him yet. An impulse struck him and he went with it before he gave it any thought. "You in a hurry?"

Sasha's first reaction was to say yes. As far back as she could remember, she'd always been in a hurry. There was always something to catch up on, something to do.

But at that moment, there was nothing actually pressing that she needed to get to. Her office was located in the medical building across the street and it wouldn't be open again until two o'clock. For once, the waiting room wasn't jammed with patients who'd been forced to restructure their day because she was called away to deliver yet another baby who had no respect for due dates.

Technically, that made her free. "A little less than usual," she told him. "Why?"

Not one to put himself entirely out on a limb all at once, he began with, "Where's a good place to eat around here?"

Humor appealingly curved her mouth. "Believe it or not," she said, knowing what people thought of hospital food, "the food in the cafeteria isn't half bad."

It wasn't the food he was actually interested in. Talking to the doctor in surroundings that put her at ease was his real goal. "I was shooting for three-quarters good."

The smile became a grin. "For that, you'd have to go to Queens."

On his own, he favored takeout, usually from a pizza place. "Why Queens?"

Without making a conscious decision one way or

another, Sasha had begun walking toward the bank
of elevators at the rear of the floor. The detective, as
she'd expected, had fallen into step with her.

"That's where my parents live," she told him.
"My mother's a fantastic cook. Dad keeps telling her
she should open her own restaurant, but she doesn't
want the hassle or the risk, she tells him."

They stopped at the elevators. Tony glanced at his
watch. "Not enough time to go to Queens and back
for lunch. Guess I'll have to chance the cafeteria." His
eyes held hers for a moment. "Want to be my guide?"

She found it took effort to stop the shiver that
threatened to sweep up and down her spine like a
runaway roller coaster. She did, however, manage to
sound cool as she instructed, "Just take the elevator
down to the basement. Can't miss it." And then, as
the elevator arrived and its doors opened, she
decided to see if she could get anything out of the
detective. "On second thought, maybe I could stand
to grab something to eat, too."

They got in and he brushed past her to press the
button. However minor, the swift, fleeting contact
was not lost on either of them. Feeling just the slightest bit awkward, Tony dropped his hand to his side.
"I'm sure your patients would appreciate it."

Sasha kept her back to the wall, wishing someone
else was on the elevator with them. "My patients?"

He nodded. Two people stepped on at the next
floor. He moved closer to her. "People think and
react better when they eat regular meals."

There was no place for her to back up into. Trapped, she forced herself to sound amused. "You a part-time nutritionist?"

The doors opened again and the two passengers got off. Tony made no effort to step back into his original space. He noticed that she shifted, inching her way to the side. He shook his head in reply. "Something my aunt used to say to us when we wanted to skip meals."

"Us?" She knew nothing about the man and saw this as a chance to give the detective some kind of depth and dimension.

"My brothers and me," he answered. He saw the interest in her eyes. He didn't have long to wait for the next question.

"Your aunt raised you?"

It hadn't been his intention to answer, but somehow the words seemed to flow naturally—even though the memories were jagged and sharp. It hadn't been a warm and fuzzy childhood by any stretch of the imagination. "I wouldn't exactly call it raised. More like stood guard as we grew."

On the second floor, several people got on, all bound for the first. This time, Sasha stepped into his space, her curiosity blocking out any claustrophobic feelings his close proximity might have aroused.

"But you lived with her," she pressed.

He tried to summon the good moments and found them lost amid a sea of bad ones. Still, Tess had done the best she could, he supposed. "Yeah."

The single word said it all, she thought. His had been a hard childhood. Probably had contributed a great deal to the man she saw in front of her today. Unsmiling. Hard. "Because you wanted to or you had to?"

It struck him as an odd way of phrasing the question. He looked at her as they came to the first floor and the same people who'd crowded on, got off. Their places were taken by people who wanted to reach the basement. Now he and the doctor were all but standing in each other's spaces. Not, he noted, an unpleasant thing. But distracting, highly distracting. "I never heard it put that way."

She found herself whispering to him in order not to be overheard or have her words mingling with anyone else's. There were at least three other conversations going on in the small enclosure.

"Is that your way of saying you're not going to answer the question?"

The woman was quick on the uptake, he thought, somewhat amused. "Something like that." He looked down at her. She had to be about five, six inches shorter than him, he guessed. And softer, remembering one feel of her hand. "I'm supposed to be the one asking questions," he pointed out.

The elevator doors opened again and the people in front of them quickly got off. "I thought you were the one who was just going to get some lunch. I didn't realize this was official."

"Off the record," he countered, getting off right beside her.

A long, brightly lit hallway greeted him. Freshly painted arrows pointed in opposite directions, one toward the out-patient pharmacy and the other toward the cafeteria.

Without looking, Sasha turned left. Striding quickly, he fell into step beside her again.

"Off the record or on, it's going to be the same information, Detective. I told you everything I knew, which wasn't much. And if anything had occurred to me, I would have called you." She wove her way in and out of the crowd like someone accustomed to doing this on a regular basis. He did his best to keep up.

"I still have your card," she told him. She carried it around with her every day. Looked at it every night as she emptied her pockets. Looked at it and conjured up an image that unsettled her as it seemed to embed its way beneath her skin.

"Good to know," he allowed. "All right, this is just lunch, then."

"Just lunch," she echoed, making it sound like a pact.

The second Sasha pushed the swinging cafeteria doors open, a wall of noise and increased warmth engulfed them. The cafeteria was filled almost to capacity.

"I guess you were right about the food," he said, lowering his head to her ear so that she could hear him. "Is it always like this?"

His breath cascaded along her neck, making her feel warmer than any of the hospital heating ducts going full blast in the winter. She did her best not to react, not to shiver in the wake of the tingling sensation that was shimmying up and down her spine.

"It's lunchtime," she pointed out. "And a lot of the staff doesn't actually get a full hour. Lauren James has a myriad of rules she wants followed and she doesn't tolerate people bending them."

Picking up a tray, he handed it to Sasha, then took one for himself before following her into the actual food area.

There were two different steam tables offering up four different kinds of entrées, while beds of ice presented a variety of salads and desserts. Tony felt his stomach tightening in anticipation, urging him to make a choice, any choice. It no longer mattered what.

He pointed to a stew and the white-attired server behind the table gingerly placed it on his tray. Tony noted Sasha selected a spinach salad. With a bit of ice still attached to the bottom of the dish, the salad slid around drunkenly on her tray until she brushed the sliver aside.

"Watching your weight, Doctor?" he asked as they both went to the coffee island. Taking the coffeepot, he poured two cups.

"No, I just like spinach." And then she smiled as she paused to pick up an apple that was nestled in another bed of ice shavings. "Me and Popeye."

It was so noisy, he was forced to read her lips in order to hear her. Dr. Sasha Pulaski had the most dazzling smile he ever remembered seeing. Not because her teeth were blindingly white, but there was something sweet and genuine about the smile. Because he was a devout cynic who questioned everything, he couldn't help wondering if the woman behind the smile was putting him on, or if she was as sweet as the smile she displayed.

He also wondered what the chances were of his finding that out before the investigation was over.

"Ring them up together," he instructed the cashier, a thin, sinewy-looking Latino with large, round eyes and an electric blue T-shirt and jeans that adhered to him like a second skin.

Sasha reached into the deep pockets of her lab coat. "I can pay for my own lunch, Detective."

He steadied her hand with his own. "I'm sure you can. Consider this a reward for steering me in the right direction."

"A reward?" she echoed.

*Okay, wrong word,* he thought. "My way of saying thanks," Tony amended.

She wasn't about to be in his debt for any reason. The ground there was uncertain. "No thanks needed." Sasha began to reach into her pocket again.

"You two want to take this mutual admiration society somewhere else?" the chunky lab technician behind them suggested, annoyed. "You're holding up the line."

"Looks like the public has spoken," Tony told her, placing a twenty into the cashier's hand.

"I'll pick up the next tab," Sasha informed him as she began to scan the area, looking for somewhere to sit.

The word *next* hung in the air, daring him to take it seriously.

# Chapter 6

"What can you tell me about Lauren James?"

The question seemed to come out of the blue after several minutes of silence between them had gone by. Tony had sampled the stew and decided that the doctor was right. The food here was more than edible. He'd consumed several more forkfuls before saying anything. Once the hollow feeling had faded from his stomach and he felt a little more human, he felt up to addressing some of the issues that had occurred to him.

Sasha raised her eyes from her salad. "What do you mean?"

He'd always felt that vague questions were the best for openers. That left interpretation up to the person being questioned. A great deal of information could be garnered that way. "What do you know about her?"

But the doctor apparently wanted him to be specific. "You mean her background?"

Tony shook his head. He wasn't after facts he could get from a human resource file. He wanted impressions. "No, I already have that—"

"Of course you do," Sasha murmured, a slanted smile making a brief appearance on her lips. He struck her as someone who left no stone unturned. And if there were no stones, he probably went out and found some.

Santini shrugged casually as he continued eating. "Part of the job."

"I know." Her father had always been thorough like that. She was fairly certain that every boy she and her sisters ever dated had a complete background check conducted on him. "You probably have everybody's background on some tiny little microchip."

"Not everybody's," he corrected, trying to decide if she considered that a job well done, or an invasion of privacy, "just the people who figure directly into the case."

Her eyes met his. "Like me."

That went without saying. "You were on the scene both times."

Sasha popped a cherry tomato into her mouth before commenting. She loved the taste of tomatoes. "Then it must have put you to sleep."

He narrowly avoided being hit on the back of his head by a woman with a large purse that could have doubled as a briefcase. He moved his head away just in time as she hurried on her way.

"What did?" he asked.

"Reading about my background. Nothing remarkable." She recited what she knew had to be in his notes. "I went to NYU for my undergraduate degree, then attended NYU medical school." She didn't add that despite the fact that she worked three nights a week as a waitress to help defray the costs, she still managed to graduate in three years instead of four. "I interned at PM, then was lucky enough to get a residency here and now I can't think of anywhere I'd rather work than here. Like I said, deadly dull." And then she paused. "Or shouldn't I use the word *deadly?*"

"You shouldn't use either word." He would have left it at that, except that she looked at him curiously, waiting for an explanation. "I don't think you're dull."

Her smile made all her features soften and stirred something within him he didn't welcome disturbed. "Then you obviously have a very low excitement threshold, Detective. I live and breathe my work and my family—not always in that order."

Tony knew all about her family. About the parents who had managed to be smuggled out of Krakow, Poland, while that country was still in the grip of communist rule. How Josef and Magda Pulaski had both worked diligently to provide a better way of life for their daughters.

"Four sisters, all younger, all doctors or almost doctors." And then he added the part he knew she didn't expect him to know about. "And each one helps the next in line until that sister graduates. And then it's on to the next one." He paused to take a sip of his coffee. And to use the cup to cover the hint of a smile. "You can close your mouth now."

She inclined her head. The man really was thorough. Or was that because he'd initially regarded her to be a suspect?

"You *have* been doing a lot of research."

He shifted the focus away from himself. "Your parents must be very proud."

Sasha smiled. "They've been known to brag a little," she allowed. Actually, given half a chance, her father bent every ear that came his way about his daughters' accomplishments.

But she had a question of her own for Santini. "If your research is that intense, Detective, what is it you want me to tell you about Lauren James that you don't already know?"

That was easy. He wanted her to tell him what he couldn't find in a report. "What do you think of her?" Before she could answer, he broadened the scope. "What does everyone else think of her?"

Sasha thought of several conversations she'd overheard, usually after Lauren had come down hard on someone. Or fired one of the staff for some minor infraction.

She shook her head. "My father taught me not to

use words like that at the table." And then she smiled.
"My mother taught me not to use words like that at
all, but my father's way is a compromise." She could
see that the detective was still waiting for some kind
of an answer. "Nicely put, no one would have the
slightest objection if Lauren was hit by a bus as she
was crossing the street. She's not exactly a people
person when it comes to the staff. Her bottom line is
profit."

"I thought that Our Lady of Patience Memorial
was supposed to be a non-profit hospital."

She liked the way Santini said the hospital's full
name. Liked, she realized, sitting here, having lunch
with him. That wasn't really a good thing, Sasha
reminded herself. Because "like" led to other things.
At this point in her life, she was too busy to get
involved with anyone and even if she wasn't, she'd
learned her lesson. Being involved meant hurting.
Unlike childbirth, this kind of pain was not worth it
in the end. Because at the end, there was only heart-
ache.

She focused on his question. "It is."

His eyes narrowed as he tried to comprehend the
connection between that and what she'd just said about
the administrator. "Then I don't understand—"

"There's profit, and then there's profit." *Clear as
mud, Sash,* she mocked herself. "Because PM is
non-profit, whatever extra money is accumulated
over the course of the year is put into updating equipment, or the facilities, in order to lure prestigious

physicians to affiliate themselves with our hospital. We have a reputation as one of the best hospitals in the state."

Tony read between the lines. "So she's on a power trip."

It was as good a summation as any. She'd already heard one of the nurses refer to Lauren as Stalin in drag, a remark that had particular meaning for her, given her family background.

"Something like that," Sasha agreed. "And there are various ways to gain from being at the helm of a thriving hospital."

"Such as?" he asked with interest. He'd known taking the doctor to lunch was a good idea. That he was having certain warm feelings was, in this case, simply collateral damage.

"Perks that come her way. Things like hard-to-come-by theater tickets and preferential treatment that she wouldn't have gotten if she wasn't the administrative head of Patience Memorial."

Tony frowned. "Isn't that unethical?"

Instead of nodding, Sasha qualified his assumption. "If you get caught."

He wasn't given to winking and looking the other way. But neither was he ready to condemn on hearsay. "These are pretty serious allegations."

Sasha knew what he was thinking, could see it in his eyes. One woman out to destroy the reputation of another. That hadn't been her intent.

"I'm not being catty, Detective. A few things have

come to light recently and several members of the board are looking into the matter. If they don't like the answers they come up with, Lauren might be in for a very rude awakening soon."

"They'd fire her?"

"In a heartbeat."

"Does she know?" If she did, he thought, that might be motive enough to do something drastic. Like damaging the reputation of the hospital that was threatening to put her out. Lauren James didn't strike him as a woman who agonized over her conscience.

Lauren didn't behave as if she knew, Sasha thought. The woman was certainly not going out of her way to make any allies or mend any fences. Still, she was too bright not to know that something was going on. "She might suspect." Sasha saw a look enter his eyes. "Why?" she wanted to know. "What are you thinking?"

"That I need to have another talk with Ms. James."

Sasha second-guessed him. She shook her head. "She's not your killer."

Tony banked down his amusement. Everyone was an armchair detective these days, he thought. "What makes you say that?"

"Because the sight of blood makes Lauren immensely queasy. I once had to give her several stitches because she cut her hand on a broken vase. Lauren passed out before I could prick her skin."

The story aroused his curiosity. "I thought you dealt mainly with, um, the other end," he finally said politely.

"I happened to be in her office when she cut her hand." She had never believed in standing on the sidelines when she could help. She hadn't been raised that way. "Seemed like the thing to do at the time."

He nodded, but he had already made up his mind. For all he knew, the murders had been committed to embarrass the administrator. Sideways thinking was the norm rather than the exception. "I'm still going to have another talk with her. In this job, you never know when a stray comment might lead to something that solves the case."

She would imagine that there were an incredible amount of pieces for him to consider and sift through. Sasha finished her coffee and set down the cup. "Your head must ache from all those pieces that you're trying to fit together."

"I manage." His tone gave nothing away as he watched her eyes, wondering where, if anywhere, she was going with this.

She trod lightly, but as a doctor, she felt obligated to point out certain things. "Drinking only intensifies headaches."

Tony looked at her, surprised at her comment. Surprised, too, that she should feel free to make it. Because the job had kept him on the move these last three weeks, there hadn't been any extra time to dwell on the black hole in his personal life that was eating him up alive. Because he was disciplined, he made sure he was always sober while working. He hadn't taken a drink in three weeks.

"What makes you mention drinking?" he wanted to know. There was an edge to his voice.

Her father had warned her more than once that she was too fearless. That she didn't allow conventions to hold her back. "That first night, you were hungover."

He drank vodka for a reason. Vodka left no telltale scent to give him away. And he prided himself on being able to navigate like a lifetime teetotaler. But he hated lies and stayed clear of them whenever possible. So he didn't bother pretending that she was imagining things.

Maybe he even had something to learn here. "So, what gave me away?"

It wasn't his behavior. It was more instinct on her part. "There was something in your eyes. Something not quite in sync."

Okay, he'd give her that, although he was pretty certain that he kept a lid on his thoughts and what little there was left of his emotions.

"Didn't have to be alcohol," he pointed out.

"No, it didn't," she agreed. "But whatever had you out of sync, you were trying to block it out with alcohol."

He regarded her for a long moment. "Lady, you're beginning to spook me." He didn't believe in clairvoyants, but he was willing to concede that there were people who were more intuitive than others. "Maybe you should be working on our side."

"I am on your side," she told him quietly. And then, because she felt she needed to explain what had given her insight into his situation, she said, "My fiancé had a cousin who tried to drown his sorrows with more than his share of Scotch. The result was the same. The sorrows didn't go away, but he very nearly did."

Tony had heard only one thing. "Your fiancé?" The background check he'd conducted made no mention of her having anyone in her life who wasn't directly related to her by blood. He glanced at her left hand. There was no ring there, but that didn't necessarily mean anything. "You're engaged?"

Sasha caught her lower lip between her teeth. Damn, how had that slipped out? Maybe because she still felt, even though he was gone, that Adam was still part of her life. "I was."

*Was.* He had no idea why the tension in his neck seemed to lessen. It was best not to go to places like that. "What happened? He have trouble competing with your career?"

"He had trouble competing with a mugger's gun," she corrected him quietly. She saw mild surprise flicker across the detective's face. Well, she'd come this far, she might as well tell him the rest of it. "Adam was killed trying to keep the man from stealing my engagement ring." She couldn't bring herself to look at it after he'd died so she sold it and donated the money to Adam's favorite charity, where it could do some good. "It was in a parking structure very similar to the one at PM," she added.

Tony took in the information, not knowing what to say, other than, "I'm sorry."

She tried to force a faint smile of gratitude to her lips and failed. "Me, too."

He understood now why she'd looked so shaken, so pale when he'd first met her. As a doctor, she was accustomed to blood, to life and occasionally, to death. But if the scene brought back personal memories, that was a completely different story.

Tony watched her push away her salad. There was still some left in the bowl. "I've made you lose your appetite."

She detected a note of self-reproach and was quick to absolve him of any guilt. "The spinach wasn't all that fresh."

He studied her face for a long moment. "You know, I'm not sure if, as an OB-GYN you'd know this, but if you lie, your nose grows."

The man had a sense of humor after all, she thought. It made her relax a little. Sasha raised her chin. "And is it?"

He looked so serious when he cocked his head, studying her, that for a moment she thought he was actually trying to verify whether her nose was growing.

"Hard to tell in this light," he finally said. She laughed and he nodded his approval. "That's better." Debating, he allowed himself to relate to her on a personal plateau, eschewing the danger of that. "I didn't mean to drag up any bad memories."

"You didn't." This time, she did smile. "All my memories of Adam are good ones."

He understood what she meant. That was the way he felt about his wife. There was a song she'd loved, "It Had To Be You," an old number from the thirties or so. One of the lyrics in it seemed to fit. "And even be glad, just to be sad, thinking of you." There were days that thoughts of Annie were the only things that kept him going.

He saw the doctor drop her napkin on the tray and then rise. She picked up the tray, ready to clear it away. "I'd better be getting back to my office," she told him. "Thank you for lunch."

"I enjoyed the company."

Tony hardly remembered rising to his feet, his own tray in his hand. He hadn't expected to say that when he'd opened his mouth. He'd expected to hear himself say something innocuous, like "you're welcome," or "maybe I'll see you." This was much too personal and revealing.

After a beat, Sasha nodded. The small smile widened just a touch. "So did I."

Whatever else she might have said was interrupted by the insistent buzz emitted by his pager. With a sigh, Tony placed his tray back on the table and reached for the device clipped to his belt. He barely had to glance at it. The number on the screen was all too familiar.

Sasha didn't know whether to linger, or take the

opportunity to drop off her tray on the conveyor belt and leave. Quickly. She didn't like what she was feeling. Attraction. It was crackling between them whenever she was near the detective. She wanted no crackling, no curiosity, no nothing.

She wanted dullness. The dullness that did not interfere with the rest of her life.

Whatever arguments she used on herself, she was still hanging back, watching him take out his cell phone and press a button that connected him to whoever was paging him.

She listened, thinking that perhaps it had something to do with finding Angela and Rachel's killer. Telling herself that it had nothing to do with gathering a few extra moments in the detective's company.

Sasha placed her tray next to his and began to combine the two, moving the plates and utensils onto one tray, then stacking it on top of the other. It bought her a few seconds. Long enough to hear him say, "This is Santini," into the cell phone.

The voice on the other end was male, but that was about all she could distinguish. The words were not clear enough for her to hear.

"You'd better get up here, partner," Henderson said to him.

"Where's 'here'?" Tony wanted to know.

He heard Henderson sigh. "Seventh floor." He paused, as if for dramatic effect. "One of the cleaning crew just found an orderly."

"And?" Tony pressed, waiting for the rest of it.

Out of the corner of his eye, he saw that the doctor was still there and that she was obviously listening to his side of the conversation. Annoyance would have been his usual response, but he found he didn't feel any.

"And the orderly was stuffed into the supply closet at the time. Tony, the guy had a hole in his forehead and the same note in his hand."

Adrenaline shot through Tony's veins. This just kept getting better and better. "Secure the area," he told Henderson.

"Already done. I was going to call for backup, but I thought you'd want me to call you first."

"You thought right, Henderson. Now call for backup." Tony closed his phone. The doctor was still watching his every move, the trays still in her hands.

"Back up, why back up?" she asked the moment he ended the call. "Did your partner find a suspect?"

His expression was sober. "No, just another body."

She stared at him, her eyes widening in horror. This was a nightmare, Sasha thought. The halls of PM were being stalked by a serial killer. "Another nurse?"

He shook his head. "Not this time. Henderson said it was an orderly."

"An orderly?" she echoed. This was making less and less sense. Now it looked as if someone had it in for the hospital. Sasha suddenly realized that

Santini was walking away from her. "I'm coming with you," she called, hurrying after him.

Sasha paused only long enough to throw the combined trays onto the conveyor belt, then she quickened her pace to catch up to him.

Tony held one of the swinging doors open for her. "I thought you had patients to see."

She darted across the threshold. "Not until two o'clock. I was going to catch up on dictation," she told him. "But there's nothing there that won't keep." Her hand covered her own pager, praying that no baby would suddenly decide to come out and see the world in the next forty minutes.

He gave her a glance that would have frozen others in mid-step. It had no such effect on the doctor.

"This isn't exactly according to the rules," Tony said tersely as they strode up the corridor to the elevators.

"Neither is death," she answered quietly, afraid that her voice might carry. There was no telling who might be turning the corner and overhear her.

She had him there, Tony thought. He supposed it would do no harm to let her come along.

The irony of the phrase he'd just used wasn't lost on him. But maybe the doctor knew the victim and could give him a jump-start on gathering information. So far, she seemed to know everyone who worked here.

He wondered, as they rode up the elevator, since

he'd already decided to talk to the administrator if it would be worth his while to corner Lauren James about this latest development. He and Henderson were going to have to start looking into recently terminated, disgruntled employees.

Most of all, he wondered, as he glanced in her direction, why he was really letting the doctor talk her way into coming along.

*Chapter* 7

Jorge Lopez was a slight man. In his late twenties and a former gang member with an arrest record, the diminutive orderly was finally getting his life together and headed in the proper direction. His job at Patience Memorial was only one of two he held down while going to school at night in order to get his G.E.D. He wanted, he'd confided to the pretty social worker he'd just begun seeing, to make something of himself.

And now, Sasha thought, heartsick as she looked at the prone body that had been discovered less than half an hour ago in the supply room, Jorge was never going to get the chance.

Tony'd examined the orderly's body as best he

could, mindful not to disturb anything until after the crime scene investigators had had a chance to photograph everything and process the scene. There really wasn't all that much to see. There was the note he'd seen on the previous two victims. Like the others, Lopez had been killed with a single bullet to the center of his forehead. Death had been instant. From all indications, a silencer had been used. That would explain why no one had heard the shot.

But not why no one noticed. The body was still warm. That meant that the murder had taken place in the last hour. This was the post-surgical floor. How had the killer escaped notice?

Perturbed, Tony rose to his feet. He exchanged places with a young woman from the crime scene unit. She was armed with a camera and immediately began taking photographs.

"I want their lives gone over with a fine tooth comb," he told Henderson as he stepped back. "The two nurses and the orderly. Everything they had in common. Where they shopped, who they saw. Any clubs they might have liked attending. Hobbies, vices. Anything," he emphasized. There had to be something more going on than just working at Patience Memorial, he thought.

Henderson pursed his lips, looking at the small, dark-haired man on the floor.

"What?" He knew the signs. Henderson was chewing on something.

"This could have been gang payback for something and they're just using the other two murders for cover," Henderson theorized, eyeing him carefully for his reaction.

Tony scrubbed his hand over his face. The thought had crossed his mind as well the second he'd found out about Lopez's former gang affiliation. "Yeah, I know. But for right now, let's just think of Lopez as belonging to this very exclusive little club. I want to make sure we shut the doors before any more members walk through them."

Stumped, frustrated, Tony turned to see that the doctor was still standing behind him. She hadn't said a word since they'd approached the supply closet and had actually listened to him when he'd told her to keep to the sidelines. There was pity in her eyes as she looked at the dead man.

Tony walked over to her. "You knew him?"

Sasha continued looking at the crumpled figure on the floor. Surprise was frozen on the handsome face. It all seemed so surreal, so bizarre to her. She'd seen more than her share of dead people when she'd done a rotation in the emergency room during her residency. Like everyone else at the hospital, she'd experienced the unnatural scenario of having a person talk to her one moment, then lapse into a deadly silence as their heart stopped beating the next. But she hadn't actually *known* any of those people, not for more than a few minutes.

She *knew* Jorge.

What was going on in the hospital was far more

personal. This was happening where she worked, where she *lived* a good portion of her life. She felt an overwhelming sadness. More than that, she felt indignant, because she felt violated.

"He was always whistling," she finally said in response to Santini's question. "Not those reedy-sounding efforts you always hear where people sound as if they were blowing out cracker bits. I could hear springtime in his whistle." She raised her eyes, aware that the detective was looking at her. "Jorge seemed very happy, like he didn't have a care in the world. But he did care," she added quickly. "He cared about his work, cared about the patients. Said that maybe in time, he'd become a nurse himself."

And then she smiled as she remembered. "He was always hanging around the OR, ready to do anything in order to be part of what went on in there, even if it was just cleaning up." She turned to look at the detective. "Why would somebody do this?" The question wasn't really directed at him, but at whatever power could supply some sort of half acceptable answer. It just didn't seem fair.

"That," Tony told her, "is the sixty-four-million-dollar question."

He looked thoughtfully down at the slain orderly. The blonde from the crime scene unit had finished taking photographs and was now lifting something from the man's shirt with tweezers. She placed it in a small plastic bag.

Tony slanted a glance at the woman next to him. "Lopez wanted to be a nurse?" He saw the doctor nod in response. "Maybe this nut job has it in for nurses," he theorized. But that didn't explain everything, either. "But if that's the case, what's this bit with the note?" he wondered out loud for the umpteenth time.

Tony was beginning to believe that the victims weren't just picked at random, or murdered in order to get back at the hospital. His gut told him that they were chosen for a reason. Whoever was doing this was too methodical to select just anyone. The killer seemed to know everyone's schedule. How else could he kill his quarry without being seen?

Which meant that it was an insider, he concluded. That narrowed it down to roughly four and a half thousand people, give or take.

"Maybe that's the key," Sasha guessed, still working with what the detective had just said. "Maybe whoever's doing this is trying to make a point, teach a lesson." She looked at the bullet hole in Jorge's forehead. "He's not just shooting them, he's executing them."

Tony raised an eyebrow. "Your father bring his cases home?"

A fond smile curved her mouth. "Sometimes. Not so Mama would see, but late at night, when she was asleep, he'd get up and sneak into the kitchen and spread his notes out on the table. Sometimes he'd sit there for two, three hours, trying to find something he'd missed."

It wasn't anything he hadn't done himself. More than a few times. "And you know this how?"

"I used to hear him and get up, too. Sometimes he'd tell me about the case." Usually after she'd begged and pleaded, she recalled. "I'm sure he kept the gorier details to himself, but he always told me enough to get me caught up in it, make me want to help him."

That would explain why she asked him so many questions, Tony thought. He stepped out of the way as the Medical Examiner arrived. Older, slightly overweight, the nature of his work had left C. S. Vaughn with a perpetual frown on his face.

Without thinking, Tony slipped his hand around Sasha's waist, moving her out of the way as well. Realizing that he was touching her, he dropped his hand. "So why didn't you become a cop like your old man?"

For a while, she'd considered it. But then she'd changed her mind. "I was more interested in life than in death. Besides, both my parents had their heart set on having a doctor in the family."

In light of what he'd learned, the comment made him laugh. "I guess that's a case of careful what you wish for. All that money for medical school," he elaborated when she looked at him quizzically. The cost of putting five daughters through college, let alone medical school, had to be staggering.

"We all pitch in," she reminded him. Education, her father had maintained, was a privilege, not a right. None of them ever forgot that.

Tony was nodding when it suddenly occurred to

him that he'd gotten distracted and veered from the case.

First time that had *ever* happened. He upbraided himself for being so careless.

Looking over his shoulder, he was relieved to see that Henderson was busy talking to the head nurse and hadn't noticed his lapse.

Still, that didn't make it any less of a transgression in his own book, Tony thought, annoyed.

He looked back at the doctor. "You work with this Lopez?"

Lopez. The detective made it sound so impersonal, she thought. Jorge Lopez was a person, not simply a statistic. It was important to her that Santini think of him that way.

"Everyone worked with Jorge," she told him. "His supervisor would send Jorge anywhere he was needed. The man worked twice as hard as anyone else. It was as if he was trying to make up for lost time."

*And now he didn't have any time left,* she thought sadly.

Santini was writing down everything she was saying in the small notepad she saw him carrying with him. "He have a family?"

She thought a minute, trying to remember. "He has a daughter with an ex-girlfriend. Monica. She's almost six. And I think he'd started seeing someone recently." Her memory became clearer and she nodded. "He showed me her picture. She's a social worker. He thought she could have been a model."

She could remember the man beaming as he showed off the photograph.

The woman had a good head for detail, Tony thought. It made his job easier. "Do you know her name?"

If Jorge had mentioned it, she couldn't remember. Sasha shook her head. "I'll ask around."

Ordinarily he would have told her that they could handle it, but in this case, to varying degrees, she seemed to be interwoven in all three victims' lives and because she was a hospital insider, he decided it was prudent to accept the doctor's offer.

"Thanks." Tony made another notation in his notepad, then flipped it closed for the time being. He tucked it away. "I'll get in touch with you later," he told her.

Tony stopped to confer with the crime scene investigator. When he turned around a couple of minutes later, the doctor was gone. And he was relieved.

With her gone, he hoped his mind would clear.

"We're going to need more manpower," he said to Henderson when the latter crossed over to him several minutes later.

"I was just about to suggest that." The wealth of data to be sorted through was increasing exponentially. It could easily overwhelm them. "Think the captain'll go for it?"

"He'll have to." Tony frowned. There was no doubt in his mind what they were facing. "Any way you slice it, we've got ourselves a genuine, dyed-in-the-wool serial killer on our hands. That means putting together a task force."

And quickly, he added silently. Before anyone else was murdered.

If there was any doubt that a serial killer was loose, the next day's edition of the *New York Daily News* vanquished it. The headline on the front page screamed Death Stalks Patience Memorial.

The second Sasha picked up the paper from her doorstep, the telephone began to ring. She was alone in the apartment. Natalya had pulled an all-nighter and was still at the hospital while Kady had left half an hour ago, saying only that she was off to see a friend.

For a moment, Sasha thought of pouring herself a bowl of cornflakes and ignoring the phone, but that lasted for only one ring. She knew who it was. Ignoring him wasn't going to make him go away.

Getting up from the kitchen table, she crossed to the telephone. One glance at the caller ID told her she was right.

"Hi, Daddy," she said, placing the receiver against her ear.

"How you know that's me?" the deep, heavily accented voice wanted to know as it rumbled in her ear.

Her father had the *Daily News* delivered and read it religiously at breakfast every morning. He'd always been an early riser. She smiled to herself as she brought the wireless receiver back to the table and sat down.

"I've known you for thirty years, Daddy. I pick things up."

Josef didn't waste time beating around the bush. He never did where his girls were concerned. "What is this serial killer thing at the hospital that I am reading about?"

She gave him a thumbnail sketch, although she knew he was asking for more. "Two nurses were killed in the parking structure at PM, and yesterday they found an orderly in the supply closet. He'd been shot like the first two victims."

She heard an impatient breath escape before he said, "I know. I can read, Sasha." Concern throbbed in every syllable. "Do you know anything about these murders?"

"Probably no more than you, Dad." Given his nature and background with the police, she imagined that her father had probably devoured all the stories about the murders. Since he'd retired, time was now a commodity that hung heavily on his hands. The model kits he'd collected for the day he would retire held no interest for him once he was free to devote himself to their construction. So he read mysteries and got himself involved in his daughters' lives. For his own good, and theirs, Sasha wished he'd do more of the first and less of the second.

"They have found nothing?" he asked incredulously. Not waiting for her answer, he said, "Maybe I should call Larry."

Larry was Larry Collins, the chief of detectives. He was a man who had swiftly risen through the ranks, but to her father he would always be the wet-behind-the-ears kid he had been partnered with. The two families got together every Christmas, at which time her father and Larry would sit by the fireplace, talking over cases that had happened "back in the day." She'd treated his wife on a number of occasions at the hospital.

That not withstanding, she didn't think that the chief of detectives would appreciate her father butting in when it came to official police business.

"I don't like you working there, Sasha," he told her. "With a crazy person loose."

She laughed. That was definitely not a reason to change hospitals. "This is New York, Dad. There're a lot of crazy people loose."

Sasha could almost see him scowling, his eyebrows drawing together, creating a formidable line above his hawk-like nose. He could look scary when he wanted to. But she knew that beneath it all was a soft marshmallow center.

"But they are not killing people," her father growled at her. The more he worried, the grumpier he tended to sound.

"That we know of," she pointed out, deliberately keeping her voice cheerful.

There was silence on the other end. Her father was accustomed to these verbal sparring matches. Accustomed, too, to her stubbornness. "Cannot you and your sisters go on a vacation?"

"No," she answered pointedly with feeling. "Daddy, the police are on it. The detective handling the case seems very competent and I'm sure—"

"You have met him?" he wanted to know, interrupting her.

"Yes." She realized that she was smiling and deliberately dropped the corners of her mouth. "He questioned me."

"Questioned you?" her father echoed, indignation rising in his voice. "Why for he question you?" And then he answered his own question, but not to his satisfaction. "He is thinking you are a suspect?"

"Daddy, you know that they have to rule people out before they can get on with the case—"

"But why you?" he pressed. He knew police procedure like the back of his hand. And he missed it more than he would ever tell anyone. "They are not talking to everyone at the hospital." And then it hit him. And he didn't like it. "Did you see something?"

"No." But that was only in the third case, she reminded herself. She'd always believed in being honest whenever possible. So with a resigned sigh, because she knew the kind of reaction to expect, she added, "But I called the police about the first two bodies."

"You?"

Josef tended to be protective of his own and in his eyes, she and her sisters would always be his little girls, in need of caring. She supposed, given a choice between having it this way and having a distant parent who remained uninvolved in her life, she would have chosen the former.

But that still didn't mean she wanted to be smothered. "Dad, please don't worry—"

"Too late," he informed her glibly. "You have children, you worry. God makes it work that way." The sigh she heard told her he was struggling to keep himself in check. "But I thought you would be safe in the hospital."

"I am safe at the hospital," she insisted.

"With a madman loose, killing everyone?" He laughed shortly.

She tried her best to reason with him as her cornflakes gradually became soggier, their wavy shapes being dragged down into the milk.

"Daddy, you're overreacting. He's not killing everyone. Three people have died. Three people too many," she quickly qualified, "but three people do not make an 'everyone' by any stretch of the imagination."

There was silence on the other end. For a second, she thought she'd won. She should have known better. "You know all the people?"

"You mean the people who were killed?"

"Yes."

"Yes," she replied, wondering if she was headed for another minefield, "I know them."

"How?" her father pressed. "From seeing, or from working?"

She was about to say that she knew the three victims from interacting with them on occasion, but then she paused to consider his question more care-fully. Angela had been present for several of the babies she'd delivered, but off-hand, she couldn't recall ever having worked with Rachel. As for Jorge, he might have been in the delivery room after the fact, but she was positive he'd never been there during a delivery.

"Seeing, mostly," she finally told him.

"You know, your mother, she says I am making her crazy, hanging around, watching her. I think I am helping and she is saying I am not."

The information had come out of left field. But she knew her father well enough to know that he was not just meandering through a conversation. Every-thing he said had a reason behind it.

"Where's this going, Daddy?"

"I am thinking," he stretched out slowly, as if to give the impression of thoughts forming, "maybe I could become a security guard. Your hospital, it needs more guards now, yes?"

Oh God, no. That was all she needed, her father following her around as she made her rounds, saw her patients. She knew he meant well, but that didn't change the fact that she didn't want him shadowing her every move.

"Daddy, it's a lovely gesture, but really, I'm fine." And then, before he could say anything, she added, "Natalya's fine. Kady's fine."

"Those nurses and that orderly," he said gruffly, "they were not so fine."

"No," she admitted, "they weren't." This was a grisly matter and she couldn't escape that. But she couldn't let it hinder her, either. "Look, Dad, if you want to be a security guard, I think that's great. But you know it's never a good idea to be personally involved." And if he worked at PM, he would be very personally involved.

"If I am not involved, I can't be doing my work," he told her simply and she knew it was true. While others maintained their sanity by separating themselves from the events of the crimes they were working on, Josef Pulaski dove in and immersed himself in the details and the situation until, on some level, he lived and breathed his work. Caring was his key when it came to solving cases. Caring defined the man.

"You do what you think is best, Daddy," she finally said. "But I am not," she warned quickly, "wearing a bulletproof vest to the hospital."

She heard him chuckle. "You were always a step ahead of me."

Sasha sincerely doubted that, but it was nice to hear.

"Gotta go, Dad."

"I will see you later."

That, Sasha thought, hanging up, was what she was kind of afraid of.

# *Chapter 8*

He couldn't catch a break.

Pulling his chair in closer to his desk, Tony suppressed an exasperated sigh. His back ached and his nerves were frayed and getting more so as he struggled to tune out the noise around him.

For the last hour, he'd been staring at the same files he'd already gone over so many times in the last few weeks, he could recite what was on each page verbatim without bothering to look.

Two weeks had gone by since the last murder. That made it a total of five weeks and nothing. No headway, no ground gained. Theories about the murders still flew around from every direction, to be discounted or placed on a list of possibilities. But five weeks after Angela Rico was first discovered on the lower level of the hospital parking structure, they were no closer to finding her killer or the killer of the other two victims than they had been when the security guard had first stumbled across her body.

Surrounded by a stack of files, Tony drummed his fingers on his desk, an outward sign of the impatience festering beneath the surface.

Each murder was the same. A single bullet to the head. An execution. Each victim had the same note clutched in his or her hand. A note that could have come from any one of a thousand printers located in the general vicinity. There were no prints on the paper other than the victim's. The only trace of a stray fiber found on any of the three bodies had come from the first victim. A single, almost imperceptible blue thread that the lab technician ascertained had come from a uniform. The kind that the security guards at Patience Memorial wore.

That brought their attention momentarily back to the initial security guard. But all it took was a simple re-questioning. Walter Stevens told Henderson that he'd bent over the body, hoping against hope, to see if the slain woman had the slightest pulse still beating.

Tony heard a squeak that seemed amplified above the rest of the noise. He glanced over in Henderson's direction. His partner was leaning back in his chair as far as it would go.

As if sensing that he had eyes on him, Henderson looked in his direction. "It's like he vacuumed and scrubbed the victim and the crime scene before he left."

There was no doubt that these murders were completely premeditated. Those were the hardest criminals to deal with, the ones who operated with no soul, who conducted their crimes with cold logic instead of being driven by heated passion. On some distant, vague level, the latter could be remotely forgivable, the former could not.

Tony tossed down the pen he'd just picked up. "This is one hell of a sick, methodical bastard," he declared.

Raising his eyes, he looked around the office, trying to clear his mind and focus on something, anything that might trigger an original thought about the case. A thought that might take him a little further than this blank wall he found himself mentally staring at.

The captain had finally been persuaded to authorize extra manpower and the extra hours that were needed to search for the Hospital Stalker, as the local papers had dubbed their killer.

Along with the task force and the publicity came the cranks. The phones rang constantly with people calling to offer information that, at this point, either proved useless or was entirely a figment of the caller's imagination. They had also started getting confessions. There were eight so far, all of which had fallen apart when further pursued.

It never ceased to amaze him how deranged and

lonely some people were that they would actually make up something like committing a murder just to garner attention, even if only for a few moments. Some things, he decided, were just outside his frame of reference, even though he knew firsthand what it meant to be so lonely. Didn't matter how lonely someone got, claiming to be a serial killer just didn't sound like a cure for the blues.

This was why the piece of information about the note found clutched in all the victims' hands had deliberately been omitted from all the news releases. The captain had insisted that Lauren James refrain from saying anything as well. The hospital administrator ate up the spotlight like a thirsty flower drew in rainwater, but she had reluctantly agreed. It was the department's only way of verifying whether or not their killer was making a legitimate full confession.

So far, none of the people who had called, confessing, could have possibly committed any of the murders, let alone all three. There were enough holes in their so-called confessions to drive a Mack truck sideways through them.

The restlessness that was so much a part of his life was beginning to surface again. Tony hated being cooped up indoors for any length of time. He supposed it came from having spent so much of his childhood confined to a corner of the small bedroom that he shared with his brothers, always for some minor infraction of Aunt Tess's rules.

"I'm going back to recanvas the hospital," Tony said abruptly as he pushed his chair away from his desk.

"Going to talk to that lady doctor again?" Henderson wanted to know.

Tony glanced in his direction.

Actually, that *was* his intent, to find the doctor again and see if she'd heard anything new herself. She had two sisters associated with the hospital and from the way she conducted herself, he was willing to bet that she was friendly with a good portion of the staff. People would be more likely to tell her things than they would a police detective.

But all he was willing to say to Henderson was, "She's part of the case," with his usual degree of carelessness. Then his eyes narrowed ever so slightly. "Why?"

Henderson's expression was affable. "No reason, just wondering." And then he added with a broad smile, "Mighty pretty lady."

Slipping on his black leather jacket, Tony shrugged off the observation. "Yeah, maybe."

The look on Henderson's face said he wasn't buying into his display of disinterest. "No maybe about it. If I were your age…" Henderson deliberately let his voice trail off.

Tony left the jacket unzipped for the time being. "You'd have another partner because I'd still be in grammar school."

Henderson leaned back in his chair in order to

continue watching him as he walked toward the doorway. "I'm not that old."

"Yeah, you are," Tony tossed over his shoulder.

"Be sure to say hello for me," Henderson called after him.

Tony raised his hand above his head and waved away the words without even turning around.

He didn't see why, after all this time, Henderson had suddenly decided to butt into his business. Maybe, Tony mused as he decided to take the stairs instead of the elevator, that was because until now there hadn't seemed to be any business to butt into.

There still wasn't, he told himself. The sound of his shoes hitting the metal steps followed him down the stairwell.

Leaving his vehicle parked in one of the spaces in the small parking lot that was directly adjacent to PM's emergency room, Tony was just about to cross the hospital's threshold when he was knocked off his feet. A disheveled-looking man in his early twenties came flying through the double glass doors just as Tony was about to enter the building.

Reflexes that had been finely honed on the job, not to mention the neighborhood where he'd grown up, had Tony grabbing the man by the leg and bringing him down before he could make good on his getaway. But not before the man had somehow managed to twist around and slash him with the knife he had clutched in one hand.

The soft black leather he was wearing was the first casualty, the arm beneath it was the second. Tony held on tighter, pinning the fugitive to the ground.

The assailant cursed his luck, the hospital and him. Within less than a minute, the security guards who'd been chasing the man caught up to their quarry.

"Thanks, mister," the tall, blond-haired guard who was first on the scene said. Grabbing the runner's arm, the security guard took possession of his quarry. Smaller, with a slighter build, the fugitive hadn't a prayer of getting away.

"Detective," Tony corrected. Refusing the hand the other, older guard extended to him, Tony rose to his feet on his own power, doing his best not to wince. He tightened his fingers around his left arm. Blood still managed to ooze through the barrier.

"Hey, you'd better have that looked at," the older guard said, concerned.

Tony bit back the urge to point out that the advice was unnecessary. He had no intention of just letting his wound bleed indefinitely. But for the moment, he was more interested in the man whose escape he'd just foiled.

Ordinarily, his first thought might have been that this was the killer they were looking for. But something told Tony as he quickly assessed his assailant that though the man looked somewhat deranged, he didn't look clever enough to be able to cover his bases. And whatever else the killer might be, there was no denying that the man was clever.

Tony nodded at the cursing captive the blond guard was holding onto. "What's he done?"

"Stole some drugs from the supply room," the younger guard said to him with a look of disgust on his face. "Somebody forgot to lock it."

"What floor?" Tony wanted to know. Maybe that somebody had deliberately left the supply room's door unlocked in preparation for another execution. After all, the first two had been in the parking garage, maybe the next two were supposed to be in the same kind of location as well. It would be a sign of an obsessive-compulsive inclination. Tony had learned long ago never to rule anything out, just in case.

"Fifth," the older guard told him. "We got the call from a Dr. Pul-something-or-other."

"Pulaski?" Tony supplied. Fifth floor. That was the maternity floor, he remembered. Where the doctor made her rounds.

The other man smiled, not attempting to repeat the name. "Yeah, that's it."

*And that's her,* Tony thought, as he saw the woman suddenly burst into the other end of the corridor located outside the emergency room.

His eyes on her, Tony took out his cell phone and called the precinct. With an economy of words, he identified himself, reported the incident and requested that a patrolman be sent out immediately to take the suspect to jail.

He'd just pushed the end-call button when the doctor reached him. She had obviously been running longer than the length of the corridor. There was something very captivating about watching the rise and fall of her chest as she tried to regulate her breathing.

And it bothered him that he enjoyed the view.

Sasha had just finished looking in on her newest patient. Carol Smith was an eighteen-year-old unmarried first-time mom who would have had her baby in an alley if Sasha hadn't spotted her less than an hour ago. She'd brought the girl into the hospital just as her contractions were coming less than two minutes apart.

Carol had no insurance, but PM never turned anyone away. The patients who ultimately couldn't pay their hospital bills provided PM with their tax write-offs at the end of the fiscal year. They also provided the hospital with an opportunity to do good works.

Carol's less-than-savory boyfriend, someone she called Duane, had tagged along for the delivery. Carol had a death grip on his hand for the first half of her ordeal. Duane told anyone within hearing range that he wasn't the baby's father.

What he was, it became painfully clear just a little while later, as Carol was being taken into recovery, was a junkie. A junkie who was looking to score something. Anything.

With the cleverness that desperation brings, Duane had managed to break into the supply room where the medicines were kept.

Returning from recovery, Sasha was looking for him when she saw Duane trying to sneak out of the room, clutching his jacket to him as if he were smuggling a kitten off the premises.

There were no kittens in the hospital—but there were a lot of valuable things stored in the supply room. Suspicious, Sasha had called out to him. Duane broke into a run immediately. She quickly called for security even as she started running after Duane herself. She'd been the one to bring Carol into the hospital, in her mind that made her responsible for the theft.

Looking at the detective's arm and what was leaking through his clenched fingers, Sasha felt even more responsible for the domino effect her one act of charity had brought about.

"Detective, you're bleeding," she said, horrified.

Tony looked down at his arm. The leather was slashed in two places. "Damn kid ruined my new jacket," he complained heatedly.

Sasha took charge. "Never mind the jacket, he could have ruined you." If there was anger in her voice, it was directed at herself. "Take it off, Detective," she instructed.

He looked at her, mildly amused. "I don't know if we know each other well enough for that, Doc," he deadpanned. The older of the two guards chuckled.

Sasha never even cracked a smile. Her guilt ran deeper than the wound she was looking at. "Hold him for the police," she ordered the security guards who seemed to come to attention at the command. "You—" she looked at the detective "—come with me." She began to lead the way into the E.R.

"You get your medical degree using the G.I. bill?" he asked, following her into the depths of the E.R. When he caught a half-quizzical look from her, he added, "You give orders like a marine."

"Only when I'm met with resistance," she tossed over her shoulder. Waving to a nurse at the nurses' station, she called out, "Eileen, I need a free bed."

Behind her, she heard the detective laugh dryly. "Doc, I'm on duty. Maybe later."

She shot him a silencing look. This wasn't funny. She still didn't know if something vital hadn't been cut, although since he was on his feet, she tended to think not. "Save it," she snapped.

"Number three is empty," Eileen told her, checking the chart located directly behind her on the wall.

"Number three it is." Without missing a step, Sasha headed in that direction. "I'm going to need a suture kit," she added.

"You got it," the nurse replied. By the time Sasha had reached number three, Eileen met them with the requested kit. She paused only long enough to give the doctor's patient an appreciative look, then returned to her post.

"No painkillers," Tony told her tersely. Feeling ill at ease and far from happy about the turn of events, he perched on the side of the bed, ready to take flight at the slightest provocation.

Sasha lowered the injection she'd prepared. Not giving it was against her better judgment. "It's going to hurt," she warned.

"No painkillers," he repeated. He had to stay focused, alert. Painkillers might take the edge off the pain, but they also took the edge off him. Not a good trade-off. "I don't mind pain. A little bit of pain makes you feel alive."

Threading the needle, she stopped to look at him for a long moment. Reading between the lines and hearing what wasn't being said.

"If that's the only thing that makes you feel alive, Detective, I'd say you have a bigger problem than just a knife wound." Without repeating her instruction, or waiting for him to comply, she placed the needle back on the tray and stepped behind him. He felt her small hands begin to pull his jacket down his shoulders. He shrugged out of the garment, careful not to move his arm any more than he absolutely had to.

He was working with her, Sasha noted with satisfaction. Very gingerly, she slid the jacket down the arm that had been wounded. "It can be fixed," she told him.

That was the whole idea behind his sitting here, preparing to be a pincushion, he thought. "It's just a cut," he pointed out.

Slipping on a fresh set of gloves, she swabbed the

area with antiseptic. Sasha spared him a glance before she took the first stitch. "I meant the jacket. My mother's cousin is a tailor. He can sew and repair anything. You won't even know it was damaged."

She felt him stiffening beneath her hand. "You double as a part-time saleslady?"

"I'm not making a pitch," she informed him. She heard him take in a breath and hold it, even though he was trying to be subtle about it. It was difficult not to grin. Men with their macho pose, she thought.

Tony released the breath he was holding. The pain was manageable if he concentrated on something else. On her. On the way her hair seemed to cascade into her face like a black sea. On the soft, subtle scent that seemed to surround her.

After a beat, his eyes met hers. "I am," he said quietly.

He was what? she wondered. When she couldn't come up with an answer, she decided to ask the question out loud. "Come again?"

"That's part of it," he allowed. Damn, but he was feeling a little light-headed. That shouldn't be happening. It was only a little needle. But the loss of blood, he realized, had not been so little. "Coming here again," he clarified when the confused look on her face only intensified.

"And the pitch?" she prodded, still not certain what he was driving at. He wasn't full of painkillers, but she'd known strong men to pass out at the sight of their own blood.

"Includes coffee," he told her. "And dinner. If you're free." He heard himself talking and was surprised by the sound of his own voice. Maybe he was out of his head, he thought. But he didn't take back the invitation. There was a part of him that wanted to hear what she had to say.

"But I'm not free, Detective." She let the remark sink in, then decided that she'd had enough fun and explained what she really meant. "I'm expensive. At least, that's what my more well-off patients seem to think. And they're right," she confided as she worked another stitch through his flesh. "That way, I can treat and buy medication for my patients who can't afford to pay for any treatment."

She pressed her lips together as she continued stitching up the wound. It went deeper than she'd first thought. Even so, the detective was as immovable as a rock. The only thing that gave him away was the involuntary twitch of his muscles. She was *very* aware of his muscles. It was enough to take her breath away if she wasn't careful, she reproached herself. He needed a doctor right now, not a fan.

She raised her eyes from her work for a split second to look at him. "I'm sorry about this."

Tony made a dismissive noise. "Not exactly your fault."

Now there he was wrong. "But it is. I brought in that thief's girlfriend." The look in his eyes told her he wanted details. So, details he was going to get. It was the least she could do. "I found Carol in the alley right behind the hospital. She was wound up into a ball and grunting. I thought she couldn't make it into PM, you know, labor pains knocking her feet right out from under her, that kind of thing," she explained, all the while working the needle back and forth through his flesh, sewing up first one layer of skin, then the next. "It turned out that she couldn't afford to stay at the hospital, but she wanted to be close by in case the baby was born in some sort of distress." Sasha sighed. "At least she had the presence of mind for that."

"What were you doing in the alley?" he wanted to know.

"Taking a shortcut. My office is in the building right across the street," she reminded him. "The back entrance faces the alley. Anyway, I brought Carol in and this boyfriend—Duane—insisted on coming along. As soon as I had her and the baby wheeled into recovery, he ran off to raid the supply room."

"How'd he get a knife past the security check?" he wanted to know.

Tony forced himself to watch as she worked. The stitches were small, precise, even. Like a seamstress, he thought. Lucky for him. Looks had never meant much to him but if he had a choice between looking like Frankenstein and not, he'd choose not.

"That wasn't a knife. That was a scalpel. He must have lifted it from the delivery room when we weren't looking." She pressed her lips together, aware that he was observing her every move. "Anyway, I owe you."

If anything, she was guilty of having a heart. He didn't see that as a punishable offense. Just an unusual one.

"Okay," he allowed, his voice rumbling along her consciousness, "you pick up the tab for dinner."

"Done," she declared, pulling through the last stitch. She raised her eyes to his. "And done," she repeated, this time more softly, her answer intended as a reply to his suggestion.

Dinner. He was asking her out. Something shimmied through her stomach. It took effort not to place her hand over it. It took further effort not to just turn tail and run from the room, the invitation and the man.

But then, she wouldn't have been Sasha Pulaski, or her father's daughter, so she stayed where she was. And smiled.

# Chapter 9

Dinner wound up being postponed.

Not intentionally, but the event was unceremoniously pushed to the rear of Tony's agenda just as he was about to leave the precinct. His plan was to go home, change and then pick the doctor up at her apartment. He had the address tucked into his shirt pocket.

An incoming call changed all that. Directed to Homicide, the call was rerouted to his desk.

"Gonna get that?" he heard Henderson ask as he stared accusingly at the telephone.

"Yeah," Tony bit off, annoyed. He should have left five minutes ago, he told himself. Yanking up the receiver, he pressed it against his ear. "Santini."

He heard the high-pitched voice of the dispatcher say, "There's been another homicide, Detective."

There was *always* another homicide in New York City. That was one of the detractions about living in an overpopulated big city, he thought.

"Have someone else catch it," he'd snapped, his voice overlapping that of the dispatcher's. The woman was rattling off the location where the body had been found. "There're eight other homicide detectives in the squad."

But no apology, no promise of taking her call elsewhere was forthcoming. "Thought you were handling the Hospital Stalker," the woman said.

He hated the name the press had affixed to the killer. It made it seem as if the police had no control over this man.

Well, did they? Tony forced himself to focus on what the dispatcher was saying.

"You just said the body was found in an office across town," he pointed out.

"It was," the woman replied. Then, before he could say anything, she added, "The patrolman who called it in said that the dead man—a doctor—had the same note in his hand."

A doctor. So the killer finally got it right, he thought cynically.

"Give me the address again," Tony instructed. Grabbing the first available piece of paper on his desk, he jotted down the address the woman was reciting. Finished, he terminated the call without bothering with any further exchange. "Henderson," he called over to his partner. "We're up." He heard the man sigh deeply as he lumbered up to his feet. Tony paused and looked at him. "You got somewhere to go?"

Henderson slipped on his hound's-tooth jacket. "Only home." It was obvious that home was where he wanted to be. "Big boxing match on pay-TV tonight."

Tony looked at him incredulously as he waited for the big man to reach him. "You pay to watch two guys beat each other's brains out? Don't you get enough of that here?"

They walked out into the hall together, and then down the corridor to the elevator. "Yeah, but on TV, I don't have to figure out who done it. I already know." He looked at Tony as they got into the elevator. The car had just been standing there, as if it knew it was going to be pressed into service. Henderson made the logical assumption. "Did someone find another body in the hospital?"

Tony shook his head. The elevator made its way down to the first floor without stopping. "No, this time it's across town. And the victim's a doctor."

They weren't called down for every murder. That was why the precinct had as large a squad as it did. "Then how—?"

Tony already knew what Henderson was going to ask. "The patrolman said he found a note."

"Same one?" Henderson asked grimly.

"Same one."

The frown on the man's beefy lips deepened. "Bastard's spreading out."

"Looks like," Tony agreed.

The elevator doors opened and they got out. Darkness wound its fingers around the world outside. And within.

The crime scene had been disturbed, Tony noted.

Despite the best efforts of the inexperienced patrolman who had responded to the initial 911 call, the late doctor's wife had sunk down to the floor, wrapped her arms around the dead man and held him to her. She'd been holding him for the last forty-five minutes.

"What is she doing here?" Tony wanted to know. He put the question to Officer Caldwell. Caldwell looked barely old enough to shave.

"The guy who found him called her. It's a partnership," Officer Caldwell offered. "Seven of them altogether. The Greater Anesthesiologists of New York." The explanation was unnecessary, since that was what it said on the door. "She's his wife," Caldwell added helplessly.

The woman was sobbing now as she rocked to and fro. Her arms were locked in a death grip around her husband. There was blood smeared on her coat, her black slacks and her sweater.

The crime scene investigators were going to have a fit, Tony thought. Making his way over to her, he politely addressed the woman.

"Ma'am, I need you to get up." She gave no indication that she heard him or was even aware of his presence. Tony tried again. "Ma'am?"

Trapped in a world whose walls were comprised of grief, the slain physician's wife didn't seem to hear him. For the time being, since the damage was already done, Tony backed away, allowing her to hold onto her husband for a while longer.

He looked over toward a very distraught man in his mid to late thirties. The man's haircut and suit alone would have set him back three months' salary, Tony mused as he crossed to him.

"You were the one who found him?" Tony asked.

The physician nodded. "Dr. Tyler Harris," he said numbly.

The name seemed to be free-floating in space. "Is that your name or his?"

The doctor blinked, as if that helped him process the question. It took a moment for him to respond. "His. Mine's Rothenberg. Julian," he added as an afterthought, then said his whole name. "Dr. Julian Rothenberg. I just looked in to say good night to Ty as I was leaving and there he was." He gestured haplessly toward the body. "Like that."

Someone had to have seen or heard something, Tony thought. "Did you see anyone leave the office?"

But Rothenberg shook his head. "I was busy in the back." He paused, then said, "Maybe Myra noticed someone…"

"Myra?" Henderson asked. Until now, Tony's partner had merely stood in his shadow, listening. Looking around. Tony knew the older detective was processing the scene in his own way.

"Our receptionist," Rothenberg clarified. "Oh, wait, Myra took off after lunch."

Tony exchanged looks with Henderson. "In the middle of the day?" That seemed a little unusual to him. Was it just a coincidence, or had Myra possibly been notified that something was going down? "Anyone covering for her?"

The doctor shook his head. "Myra does the billing, mostly and keeps tabs on the surgeries being scheduled. We're not those kind of doctors."

It sounded like an odd thing to say. "What kind?" Henderson wanted to know.

"The kind who see patients in our office. We see them in the hospital, the day of the surgery. And we usually call the night before to go over things with them," he added, then explained, "but no one ever comes to the office."

Tony looked around. He was no expert, but he knew expensive when he saw it. "Pretty elaborate decorating for a place no one ever sees."

"We see it," Dr. Rothenberg pointed out. There was just enough snobbery in his voice to be off-putting.

"Yeah, right," Tony muttered under his breath. He took out his notepad and flipped to an empty page. "What hospital was Dr. Harris with?"

"The group is affiliated with several hospitals,"

Rothenberg told him. When Tony continued to look at him expectantly, the doctor rattled off the names of the hospitals.

None of them were Patience Memorial.

Where was the connection? Tony wondered. *Was* there a connection or just some psycho running around, terrorizing people? "Did Harris ever freelance? Fill in for another anesthesiologist?" Tony asked.

Rothenberg didn't look as if he was sure what he was being asked. "We cover for each other if some kind of emergency arises, but those are the only hospitals we're affiliated with. Why?" And then genuine fear contoured his features. "Does this have anything to do with the Hospital Stalker?"

Tony didn't answer him directly. Instead, he said, "The other three victims were associated with Patience Memorial Hospital."

Rothenberg's head bobbed up and down, as if everything was making perfect sense to him. "Tyler's last group was associated with that hospital."

"Last group?" Tony repeated.

On firmer ground, Rothenberg looked a shade more confident again. "Doctors recruit just like everyone else, Detective. As an anesthesiologist, Tyler had an excellent record. Better than most. We made him an offer he couldn't refuse."

"Looks like the killer did, too," Tony commented more to Henderson than to Rothenberg as he looked down at the dead man.

\* \* \*

Sasha tossed the magazine she'd restlessly been paging through for the last twenty minutes onto the coffee table. If pressed, she wouldn't have been able to repeat a single thing she'd read.

Pretty bad for a woman with a photographic memory, she thought ruefully.

She resisted looking at the clock again. It had to be approaching ten o'clock, or perhaps even later. That would make Santini three hours late. If he were coming, which, it seemed, he wasn't.

The detective had told her that he would be at her apartment by seven. He hadn't come, hadn't called. Obviously, she'd slipped his mind. Or maybe he'd thought better of his invitation.

Sasha frowned, telling herself not to make a big deal out of it. But she'd never been stood up before, she thought.

It didn't matter, she silently insisted, except that she had been looking forward to going out to some place different for a change. These days, "going out" meant going back home to Queens, to the house where she'd grown up, to spend time with her parents and younger sisters. That is, if Tatania and Marja were home. These days, that usually wasn't the case. Tatania was an intern. Asserting her independence, she'd chosen a hospital that *wasn't* Patience Memorial and right now, Sasha was secretly glad that Tatania was somewhere else. As for Marja, the youngest of the Pulaski sisters, she was in her last year of medical school. Free time for either of them was rare.

The apartment was too quiet, Sasha thought. So quiet she could swear she could hear the paint aging on the walls. Ordinarily, one or both of her other sisters were here, barring some last-minute emergency at the hospital. But Natalya had gone off with a couple of friends to spend a hard-earned weekend in Atlantic City and Kady, well God only knew what Kady was doing. The most rebellious sister of the group, Kady liked to come and go as she pleased "without having to punch a clock," as she put it. The remark was a blatant reference to all those times as teenagers when they'd had to account for themselves to their father.

It wasn't so much that Josef Pulaski was unreasonably strict, he just worried about them. As a policeman, he'd been privy to the lowest forms of humanity and more than anything, he wanted to keep his wife and daughters safe from that world.

It was a sweet sentiment, she thought. Confining, but nonetheless a sweet sentiment.

Sasha blew out a breath, looking around for the umpteenth time. Here she was, with the apartment all to herself and nothing to do.

She supposed it was better this way. If the detective had taken her out, he might have insisted on walking her back home. Since it was empty, she might have been tempted to ask him in....

*Tempted,* now there was a word she hadn't used

in a long time, Sasha thought. That was because she hadn't felt that way in a long time.

*Tempted.*

She hadn't been tempted by anyone or anything since Adam had been killed. Hadn't felt anything since he'd been killed. Nothing except for a sense of duty.

Until now.

*Not now,* she insisted silently.

Rotating her neck from side to side, she rose from the sofa. As she did, she slanted a glance at the clock above the TV monitor. It *was* past ten. Maybe what she should do was go to bed before one of those babies she was scheduled to bring into the world in the next few weeks decided to pop early. God knew she was always complaining about never getting enough sleep. Now was her chance to catch up.

It was as good a plan as any.

Sasha switched off the light in the living room and reduced the lamp closest to the hallway down to its lowest setting. That way, the small foyer would have some illumination in case Kady came home before dawn.

She was on her way to her bedroom when she heard the doorbell ring.

Instantly, every muscle in her body tightened. Thoughts of those two murdered nurses, not to mention poor Jorge, were never all that far from her thoughts. She stared at the front door.

*The killer hasn't changed his MO, Sash. He's not*

*going from door to door ringing doorbells like some demonic trick-or-treater,* she upbraided herself.

Nonetheless, she made no effort to cross to the foyer.

When the doorbell rang again, Sasha was forced to abandon the idea that if she simply ignored the person, whoever was ringing her doorbell would just go away.

It was probably just one of her sisters' boyfriends, looking for them, Sasha reasoned. Squaring her shoulders, she approached the door.

"Who is it?"

There was a pause, as if the person on the other side of the door didn't know what to call himself.

The murderer?

A chill raced down her spine. Deciding that it was better to be safe than sorry, Sasha pulled out the cell phone she kept in her pocket at all times and quickly pressed the buttons that would connect her to Santini. The detective had picked a hell of a time to stand her up, she thought, annoyed.

The second she pressed Send, Sasha heard a phone ringing somewhere in the hallway outside her apartment. With the cell phone still against her ear, she looked through the peephole. And saw the man she was calling standing on the other side of her door.

"Detective?"

With one hand braced against the side of the peephole, Tony leaned against the door. "Look, I know it's late, but could you open up the door, Sasha?"

Sasha. She suddenly realized that in all the exchanges they'd had, Santini had never called her by her given name before. It kind of rumbled from his mouth, she thought, amused despite the fact that she knew she was supposed to be really annoyed.

She slipped her cell phone back in her pocket. Flipping open the lock, she removed the chain and then opened the door.

"Someone steal your watch, Detective?" she asked politely as she stepped back.

Tony walked in, feeling awkward. Knowing he'd only feel more awkward if he'd skipped coming here and gone directly home from the crime scene.

He held up his left hand, allowing her to glimpse the watch that was strapped to his wrist. The watch that he only removed when he showered.

"No, it's still there." He dropped his hand to his side again as he turned to look at her. "I forgot about picking you up for dinner."

Sasha closed the door. "Now there's something every woman loves to hear," she commented drolly. "That she's forgettable."

Sasha Pulaski might be many things, Tony thought, trying not to stare at the way the electric-blue dress she had on clung to the outline of her breasts, but forgettable was certainly not one of them.

He tried again. "The reason I forgot," he told her, "was because there's been another homicide."

Every other thought flew from her mind, crowded

out by horror as she looked at him. "At the hospital? When? Who?"

She was firing questions at him like a seasoned veteran at a target range. Taking a deep breathe he addressed the first one. "No, not at the hospital. At the Greater Anesthesiologists of New York's office."

That wasn't good, she thought. She felt a chill had gripped her heart. She already had patients who wanted to know if they could deliver their baby at another hospital. People were getting leery of PM. "The killer's spreading out his base?"

In response, Tony shook his head. "I don't think so."

"But you just said—"

"The victim was a doctor," he told her. "Dr. Tyler Harris."

Sasha's eyes widened in disbelief. This was becoming very, very weird. "Ty?"

"You knew him?" It was a rhetorical question, given the tone of her voice.

"Everyone knew him." She couldn't believe it. Ty, who liked being the center of every gathering. Ty, who was funny and gregarious. *Murdered.* It just didn't seem possible. "He was one of those people who had a story for everything and was willing to share it at the drop of a hat." A bittersweet smile twisted her lips. "They used to say that he didn't need to bother with applying anesthesia, he could just talk the patient to sleep." The nightmare was escalating. "When did it happen?"

"One of his associates found the body at five." Tony looked around. Her apartment looked warm, homey, with just enough scattered around to give it a lived-in look. In contrast, his apartment was as personal as a bus depot. "He called the police and then the doctor's wife. We found Mrs. Harris holding him when we arrived."

Maybe it wasn't the same person who had killed the people at PM. "He was still alive?"

Santini's expression was grim as he said, "No."

His meaning sank in. She looked at him in horror. "Oh God, that poor woman."

Interest entered his eyes. "You were acquainted with her?"

She didn't want him to misunderstand. "Only by reputation. Hers," she emphasized. "Linda Harris is a very jealous, suspicious woman. She thought that every woman in the room was after her husband, that every woman was out to take him away from her." Sasha's words played back to her in her head. "I guess now she won't have to worry about that."

"Jealousy." Santini said the word as if he was chewing on it. Sasha looked at him. "Ordinarily, that would be a motive for us to explore."

Tyler Harris's wife was a shrew, but she didn't think that the woman was capable of murder. Still, she wondered about Santini's reasoning. "But?"

"But," and it was an all-important *but,* "Harris had one of those notes in his hand. Or on the floor next to him, actually." That was where the note had been when he'd arrived on the scene. "The patrolman who was there first said that Mrs. Harris pulled the paper out of the doctor's hand, thinking it was some kind of suicide note."

Or love note, Sasha thought. That was probably what was running through the woman's mind. "Any chance that she planted the note?"

He couldn't help the weary smile that came to his lips. She was making noises like a police detective. "The note's not a piece of common knowledge. We've kept that from the media."

She knew how that worked. The police held back some small, telling piece of information that only the killer would know. "Smart."

"Thanks." He was enjoying this bit of conversation and reminded himself that he'd come here to apologize for not showing up at seven, and then he'd go home. He'd done the former, in a fashion. But for some reason, he couldn't quite get himself to follow through on the latter. He didn't want to go home to his studio apartment, to the emptiness. Not yet. "Any chance I might be able to get a cup of coffee?"

According to the rules of engagement set down by Rita Riley, her best friend in college, Sasha knew that she was supposed to be indignant at how easily she'd slipped his mind. In keeping with that, she should be showing him the door. But then again, last time she'd heard, Rita was on her way to divorce court for a second time.

Sasha smiled and nodded. "I think the odds are pretty favorable. Come with me."

Turning on her heel, she led the way to the kitchen. The woman, Tony noted almost against his will as he followed her, looked almost as good going as she did coming.

*Chapter 10*

Tony sat down on the outermost stool and rested his hands on the counter. It wasn't a kitchen that had room for a table, but it was a bright, cheery-looking space, even under artificial light. It seemed hard to imagine that creatures like serial killers and stalkers existed in the same world occupied by someone like Sasha Pulaski.

For a moment, there was no other sound than that of the coffeemaker, percolating. He watched Sasha stretch as she reached up into the cupboard for two mugs. There didn't appear to be an ounce of excess fat on her. He wondered when she found time to work out, given her schedule.

Rousing himself, Tony focused on the reason he'd

been late. The anesthesiologist no longer worked at Patience Memorial, yet he'd been killed. It seemed to him that everyone associated with the hospital was at risk.

"You know," Tony finally began, measuring out his words slowly, "maybe you should go on vacation for a while."

The mugs secured, she turned around and placed both on the counter beside the coffee machine. Amusement curved her lips. "Are you propositioning me, Detective, or trying to get rid of me?"

If her question surprised him, he didn't show it. "Neither. I'm just trying to keep you safe."

She looked at him for a long moment. A warm feeling descended over her, wrapping her in its arms before dissolving again. She smiled at him.

"Thanks for the thought, but that's just what we're trying to avoid at PM—a mass exodus by the staff." The last few weeks, especially after finding the orderly, had been hell. This newest development was just going to make things worse. But she had no desire to flee. Only a fierce desire to catch whoever was responsible for the killings. "It's bad enough that the patients are getting jittery."

Other than looking into whether any patients had lodged complaints against any of the victims, he hadn't given the patients at the hospital much thought.

"Oh?"

Sasha nodded. Because the coffee was still brewing, she leaned forward over the counter, sharing a moment with him. "I've had some of mine ask if they could deliver their babies at another hospital."

"This guy's not killing patients," he pointed out, "just staff members."

"Still not a warm and toasty thing to contemplate." Sasha searched his face for any additional clues. "You think it's a man?"

He tended to think of all brutal crimes in terms of men having committed them. He supposed, in a way, there was a bit of the old-fashioned chauvinist left within him. The department shrink would have accused him of being sexist. "Most serial killers are."

Sasha recalled one of the books her father had in his library. It was an encyclopedia of serial killers. All aspects of law enforcement had always fascinated her father. "But not all."

"No," he allowed, "not all."

The coffee machine had settled down. Sasha took the pot and filled first his mug and then her own. With an economy of movement, she set out a container of milk and placed the sugar bowl within his reach. Santini ignored both. He liked his coffee like his world—black.

She added enough milk into her coffee to make it turn into a light shade of chocolate. She took a sip before asking, "Have you eaten?" And then she flashed a smile that was just a tinge rueful. For a second, in light of the newest development, she'd almost forgotten. "No, of course you haven't." And he had the look of a hungry man about him, she thought. "I can throw something together for you."

Tony shook his head, taking another long sip of the black liquid and letting it course through his veins. "You don't have to bother." It wasn't meant so much as a protest as a dismissal. "Coffee's fine."

Her parents had always emphasized the importance of hospitality to her. Even when they had next to nothing, they always made it a point to share with anyone who came to their door. Her smile broadened. "No bother," she assured him.

Another, more forceful protest rose to his lips, but died there for lack of conviction; he was hungry and the only thing in his refrigerator was a third of a loaf of bread. The last time he'd looked, the slices were tinged with green and growing greener.

Closing the refrigerator with her elbow, Sasha deposited two kinds of peppers, green and red, and a package of chicken onto the counter. She turned her attention to the crowded carousel of spices in the corner and began selecting containers.

"How do you feel about curried chicken?" she asked him, her voice echoing from inside the lower cabinet as she squatted there, locating the largest frying pan she had.

Her bounty in her hand, Sasha rose again and placed the pan on the largest burner when he didn't answer. She slanted a glance in his direction.

"Never thought about it one way or another," he told her with a shrug.

She put her own interpretation to his words. Taking a drop of oil, she jiggled the pan until the single drop coated the surface.

"Never had it?" was her conclusion.

She was good, he thought, then shook his head. "Not that I recall."

Like a child facing the prospect of a new toy, she grinned. "Ah, a fresh palate. This should be fun." Recruiting a heavy chopping block, she began dicing peppers with a steady rhythm he found almost hypnotic. She made quick work of the peppers and turned her attention to the chicken. "So, Detective," she began cheerfully. "What's your story?"

He thought they'd already covered that. But since she had given him coffee and was determined to feed him, he decided to humor her to an extent. "I just told you. There was another homicide and—"

Sasha looked up at him. The rest of the sentence disappeared. He lost his train of thought as he felt something stir inside him again. Damn it, he was overtired, he thought. Overtired and stimulated at the same time. Not a good combination, he told himself. Cops got sloppy when they were both. And he couldn't afford to get sloppy. On or off the job.

"No," Sasha countered firmly, shaking her head at what he was about to say. "*Your* story," she emphasized. When he said nothing, she tried again. "What's behind the badge, Santini?"

His eyes met hers when she turned to look at him. "Muscle and bone."

It was, she thought, like playing chess. He blocked her every move. "You ask a lot of questions, but you never answer any."

"Maybe because the answers don't make a difference." He didn't welcome people into his life. There were no invitations issued. Not anymore.

Meaning his answers would be evasive. She didn't want him to evade her. She wanted the truth.

"The answers always make a difference," she told him, then paused as she studied his face. "Who are you, Detective Santini?"

"Just a guy trying to get to the bottom of things."

He was defining himself by his work. But there was more to him than that. Much more.

"When you're not trying to get to the bottom of things," she insisted. "What makes you laugh?"

That was simple enough to answer. "I don't laugh." The last time he had, it was with Annie, over some silly thing she'd done.

Sasha stopped chopping. Her hand on her hip, she looked at him for a long moment. When she spoke, her voice was filled with compassion. And understanding. Because she'd been there herself. "You need to change that, Detective Santini."

Watching Sasha move around the tiny kitchen brought back memories. Memories that he'd thought he'd buried when Annie had been taken from him. But being here with this woman tonight after a long, hard day, sipping coffee and watching her prepare a meal, felt damn near normal.

When was the last time he'd felt normal? When had he felt like something other than a machine, going through the paces because he knew if he stopped he couldn't go on? Couldn't go on because he'd been to the other side, been allowed to glimpse what life could be like for him, and now he missed it like hell.

But that was for only him to know. Him and no one else. Not even a woman with hair the color of midnight and a smile that cut clear down to the bone.

"Maybe," he said very slowly, toying with what was left in his cup, "for the space of the evening you could stop calling me Detective Santini."

"Fine." Pausing, she poured him a fresh cup, then continued working. "What would you like me to call you?"

"My given name's Anthony," he reminded her.

"Anthony," she repeated with a nod, saying the name as if she was tasting it, one letter at a time. "Yes, I remember. Tony." A smile seemed to vibrate around the name. "I'm Sasha."

A small ring formed beneath the mug. Tony erased it with his thumb, then set the mug back on the counter. "I know."

She hadn't meant to suggest that he'd forgotten it. Sasha had no doubt that somewhere within the recesses of his memory, Detective Santini could access everything he'd ever come across.

"I meant, for tonight. You keep calling me Doctor." They were both guilty of trying to keep their distance. She no longer wanted to. "Maybe we should both stop standing behind our titles."

The moment seemed to stretch out forever. "Maybe," he allowed.

He was agreeing, but Sasha heard the caution in his voice. Swiftly, she gathered up everything on the chopping block and deposited it into the frying pan. Turning the heat up, she stirred the peppers, chicken and onions together, then began adding the battalion of spices, one by one.

A smile feathered along the corners of her mouth. She slanted another look at him as she stirred. "Now tell me something personal."

Maybe coming here was a bad idea after all. Something had drawn him here. The need to apologize for not calling wasn't the real reason. He could have left a message on her answering machine if that were the case.

He'd wanted to see her. And now, he was paying the price. "What?"

She lowered the heat and covered the pan. "Well, for all intents, this is a date." Saying the word felt strange. And yet, what else could she honestly call this? "We've known each other for what, six weeks now?" She didn't wait for affirmation. She knew exactly how long she'd known Tony. "I think it's time we shared something more than coffee." Lifting the lid, she stirred once, then replaced it again. "So, tell me something personal."

The coffee cup was empty. He debated taking a

third mugful, then decided against it. "You're a very attractive woman."

He wasn't going to get away that easily. "Something personal about you."

"I'm *not* a very attractive woman," he responded gamely.

Sasha laughed and shook her head. He was a challenge, she'd give him that.

"Okay, I'll go first." And then she sobered just a little, the way she always did when she thought about Adam and how quickly his life had been cut short. "My fiancé's name was Adam and I thought I was going to die when he did. I almost did, inside."

"What brought you around?"

"My parents and sisters." If it hadn't been for them, that dark place she'd slipped into would never have let her go. "Adam was my first and only real relationship. That night in the hospital parking structure, when I first saw Angela, it brought it all back to me." She took a deep breath, realizing she'd gotten far too serious. "You have to find who's doing this."

There was no doubt in his mind how this would be resolved. "We will."

The smile she flashed told him that she believed him. He would have thought an intelligent woman would have been more skeptical.

"Okay," she said, stirring again. "Your turn."

He didn't want a turn. Didn't want to bare his soul to anyone. He'd long since left behind the notion that confession was good for the soul—if he'd ever believed it in the first place.

"I didn't agree to this game."

She heard things in his voice, heard barriers being reinforced. Her heart went out to him.

"What are you afraid of, Tony?" she asked softly.

"Same thing you are."

She turned down the heat beneath the frying pan even further, allowing the ingredients to simmer, before she turned all her attention to him.

"You're afraid of feeling something again?" Before he could shut out her questions, she came around the counter to stand next to him. "That's the only way we have of proving that we're alive, Tony. Feeling."

Feelings were highly overrated, he thought. "I'll prove I'm alive by catching this bastard."

"And then the next one? And the next one after that?" she guessed.

Now she understood, he thought. "Yes."

He was running. Hiding from himself. Just as she had been, she thought. Even now, there was this urge to flee. But she knew she couldn't give in to it. She had to stand up in order not to be dragged down. "When do you have time for you?"

Maybe he'd given her too much credit. He would have thought she would have caught on by now. "With any luck, I won't."

Sasha didn't back away. Her eyes looked into his. Seeing herself there. "You can't outrun it."

"It?" he mocked, his manner meant to get her to back away.

He knew perfectly well what she was talking about, she thought. "The pain. You have to come to terms with it and move on."

He hated people who thought they knew what was best for you. Even beautiful people. "Have you?" he challenged, turning the tables on her.

She surprised him by saying, "To some extent. Doesn't mean I love Adam any the less," she added quickly, "just that I didn't shut down my heart. All systems are still up and running."

"Good for you." The response was meant to be dismissive.

"Yes," Sasha said quietly, "it is."

She was still standing near him, so close that their breath was mingling, that her words could have fit into his. He needed only to reach up, to cup the back of her head and bring his mouth down to hers. The debate raged hot and heavy for a few moments. He managed to refrain, but it wasn't easy.

She could almost read his mind. Or was that wishful thinking on her part? Anticipation laced fingers with a jittery panic. Finally, Sasha stepped back. "Dinner's ready."

He wanted to say the hell with dinner. He wanted to act on this feeling that was suddenly surging through him before he could think better of it. Before he could stop himself again. There was a tiny part of him that ached to feel again. To recapture what he'd once had.

But that was impossible and he knew it. He wasn't one of those men who fell easily into love. He was one of those men who had to be ambushed by it, to be captured and taken prisoner. It had happened once. He damn well doubted that it would ever happen again.

"This is good."

The compliment was almost grudgingly given, following several minutes of silence while they both sat at the counter.

"Thanks." She wanted to ask why he looked so surprised, but she decided to hold off. Maybe he'd actually offer a little more conversation on his own.

And he did after another two minutes had passed. "Where you'd learn to cook like this?"

"It's in the genes," she told him with a grin. "My mother can almost literally create something out of nothing. When I was growing up, there was no money for things like prepackaged meals and frozen entrées. Mama would come up with meals using whatever she could find at home in the pantry." A fond look came into her eyes. "Mama was right up there with the miracle of the fishes and loaves. I think, if I hadn't gone into medicine, I might have opted to start my own restaurant."

He had her pegged right. She was a dreamer. "Most businesses fail in their first year," he told her, his attention devoted to his meal. He hadn't realized he was this hungry until he'd begun to eat. "Those that don't usually fold in the first five."

Sasha blew out a long breath. "You have got to be the least cheerful person I have ever met," she commented. And that bothered her. "Don't you ever see the upside of anything?"

"I did, once," he admitted in what he felt, in the next second, was a moment of weakness.

He didn't make it a habit of admitting things to people, of letting them into his head. Not even his brothers. But there was something about this woman, something that warmed him. That tempted him. That stood at the door of his self-imposed prison and threatened to splinter the wood.

"So what happened?" she asked, her voice low, coaxing. Understanding.

He knew she was asking about his wife. About the circumstances that took her from him. This was where he slid off the stool, said something like thanks and went on his way.

Except he didn't.

"She died," he heard himself saying. "In a hit-and-run accident. Whoever hit her just left her there, on the side of the road. When she died," he said heavily, feeling the ache all over again, "everything else did too."

Sasha placed her hand over his, one grieving soul touching another.

"I'm so sorry," she whispered.

When he raised his eyes to hers, he knew that she was serious. That she wasn't just mouthing empty words. And that spoke to him.

Her eyes still on his, Sasha brushed her fingers along his cheek. He felt as if something broke loose inside. Rising, he drew her up to her feet with him. The next moment, he took her face in his hands and kissed her. Kissed her because something inside of him hurt so badly, he could hardly stand it. Kissed her because he wanted to put an end to that ache.

As he brushed his lips against hers, something rose up from the depths of him and seemed to explode. The sweetness he discovered on her lips caused him to deepen the kiss. To fall headlong into it.

And with each passing fraction of a second, the power increased. The pull drew him into the very center of this unexpected hurricane that had suddenly risen up all around him.

She felt soft against him.

Her body seemed to fit right into his, so much so that it was as if they had been created as two complementary puzzle pieces.

*What the hell was he doing?* Another second and he'd drop off the face of the earth, go plummeting over the side of the abyss that he hadn't even suspected was there. Kissing her wasn't just a pleasurable experience, it was an experience that defied description, defied being pigeonholed. And he wanted to take it to the next plateau.

With a burst of superhuman energy, Tony forced himself to pull back. He felt shaken. The air that he sucked into his lungs didn't steady anything.

"I'm sorry. I had no right to do that. I'll go. Thanks for the meal."

She felt as if the short sentences were attacking her, one after another, as Tony drew back making his way toward the door. Away from her.

Snapping to, Sasha quickly caught up to him before he could leave.

She began at the end and worked her way to the beginning. "You're welcome for the meal. You don't have to leave. And you have every right to do that. There's no reason to be sorry." She looked at him pointedly. "I wanted you to kiss me."

"Look—" He felt as if he was stumbling over a tongue that had somehow gotten to be five feet long and incredibly unwieldy. "—you're vulnerable—"

There was no denying that, Sasha thought. Today marked five years since she'd gotten engaged to Adam and maybe, in between all the patients she had seen today during her hectic schedule, she'd been feeling sorry for herself.

But she'd meant what she'd said. It was time to move forward. At least a little. Denying herself the right to feel was cruel and unusual punishment. It was time to stop beating herself up because she was still alive and Adam was not.

Adam wouldn't have wanted that.

"Yes, I am," she agreed, wrapping her arms

around Tony's neck and once again drawing herself closer to him than a soft whisper. "But don't worry," she added, rising up on her toes, bringing her lips close to his. "It's not catching."

He didn't know about that, he thought, taking what was offered.

But, catching or not, he had no choice but to do what every fiber in his body begged him to do.

He brought his mouth down on hers and utterly shattered every promise he'd made to himself about keeping his distance and remaining uninvolved.

# Chapter 11

Sasha made him feel strong and weak at the same time. Powerful, invincible and yet completely vulnerable and exposed. Had he been able to think, Tony would have said that the woman in his arms had turned him inside out and spun him around until he wasn't sure which end was up.

But thinking was the last thing he was capable of right now. Not with this myriad of sensations bombarding him from every conceivable direction. And at the very center of the emotional hurricane that was raging within him was desire. Desire, fiery and strong and so unrelenting that he couldn't even manage to draw a complete breath without every fiber of his being shouting that he wanted her.

Where had all this come from?

Had it been hiding in the wings, waiting to capture him while he was still unaware?

But that was just it, he *was* aware, aware of every nuance of her body, every movement, every curve that called to him. He hadn't felt this vibrant, this alive since Annie had been in his life.

He felt like exploding.

It took everything he had within him not to give in to what was happening, not to quickly take this woman who stirred him so much. The hunger that seemed to have risen out of the shadows and taken him prisoner begged to be satiated.

With extraordinary effort, he banked it down as best he could. He wasn't some rutting pig, some soul-less, lusting beast who suddenly had an appetite that needed satisfying. He was a man, a man who could think, who could reason. Who could exercise control over himself.

The last thing he wanted was to frighten Sasha. Or offend her.

So he caressed her, kissed her and gave up part of his resistance. He found himself lost in the taste of her. In the feel, the scent, the softness of her. From where he stood, it was a good bargain.

Tony hardly remembered how they managed to get from the stool to the sofa. All he knew was that the second he'd begun kissing her, he couldn't pull himself away, couldn't stand back and create that small, necessary distance he'd always been able to maintain. There'd always been a part of him that could observe, that could separate him from what was going on. Even with Annie, he was able to maintain that small, uninvaded space.

That space didn't exist any more. He couldn't find it, couldn't take refuge in it. He was hopelessly lost in her.

Tony kissed her mouth, her face, her throat and all the while his hands roamed over her body, memorizing every subtle curve, every inviting dip, every single hollow that he found.

And even while he was losing himself in her, Tony could feel her fingers as they worked the buttons from their holes on his shirt, heard her deep intake of breath as she dragged the shirt from his waist, then pushed it from his torso. Felt his own breath catch in his throat as her fingertips moved along his chest, his skin. Branding him.

This was wrong.

He shouldn't be letting this happen, his mind argued silently. Shouldn't be with her like this. And yet, he wanted nothing more. Even though it shattered every single promise, broke every rule, tore him out of his solitary cell where he'd been bathed in darkness.

She made him feel alive. Feel glad to *be* alive. He didn't even have time to feel disloyal to Annie.

Everything seemed to be happening in some sort of warm haze. And yet, he was aware of everything. Aware of the feel of her lips, the silkiness of her skin, the zipper as it flowed down her back. Aware of her dress as it floated away from her body and to the floor.

He was supposed to stop now. It had gotten out of hand.

He hadn't meant for this to happen when he'd taken that right turn down the street that led to her apartment building. He'd only meant to offer his apologies for neglecting to call her earlier and then go. That was all. Nothing more.

*Liar.*

The word vibrated in his brain, mocking him. And then it disappeared, burned away in the heat of his desire.

She was naked and beautiful and, for this single, precious moment in time, his. And he wanted her with a need that was almost uncontrollable.

A small kernel of feeling that was deeply rooted within him demanded that he hold off taking her, hold off from the ultimate moment. It demanded that he do his very best to place her needs before his own. It wasn't a conscious thought, more like a sense of order. Of how things had to be, to be right.

It wasn't until Tony's lips touched hers that she realized just how much she had ached for this. How much she'd truly missed the physical aspects of a good relationship. Since Adam had died, there had been no one to take his place, no one to turn to. To escape the grief, the pain, she had buried herself in her work. Pretending that it and her family were enough. That she had no other needs, no great desire to savor the physical pleasures that came from loving and being loved by a man.

There'd been men since Adam had died, men who had been interested in her. But she'd refused any attempts on their part to get closer. She'd become celibate because making love had always been just that to her, making love. Not having sex. Adam had been her first, her only. It was because she'd loved him that she'd made love with him. It had been a natural outpouring. Her love had just spilled out, impossible to contain or manage any longer without an outlet.

That couldn't be the case here, she thought, even as her body heated in response to Tony's touch. She didn't love this detective. She felt for him. Related to him and was drawn to him because of the similar circumstances in their backgrounds. And because of the life-and-death situation they found themselves on the edge of. Tony was a protector and she appreciated that, but it wasn't as if she actually needed protecting.

What she needed, she realized, was to feel like a woman again. A desirable woman. And if she were being honest with herself, he made her feel just that. From the first covert look of interest in his eyes when he'd slanted a glance in her direction, something electric had telegraphed itself to her, slicing through protocol, through logic. Through all the barriers she'd constructed around herself. She'd wanted Tony long before she'd given in to him.

His tenderness surprised her. Touched her. More than she could ever say. She'd thought to get lost in the wild rapture that would overtake her the moment they came together, but he somehow managed to be tender within the frenzy that seized them, the frenzy that sent clothes flying, along with any lingering inhibitions she might have possessed.

But it wasn't a wild flash in the pan, a simple wham-bam-thank-you-ma'am. It was so much more.

The taste of his lips inflamed her. His breath sent her pulse racing even faster than it already was, stirring every dormant thing inside her. There was an overwhelming need to be swept away and another, equally great need not to drown within the tidal wave that had been created.

She needed to make Tony feel something as well, needed to leave a mark, an impression on his soul that would make her different in his eyes, different from all the other women she assumed he had had over the years.

Grasping his arms, she caught him off guard and reversed their positions before he realized what he was doing. She scrambled up, moving until she was on top of him. The flicker of surprise in his gray eyes pleased her to no end.

Sasha lost no time. She dusted his chest with kisses, snaking her body along his. Succeeding, she thought triumphantly, in arousing him to an even greater level. She knew she was on borrowed time, that any second, he would be taking over again. He was already making her head spin and there was a rushing noise in her ears that continued to grow louder. There was no doubt that at any moment, she was going to lose control and she wanted desperately to bring him up to as high a plateau as she could before that happened.

And, just as she had come to both her own limit and his, Tony suddenly reversed their positions again. And then he was the one looming over her. He laced his hands with hers, holding them overhead and then to the side as he worked his mouth slowly down her torso.

Electrical charges shot through her. Sasha twisted and wiggled both into the sensations and away from them. Trying to savor, to sustain. Trying to forestall the ultimate detonation, keeping it back for just a little longer.

He was smiling, as he raised himself back over her again. Her whole body was humming like a newly tuned generator, but it was his smile that registered most of all. His smile that had the greatest effect on her.

And then he was inside her and they were one. One and racing together to the final destination. The final summit before they plunged back down to the earth that was waiting for them.

The sound of Sasha's growing agitation, released in small gasps and garbled words that completely defied understanding, excited Tony to a point he was completely unfamiliar with.

And then the explosion came, wrapping itself around them both. Sealing them together in desire and sweat. They hung suspended in midair.

Sasha felt part of Tony's weight against her. Felt her heart hammering so hard, she was certain it would pop out of her chest and into his. She wrapped her legs around his, unwilling to have the moment end, even after it had.

The descent was slow, but inevitable. When she felt him roll off, the emptiness hovered on the brink of her consciousness, threatening to oppress her. She held it at bay as best she could.

What felt like a hundred years later, Tony propped himself up on his elbow and leaned his head against his hand. She could feel him looking at her for a long moment. When she finally turned her head toward him, she couldn't read his expression. Was he angry? Pleased? As blown away as she was?

"Why?" he asked.

"Why what?" Sasha managed to push the words out after one failed attempt. Her throat was so dry, it felt as if it was sticking to itself, sealing off almost all of her air.

He didn't explain, didn't enlighten. All he did was repeat the question. "Why?"

She didn't know why. All she knew was that if she hadn't, she would have burst into flames on her own. Until it had happened, she hadn't known how much she had wanted it to happen. But that was all too serious, too much to burden him with. There were no strings here.

So she forced a smile to her lips and said, "I didn't have any dessert to offer you."

Her flippant response surprised him. He didn't think she was capable of flippant answers. But then, he wouldn't have thought her capable of what had just happened here, either.

No, that wasn't exactly right. He'd felt, sensed really, that beneath her cool exterior there was a passionate, vibrant woman. What he hadn't been prepared for was the degree to which that was true. And was unequally unprepared for his own reaction to her. Granted he'd been attracted to her, maybe even from the very start, but the degree to which he'd found himself responding had caught him completely off guard.

Even now, spent and exhausted, Tony could feel the beginnings of desire starting to stir him. Could feel himself wanting her all over again. It didn't seem possible and yet, there it was. Desire, fully clothed and waiting to be stripped down to its barest essence all over again.

"That's one hell of a menu," he finally said in response to her comment.

She smiled. She felt very close to him at this moment and the fact that they were both naked, their flesh warm from the press of feverish skin against skin, had nothing to do with it. It was the honesty and not the proximity that made her feel so close to him.

"Yes, it kind of surprised me, too." Moving on instincts, Sasha turned her body into his.

Tony felt himself responding even more fiercely to her than before. It was no longer simply mind over matter. His mind kept slipping away.

With effort, he attempted to regain some ground. "Look, I'm sorry if—"

"No." Sasha pressed her finger against his lips, stopping him before he could say anything more. Before he could say something that hurt. "No 'sorry.' I'm not sorry," she told him softly. "And if you are, I don't want to hear about it. Not tonight. There're no strings attached, Tony. Just don't spoil it for me, that's all I ask." And then, because she could feel his desire for her growing, she allowed a smile to slip along her lips. "You can even have seconds if you want."

It was as if she'd read his mind. The spirit was willing, but the flesh was going to take a wee bit longer. "Give me a minute."

"I'll give you as long as you like," she told him. She lowered her eyes just a little. And smiled again. "But I don't think you'll need it."

And neither did he, he realized. His desire had taken full possession of him. Again. As he wove his fingers through her hair, his mouth curved in anticipation.

She was right. Tony had a heart-melting smile. Even a little went a long way. "You should do that more often."

He was just about to kiss her and stopped a fraction of an inch short of Sasha's lips. "What, make love with you?"

That, too, she thought. "I meant smile." Even a hint of one transformed his face, softening it. "You have a nice face." As if to underscore her words, she slid her hand along his cheek. She felt a muscle leap beneath her palm. Felt something tighten within her in response. "When you're not trying to scare people."

"I don't 'try' to scare people." He just went about business the only way he knew how. Doggedly.

"Right." She laughed quietly, the smile slipping into her eyes. And his gut. "It just comes naturally to you, I guess."

"You're not scared," he pointed out, his voice rumbling along her skin. Exciting her.

Slipping one hand beneath his head, she laced her hands around his neck. "Actually," she confessed, fitting her body against his, reveling in the heat that she felt emanating from his torso, "I'm terrified."

She couldn't help wondering if he realized that there was more than a little truth in her admission. Because she *was* afraid. Afraid of what she had just felt. Afraid of what she was feeling. She knew that, unlike with Adam, this couldn't lead anywhere. But somehow, she couldn't make herself pull back. Couldn't get herself to dive for shelter again. She was so weary of being numb. Of having a heart that pumped only blood and nothing more.

"I would have never guessed." But now that he looked into her eyes, there was something there, something that told him she wasn't merely being witty, or wry.

"I'm almost as good at hiding my feelings as you are."

She was striking too close. It was, he thought, bringing his mouth down to hers, as if she could look into his soul. Because, much as he tried to deny it, he was feeling something. And that scared the hell out of him.

Blocking out his thought, he focused only on the moment. Only on making love with Sasha again and nothing else.

The second time seemed even more intense, more pleasing, more of everything than the first had been. And it served to open his eyes even further.

He hadn't thought it was possible to feel this way again. To feel this surge through his veins, this need coursing through his body. He would have bet any amount of money that all of that had died for him the day that Annie had.

But here it was again, that wild, exhilarating feeling of being alive, of having things open up for him.

And yet, somehow, it was different.

He couldn't explain it, couldn't put his finger on it, but all Tony knew, dead center in his soul, was that it was different. Not better, not worse, than what he'd had with Annie, just different.

*Damn it, don't analyze, just enjoy,* he upbraided himself.

And so he did. Less urgently than before, because this time he allowed himself time to explore, to savor, to absorb and remember. Because he'd had one true love in his life and that was more than most. To think that he could get that lucky again would be taking up residence in a fool's paradise.

Spent, exhausted beyond words, Tony drew his body away from hers and tucked Sasha against him. He held her in silence, listening to the beat of her heart mimicking the rhythm of his own. He'd believed that moments like this were beyond his reach. To be allowed to revisit the peace, just this one more time, was something he was truly grateful for.

The next moment, peace flew out the window and adrenaline kicked in.

Someone was unlocking the front door.

# Chapter 12

Tony bolted upright. Grabbing his jeans, he tossed his shirt at Sasha. He had his pants on and zipped before she had a chance to slip the shirt on.

"You expecting someone?"

"No."

The word was no sooner out of Sasha's mouth than the front door opened and a slender woman with auburn hair almost as vibrant as she was came in.

Sasha slanted a glance toward Tony. He amazed her. She'd never seen anyone get dressed so fast in her life. All she had managed to do was jam her arms into the shirtsleeves and close one strategic button before Natalya came walking in.

It could have been worse, Sasha thought. It could

have been her mother. She didn't even want to begin to think about the consequences if it had been her father.

"Lock's sticking again," Natalya complained. And then her mouth dropped open as she finally looked into the room. The key she'd been wrestling with was forgotten as it hung from the lock like a trapeze artist suspended in midair. Blinking to make sure her eyes weren't playing tricks on her, Natalya remained where she was, staring.

"Sasha?" she asked uncertainly.

Dragging a hand uncomfortably through his hair, Tony spoke first. "Let me take a look at that lock." Without waiting for an invitation, he padded barefoot over to the door.

*And let me take a look at you,* Natalya thought, her eyes slowly and appreciatively washing over the stranger's torso. This was certainly a much better specimen of manhood than she had just walked away from. When the latter had tried to hurry the evening into bed, she'd decided to cut short her plans for the weekend and come home.

She'd had no idea she'd be interrupting something. Sasha never brought men home.

Natalya sidestepped the handsome stranger as he came closer. "Um, Sash, there's a man in our apartment and he doesn't belong to either Kady or me."

Sasha took a deep breath. She was going to hear about this for weeks to come. Maybe months. "Yes, I know."

Natalya turned to the man, whose chest looked as if it had been chiseled out of rock and put out her hand. There was no attempt to hide the admiration in her eyes. "Hi, I'm Natalya, Sasha's sister."

"Anthony Santini," came the terse reply, coupled by an even terser handshake. He looked over her head toward Sasha. "Do you have any WD-40?"

"I'll get it," Natalya volunteered, glancing toward Sasha. The shirt her sister had on was hardly long enough to cover the bare essentials. "You don't look as if you're dressed for rummaging under the sink."

Natalya was back before Sasha could put on her own clothes. She'd had a chance to match the stranger's name with a scrap of information that had surfaced in her brain. Holding the small can out to him, Natalya said, "You're one of the police detectives investigating the murders at PM, aren't you?"

He took the can from her, then pulling a handkerchief out of his pocket, he held it around the wood surrounding the lock. Tony applied some of the spray before answering. "Yes."

Natalya glanced at her sister, then back at him. "Is this the way you usually question witnesses?" The woman's mouth, he noted, curved just the way that Sasha's did.

He squirted the spray into the lock a second time. "I was just getting ready to leave."

"Without your shirt?" Natalya asked innocently. She glanced toward Sasha, taking in the way her sister filled out the garment. "I don't think so." Finished,

Tony easily removed the key from the lock and tossed it to her. She caught them handily. "Take your time, Detective. There's this all-night deli that's just around the corner. I've got a sudden craving for a pastrami sandwich on rye. All things being equal, I should be gone for about an hour." She was already edging her way over to the door. "Longer if you need it."

"Natalya—" Sasha began to protest.

Natalya ignored her. "And be good to her," she added, opening the door. "Sasha doesn't do this kind of thing. Ever." Natalya paused to insert her key into the lock again, testing its mobility. "Perfect," she declared. Her eyes slid over his torso again as she stretched out the word. "I guess a little lubrication does do wonders." A mischievous smile curved her mouth just before she closed the door behind her.

Tony blew out a breath as he placed the can of WD-40 on the coffee table.

"Well, that was awkward." Sasha ran her hand through her hair. "I'm sorry. I didn't think she'd be home this weekend. Something must have happened," she realized. Sasha pressed her lips together. What was he thinking, she wondered. Was he angry at the interruption, or at being discovered in a compromising situation? His expression was unreadable. "Natalya tends to be a little outspoken. Sometimes she engages her mouth before her brain has had a chance to catch up. What she said about my not doing this sort of thing—"

"I already know that," he told her, his voice so low

she almost felt the words rather than heard them. His eyes held hers. "Neither do I."

So where did that put them? Sasha was afraid to ask. Afraid of the answer she might receive. Because she knew what she wanted to hear and knew that she would most likely hear the exact opposite. Better not to hear it said at all.

"Your sister was right about one thing," he finally said.

Sasha realized she was still holding her breath and let it out slowly. "And that was?"

Tony nodded toward her body. "I am going to need my shirt."

"What?" It took her a second to replay his words. And then she flushed, embarrassed. "Oh, right. Sure."

But before she could slip the shirt off and quickly put on the dress she'd shed earlier, Tony was doing it for her. He slowly slipped the shirt from her shoulders. But instead of putting it on or offering her the dress that had been discarded, he just stood there, his hands on her shoulders. She could have sworn that his breath had grown short. So had her own.

"Your sister said an hour?"

"Yes." Sasha could feel everything inside her begin to vibrate again as anticipation started to rise. Her reply was hardly more than a whisper.

"Does that mean an actual sixty minutes?" At this point, Tony wasn't taking anything for granted.

"Maybe more." Sasha drew her tongue along her lips. "Natalya has a tendency to run late."

"Good."

It was the last thing he said for a while.

The next time Natalya unlocked the apartment door, an hour and a half later, she did it with a great deal of commotion. She wanted to make sure that her re-entrance caught no one by surprise. Once the door had parted from the doorjamb, she stuck in a white handkerchief and waved it just for good measure.

Sasha was sitting on the sofa. The same sofa that had seen a great deal of activity in the last few hours. Seeing the white flag she laughed. "You can come in, Nat."

"The hunk is gone?" Opening the door all the way, Natalya looked around the living room, as if to see for herself.

"The hunk is gone," Sasha confirmed. She couldn't help the small, satisfied smile that escaped her lips. She slanted a look at her sister to see if she'd noticed. Natalya's wide grin told her she had. "What happened to your weekend?"

Natalya frowned, waving a dismissive hand. "Jerry's a jerk." And then her face brightened. "Tell me everything!"

In a flash, she crossed the room and grabbed both of Sasha's hands in hers, as if she intended to pump the story out of her if Sasha was unwilling to comply with her request.

Sasha laughed, disengaging herself from her sister. "You saw everything."

Natalya's grin turned from engaging to mischievous. Her eyes were sparkling.

"Not everything." A heartfelt sigh accompanied the words. "But from what I saw, this detective of yours was beautiful. So tell me," she said as she settled in for a lengthy story, "how long has this been going on?"

"He's not *my* detective," Sasha corrected. "And *this* has not been going on at all." She saw the impatient look on Natalya's face. Her sister clearly wasn't buying into this. She began to explain. "We were supposed to go out tonight for dinner—"

Natalya cut in, surprised. "Dinner? A date? And you didn't tell me?"

Sasha ignored the surprised accusation and pushed on to the conclusion of her short story. "But he was called away to another homicide. Except that he forgot to let me know that he wasn't coming to pick me up. So he came by later—to apologize."

Natalya whistled. "That man certainly knows how to offer up an apology." There was more than a touch of envy in her voice. "Can you get him to apologize again?"

"Natalya." There was a warning note in Sasha's voice, one that Natalya gave no indication she had even heard.

"Seriously," Natalya pushed on, "maybe you could offer to help him with his investigation and when he snaps at you—he looks like the snapping type—" she confided, "he'll feel guilty and apologize again." Natalya sighed, thinking of what she'd almost walked in on. "Does he have any brothers who like to apologize—?"

Sasha knew that Natalya could go on like this indefinitely. She didn't want a big deal being made of what had just happened, even if Tony was the first man she'd been with since Adam. It would all soon be in her past. The best way to stop her sister was a cold dose of reality.

"Natalya, Tyler Harris is dead."

"Tyler Harris?" Skidding to a verbal halt, Natalya then repeated the name slowly. "Tyler Harris?" She was drawing a blank and shook her head, looking at Sasha for enlightenment.

"He's an anesthesiologist, or was," Sasha amended. God, but she was having trouble accepting all this as being real. She kept hoping it was all a nightmare and that she'd wake up. "Tyler used to work at PM." Even as she said the words, something came back to her. A wisp of a memory that went through her fingers like smoke when she tried to catch it.

"Sasha? What's the matter?" Natalya asked, concerned. "You look pale."

And then it came to her. Not a fragment but the entire scenario. Her eyes widened with surprise as she looked at her sister. Why hadn't she remembered earlier?

"Tyler and I once were in the O.R. together. It was the Sunday after Thanksgiving and there was almost no one in the E.R." As more bits and pieces returned to attach themselves to the memory, her voice began to grow progressively more agitated. "The EMTs brought in a woman who'd been in a hit-and-run car accident. Tyler administered the anesthesia and I operated. There wasn't time to get a specialist." She hadn't thought about that in a long time, had put the entire incident in the back of her mind because the results had not been good. Despite all her best efforts, the woman had died on the table.

*Died.* The single word vibrated in her brain. Her eyes widened.

*Omigod.*

She became aware of Natalya's hand on her arm. "Sasha? Sasha, what's wrong? You look as if you'd seen a ghost."

She had. A ghost from the past. She looked at Natalya. "Angela and Rachel were the nurses in the O.R. that day. We were short-staffed. The woman's body was a mess. I couldn't find the source of her internal bleeding. I sent Jorge to get more blood…" Her voice trailed off. "I sent Jorge," she repeated. "Jorge was there."

Everyone she'd just mentioned was dead.

Except for her.

A cold, clammy feeling descended over her.

And then, through the haze that had suddenly enshrouded her, she heard Natalya's voice. "Are you trying to tell me that everyone who was in the O.R. with you that day has been killed by that psycho who is stalking PM?"

Spoken out loud, that sounded absurd. Sasha let out a long breath. She was letting her imagination run away with her.

Sasha shook her head in response to Natalya's question. "Maybe it's a coincidence."

But Natalya was far from convinced. She shook her head grimly. "You don't believe in coincidences, Sasha. Remember? And neither do I."

She was about to protest that a coincidence was more likely than the scenario she'd just mentioned, but then another thought came to her. A horrifying thought. She looked at Natalya.

"Oh my God, Joshua."

"Joshua?" Natalya repeated, confused. She narrowed her eyes, trying to fathom what her sister was telling her. Sasha had her hand on her wrist and was squeezing. Hard.

"Joshua Palmer," she cried. If this outrageous thought had any merit to it, the young physician could be next. "He was the assistant at the surgery." Natalya said nothing, continuing to listen. "He's a primary-care physician, Nat, specializing in internal organs. We thought, between the two of us, we could keep the injured woman alive until Norman Fernandez could be located and answered his page."

"Anyone else in the operating room?" Natalya wanted to know.

Sasha shook her head. "No. Just the five of us. And Jorge."

"Six, with four dead," Natalya reviewed, no

longer smiling. No longer thinking about the scene she'd just walked in on. "Sasha, you've got to tell your hunk about this."

Sasha was already striding across the floor to the phone on the coffee table. More than anything else, she hoped she was wrong, that this really was just a bizarre coincidence. "I already told you, Nat. He's not my hunk."

Natalya joined her at the telephone. "Then I'd let him down easy, because I think he thinks he is." And she meant that, seriously. "And I wouldn't tell him until after this psycho stalker, whoever he is, is caught. You're going to definitely need that sexy detective for protection."

Sasha began to protest, then fell silent as she heard the phone on the other end of the line begin to ring. She waved her hand at Natalya, indicating that she should hold her tongue.

A deep, sleepy voice muttered, "Santini."

She immediately felt guilty and would have hung up had Natalya not been right there at her side, watching. So she pushed on, telling herself that she was right to call. "Did I wake you?"

She heard Tony let out a long breath, as if he was getting his bearings. And putting a lid on his temper. He didn't answer her question.

Instead, he responded to what he heard in her voice. "Something wrong, Doc?"

So, they were back to that. To their job descriptions. She'd hoped they had moved beyond that. But then, she reminded herself, she had known going into this that he was the type who wanted to maintain his distance.

"It might be," she began slowly, trying hard to sound as if she was rational. "I'm not sure, but I think I might have found your connection between the dead people."

"I'm listening."

She could detect a note of electricity crackling between the lines. She'd gotten his undivided attention.

"Three years ago, on the Sunday after Thanksgiving, we all operated on a hit-and-run victim." She enunciated every word as if she as waiting for him to absorb them one at a time.

"Hold it, hold it," he ordered gruffly. He was certain his foggy brain had caused him to mishear her. Or at least he fervently hoped so. "You said 'we.' Is that a royal 'we'?"

Sasha took a breath before answering. That meant that she was in danger, too, didn't it? She refused to allow her mind to go there, to deal with that thought.

"No, it's not a royal 'we', Detective. I was there, too. It was a hit-and-run," she said again with emphasis. "The paramedics brought her in, a young woman about twenty-five years old. There was no one on duty that night who specialized in internal surgery. If we'd waited until a specialist arrived, there was a hundred percent chance she would be dead before the surgeon ever crossed the threshold." Sasha paused.

"Did you save her?" Tony asked the question for form's sake. He had a feeling that he already knew the answer.

The next moment, she confirmed it. "No, she died while we were operating." Sasha sighed, remembering. Feeling helpless and awful. The woman had been young. And three months pregnant.

He heard the sadness in her voice and ignored the urge to say something to comfort her. There were more important things at stake right now. There was nothing to be gained by feeling guilty about the woman's death. It wouldn't change the results. He was certain that Sasha had done all that had been humanly possible. At the moment, he was far more interested in keeping her and whoever else had been involved in that emergency surgery alive.

"Can you remember if the woman was married or about to be married?"

Sasha heard rustling on the other side of the line, as if Tony was moving around, getting dressed. She tried not to allow herself to get distracted by that thought, by the image of him slipping into clothes the way he had done earlier.

Instead, she concentrated on his question. On the memory of an operation that was three years in the past. "Yes, she was. Her husband threatened to sue everyone." She remembered that the man had been angry and abusive to her when she came out to break the news to him. She'd had the woman's blood on her surgical livery and it had nearly sent him over the edge. "But in the end," she said, struggling to regain her calm, "the whole thing just blew over."

Tony had a different view of it. "Maybe not. I'll be right down there. In the meantime, try to remember as much as you can about the operation, who was there, what the husband might have said, things like that."

"You don't need to come rushing over, Tony," she protested.

Maybe they weren't back to square one after all, he thought. That should have bothered him, he told himself. But the exact opposite was true. "Is your sister back yet?" he wanted to know.

Sasha glanced at Natalya, who'd remained only a couple of feet away from her during the entire phone call. Maybe he wasn't worried about her. Maybe, since she'd woken him, he'd decided to come back for an encore. She could feel tiny nerve endings priming, sending off alarms. "Yes, but—"

"Good. Keep the door locked and don't let anyone else in until I get there."

He *was* worried. She could feel her uneasiness increasing even as she silently insisted she was making something out of nothing. "I might be all wrong about this."

"And then again, you might be all right," he countered grimly. "Keep the door locked."

Ten minutes later, he was there, banging on her door and calling through it for her to let him in.

Sasha all but flew to the door, taking the chain off even as she flipped the lock.

"I didn't realize you lived so close by."

"I don't," he told her, crossing the threshold. Turning, he closed the door and secured the chain. "One of the advantages of having a police siren in your car is that you get to use it once in a while to prevent crimes instead of getting there after the fact." He nodded at Natalya, but his attention was completely centered on Sasha. "Was there anyone else in the operating room that night?"

She'd thought and rethought that surgery the minute they hung up the phone. "Just Joshua Palmer. He's a primary-care physician."

Tony frowned. He hated the labels that society had slapped on everything. He missed the days when a doctor like Palmer was simply referred to as a family physician and that was enough to speak volumes.

"Anyone else?" he wanted to know. Sasha shook her head. "And everyone who's been killed so far," he repeated the names of all four victims slowly, "Angela Rico, Rachel Wells, Jorge Lopez and Tyler Harris, they were all in the operating room that night, too?"

Sasha was beginning to feel hollow inside. And extremely uneasy. "Yes."

"Can you remember the woman's name?"

That she wasn't liable to forget any time soon, Sasha thought. She nodded as she pressed her lips together. "You tend to remember the one you lose, no matter how hard you try to forget them. Her name was Gloria Jean Anderson."

The first order of business, Tony thought, after calling the captain and getting authorization for Sasha and the other doctor to have bodyguards posted, was having a talk with the late Gloria Jean's husband.

It felt good to finally have some kind of lead to work with. He nodded at Sasha as he took out his cell phone. "It's going to be all right."

The optimistic promise surprised her.

# Chapter 13

"Dr. Pulaski, have you seen the paper this morning?"

The breathless question came from one of the newest nurses on the floor, Jennifer Cruz, as Sasha was quickly walking past the nurses' station on the maternity ward the following morning.

It was a little before nine and she was running behind. She always did her rounds at the hospital before going to her office. Today, mercifully, was a light day. Only three of the patients on the floor were hers, and one was going home this morning as soon as she signed the discharge papers.

Without looking, Sasha had a feeling she knew what Jennifer was referring to. "No, I didn't have time." She glanced toward the nurse. "I'm running late. Oh God." The groan was an involuntary reaction to the headline that was splashed across the first page of the newspaper that the nurse was holding up for her to view. "Hospital Stalker Strikes Again." The headline fairly vibrated. Sasha sighed. It didn't take the media long. "Just what we need. More panicked patients."

Sasha saw the animation drain away from the nurse's face. The next moment, she discovered why.

"The medical staff isn't feeling too good about this killer being at large, either," Lauren James complained.

The administrator came up behind her. The woman looked slightly harried beneath her perfectly made-up features. The board, Sasha knew, was not taking this well. Which meant that they were, in turn, taking it out on Lauren.

Despite the differences they'd had, Sasha felt sorry for the woman.

"Everyone's looking over their shoulder. Patients are canceling elective surgeries, or postponing them." For a moment, Lauren paused, as if debating her next words. It was a known fact that the woman had no friends. Up until now, Sasha would have said that Lauren felt she didn't need them. But now, judging by the look on Lauren's face, she wasn't so sure. "The board is threatening to have my head."

Though she felt certain that the board was not happy about this unwanted publicity the hospital was getting, she had a feeling that the members were using the fallout as an excuse to make Lauren's life difficult. Difficult enough perhaps to make the woman hand in her resignation of her own accord. It was no secret that, education and credentials notwithstanding, the woman was no one's candidate for hospital administrator of the year. Or even the month.

Still, Sasha felt obligated to lend a sympathetic ear. "They can't blame you for these murders."

Lauren had purposely moved away from the nurses' station and Jenny's rather unsubtle attempt to listen in. She kept her voice low as she said, "Tell that to the board."

"Well, unless you're responsible for killing these people—and everyone knows how you hate to get your hands dirty," Sasha quipped with a wry smile, "there's really no way that you could be behind this."

The icy blonde shrugged her shoulders as her lips curled into a deep frown. And then her eyes seemed to grow alert as she looked over Sasha's shoulder. "Who's that?" she wanted to know.

Sasha turned to look. Lauren was referring to a man not more than several paces away. To the casual observer it was obvious that the stranger didn't look like either an anxious husband or a happy one.

She'd told Tony the man didn't blend in, Sasha thought, frustrated. She'd left the apartment quickly this morning, hoping to ditch the detective assigned to her. She should have known better.

"My police protection," Sasha told Lauren.

This was not going to work. Harry Ackerman had been introduced to her last night. Last night, she'd assumed that the detective would be outside her apartment, in his car, unobtrusively standing guard. It wasn't just herself needing protecting last night.

But today, it was a whole different story. Today the detective would only be getting in her way. And she couldn't have that. Her first allegiance was to her patients.

"You have police protection?" Lauren looked at her, stunned. "Why? What else has happened?" she wanted to know.

But Sasha ignored the questions as she crossed over to the dour, slightly rumpled-looking man. He towered over her by almost a foot. He hadn't been picked for his ability to blend in, she thought.

"Look, Detective Ackerman, I'm sorry but this just isn't going to work. No offense, but having you around is going to get my patients nervous. Not to mention that I've got exams to perform." She looked up at him pointedly. "And you can't be present."

"It's Harry," he told her. Willing to work within the situation he said, "Then I'll be in the reception area."

She took a breath, knowing this was going to make her seem as if she were being difficult, but that wasn't her intent. "Can I refuse police protection, Harry?"

"Yes," he allowed, saying the word slowly. "But I don't recommend it."

It wasn't his place to recommend that he not be around, she thought. Especially since Tony had gone through channels to obtain his services. But if she'd found the idea of having protection comforting last night, in the light of day, she knew that her own fears had to take second place to her patients' needs.

"Duly noted, Harry. And it's not that I don't appreciate it, I do. But I have to officially refuse protection." She offered the older man an apologetic smile. "Tell Detective Santini thanks but no thanks."

"He's not going to be happy about this," Ackerman warned her.

That she already knew. Santini was a headstrong man. But she was well acquainted with headstrong.

"You're sending the police detective away?" Lauren was still trying to fathom what was going on in her hospital.

Sasha nodded. Returning to the nurses' station, she went to the main desk and pulled a chart. "It wouldn't work out."

"You didn't answer me before," Lauren reminded her. She rephrased her question. "Why do you merit special police protection while the rest of the hospital staff doesn't? Is there something I should know?" Suspicion was all over her face.

More than anything else, Lauren James hated being out of the loop. About *anything*. Annoyance creased her brow, creating tiny furrows of disapproval. Had she been of a different temperament, Sasha would have played the moment out for a while for her own amusement. But there was nothing to be gained by that.

So she told Lauren, even though she knew she was probably opening up a can of worms. "Because the investigating detective thinks there's a connection between me and the four victims, including the latest one." She nodded toward the newspaper.

"A connection?" Lauren echoed, clearly horrified. "What kind of a connection?"

"We all worked on a hit-and-run patient three years ago. She died on the operating table. I was the surgeon, Tyler was the anesthesiologist. Joshua Palmer was the assistant."

"Three years," Lauren repeated. "That was before I came to Patience Memorial."

And glorious times they were, too, Sasha thought, although her expression never changed. "Yes, I know. At the time I'd only been here, as an attending, for six months."

Making a notation in the chart, she closed it and placed it back on the desk. Ackerman, she noticed, was still lingering in the corridor, uncertain as to whether or not he should leave.

As she came out of the nurses' station, Sasha made eye contact with him. "Really, go," she urged. "If there's any heat, I'll take it. Tell Detective Santini it was my doing, my choice."

With that, she put the matter of killings and stalkers out of her mind and walked into the first room. She had patients to attend to and that came before anything.

"So," Sasha said cheerfully, addressing the woman in the hospital bed, "are you and your beautiful daughter ready to go home, Sandy?"

"The guy's alibi checks out." It was the second time Henderson had said the sentence to Tony. There was still no response from the man. Henderson leaned over his partner's desk, peering at his face. "Santini, did you hear me? Gloria Jean Anderson's husband, his—"

Tony waved a hand at his partner. He and Henderson had brought Anderson in for questioning first thing that morning. The college professor's haughty attitude had made it a case of instant dislike on his part. He'd grilled the man intently, getting his whereabouts for the time of death for all four victims.

The alibis hadn't been creative, but they'd obviously been genuine. Henderson had been checking them out for the remainder of the morning.

"Yeah, I heard you," Tony grumbled. "I just didn't want to hear you."

Henderson blew out an audible breath, leaning against the side of Tony's desk.

"Yeah, I know what you mean." He shook his head. "It really looked like you were onto something there. But the guy was in Vegas for the first killing. And at some seminar for the college for the second. He was giving a lecture when Harris was killed. Lots of people saw him all those times." Henderson flipped the pages of his small, battered notepad, as if he expected something magical to pop up, something that hadn't been there all the other times he'd opened the notepad. With a helpless shrug, he tucked it back into the pocket of his hound's-tooth jacket. "Maybe there's something else that ties all those victims together. You came up with one operation, maybe there's another. It's a busy hospital."

He hadn't come up with the operation. Sasha had. He would have liked nothing better than to take her out of the equation. Except that his gut told him she belonged in it. And that she was right about this.

Tony didn't liked the late Gloria Jean Anderson's husband. A tall, rangy man with dirty blond hair, condescending brown eyes and a nasty disposition that had flared once he'd discovered he was being approached by a member of the police. An English professor who had no qualms about showing that he felt superior to everyone he spoke to, Simon Anderson blamed the entire police force for never apprehending the hit-and-run driver responsible for his wife's death.

A little delving into records showed that Simon and his late wife had had marital problems. The counsellor they'd gone to see had recommended Simon sign up for anger-management classes. The man had attended one class before dropping out.

It took very little effort for Tony to envision Anderson plotting and exacting revenge for his wife's death. Since he couldn't find the hit-and-run driver, wiping out the medical team who had failed to save her would have undoubtedly been a close second.

Except that he had alibis. Or so it looked on the surface, Tony thought.

"Maybe," he agreed. "Why don't you dig a little deeper, make sure that our boy didn't hire someone to do his dirty work. Check into his finances, see if any large sum of money moved out of his accounts recently. Hit men don't come cheap. Maybe—" Tony stopped abruptly as he saw Harry Ackerman walking into the squad room.

Leaving his thought, and Henderson, hanging, Tony got out of his chair and crossed over to the detective. The latter obviously hadn't seen him and was walking to the rear of the squad room, to the captain's office.

"Hey, Ackerman," Tony called. "What's up? Why aren't you with Dr. Pulaski?" And then a partial answer occurred to him. His expression drew deadly serious. "Something happen?"

Ackerman stopped walking. He frowned. The jowls on his face resembled that of a well-fed hound dog. "Yeah, something happened. The doc told me to tell you that she's decided to refuse police protection."

"What?" That was a stupid move and Sasha did not strike him as a stupid woman.

"She told me to tell you she's decided to refuse police protection," Ackerman repeated a little more slowly. He knew better than to flippantly ask Santini if he was going deaf.

Tony waved an impatient hand at Ackerman. He could feel Henderson staring at him. It just served to heighten his annoyance. What the hell was going on here? Why would the woman suddenly decide to play hero?

"I heard you the first time." His eyes narrowed as he looked at Ackerman. "What did you do to make her change her mind?"

Ackerman straightened, like a man bracing himself for a blow. "Nothing."

"You must have done something," Tony insisted, doing his best not to lose his temper. He'd never been on the easygoing side but lately it felt as if all his emotions were closer to the surface than they'd ever been. Ready to explode. "Everything was all right last night when I left you there outside her apartment."

Ackerman moved his wide shoulders in a hapless shrug. "Don't look at me. It wasn't my idea. She said I scared her patients. I offered to stay in her reception area, but she didn't think that was good enough, or far enough away," he added, annoyed himself.

The man wasn't exactly warm and cuddly, but he wasn't Frankenstein either, Tony thought in exasperation. Pulling out his cell phone, he punched in Sasha's number. He listened to the phone ring five times before her voice came on. But as he began to speak, he realized he was talking to a pre-recorded message.

Tony bit off a curse as he waited for the beep as instructed.

"Listen," he said into the phone after the beep had sounded, trying to ignore the fact that he was conversing with a machine, something he hated, "you don't get to call off police protection. Only *I* get to do that. Damn it, I hate talking to machines," he shouted.

It was the last thing he said into the phone before terminating the call.

When Tony started striding through the squad room, heading toward the exit, Henderson was quick to follow. He was only a step behind the primary investigator as they walked out into the corridor.

"Okay, so what's the plan, Santini?" he wanted to know.

The plan. He hadn't anything as clear-cut as a plan. He was back to flying by the seat of his pants—and following his gut. And his gut told him that Sasha might be the next target.

"I'm going back to the hospital. The key to all these murders has to be there. Maybe I can get the administrator to have one of her people cross-reference all the patient records against the staff they interacted with." If the woman refused because of some doctor-patient privilege, he had a few other options to try that weren't quite so much on the straight and narrow. But he'd learned to give protocol a try whenever possible. "Maybe there's a connection there."

"No more bodyguards?" Henderson wanted to know.

"I didn't say that," Tony bit off. His tone told Henderson to back off.

Henderson was very good at picking up on tones. It was part of the secret of his longevity on the force— and why he'd managed to survive for as long as he had with Tony. He knew better than to rock the boat.

"No, no, Dad, I'm okay. We're all okay. You don't have to come out of retirement. Really," Sasha insisted. The second she'd seen the story on Tyler Harris's murder, she'd been expecting her father's call. She'd already had one from her mother.

She was beginning to think of the cell phone as an evil invention, meant to bedevil her.

"I have already made up my mind, Sasha. Conrad has been after me to join the security firm he is running. Now I have a reason."

Conrad Zemanski was her father's oldest and best friend. Both had served on the police force together. Conrad had taken early retirement after having been wounded on the job. A small inheritance from his wife's uncle had given him enough money to start his own security firm. A firm her father seemed dead set on joining now.

"Daddy, even if you do become a guard, that doesn't mean that you'll automatically be sent over to PM. Conrad might not even have a contract with the hospital." She crossed her fingers as she said it.

"Yes, he does," her father's voice boomed in her ear. "Conrad's firm has a contract with many of the hospitals in the area. I told him what was happening, and your hospital is looking for more security even as we are talking."

Sasha closed her eyes, searching for strength. "Daddy, you don't have to do this. Detective Santini's already assigned a bodyguard to me." *And I got rid of him, but you don't have to know that.*

"Why? Why just you? What is it you are not telling me?"

She realized her mistake too late. "I always tell you everything, Daddy. And I'm not the only one getting a bodyguard. There're several other doctors as well." It was a white lie, but under the circumstances, she could be forgiven, she thought. She was only out to give her parents peace of mind. Instead of losing her own. "So you see, I'm fine. You can stop worrying." The sun, she knew, would stop rising sooner than her father would stop worrying, but she was bound to go through the motions.

"Sasha, you know that I—"

She could smell an argument coming. "I've got to go, Daddy. I'm being paged. Oops, that's Mrs. Miller. Twins," she told him hurriedly. "Babies don't wait to be born. Love to Mom."

She disconnected the call before he had a chance to make another protest or mount another argument. With a sigh, she leaned back in her chair, eyes closed.

"It's not nice to lie to your father."

Startled, Sasha swung her chair around to face the doorway. Her pulse accelerated when she saw Tony standing there. She drew in a long breath to steady it, hoping that she hadn't suddenly become flushed. Flushed was for teenagers. Not even teenagers, she amended.

She watched Tony enter the room. It was more as though he took possession of it. "What are you doing here?"

His expression was unreadable. "Listening to you lie to your father."

She straightened her shoulders defensively. "I wasn't lying."

"Oh?" Crossing his arms before him, he leaned a hip against her desk. Parking his torso much too close to her. "What do you call untruths in your world?"

"I call it making him feel better." She loved her father, but he was the poster child for the overprotective dad. "If he had his way, my sisters and I would all be wrapped up in cotton batting and stored in some large closet."

"The man was a cop," Tony reminded her. He felt a smile attempting to curve his lips. She had that effect on him, he thought as he banked it down. "He knows better than most what could happen."

"All of life's a risk. By definition," Sasha added with emphasis. She deflected the conversation back toward him. "Now, what are you really doing here?"

The smile faded on its own. "Why did you send Ackerman away?"

"I told him why. I can't do my work and have him looking over my shoulder. My patients expect privacy and rightly so."

She was smarter than that, he thought. Ackerman wasn't going to be standing two inches away from her while she was in her office. He was supposed to provide protection for her as she went from one place to another.

"He'd keep out of your way," he told her.

A good number of her patients were pregnant right now. Which meant that their hormones and emotions were in flux. It didn't help to see a hulking man sitting in the waiting room.

"None of my patients are going to suddenly pull out a gun on me."

"No." He did his best to keep his temper, but there was no denying that he was wasting time trying to convince her of something that he felt was necessary. "But someone else might."

She didn't want to think about that. "Did you check out the husband?"

Tony nodded. "He's clean. Nasty son of a bitch, but clean."

She smiled, storing her frustration for a moment as she touched his face.

Sasha felt stirrings. Too fast, too intense. She dropped her hand, needing to get a handle on this before it overwhelmed her.

"Maybe it was just a coincidence, all the victims being in the O.R. with that patient." She shrugged ruefully. "My fault for thinking there was something to it."

They both thought there was something to it. "I don't believe in coincidences."

"But if the husband's clean…"

"Maybe we didn't dig deep enough," he countered. He surprised himself by letting her into his thought process. "You remember ever being in the O.R. with them on any other occasion?"

She shook her head. "No. We interacted, saw each other in the halls, but our fields of expertise didn't bring us into the O.R. together—except for that one occasion."

"I've got Henderson at the hospital, having Lauren James dig into the records, cross-referencing them to see if the victims ever had any joint dealings with any other patient. You might not even figure into the equation," he added.

Her eyes met his. He didn't really believe that, she thought. But for the sake of argument, she said, "Then I really won't be needing police protection."

Tony looked at her for a long moment. "Don't be so quick to refuse police protection."

"Do I get to choose which detective I have protecting me?" she said playfully.

She already had the answer to that, he thought. "I'll be by later to take you home. You'll be here?"

"Here or at the hospital."

"You'll be here."

This time, it wasn't a question. It was an order. She felt herself bristling slightly. And then the buzzer on her telephone went off. "That's Lisa," she told him, referring to her nurse. "She gets on my case if I start falling behind."

"I'll let you get back to your work," he told her, crossing to the threshold. He paused for a moment longer. "Don't leave without me."

The order made her feel simultaneously protected, rebellious—and nervous. For a whole barrage of reasons.

# *Chapter 14*

Tony finally got Sasha to agree to let him bring her home when she was finished. And then he was faced with waiting for her day to end. He discovered that she actually kept worse hours than he did.

Long after his own workday was officially closed—and for once, there were no calls on his cell—she was still on the job. The moment he finished the last of his paperwork at the precinct, he called Sasha to make sure she was still at her office. It wasn't that he didn't trust her, but he'd learned in a very short matter of time that the woman was unbelievably headstrong. Willful even as she flashed that innocent smile at him.

Lisa had left for the day and Sasha answered her

own phone, just in case it was one of the mothers-to-be. Her voice grew warm and intimate the moment she recognized his voice.

"I'm just heading out to the hospital to make my rounds before I go home," she told him. "Barring an emergency, I should be done in about half an hour or so."

"Wait for me," he instructed.

She could hear movement on the other end of the line and could almost see him slipping on his jacket, heading for the door. Trying to outrun her.

Sasha smiled. "Tony, I am perfectly capable of crossing the street and walking into the hospital on my own."

He knew she'd say that. Knew, too, that it was useless to argue with her. She'd do what she wanted to do. All he could hope for was compromise. "Don't take any shortcuts."

He heard the smile in her voice and could envision her giving a mock salute. "Yes, sir, Detective, sir. Only long cuts."

He wondered if she actually thought this was a joke, or if she was doing this for his benefit. "In plain sight, Sasha."

"Does Dr. Palmer get this kind of up-close-and-personal service?" she wanted to know.

"No."

"Why?" she teased.

There was a long pause on the line before she heard him say in a low whisper that fairly raised goose bumps on her flesh, "I haven't slept with Dr. Palmer."

"Good to know. See you at the hospital." With that, she broke the connection.

She'd made a joke in response to his answer because the implications of his words might have been serious. The trouble was, she *wanted* them to be serious. But she couldn't afford to go there just in case they weren't. Just in case he was only talking and nothing more.

Sasha sighed as she went down in the elevator. She didn't want to open up her heart and risk having it snatched out of her chest again. Loving a man had taken its toll on her, had had its price. Allowing love to take her prisoner again, well, she didn't know if she was up to that.

As if she had a choice, she thought ruefully, hurrying across the street to the hospital entrance.

Love, her mother had once told her, although not in these exact words, was not like a faucet that you could turn off and on. It happened of its own accord and you could chose to follow your heart or not, but you couldn't dictate who you did or didn't love. It just wasn't that easy.

And nothing about Detective Tony Santini was easy, she thought later that night as he brought her not just into her building, but to her apartment door. The man would have made the word *hello* difficult.

She paused at her door just before she began the search for her key. "Would you like to come in?"

*More than you'll ever know,* he thought. And his professional responsibility had nothing to do with it. Interwoven into his investigation, into all the reams of facts and databases he'd gone through, had been thoughts of this dark-haired, blue-eyed doctor. Of the night they'd spent together. Of the nights to come that he wanted to spend with her.

This wasn't like him, he berated himself. He had ironclad control over his feelings, over his thoughts.

Or at least he had had.

Until he'd taken on this case. And her.

He shrugged at her invitation, trying to appear indifferent. Trying, without success, to maintain a professional relationship. "I thought I'd just, you know, stay in the car for the night."

It was downright cold tonight. He'd freeze sitting in his car and he couldn't leave the heater on all night. The fact that he didn't want to remain in her apartment told her that maybe she'd misinterpreted the signals he'd been sending.

She looked up into his eyes. Trying not to get lost. "I thought we decided that I don't need a bodyguard."

He shook his head in response. "No, you decided you didn't want someone looking over your shoulder while you worked. There were no actual decisions made about you not having a bodyguard."

She made one more attempt to bow out gracefully. "I'm safe," she insisted. He raised one eyebrow, obviously waiting to hear what led her to this conclusion. "My sisters are probably in the apartment. The murderer only kills his victims, no collateral damage."

"So far," Tony was quick to point out, his tone indicating that it was just a matter of time. "Our boy's not a serial killer, he's a dedicated executioner. We're not dealing with an obsessive-compulsive. He could easily change his pattern just to get what he's after." He pinned her with a penetrating look that went clear back to her spine. "You want to take that chance with your sisters' lives?"

He knew he had her there.

"If you're going to be my bodyguard, then you can stay in the apartment." She raised her chin. Her breath skimmed along his skin. "Closer to the body you're supposed to be guarding."

He found himself only an inch away from her. And wanting even that distance to melt away. Tony felt his belly tighten. "How close?"

She smiled at him, knowing she was going to regret this in the morning. Or the next morning. Or the morning after that. But right now, she didn't have enough willpower to push him away. To hold herself in check. Nor did she really want any.

"As close as you like."

He knew how close he'd like. But that would require his putting his very job description on hold and he just couldn't afford to get distracted. Her life might depend on it.

Besides, her sisters were inside the apartment and

he wasn't one of those people who could block out the world and allow himself to indulge in his fantasy. But, if he were being honest with himself, he'd been blocking out the world, standing on the outside, for most of his life.

There was a war going on inside of him and no matter which side won, he'd lose.

Framing Sasha's delicate face with his hands, he brought her mouth closer to his and then he kissed her. Slowly. As if they had all the time in the world instead of a finite amount, after which he would return to his duties, his world, and she would go back to hers.

But the kiss satisfied nothing.

It only made him want more. Made him want her more. So much that he felt desire become almost overwhelming in proportion.

The kiss deepened, taking him on an exhilarating ride that demanded more. He could almost hear a small voice in his head crying: *Again!*

Her arms were around his neck, her body pressed close to his. So close that the coat she was wearing and the jacket he had on seemed to burn away at the first sign of contact.

She didn't want this to stop. She wanted to make love with Tony again. Here, now, in the hall, it didn't matter where as long as it happened.

Quickly.

Where had her common sense gone? Her restraint? Her grasp of decorum?

All of it seemed to have burned at the very first

contact of his mouth to hers. It was as if her very body was on fire. She needed to feel his hands on her. To feel them skimming along her curves.

To feel his body, his skin, hot and hard, against hers.

Sasha moaned as the kiss made her head spin and her breathing become labored. She didn't want this to end. Not yet. She needed to store up the wild, erratic emotion coursing through her veins. Store it up for when there would be nothing again.

It took them both a second to realize that the door to the apartment had opened.

Tony was the first to sense the difference, to feel the slight shift of air that indicated the change of surroundings. Pulling back from Sasha, his hand flew to the hilt of his weapon in a motion that defied visual verification. One second he was holding her, the next, he had his gun out and trained on the opened doorway.

Natalya swallowed a squeal, her initial reaction to seeing the drawn weapon. Instead, she quipped, "Get a room, you two." There was no denying that she'd been waiting for the sound of Sasha's return. This stalker business had all of them nervous. "Preferably Sasha's," she told Tony, then nodded at the weapon. "Or a firing range if you'd feel more comfortable."

Tony holstered his firearm. He wondered if Sasha's sister knew how close she'd come to needing medical attention.

"Sorry," he murmured. "You move too quietly."

"Maybe you were too busy to hear me." And then Natalya looked at the gun that was now safely holstered. "And then again, maybe not." She shifted her attention to Sasha. "You're late. Call next time."

"Since when?" Sasha wanted to know.

They never called one another to say that they were going to be extra late. It was understood that erratic hours went with the territory. That was one of the reasons they had all moved in together instead of remaining in their parents' house in Queens—the freedom to come and go as they needed to with no explanations. The close proximity to the hospital was just an added bonus.

For once, Natalya's expression was very serious. "Since you started being stalked."

"There's still no indication of that," Sasha was quick to remind her. "The fact that we'd all worked together that one time could just be a coincidence, especially since that woman's husband can't be connected to any of the killings."

Tony found himself exchanging looks with Natalya. He realized that Sasha's sister didn't believe in coincidences either. But for the time being, he let Sasha's protest go. He walked into the apartment after Sasha.

Sasha paused to close the door. Out of the corner of her eye, she saw Tony slip the chain into place. "Tony's staying the night," she told her sister.

Natalya nodded, as if to say it was about time. "Good."

"In an official capacity," Tony felt compelled to clarify.

At that, Natalya's serious expression vanished. "Hey, whatever rings your chimes," she said. "Me, I'm catching up on my favorite show thanks to the magic of VHS recording and then going to bed." She flashed a wicked smile at Tony. "I'm a very sound sleeper," she confided.

"I'll be on the couch," Tony responded.

Natalya's grin grew larger. The look in her eyes said she didn't believe him for a minute.

"Of course you will." She paused to look at Sasha before going to her room and the wide-screen TV she'd treated herself to. "G'night."

"Where's Kady?" Sasha called after her. There was no light coming from beneath Kady's door to indicate that she was home. And Sasha felt certain her sister would have come out to join in the second she'd heard voices in the living room.

"At PM. She just got called down about twenty minutes ago. One of her patients had a minor Transient Ischemic Attack. Nothing serious, but the man's wife wanted Kady to check him out." There was an unmistakable touch of pride in her voice as she added, "Wouldn't let anyone else touch him. Well, good night again. Happy guarding, Detective," she said with as straight a face as she could manage. And then she was gone.

Sasha turned away from the hall and saw that Tony had walked over to the sofa. He looked about to plant himself there for the duration of the night. She knew he'd remain there, too, unless she said something.

"You know," Sasha began innocently, "if guarding me is your intent, you could probably do a better job if you were closer."

He wasn't the kind who was schooled in the games that men and women played. But he knew an invitation when he heard one. It took him less than thirty seconds to debate the merits of remaining on the sofa or of staying in her room. It really wasn't much of a contest.

"You might have a point," he allowed, rising to his feet.

Sasha laughed. "I'm the doctor. I *always* have a point." She held out her hand to him.

The next moment, Tony laced his fingers with hers and allowed Sasha to lead him to her room. Where he guarded her. Up close and very personal.

Leaving the delivery room, Sasha wiped her brow with the side of her forearm. She was exhausted. Not as exhausted as Edie Wilson, she was willing to bet, but still pretty exhausted.

Edie Wilson had gone into labor at 6:32 a.m. when her water had broken as she was getting out of bed. This was her first baby and she panicked. Her husband, Miles, broke all the speed postings and got to the hospital in record time, leaving more than a few drivers, she was willing to bet, cursing in his wake. He needn't have bothered hurrying, because Edie's labor went on and on. And on.

With each hour that went by, the frustration and the pain seemed to grow, as did Edie's feelings of hopelessness. Sasha had attended her first thing this morning. But after an hour and a half, when it appeared that Baby Wilson was not about to make an appearance any time soon, Sasha had gone to her office—only after swearing that she would check in on Edie at regular intervals.

The hospital, she'd reminded Edie, was only five minutes from the office by foot. Three if those feet were running.

At six that evening, with Edie's screams ringing in her ears, Sasha made a decision that it was time to seriously consider performing a C-section. To her surprise, Edie said no. Edie, it turned out, was terrified of surgery.

Another forty-five minutes of labor had her changing her mind. The woman begged her for either the C-section, or death. Sasha assured her that the C-section was by far the better option.

Just like her labor, Edie's surgery turned out to be not without its tricky moments. The monitor indicated, as they were about to begin, that there was fetal distress. The umbilical cord was wrapped around the baby's neck.

Because of the monitor, Sasha had a neonatal team in place, ready to take the baby the moment he made his entrance into the world. The team did what needed to be done in order to bring him around. There were some very tense moments before the ultimate happy ending.

Sasha found herself on the receiving end of an incredibly fierce hug from Edie's husband once he'd heard his son let out a lusty wail for the first time.

"Thank you. Thank you," Miles had sobbed. "Isn't that the most beautiful sound you've ever heard?" he'd demanded happily.

That would change soon, Sasha thought. She nodded, allowing him to have his revelry without comment. It looked, she thought while pulling off her surgical mask and letting it hang about her neck, as if mother and baby were going to be just fine.

It was a good feeling.

So was finally going home. Sasha made her way to the locker room, her feet shuffling along on the freshly washed floor, too tired to lift them properly.

Stripping off her surgical livery and changing back into her own clothes took more time than she'd anticipated. She hadn't realized just how drained she felt until this very moment. Until the drama was over.

When she was finally in her street clothes, the light green surgical pants and top stuffed into the laundry hamper in the corner, it vaguely occurred to her that she hadn't eaten lunch yet. It was hours past dinnertime, but for some reason, she wasn't hungry.

She supposed that she'd been running on the high she'd sustained in the delivery room. Each and every successful birth left her feeling as if she could walk on clouds for the next hour. The miracle never left her untouched, never grew old.

But its effects were fading now, leaving her craving her bed and sleep. Taking out her purse, she closed the locker with her elbow and began to rummage around, looking for her cell phone. She'd promised Tony to call once baby made three.

Tony had opted to stay late in the squad room, instructing her to give him a call once she was finally finished. For the first time in a week, he hadn't brought her in this morning. She'd gotten the call from Miles Wilson while Tony was in the shower. She'd left him a note and quickly left for the hospital. He hadn't been happy about it when he'd finally connected with her.

She knew that he didn't want her going home alone, but she didn't want to leave her car in the structure for the night. Besides, it had been quiet this last week, with no sign of the killer. She was certain that he had probably been intimidated by the presence of the police and the extra security at the hospital.

Maybe he'd decided it was too dangerous to continue and had aborted any plans to continue his spree, she thought hopefully.

There was no need to bother Tony, she told herself. Closing her cell phone, she dropped it back into her cavernous purse. He'd been looking exhausted himself lately. And that was because he'd been putting in what amounted to double duty. He worked on the case all day and then spent the night with her. Not necessarily sleeping.

She'd woken up several times in the last week to see him sitting in a chair, wide awake. Guarding her. Each time she'd urged him back to bed, and he'd slip in between the sheets. But as soon as she was asleep, she knew he got up again. The man definitely deserved a night off, she decided.

Sasha pulled her coat closer around her as the elevator doors opened on the lower level. Taking a deep breath, she stepped out and then hurried to get to her vehicle. She'd managed to get a parking space near the elevator door this morning. That meant she didn't have to walk too far.

She walked quickly nonetheless, every step she took echoing endlessly through the structure.

The parking facility was far from deserted, even at this time of the evening. But it was filled with vehicles, not people. She would have rather it'd been the other way around.

There it was, she thought, seeing her car in the distance. She already had her keys in her hand and she pointed it toward the vehicle, pressing on the alarm deactivator. She heard a distant "click-click."

"Where's your shadow?"

The voice came from behind her. Sasha swallowed a scream as she swung around. Her heart was pounding in her chest, the sound duplicated and echoing in her ears.

The next moment, she was silently calling herself an idiot. She found herself looking into the face of Walter Stevens, the security guard.

She could have hugged him.

Hiking her purse strap up higher on her shoulder, she slipped her hand over her heart for a second. It was still pounding hard.

"Oh God, Walter, you really scared me." She took a deep breath in an attempt to regulate her pulse. "My shadow?" she asked.

He nodded. "Yeah, that police detective. The one who's doing the investigation."

She smiled fondly. "You mean Detective Santini." Funny how her tongue seemed to enjoy wrapping itself around even his surname. "He's not here tonight."

Walter looked at her with mild interest. "Off investigating another homicide?"

"Not that I know of. Although I guess he could be," she admitted. "I just decided to give him the night off."

The guard nodded, a slight smile forming on his cherubic face. "Figured you would, eventually. And that I could wait you out. You're the important one, you know. The main one."

Sasha was about to ask him what he meant by that, but the words died in her mouth. She saw him slip his hand over the hilt of his weapon, his fingers curling around the handle.

There was a look in his eye that made her blood suddenly run cold.

# *Chapter 15*

How long did it take for a baby to be born? Tony wondered irritably after checking his watch again. He'd done it so many times in the last couple of hours, he'd lost count. It seemed as if the minute hand had been dipped in molasses. As had this baby who refused to come.

Tony flipped the file closed. Pages slipped out, scattered by the sudden movement.

The last he'd heard from Sasha, or rather, from her nurse who'd said that the doctor had asked her to call, she was going back to the hospital because the woman who'd gone into labor early this morning was *still* in labor.

By now, he knew how Sasha operated. She wasn't

going to leave the hospital until that baby had left the womb. And who knew when that would be?

How long did these things take, anyway? he thought again irritably.

He took a sip of his coffee and frowned. He had this uneasy feeling that refused to recede. It had been riding him all day. The same kind of uneasy feeling he'd had just before he'd learned that Annie had been in a fatal car crash.

He wasn't the kind of man who was superstitious, but something was wrong. Something, but he just couldn't put his finger on it.

Probably being paranoid, he told himself. What was more likely was that Sasha might just get it into her head to go home without him after she was finished, if only to prove that she could. He both loved and hated her independent streak.

One thing he knew for sure, this wasn't the time to prove things. Not with a killer with an agenda loose, he thought darkly.

He heard a chair over to his right squeak. Glancing in that general direction, he saw that Henderson was on his feet.

"Dunno about you, but I'm going to call it a night and go home," Henderson told him. "There's a piece of Boston cream pie in the refrigerator that's been calling to me for the last three hours."

Tony eyed his partner's expanding girth. When they'd first been partnered, Henderson's waist had measured five inches less than it did now. "Tell it that it has the wrong number."

Henderson feigned indignation. "Hey, we all can't be Mr. Universe." He crossed to his desk. "If not for us pudgy, out-of-shape guys, guys like you wouldn't look half as good."

"Whatever."

Sideways logic. It was what Henderson was good at. But right now, he wasn't in the mood to hear it. He was going to call her, Tony decided, taking out his cell phone. And keep calling her until she or someone else around her finally answered.

But before Tony could press the first button to her number, he saw Simon Anderson come barreling into the squad room. The university professor looked as if he was scanning the area. The man stopped just long enough to talk to the first person he encountered. The exchange was too far away to hear, but Tony saw the detective he was talking to point in his direction.

Tony flipped his phone shut, tucked it back into his pocket and braced himself.

"Who the hell do you think you are?" Anderson demanded as he crossed the room, heading straight for him with the rhythm of an oncoming freight train.

"Detective Anthony Santini," Tony replied calmly, then nodded at the battered nameplate sitting on the front of his desk. "It says so right there."

"Don't get smart with me, Santini," Anderson warned. He was as big as Henderson and in far better shape as he eyed the other detective. "I should sue your ass off. Yours and the whole damn police department's."

"The department doesn't have an ass," Tony replied, his tone low. Nothing got his back up more than being threatened. "Want to tell me what the problem is?"

"The 'problem' is that you've been digging into my finances," Anderson shouted. "I just got home and played my messages. There was a call from my bank, saying that the police department requested a statement showing all my transactions for the last year. They're putting a hold on my loan application until this 'matter' is resolved to their satisfaction." By now, he was all but breathing fire. "You have no damn right to be disrupting my life this way."

Tony remained sitting, his face impassive. He was aware that Henderson looked as if he was ready to spring into action at the least sign of trouble.

"It's just routine, Professor Anderson, nothing personal." Each word was slowly measured out. "We wanted to make sure you hadn't made any large withdrawals lately."

"And what business is that of yours if I had?" he wanted to know. "Is this because of my wife, is that it?" He spat out the question contemptuously. "You want to harass someone about knocking off people who were in that operating room, talk to my father-in-law. He's the one who went berserk when Gloria Jean died."

Tony's back straightened. This was the first they'd

heard of the woman having any other family members beyond an apparently not-so-grieving husband. He glanced toward Henderson before looking back at Anderson.

"Her father?"

"Yeah." The strained relationship was evident in the single word. "He's got the brain of a flea, but he took her death hard. Hell, the last I heard, he'd even taken a job at the hospital, saying something about being around the last place where Gloria'd been alive. I figured he went over the deep end."

Tony was on his feet. The uneasy feeling he'd been harboring all day mushroomed into overwhelming proportions. "What's your father-in-law's name?"

"Stevens. Walter Stevens." He looked at them with angry contempt in his eyes. "You going to question him?"

Henderson's mouth dropped open. "Hey, isn't that the—?"

"—security guard who found the first body," Tony ended his partner's thought. Damn, he'd never made the connection. The last names were different and there was no mention made of the relationship.

The back of his neck began to prickle. Tony hurried for the door. He heard Henderson trotting right behind him.

"You go to Stevens' apartment, see if he's there," Tony instructed Henderson.

Henderson stopped and doubled back into the office. The address was noted down in the case file.

"Where are you going to be?" Henderson wanted to know.

Anderson was cursing in the background. Tony ignored him.

"I'm going to the hospital," he told Henderson. "Sasha should have called me by now, or at least answered her cell phone. Something's not right."

Tony called several more times as he sped to the hospital. Frustrated because he kept getting her voice mail, he called the hospital switchboard. They put him through to the maternity ward. The nurse who finally answered informed him that he had "just missed Dr. Pulaski. She just left."

Without calling him, he thought. That meant she was going to take her car back to her apartment.

Why the hell couldn't she listen?

He tried to tell himself that he was allowing his natural pessimism to get the best of him and that everything was all right.

The uneasy feeling was almost unmanageable.

"Walter, why are you doing this?"

Staring down at the small handgun in the security guard's hand, Sasha struggled to sound calm. She had to find a way to stall until someone came. Someone *had* to come. There were so many cars here, waiting for their owners. All she needed was for one of them to arrive. The odds were on her side.

If only luck was.

Walter Stevens tightened his grip on the firearm. "Don't play dumb, Dr. Pulaski. You know why I'm doing this. I'm doing it for Gloria Jean. For my Jeannie." His expression hardened. "Because no one else will. That pompous ass she was married to was glad to be rid of her. All he wanted was to make money off her death." Hatred dripped from every word. It didn't take much of a stretch to envision the last name on Walter Stevens' elimination list. "She was a wonderful, sweet girl. And smart." For a second, he could have been any father, bragging about his daughter. If not for the gun in his hand. "Did you know they made her teacher of the year at her school three years in a row?" And then anger contorted his features. "No, you wouldn't know that. All you saw was someone to practice on."

Was that what he thought? Was that what had festered in his chest, finally prompting the man to go off the deep end? "Walter, it wasn't like that."

Her words seemed to bounce off him. "Sure it was. Otherwise, you would have waited for the specialist to come."

But that was just the point. She had to make him see that. "There wasn't time, Walter. Gloria Jean was going to die if something wasn't done quickly—"

He cut her off, shouting, "She died anyway, didn't she?"

"Yes," she agreed heavily, never taking her eyes off the weapon that was trained on her. "She died anyway." Sasha thought of her parents, of how they would feel if she died here tonight. They'd already been through so much in their lifetime, she wasn't going to let that kind of grief touch them if she could help it. "Walter, we did all we could. You have to believe that. You said that Gloria Jean was a good person—"

"She was," he snapped, fury coming into his eyes.

Sasha kept her voice low, calm. It was the only chance she had. "Then she wouldn't want you to do this. To kill people in her name."

But he shook his head, as if shaking off her words. "I have to. It's all I got left. To make you people pay for killing my little girl." With his left hand, he dug into his pocket. Walter pulled out the carefully folded note he'd printed out on his machine the night after he'd killed Tyler Harris. "Here, take this," he ordered. "Hold it in your hand."

She already knew what it was. "No."

Her refusal incensed him. "I said take it!" he shouted. Taking a step forward, he shoved the paper at her.

Sasha swung her purse at him with all her might. Trying to ward off the block, Walter toppled backwards and fell down. Sasha took off, running as fast as she could back toward where she'd come. If she could just get back to the next level, street level, she'd be all right. There'd be people there. People who would come between her and the deranged security guard.

She just prayed that the man wouldn't have a complete meltdown and start firing at people at random.

Why hadn't she called Tony and waited for him? She made herself a promise to apologize. If she lived long enough.

As she rounded the corner, Sasha heard the squeal of brakes and the sound of a car traveling at a high speed. For a second, she wasn't able to discern if the noise was coming from behind her or in front of her.

Was Walter going to run her down?

And then she saw it, the low-slung sports car coming directly at her. At the last minute, the driver swerved. Tires screeched as the car came to an abrupt, sudden halt.

Tony had always said it could stop on a dime.

Leaning over, he threw open the passenger door. "Sasha, get in!" Tony ordered. The smell of burning rubber permeated the air.

Her heart pounding, she could have cried. Quickly, she did as he instructed, pouring herself into the passenger seat. Idling, the car rumbled, like a bull pawing the ground before charging.

Tony's facade cracked. "Are you all right?" he demanded.

She nodded her head vigorously. She was fine. Now that he was here.

"It's Walter. The guard," she gasped, her lungs aching from the cold air she'd dragged in as she'd run. "He's the hit-and-run victim's father and he's the one who's been killing everyone."

"I know."

He could have kicked himself for not knowing

sooner. For not suspecting. But the man had looked like an overgrown Christmas elf and his suspicions had been lulled. Stupid, Tony reprimanded himself. His oversight had almost gotten Sasha killed.

Tony searched her face, her body, looking for wounds, not bothering to hide his concern. "Did he hurt you?"

Sasha realized that there were tears in the corner of her eyes. Tears of relief, of tension. She blinked them back.

"No, but he was going to. He has a gun, Tony. With a silencer." As she said it, she realized that explained why she hadn't really heard anything that night when Angela had been killed only a few feet away from her. The security guard had used a silencer. "He wanted me to take the note, the same one you found all the other victims holding in their hand." With effort, she forced herself not to think about what had almost happened. And then another thought assailed her. "Tony, he's still out there."

"Yeah, I know." The next moment, Tony got out of the car. He paused only long enough to give her a warning look. "Stay here."

She was about to negate the order. There was no way she was going to let him confront the deranged security guard alone. But before she could get out of the vehicle, Walter suddenly appeared, coming around the corner. His gun was drawn and aimed straight at the windshield.

Sasha cried out a warning. "Tony!"

Tony's weapon was drawn before he ever completed turning away from her. He held it steady in both hands, his eyes trained on the guard. "Drop the gun, Stevens."

Walter stopped walking. "She needs to die, Detective. Just like the others did."

"There'll be no more killing, Stevens." It was an edict, coldly issued. "Now drop the gun," he repeated.

Walter's hands trembled slightly as he continued to hold the weapon. "Don't you see? She killed my daughter."

"She tried to save your daughter," Tony countered. "The hospital records showed that your daughter sustained multiple injuries from the car accident. She was bleeding internally in half a dozen places." He was making it up as he went along, using what he could remember from a Discovery Channel program he'd once seen. "No one could have saved her."

"You're lying!" Walter shouted, growing agitated. The gun shook. "Lying to protect her. She has to die. They all have to die."

Walter let loose with an anguished cry. He raised his gun higher, aiming it straight at Sasha's head. Uttering a curse, Tony fired. The bullet struck Walter dead center in the forehead. Just the way the guard had executed all the other victims.

A second shot rang out, this one coming from Walter's gun. The security guard fired the weapon as he went down, a stunned expression frozen into his features.

Sasha bolted from the shelter of the vehicle, rounding the engine until she was next to Tony's side. Frantically, she scanned him for any signs of a wound.

"Are you all right?"

Tony nodded. "Yeah."

She closed her eyes, uttering a silent prayer of thanks. When she opened them again, Sasha crossed to the body lying on the ground a few feet away from them.

"He's dead, Sasha," Tony called after her. He holstered his weapon, knowing he was going to have to turn it into Internal Affairs until all the facts about the shooting were duly taken into account.

Sasha felt the man's neck for a pulse anyway. There was none. Steeling herself, she passed a hand over Walter's lifeless eyes, closing them. "I had to be sure."

Tony joined her and slipped an arm around her shoulders. She was trembling, he realized, even though she was struggling not to show any emotion. "To stop the nightmares?" he guessed.

"Because I'm a doctor," she corrected. "And if he was alive, I took an oath to keep him that way."

Tony thought that was rather ironic, seeing as how the man had been trying to kill her. In her position, he didn't know if he would have been able to think that way. Not about someone who had gone to such lengths to try to eliminate him.

A sigh shuddered its way out of his throat as he placed a call in to dispatch to apprise them of the situation.

He was vaguely aware that the uneasy feeling haunting him all day was gone.

"I can't believe it's really over."

Sasha sank down on a stool beside Tony, a mug of hot tea in her hand. It was more than three hours later and they were finally in her apartment. She'd gone to the police station with him, insisting on giving her statement now instead of in the morning the way he'd suggested. There was no way she was going to allow this to linger. She'd wanted to purge as much of the incident as she could before going home.

The moment she and Tony had walked into the apartment, her sisters had surrounded her. They'd fussed over her as much as she would allow them to. She'd answered their questions and assured them more than once that she was all right. Tony was about to take his leave when she'd stopped him, asking him to remain a few more minutes.

That had been Natalya and Kady's cue. To their credit, they'd taken it quickly and retreated back into the bedrooms from which they'd emerged.

Natalya had paused to give her an extra hard hug. "We'll figure out how to sugarcoat this for Mama and Daddy in the morning," she whispered. All three of them knew that their parents would be after them to move back home.

Sasha had smiled and nodded. "I'd appreciate the help." Natalya had always been the more creative one of the three.

Tony had sat quietly, studying his coffee mug until her sisters finally left them alone. And then he looked at her, trying not to think of the way things could have gone tonight. Focusing only on the fact that she was alive and out of danger.

"It'll take some time for you to get it out of your system," he warned. "Sometimes our emotions won't accept what our minds tell us is really true."

She raised her eyes to his. Her intuition told her that he wasn't referring to the fact that there was no more need to be afraid. "You're talking about your wife, aren't you?"

He began to deny it, then shrugged. Wasn't much point in doing that. She seemed to be able to see right through him. The next moment, he realized that that didn't scare him any more. "Among other things."

She smiled, affection in her eyes. "I had no idea you could wax so poetic."

He laughed shortly. That wasn't what some people called it. "I have my moments."

"Yes," she said softly, running the back of her hand across his cheek, creating all sorts of tidal waves inside his stomach, "I know."

Tony knew he should be leaving. Closing this chapter of his life and going back to the routine that he knew best. Being a cop. He didn't belong in her life. She was too good and he was too jaded.

And yet, he found himself reaching for her. With his arm hooked around her waist, he drew her onto his lap. She nestled in, adding more friction to the already existing tidal waves.

"I guess you'll be relieved not to be needing a bodyguard anymore."

He couldn't quite read the expression on her face. It was a cross between whimsical and thoughtful.

"Oh, I don't know about that. New York City is a pretty dangerous place at times. A woman can't be too careful these days." And then she smiled into his eyes. "A little extra protection would be very welcome."

He shouldn't be thinking what he was thinking. Shouldn't allow himself to grow optimistic. But he did. "It would?"

"Uh-huh." She only half succeeded in looking serious. "Any idea where I might be able to find that kind of protection?" She laced her fingers around his neck. "The kind that would be available at odd hours of the day or night?"

Tony nodded, never taking his eyes off her face. "I think I know just the guy."

Sasha's smile widened. "I was hoping you'd say that."

He never missed a beat. "Henderson's been looking to pick up a little extra cash."

About to kiss him, Sasha pulled her head back. "Henderson?"

"Yeah." And then, unable to help himself, Tony grinned. "I'm just going to have to tell him to find someone else to guard. That this body," he tucked his hands around her, "is spoken for."

He'd had her going for a second. Paying him back, Sasha whacked his shoulder with the flat of her hand. He looked at her in surprise. "That's for Henderson."

He laughed, pulling her even closer. "I'll deliver it when I get a chance."

He didn't make it sound as if he was going anywhere anytime soon. "Planning to be busy for a while?"

"For a very long while," he told her, as he began to lower his mouth to hers. "Say like the next ten or twenty years."

Sasha looked at him pointedly. "Ten or twenty years? That's all?"

"We'll negotiate."

Tony tasted her laugh against his lips and felt rays of hope and sunshine spread out all through him as he deepened the kiss.

In his mind, he amended the length of time to forever.

*Watch out for Marie Ferrarella's next page-turning romance,* Diagnosis Danger, *out in February 2008!*

*Turn the page for even more from Intrigue.
We've an exclusive extract of
Dani Sinclair's* Sleeping Beauty Suspect
*out next month!*

# Sleeping Beauty Suspect

### by

### Dani Sinclair

Flynn yanked off his mask and sucked in fresh air thankfully as Lew led him to the rescue vehicle. The victim lay on her back in the grass. Paramedics, Arlene and Murray, were working over her. Flynn paused to gaze down at her delicate features covered in thick black soot.

"Pretty little thing," Lew remarked.

Pretty was an understatement. Beneath the soot she appeared fragile, almost porcelain-doll lovely. She reminded him of a fairy-tale princess on the cover of some book.

A very dirty princess.

"Now what was someone like her doing in there, I'd like to know," Lew grumbled.

An excellent question.

Flynn watched them work on her, willing her to live

while wishing there was something more he could do to help.

"I should have got her out sooner."

"Man, you guys barely got out at all. Count your blessings."

"I do. Thanks, Lew."

He let Lew guide him away. Standing suddenly lost its appeal. His legs complied as Lew pressed him down on the ground.

"I'm okay."

"Let them be the judge of that."

The new voice jerked his head up. Flynn tried to focus on the lined features of the battalion chief, who stood over him. It took his groggy head a long moment to process the identification, yet there was no mistaking that craggy face. He let his gaze sweep the scene. They'd called a box alarm and the area was flooded with responders and their vehicles.

The wind gusted steadily, sending sparks drifting in multiple directions. Brush near the side of the house had ignited as the big Victorian swelled with smoke and flames. The house was fully engulfed now. He could feel the intense heat clear over here by the engine.

"Anyone else inside?" the chief demanded.

"We cleared most of the house, sir, but I don't know for sure."

The man nodded and turned to speak with the lieutenant.

"You all right?" Lew demanded.

"Yeah. Carey?"

"They think his ankle's broken."

Flynn grimaced. "What about the victim?" He indicated the woman being loaded onto a stretcher. Long, soot-coated blondish hair spilled over the side.

"Unconscious, but alive. She took in a lot of smoke."

The battalion chief turned back to him. "She a victim or the arsonist?"

Flynn shrugged and wished he hadn't as his shoulder twinged. "I'd say victim. She was unconscious on a mattress when I found her."

He scowled. "You'll need to talk to the fire investigator."

"Figured as much," Flynn agreed.

The chief moved away and Murray and Arlene shouldered Lew aside. "Let's have a look at you."

"I'm fine."

"We're taking you to go to Community Hospital to get checked out," Murray told him.

"No need. I'm fine."

"Lieutenant's orders," they chorused.

"Okay, but I'm not lying on any gurney."

Murray grinned evilly.

"Who's your sleeping beauty?" Arlene questioned. "She sure isn't from this part of town. That was an expensive designer evening gown she was wearing."

Flynn focused on Arlene's long face. "Evening gown?"

"Yeah, you know, formal dances, that sort of thing?"

"I didn't know women still wore evening gowns outside of television."

"You move in the wrong circles, O'Shay. Now if you were rich or famous—"

"He'll probably be famous." Murray grinned. "I saw

Dick Scellioli snapping pictures when he passed the woman outside. And I think he got a good one of you falling through the roof."

Flynn groaned. They all knew Scellioli. The freelance photojournalist was making quite a name for himself following police and fire calls, where he'd snap pictures to sell to the highest bidder. He'd shown up at more than one fire scene recently.

"Can you stand?" Arlene asked.

"Of course I can stand." But it took a little help as it turned out. He swayed unsteadily.

"Come on, hero, let's ride."

# 4 FREE

## BOOKS AND A SURPRISE GIFT!

We would like to take this opportunity to thank you for reading this Mills & Boon® book by offering you the chance to take FOUR more specially selected titles from the Intrigue series absolutely FREE! We're also making this offer to introduce you to the benefits of the Mills & Boon® Reader Service™—

- ★ **FREE home delivery**
- ★ **FREE gifts and competitions**
- ★ **FREE monthly Newsletter**
- ★ **Exclusive Reader Service offers**
- ★ **Books available before they're in the shops**

Accepting these FREE books and gift places you under no obligation to buy, you may cancel at any time, even after receiving your free shipment. Simply complete your details below and return the entire page to the address below. You don't even need a stamp!

**YES!** Please send me 4 free Intrigue books and a surprise gift. I understand that unless you hear from me, I will receive 6 superb new titles every month for just £3.10 each, postage and packing free. I am under no obligation to purchase any books and may cancel my subscription at any time. The free books and gift will be mine to keep in any case.

I8ZED

Ms/Mrs/Miss/Mr ..............................................Initials ..........................................

BLOCK CAPITALS PLEASE

Surname ..................................................................................................................

Address ..................................................................................................................

..................................................................................................................

..........................................................Postcode..........................................

## Send this whole page to:
### UK: FREEPOST CN81, Croydon, CR9 3WZ

# AIR BRIDGE

"Hammond Innes is in the forefront of modern writers of the straight-forward action story. He writes in a flexible, economic style, the pace of his stories is rapid, his detail authentic . . . Mr. Innes achieves a masterly sense of urgency as the story rises to the climax." *Daily Telegraph*

"Highly exciting . . . As always with Mr. Innes, the background has an authenticity which intensifies the novel's gripping power." *Scotsman*

"First-class . . . Hammond Innes obviously knows the technical side of aviation, which gives the book an air of reality. Not only does he tell a story well, but he creates vivid characters." *Glasgow Herald*

"Tremendously exciting . . . Hammond Innes knows how to tell a story so that the reader's attention will not only be gripped, but so that he will begin to share the tension, the excitement, the cold and the danger." *Sphere*

HAMMOND INNES

# *Air Bridge*

*Collins*

FONTANA BOOKS

First published 1951
First issued in Fontana Books 1955
Fourteenth Impression August 1971

Printed in Great Britain
Collins Clear-Type Press
London and Glasgow

*For*
*Daphne and Bill*

## Note

In the sections of this book dealing with the Berlin Airlift I am indebted to the Royal Air Force, who flew me into blockaded Berlin and who gave me every facility for studying the lift both on the ground and in the air. I should like to take this opportunity of expressing my appreciation of the Air Ministry's willingness to assist me and of the friendly co-operation I received from lift personnel at Wunstorf and Gatow at a time when they were very overworked.

It is inevitable, in a story of this nature, that the types of aircraft and the titles of air-force personnel should be those that operated at the time and at the bases concerned. I wish to make it clear, therefore, that the story is not founded on anything that actually occurred and, in particular, that the characters in the story who hold official positions are entirely fictional.

# CHAPTER ONE

It was dark and I was very tired. My head ached and my mind was confused. The road ran uphill between steep banks and there were trees with gaunt branches spread against the pale glimmer of the Milky Way. At last I reached the level and the high banks gave place to hedges. Through a gap I caught a glimpse of an orange moon lying on its back on the far side of a ploughed field. Nothing stirred. All life seemed frost-bound in the cold of night. I stood for a moment, exhausted, my knees trembling weakly and the sweat drying like cold steel against my skin. A little wind ran chill fingers through the bare spikes of the quick-thorn and I went on then, driven by the shivers that ran through my body. It was the reaction after the crash. I had to find somewhere to lie up—a barn, anything, so long as it was warm. And then I had to get out of the country. I was meeting the wind now, even as I walked, it chilled the sweat on my body. My steps no longer rang firm. The sound of them became a shuffle that was lost every now and then in the lashing of the trees in a small copse.

The country around was quite flat now—a familiar flatness. The sharp edges of a large rectangular building stood for a moment black against the moon. It was there for an instant, gaunt and recognisable, and then it was lost behind the high earth mounds of a dispersal point. I stopped, my body suddenly rigid. The dispersal point and that distant glimpse of a hangar confirmed what I had already sensed almost automatically. The flatness that stretched before me was an aerodrome.

If I could get a plane! Damn it—I'd done it before. And it had been far more difficult then. I could remember the fir trees and the feel of the sand, almost silver in the moonlight, and the dark shadows of men against the hangar lights. The picture was so vivid in my mind that the same surge of excitement took hold of me now, tensing my nerves, giving me strength. I turned quickly and slid into the woods.

It was less cold in the woods or else the sudden urgency of hope gave me warmth as well as energy. It was darker, too.

I might have lost my sense of direction, but always there was Jupiter, like a candle flickering amongst the branches, to show me the way the road had run. The trees clutched at me, whipping across my face, and in a moment I felt the warm trickle of blood from the cut on my forehead. The thick, salt warmth of it reached my tongue as I licked at the corner of my mouth. But it didn't hurt. In fact, I barely noticed it. I was intent upon one thing, and one thing only—a plane.

I came out of the wood on the very edge of the perimeter track, a fifty yard wide ribbon of tarmac, rutted and hillocked by the frosts and marked with the dead stalks of summer's weeds. Left and right it seemed to stretch to the horizon, and across the track was the airfield, a bleak, open hilltop, black under the moon, for the grass was gone and it was all plough. The curve of that hilltop was smooth and even like the curvature of the earth's surface, a section of a globe hung against the stars. The only relief to that impression of void was away to the left where the black edge of a hangar seemed to be shouldering the moon up the sky.

I stood there for a moment, conscious again of the wind cutting through my clothing as the sense of emptiness drained the excitement out of me. The story of the ploughed-up grassland, the dead weed stalks and the frost-broken tarmac was evident in the dead atmosphere of the place. The airfield was deserted. It was one of the great bomber stations that had died with the end of the war. It was easy to see it as it had been, full of activity with the roar of planes coming in from a raid—big, graceful shapes, in silhouette against the flarepath, settling clumsily on to the runway. This sort of place had been my life for six and a half years. Now the planes only existed as ghosts in my mind. All about me was empty desolation, a slow disintegration moving inevitably back to the land from which it had sprung up.

With a feeling of hopelessness I started along the perimeter track towards the hangars. They would be just derelict shells, but at least they would give me shelter for the night. I felt suddenly sick and very tired—a little scared, too. The desolation of that airfield ate into me, bringing with it an awareness of my own loneliness.

The perimeter track seemed unending, growing wider and more desolate at every stumbling step as the wind thrust into my stomach till it chilled and stiffened my spine. Dizziness overtook me. It was the crash, of course, and the awful crack I'd got on the head. And then a flicker of hope came to steady me. The hangars now loomed black against the moon, big rectangular skeletons slowly crumbling away. But at the far end of the concrete apron there was one that looked whole and solid. The line of windows along its side was intact and reflected a glimmer of starlight.

I quickened my pace. It was just possible that some private owner, a local farmer or landowner, kept his plane up here on this deserted aerodrome. That was the hope that sent me hurrying across the apron to the deep shadows of the hangars. And as I slid from one hangar to the next I prayed to God there would be petrol in the tanks.

I was a fool perhaps to build my hopes on such slender foundations as the fact that one hangar was intact. But when you're desperate you clutch at anything. Before I'd even reached the hangar I was already mentally in the cockpit of some tiny aircraft winging my way through the night towards France. I knew exactly how the coast would look as it slid beneath me and how the Channel would be gently corrugated at right angles to my line of flight as the waves reflected the slanting rays of the moon. I could see myself checking in at the little hotel in Montmartre where I'd stayed several times before and then after a rest, going to Badouin's office. Badouin would fix it all for me. Everything would be all right as soon as I'd seen Badouin.

I reached the hangar and stood for a moment in the shadow of its bulk. I was panting. But I no longer felt sick or dizzy. I was trembling slightly, but that was just nerves. I had plenty of energy. Nothing could stop me now. I slid round the corner of the building and along the face of the huge sliding doors.

My luck was in, for the little wicket door in the centre yielded to the touch of my hand, revealing a dark void full of vague shadows. I stepped inside and closed the door. It was still and very cold with that queer musty smell of damp on concrete. Some glimmer of moonlight seemed to penetrate into the rear of the hangar, for the shadows resolved themselves into the nose and wings of a large four-engined plane. It was facing me head-on and it seemed enormous in the gloom of the hangar.

The incredible luck of it! I ducked under the port wing

and moved along the fuselage, running my hand along the cold metal of it, searching for the door.

"So. His work is not to be remembered."

I stopped with a jerk. It was a girl's voice that had spoken. A man answered her: "I'm sorry. War is a dirty business."

"But the war is finished."

"Yes, but you lost it, remember."

"And because Germany loses a war, my father must suffer? My father has suffered enough, I think."

"You father is dead." The brutal words were said in a hard, matter-of-fact voice.

A silence followed. Peering over the tailplane I could see the outline of two figures against the steady glow of a pressure lamp. The man was short, thick-set and powerful-looking and as he moved towards the girl he unmasked the lamp so that its dim light showed me the litter of a work-bench running the width of the hangar and the dark shadow of a belt-driven machine lathe.

I turned quickly. The lamplight was glowing on the metal of the plane and as I slid along the fuselage towards the door I saw that it was a Tudor and its inboard engine was missing.

If I had gained the door unnoticed I should not now be setting down what must surely be the most extraordinary story of the Berlin Airlift. But my foot caught against some scrap metal and with the sudden clang of sheet tin I froze.

"Who's that?" It was the man's voice and it had the drive of a man accustomed to absolute authority. "So you've got friends here, have you?" The beam of a torch swept the plane and then spotlighted me with its dazzling light. "Who are you? What do you want?"

I just stood there, blinking in the glare, incapable of movement, panic lifting my heart into my mouth.

The torch moved suddenly. There was a click by the wall and the sound of an engine starting up outside. Then lights glowed and brightened.

The man was facing me across the tail of the plane now and he had a gun in his hand. He wasn't tall, but he was immensely broad across the shoulders. He was thick through like a bull and he held his head slightly forward as though about to charge. I hardly noticed the girl.

"Well, who are you?" the man repeated and began to move

in on me. He came slowly and inevitably like a man sure of his ability to handle a situation.

I broke and ran. I wasn't going to be caught like this, trapped in a hangar, accused of attempting to steal an aircraft as well as a car. If once I could get to the shelter of the woods I'd still have a chance. I ducked under the wings with the sound of his feet pounding on the concrete behind me. As I wrenched open the door of the hangar he shouted at me in German: " *Halt! Halt, Du verrückter!*" That damned language with its memory of endless, unbearable days of prison and the nagging fear of the escape gave me a last burst of energy.

I shot through the door and in a moment I was out on the perimeter track racing for the dark line of the woods. I crossed the concrete of the runway-end, my breath a wild hammering in my throat. My mind had become confused so that I seemed to be running again from the tunnel mouth to the dark anonymity of the fir woods. At any moment I expected to hear the deep bay of the dogs and my skin crawled between my shoulder blades just as it had done that night in Germany so long ago, cringing in anticipation of the shattering impact of a bullet. The concrete was broken and matted with weeds. Then I was on plough with the clay clinging to my shoes and the sound of my flight deadened in the sticky earth.

I stumbled and clawed my way to the woods. I heard my pursuer crash into the undergrowth close behind me. Branches whipped across my face. I barely noticed them. I found a path and then lost it again in a tangle of briar that tore at my clothes. I fought my way through it to find that he'd skirted the brambles and was level with me. I started to double back, but the undergrowth was too thick. I turned and faced him then.

I didn't stop to think. I went straight for him. God knows what I intended to do. I think I meant to kill him. He had shouted at me in German and my mind had slipped back to that earlier time when I had been nearly hunted down. His fist struck my arm with numbing force and I closed with him, my fingers searching for his windpipe. I felt the knobbly point of his Adam's apple against the ball of my thumb, heard him choke as I squeezed. Then his knee came up and I screamed

in agony. My hands lost their grip and as I doubled up I saw
him draw his fist back. I knew what was coming and I was
powerless to stop it. His fist seemed huge in a shaft of moonlight and then it shattered into a thousand fragments as it
broke against my jaw.

What followed is very confused in my mind. I have a vague
memory of being half-led, half-carried over ground that
seemed to rise and fall in waves. Then I was lying on a camp
bed in an office full of bright lights. I was being interrogated,
first in German, then in English. There was only one person
there—the man who had hit me. I didn't see any sign of
the girl. He sat in a chair, leaning over me so that his big,
solid head seemed hung in space, always on the verge of falling
on me and crushing me. I tried to move, but my hands and
feet were bound. The light was above me and to the left.
It was very bright and hurt my eyes. My jaw ached and my
head throbbed and the interrogation went on and on through
periods of black-out. I remember coming round once with a
cry of pain as the searing burn of disinfectant entered the
wound on my forehead. After that I slept.

When I woke it was daylight. I lay staring at the ceiling
and wondering why it was plain, untreated concrete. The
walls were bare brick. In the opposite corner the mortar had
crumbled away and there was a long, jagged crack stuffed
with newspaper. Slowly the events of the night before came
back to me—the airfield, the hangar, the struggle in the woods.

I sat up with a jerk that sent a stab of pain shooting
through my head. My jaw was painful and slightly swollen,
the cut on my forehead was covered with lint secured by
adhesive tape. There was a patch of dried blood on the grey
Army blanket that had been pulled over me. I swung my legs
out of bed and then sat there for quite a while staring at the
unfamiliar room and fingering my jaw.

It was quite a small room and had obviously been used as
an office. There was a cheap desk with a portable typewriter
in its case, an old swivel chair, a steel filing cabinet and an
untidy litter of books and papers. The books, I saw at a
glance, were all technical manuals—engineering, mechanics,
aviation. They were thick with dust. The floor was of bare
boards and a rusty stove stood against one wall, the chimney
running out through a roughly-patched hole in the ceiling.
The windows were barred and looked out on to a pile of

rubble and a vista of broken brick foundations, half-covered with dead sorrel stalks. There was an air of disintegration about the place. My gaze focused and held on the bars of the windows. They were solid iron bars set in cement. I turned quickly to the door with a feeling of being trapped. It was locked. I tried to find my shoes, but they had been removed. Panic seized hold of me then and I stood quite still in the middle of the room in my stockinged feet and fought it down.

I got control of myself at last, but I was overcome with a feeling of sickness and lay down on the bed. After a time the sickness passed and my brain became active again. I was in a hell of a spot! Oh, I was being quite honest with myself then. I knew I'd tried to kill a man. I could remember the feel of his windpipe against my thumb. The question was, did he know that I'd meant to kill him?

I looked slowly round the room. The iron bars, the locked door, the removal of my shoes—he knew all right.

My hand groped automatically for my cigarette-case. My jacket hung over the back of a chair and as I felt for the case, my fingers touched the inside breast pocket. It was empty. My wallet was gone.

I found the case and lit a cigarette. And then I leaned back. That wallet had contained something more important than money—it had contained my pilot's certificate and my false identity. Hell! He'd only to read the papers . . . I dragged at my cigarette, trying to think through the throbbing ache of my head. I had to get out of here. But how? How? My eyes roved desperately over the room. Then I glanced at my watch. It was eight-fifteen. Probably the papers had arrived already. In any case he would have phoned the police.

A door slammed somewhere beyond the brickwork of the walls. I sat up, listening for the sound of footsteps. All I could hear was the beating of my heart and the buzzing of a fly trapped in a web at the corner of the window. Nobody came. Time passed slowly. Occasionally I heard the sound of movement somewhere in the depths of the building. At eight thirty-five a car drew up at the back. There was the slam of a door and the sound of voices. Five minutes later the car drove off.

I couldn't stand it any more. The feeling of impotence was getting on my nerves. In a sudden mood of anger I got up and beat on the panels of the door. Footsteps approached, a heavy, solid tread, boots ringing metallic on concrete. Then a voice asked, " Are you awake?"

" Of course I'm awake," I replied angrily. " Do you mind opening the door?"

There was a moment's pause and then the voice said, " That depends. I'm a bit cautious after last night. You damn nearly throttled me."

I didn't say anything and a moment later the key turned in the lock and he opened the door. It was the same man all right—short and broad and very solid. He had thick dark hair slightly grizzled at the temples and a wide jaw that seemed to compress his lips into a thin, determined line. He was dressed in oil-stiff overalls and the silk scarf round his neck didn't entirely hide the livid marks left by my fingers.

" I'm sorry—about last night," I murmured.

He didn't come in, but stood there in the gap of the doorway, his legs slightly straddled, staring at me. He had hard, slate-grey eyes. " Forget it." His voice was more friendly than his eyes. " Have you had a look at yourself in the mirror? Afraid I made a bit of a mess of your jaw."

There was an awkward silence. Somehow I couldn't bring myself to ask when the police would arrive. " I'd like to get cleaned up," I said.

He nodded. " Down the passage." He stood aside to let me pass. But though he didn't seem angry, I noticed he took good care to keep well out of my reach.

Outside I found myself in a brick passageway filled with sunlight. An open doorway showed the woods crowding right up to the side of the building and through the lacework of the trees I caught a glimpse of the flat, bare expanse of the airfield. It all looked very quiet and peaceful. Through that door lay freedom and as though he read my thoughts, he said, " I shouldn't try wandering about outside, Fraser. The police are searching this area."

" The police?" I swung round, staring at him, trying to understand the sense behind his words.

" They've found the car. You'd crashed it about half-way down Baydon Hill." He glanced up at my forehead. " I did the best I could with the cut. You've probably scarred your-self for life, but I don't think any dirt has got into it."

I didn't understand his attitude. " When are the police coming for me?" I asked.

" We'll discuss that later," he said. " Better get cleaned up first. The lavatory is at the end there."

Feeling dull and rather dazed I went on down the passage. I could hear him following behind me. Then his footsteps stopped. " I've left my shaving kit out for you. If there's anything you want, shout." And then he added, " I'm just knocking up some breakfast. How many eggs would you like —two?"

" If you can spare them," I mumbled. I was too astonished at the calmness of his attitude to say anything else.

" Oh, I'm all right for eggs. A girl brings them from the farm each day with the milk." A door opened on the sound of sizzling fat and then closed. I turned to find myself alone in the passage. Freedom beckoned through the sunlit doorway at the end. But it was hopeless. He wouldn't have left me alone like that if he hadn't known it was hopeless. I turned quickly and padded down the corridor in my stockinged feet.

The lavatory was small with an open window looking out on to a tangle of briar. It was a reminder of service quarters with its cracked basin, broken utility seat and initials and other pencil scratchings still visible on the crumbling plaster. Shaving kit had been left out for me and a towel. Hung on a nail on the window frame was a cracked mirror. I stared at myself in its pock-marked surface. I wasn't a particularly pleasant sight. Apart from the black stubble that I'd met every day for at least fifteen years, the side of my jaw was puffed and swollen, producing a queer variation of colour from red to dark purple and culminating in an ugly split of dried blood. My eyes were sunk back in dark sockets of exhaustion, the whites bloodshot and wild-looking, and to cap it all was a broad strip of adhesive tape running right across the right side of my forehead.

" You bloody fool," I said aloud. It was like talking to a stranger, except that the lips of the face in the glass moved in echo of my words. I almost laughed at the thought that I'd wanted to try and escape into the outside world looking like that.

I looked better after I'd shaved—but not much better. I'd had to leave the stubble round the swollen side of my jaw and it gave me a queer, lop-sided appearance. The cold water had freshened me up a bit, but the dark shadows round my eyes remained and there was still the adhesive tape across my forehead. "Breakfast's ready."

I turned to find him standing in the doorway. He nodded for me to go ahead and at the same time stepped slightly back. "You're taking no chances," I said. The bitterness in my voice was for myself, not for him.

"Last door on the right," he said as though I hadn't spoken.

Inside was a trestle table, the sort we'd had in forward bases. Two plates heaped with bacon and eggs and fried bread steamed slowly and there was a pot of tea. "By the way, my name's Saeton. Bill Saeton."

"I gather—you know my name." My voice trembled slightly. He was standing just inside the door, solid and immovable like a rock, his eyes fixed on my face. The personality of the man seemed to grow in silence, dominating me and filling the room.

"Yes, I think I know all about you," he said slowly. "Sit down."

His voice was remote, impersonal. I didn't want to sit down. I wanted my shoes and my wallet. I wanted to get out of there. But I sat down all the same. There was something compelling about the way he stood there, staring at me. "Can I have my wallet, please?"

"Later," was all he said. He sat down opposite me, his back to the window and poured the tea. I drank thirstily and then lit a cigarette.

"I thought you said you could manage two eggs."

"I'm not hungry," I answered, drawing the smoke deep down into my lungs. It soothed me, easing the tension of my nerves. "When are they coming for me?" I asked. I had control of my voice now.

He frowned. "Who?" he asked, his mouth crammed full.

"The police," I said impatiently. "You've phoned them, haven't you?"

"Not yet." He pointed his fork at my plate. "For God's sake relax and get some breakfast inside you."

I stared at him. "You mean they don't know I'm here?" I didn't believe him. Nobody would calmly sit down to eat his breakfast with a man who'd tried to throttle him the night before unless he knew the authorities were on their way. Then

I remembered the car and the way he'd advised me not to wander about outside. "The police were here about half an hour ago, weren't they?" I asked him.

For answer he reached over to a side table and tossed me the morning paper. I glanced down at it. The story was there in bold headlines that ran half-across the front page: PALESTINE FLIGHT FOILED—Police Prevent Another Plane Leaving Country Illegally—Mystery of "Mr. Callahan." It was all there in the opening paragraph of leaded type—the whole wretched story.

I pushed the paper away and said, "Why didn't you hand me over?" I spoke without looking up. I had a peculiar sense of being trapped.

"We'll talk about that later," he said again.

He spoke as though he were talking to a child and suddenly anger came to bolster my courage. What was he doing living alone up here on this deserted aerodrome tinkering about with a Tudor in the dead of night? Why hadn't he rung the police? He was playing some sort of cat-and-mouse game with me and I wanted to get it over. If it had to come, let it come now, right away. "I want you to call the police," I said.

"Don't be a fool! Get some breakfast inside you. You'll feel better then."

But I'd got to my feet. "I want to give myself up." My voice trembled. It was part anger, part fear. There was something wrong with this place. I didn't like it. I didn't like the uncertainty of it. I wanted to get it over.

"Sit down!" He, too, had risen and his hand was on my shoulder, pressing me down. "Nervous reaction, that's all."

"There's nothing wrong with my nerves." I shook his hand off and then I was looking into his eyes and somehow I found myself back in my seat, staring at my plate.

"That's better."

"What are you keeping me here for?" I murmured. "What are you doing up here?"

"We'll talk about it after breakfast."

"I want to talk about it now."

"After breakfast," he repeated.

I started to insist, but he had picked up the paper and ignored me. A feeling of impotence swept over me. Almost automatically I picked up the knife and fork. And as soon as I'd started to eat I realised I was hungry—damnably hungry. I hadn't had anything since midday yesterday. A silence stretched over the table. I thought of the trial and the prison sentence that must inevitably follow. I might get a year, possibly more after resisting arrest, hitting a police officer and stealing a car. The memory of those eighteen months in Stalag-Luft I came flooding back into my mind. Surely to God I'd had enough of prison life! Anything rather than be shut up again. I looked across at Saeton. The sunlight was very bright and though I screwed up my eyes, I couldn't see his expression. His head was bent over the newspaper. The quiet impassive way he sat there, right opposite me, gave me a momentary sense of confidence in him and as I ate a little flicker of hope slowly grew inside me.

"When you've finished we'll go up to the hangar." He lit a cigarette and turned to the inside of the paper. He didn't look up as he spoke.

I hurried through the rest of the meal, and as soon as I'd finished he got up. "Put your jacket on," he said. " I'll get your shoes."

The air struck quite warm for November as we went out into the sunlight but there was a dank autumnal smell of rotting vegetation. A berberis gleamed red against the gold of the trees and there were some rose bushes half-covered with the dead stalks of bindweed. It had been a little garden, but now the wild had moved in.

We crossed the garden and entered a path leading through the woods. It was cold and damp amongst the trees though the trunks of the silver birch saplings were dappled with sunlight. The wood thinned and we came out on the edge of the airfield. The sky was crystal clear, bright blue with patches of cumulus. The sun shone white on the exposed chalk of a dispersal point. Far away, beyond the vast curve of the airfield, a line of hills showed the rounded brown of downland grass. The place was derelict with disuse—the concrete of the runways cracked and sprouting weeds, the buildings that dotted the woods half-demolished into rubble, the field itself all ploughed up for crops. Only the hangar, fifty yards away to our left, seemed solid and real.

"What's the name of this airfield?" I asked Saeton.

" Membury."

" What are you doing living up here on your own?"

He didn't answer and we continued in silence. We turned

the corner of the hangar and walked to the centre of the main doors. Saeton took out a bunch of keys and unlocked the wicket door that I'd pushed open the previous night. Inside, the musty smell of concrete and the damp chill was familiar. Both the inboard engines of the plane were missing. It had a sort of toothless grin. Saeton pressed his hand against the door till the lock clicked and then led the way to the back of the hangar where the work bench stretched along the wall. "Sit down," he said, indicating a stool. He drew up another with his foot and sat down facing me. "Now then——" He took my wallet from his pocket and spread the contents on the oil-black wood of the bench. "Your name is Neil Leyden Fraser and you're a pilot. Correct?"

I nodded.

He picked up my passport. "Born at Stirling in 1915, height five-eleven, eyes brown, hair brown. Picture quite flattering compared with what you look like at the moment." He flicked through the pages. "Back and forth from the Continent quite a bit." He looked up at me quickly. "Have you taken many planes out of the country?"

I hesitated. But there was no point in denying the thing. "Three," I said.

"I see." His eyes didn't move from my face. "And why exactly did you engage in this somewhat risky business?"

"Look," I said, "if you want to get me under cross-examination hand me over to the police. Why haven't you done so already? Do you mind answering me that?"

"No. I'm quite prepared to tell you why—in a moment. But until I have the answer to the question I've just asked I can't finally make up my mind whether to hand you over or not." He leaned forward then and tapped my knee. "Better tell me the whole thing. I'm the one person, outside of the organisers of your little racket, who knows that you're the pilot calling himself 'Callahan.' Am I right?"

There was nothing I could say. I just nodded.

"All right then. Either I can give you up or I can stay quiet. That places me in the position of judge. Now, why did you get mixed up in this business?"

I shrugged my shoulders. "Why the hell does anyone get mixed up in something illegal? I didn't know it was illegal. It wasn't at first anyway. I was just engaged to pilot a director of a British firm of exporters. His business took him all over

Western Europe and the Mediterranean. He was a Jew. Then
they asked me to ferry a plane out. They said it was being
exported to a country where the British weren't very popular
and suggested that for the trip I used a name that was more
international. I agreed and on arrival in Paris I was given
papers showing my name as ' Callahan.' "

" It was a French plane?"

" Yes. I took it to Haifa."

" But why did you get mixed up with these people in the
first place?"

" Why the hell do you imagine?" I demanded angrily. " You
know what it was like after the war. There were hundreds of
pilots looking around for jobs. I finished as a Wing Co. I
went and saw my old employers, a shipbuilding yard on the
Clyde. They offered me a £2 rise—£6 10s. a week. I threw
their offer back in their faces and walked out. I was just about
on my uppers when this flying job was offered to me. I jumped
at it. So would you. So would any pilot who hadn't been in
the air for nearly a year."

He nodded his head slowly. " I thought it'd be something
like that. Are you married?"

" No."

" Engaged?"

" No."

" Any close relatives who might start making inquiries if
Neil Fraser disappeared for a while?"

" I don't think so," I answered. " My mother's dead. My
father remarried and I'm a bit out of touch with him. Why?"

" What about friends?"

" They just expect me when they see me. What exactly are
you driving at?"

He turned to the bench and stared for a while at the contents
of my wallet as though trying to make up his mind. At length
he picked up one of the dog-eared and faded photographs
I kept in the case. " This is what interested me," he said
slowly. " In fact, it's the reason I didn't ring the police last
night and denied that I'd seen anything of you when they
came this morning. Picture of you with Waaf girl-friend. On
the back it's got—*September, 1940: Self and June outside our
old home after taking a post-blitz cure.*" He held it out to me
and for the first time since I'd met him there was a twinkle in
his eyes. " You look pretty tipsy, the pair of you."

"Yes," I said. "We were tight. The whole place collapsed with us in it. We were lucky to get out alive."

"So I guessed. It was the ruins that interested me. Your old home was a maintenance hangar, wasn't it?"

"Yes. Kenley Aerodrome. A low-flying daylight raid—it pretty well blew the place to bits. Why?"

"I figured that if you could describe a maintenance hangar as your home in 1940 you probably knew something about aero-engines and engineering?"

I didn't say anything and after staring at me for a moment he said impatiently. "Well, do you know anything about aero-engines or don't you?"

"Yes," I said.

"Practical—or just theory? Given specifications and tools can you build an engine?"

"What are you getting at?" I asked. "What do you——"

"Just answer my questions. Can you operate a lathe, do milling, grinding and boring, screw cutting and drilling?"

"Yes." And then I added, "I don't know very much about jets. But I'm pretty sound on all types of piston engines."

"I see. And you're a pilot?"

"Yes."

"When did you become a pilot?"

"In 1945, after I escaped from Germany."

"Why?"

"I don't know. I wanted a change. In 1944 I was posted to bombers as flight engineer. I started learning to fly. Then we were shot down. I escaped early in 1945 and remembered enough about flying to pinch a Jerry plane and crash-land at an airfield back home. Shortly after that I got my wings."

He nodded vaguely as though he hadn't been listening. He had turned slightly on his stool and was staring sombrely at the gleaming fuselage of the Tudor. His eyes caught a shaft of sunlight from the high windows and seemed to gleam with some inner fire. Then he turned back to me. "You're in a spot, aren't you?" It wasn't said unpleasantly—more a statement of fact. "But I'll make you a proposition. See that engine over there?" I turned. It stood against the wall and was chocked up on wooden blocks. "That's finished—complete. It's hand-built, mostly right here in this hangar. Well, that's one of them. But there's got to be another before I can get this crate into the air." He nodded towards the Tudor. "It's

due to fly on the Berlin Airlift on 25th January—fuel freight-
ing. We've got the tanks installed. Everything's ready. All we
need is a second engine. We've started on it already. But I'm
pressed for time. That first one took us six months. And now
Carter, who's been working on it with me, is getting impatient.
I'm a pilot, not an engineer. If he walks out on me, which is
what he threatens to do, I'll have to pack up—unless I've got
somebody else to carry on." He looked at me, eyes narrowed
slightly. " Well, what about it? Can you build another engine
like that, if necessary on your own?"

" I don't know," I said. " I haven't examined it and I don't
know what equipment you've got." My eyes roved quickly
along the bench, noting the lathes, the racks of taps, boxes of
dies, the turning tools, the jigs and the welding equipment. " I
should think I could," I added.

" Good." He got up as though it were settled and went over
to the completed engine. He stood there staring at it, and then
he turned away from it with a quick, impatient movement of
his shoulders as though throwing off something that was constantly at the back of his mind. " You won't get any pay.
Free board and lodging, beer, cigarettes, anything that is absolutely necessary. You'll work up here until the thing's complete. After that . . . well, we'll see. If things work out the
way they should, then you won't lack a permanent job if you
want it."

" You seem to be taking my acceptance rather for granted,"
I said.

" Of course I am," he said, swinging round on me. " You've
no alternative."

" Look—just what's your racket?" I demanded. " I'm in
enough trouble without getting deeper——"

" There's no racket," he cut in angrily. " I run a company
called Saeton Aircraft Ltd., and I rent these premises from
the Air Ministry. It's all perfectly legal."

" Then why pick on a lonely spot like this? And last night
—you were scared of something. And you shouted at me in
German. Why in German? And who was the girl?"

He came towards me then, his head thrust forward, his
thick neck hard with the tautness of the muscles. " Take my
advice, Fraser—accept my offer and don't ask questions." His
jaw was so tight that the words came through his teeth.

I had got to my feet now. " Are you sure you haven't

pinched this plane?" I asked. Damn it! He wasn't going
to get me in a worse mess.

For a moment I thought he was going to strike me. But
instead he turned away with a little laugh. " No. No, I didn't
pinch it." He rounded on me and added violently, " Nor
this engine, nor these tools, all this equipment. There's three
years of my life in this hangar—three years of sweating my
guts out, improvising, struggling, trying to make fools see that
if only . . ." He stopped suddenly. Then in a voice into which
he had forced mildness he said, " You've nothing to worry
about, Fraser. It's all perfectly legal. And once this plane is
in the air and——" He was interrupted by someone banging
on the hangar door. He hesitated and then glanced at me.
" That could be the police. Which is it to be—complete the
second engine for me or do I hand you over? You'll be quite
safe up here in a day or so," he added.

The banging on the door seemed to merge with the hammering of my heart. The possibility of arrest, which had gradually
receded, now became real and instant. But I had already suc-
cumbed to a flicker of hope that had grown up inside me. " I'll
stay," I said.

He nodded as though there had never been any doubt of it.
" Better nip into the fuselage. You can hide in the toilet at
the rear. They won't think of looking for you there."

I did as he suggested and climbed into the fuselage. In
the dark belly of the plane I could just make out the shape of
three large elliptical tanks up for'ard. I heard the click of the
door being opened and the sound of voices. The door slammed
to and for a moment I thought they'd left the hangar. But
then their footsteps were echoing on the concrete as they came
down towards the bench. There was the drone of a man's
voice, low and urgent. Then Saeton cut him short: " All right.
Throw in your hand if you want to. But we'll talk about it
back at the quarters, not here." His voice was hard and angry.

" For God's sake, Bill, be reasonable. I'm not throwing in
my hand. But we can't go on. You know that as well as I do."
They had stopped close beside the fuselage. The man was
breathing heavily as though he were out of breath. He had
a slight cockney accent and his voice was almost pleading.
" Can't you understand—I'm broke. I haven't a bean."

" Well, nor have I," Saeton said harshly. " But I don't
whine about it. In three months from now——"

"It's been two years already," the other put in mildly.

"Do you think I don't know how long it's been?" Saeton's voice softened. "Listen, Tubby, in three months we'll be on top of the world. Think of it, man—only three months. Surely to God you can pull in your belt and stick it as long as that after all we've been through together?"

The other grunted. "But you're not married, are you chum?"

"So your wife's been getting at you. That's it, is it? I ought to have known it. Well, if you think your wife's going to stop me from getting that plane into the air . . ." Saeton had been lashing himself into a fury, but he stopped suddenly. "Let's go back to the quarters. We can't talk here."

"No," the other said obstinately. "I'll say what I've got to say here."

"We're going back to quarters," Saeton said gently. "We'll talk about it over a cup of tea."

"No," the other repeated, still in the same obstinate tone. "We'll talk it over here and now if you don't mind. I'm not going to have you rowing Diana for something that isn't her——"

"Diana!" Saeton's voice was suddenly harsh. "You haven't brought her back——"

"She's down at the quarters now," the other said stolidly.

"At the quarters! You bloody fool! This is no place for a woman. They can't keep their mouths shut and——"

"Diana won't talk. Besides, she's nowhere else to go."

"I thought she was sharing a flat with a friend in London."

"Damn it, man," the other shouted, "can't you understand what I'm trying to tell you? We're broke. I'm overdrawn by twenty quid and the bank has warned me I've got to settle my overdraft within three months."

"What about your wife? Didn't she have a job?"

"She got fed up and chucked it."

"And you're supposed to throw up all you've worked for just because she's bored. That's typical of a woman. If you can take it, why can't she? Doesn't she understand——"

"It's no good kicking at Diana," the other cut in. "She's not to blame. She's stuck it pretty well if you ask me. Now it's come to this—either I find a job that'll bring us in some money so that we can live together like normal human beings, or else——"

" I see."

" You don't see at all," the other snapped, his voice rising on a note of anger. " All you can think of is the engines. You're so crazy about them you don't behave like a human being at all. Well, I'm not made that way. I'm married and I want a home. I'm not busting up my marriage because of your engines."

" I'm not asking you to go to bed with them, am I?" Saeton snarled. " Well, all right. If you're so in love with your matrimonial pleasures that you can't see the future that's within your grasp——"

" I think you'd better withdraw that remark." The man's voice was low and obstinate.

" Oh God!" Saeton exploded. " All right, I withdraw it. But for Christ's sake, Tubby, stop to think what you're doing."

It seemed to me it was about time I showed myself. I slammed the toilet door and stumped across the steel-sheeted floor of the plane. From the open door of the fuselage I could see them standing, staring up at me. Saeton's companion was dressed in an old pair of grey flannels and leather-patched sports jacket—a round, friendly little man with a shock of unruly hair. His fresh, ruddy complexion contrasted oddly with Saeton's hard, leathery features. By comparison he looked quite boyish though he was about my age. Little creases of fat crinkled the corners of his eyes giving them a permanent twinkle as though he were perpetually on the verge of laughter. " Who's this?" he asked Saeton.

" Neil Fraser. He's an engineer, and he's come up here to work with us on that last engine."

" My successor, eh?" the other said quickly. " You knew I'd be leaving."

" Don't be a fool. Of course, I didn't. But I knew time was getting short. With an extra hand——"

" How much are you paying him?"

" Oh, for God's sake!" Saeton explained angrily. " His keep. That's all." He turned to me. " Fraser. This is Tubby Carter. He built the engine I've just shown you. Did you fix that toilet door?"

" Yes," I said. " It's all right now." I got down and shook Carter's hand.

" Fraser is an old friend of mine," Saeton explained. Carter's small, button-brown eyes fixed themselves on my face in a puzzled frown. " You look as though you've been in a rough house." His eyes stared at me, unwinking, as I searched desperately for some reasonable explanation.

It was Saeton who supplied the answer. " He got mixed up in some trouble at a night-club."

But Carter's eyes remained fixed on my face. " Neil Fraser." He seemed to be turning the name over in his mind and my heart sank. Suppose the police had discovered who Callahan was. After all, I'd only seen one of the daily papers. " Are you a pilot by any chance?"

I nodded.

" Neil Fraser." His face suddenly lit up and he snapped his fingers. " 101 Bomber Squadron. You were the type who made a tunnel escape from prison camp and then pinched a Messerschmitt and flew it back to England. We met once— remember? At Mildenhall." He turned to Saeton. " How's that for a photographic memory, eh? I never forget a face." He laughed happily.

Saeton glanced at me with sudden interest. Then he turned to Carter. " You stay here with Fraser and talk over your boyhood memories. I'm going to have a word with Diana."

" No, you don't, Bill." Carter had caught his arm as he turned away. " This is between you and me. You leave Diana out of this."

Saeton stopped. " It's all right, Tubby," he said and his voice was almost gentle. " I won't upset your wife, I promise you. But before she forces you into some dead-end job she must be given the facts. The situation has altered since you left on Saturday. With Fraser here we can still get on to the airlift on schedule."

" It took us six months to build that one." Carter nodded to the completed engine.

" That included tests," Saeton answered. " And we came up against snags. Those have been ironed out now. Damn it, surely she'll have the sense to give you two months longer. As for money, leave that to me. I'll wring some more out of Dick if I have to squeeze it out of him with my bare hands. It's a pity he's such a——" He stopped abruptly, his lips compressed as though biting on the words. " You stay here. I'll talk to Diana. She's no fool. No woman is when it comes to looking to the future. We've got all the metal and castings. All we've got to do is build the damned thing." His eyes swung towards the plane. "Then we'll have 'em all licked." He stood staring at it as though by mere effort of will he could get it into the air. Then almost reluctantly his gaze came back to Carter. "You can have that front room that used to be the office. It'll work out. You'll see. She can do the cooking for us. That'll keep her busy, and it'll give us more working time."

"I tell you, her mind's made up," Carter said wearily.

Saeton laughed. It was a slightly cynical laugh. "No woman's mind is ever made up," he said. "They're constructed for the purpose of having their minds made up for them. How else do you imagine the human race survives?"

Carter stood quite still watching Saeton as he left the hangar. Then he turned and went straight over to the end of the work-bench by the telephone and took down a pair of overalls. As he got into them he glanced at me curiously. "So you're an engineer?" He zipped up the front of the overalls. Then he went over to a small petrol engine and started it up. "We're working on the pistons at the moment." He pulled a big folder towards me across the bench and opened it out. There were sheafs of fine pencil drawings. "Here we are. Those are the specifications. You can work a lathe?" I nodded. He took me down the bench. The lathe was an ex-R.A.F. type, the sort we'd had in the maintenance hangar at Kenley. The belt drive was running free. With a quick movement of his hand he engaged it and at the same time picked up a half-turned block of bright metal. "Okay, then. Go ahead. Piston specifications: five-inch diameter, seven-inch depth, three-ring channels, two to be drilled for oil disposal, and there's a three-quarter inch hole for the gudgeon-pin sleeve. And for the love of Mike don't waste metal. This outfit's running on a shoe-string, as you've probably gathered."

It was some time since I'd worked at a lathe. But it's a thing that once you've learnt you never forget. He stood over me for a time and it made me nervous. But as the shavings of metal ran off the lathe my confidence returned. My mind ceased to worry about the events of the last twenty-four hours. It became concentrated entirely in the fascination of turning a piece of mechanism out of a lump of metal. I ceased to be conscious of his presence. Hands and brain combined to recapture my old skill, and pride of craftsmanship took hold of me as the shape of the piston slowly emerged from the metal.

When I looked up again Carter was leaning over the specifications, his eyes staring at a bolt he was screwing in and out of a nut. His mind was outside the shop, worrying about his own personal problems. He looked up and caught my eye. Then he threw the bolt down and came towards me.

I bent to my work again and for a time he stood watching me in silence. At length he said, " How long have you know Saeton?"

I didn't know what to say so I didn't answer him. " Saeton was a Coastal Command pilot." The metal whirled under my hands, thin silver slivers streaming from it. " I don't believe you've ever met him before in your life."

I stopped the lathe. " Do you want me to balls this up?" I said.

He was fidgeting with the metal shavings. " I was just wondering——" He stopped then and changed his line of approach. " What do you think of him, eh?" He was looking directly at me now. " He's mad, of course. But it's the madness that builds empires." I could see he worshipped the man. There was a boy's admiration in his voice. " He thinks he'll lick every charter company in the country once he gets into the air."

" They're most of them on the verge of bankruptcy anyway," I said.

He nodded. " I've been with him for two years now. Working in partnership, you know. We had one plane flying— single-engined job. But that crashed." His fingers strayed back to the metal shavings. " He's a crazy devil. Incredible energy. The hell of it is his enthusiasm is infectious. When you're with him you believe what he wants you to believe. Did you hear what we were talking about when you were fixing that door?"

" Part of it," I said guardedly.

He nodded absently. " My wife's got a will of her own. She's American. Do you think he'll persuade her to agree to give me three months more?" He picked up a block of metal destined to be the next piston. " He's right, of course. With the three of us working at it we ought to be able to complete the second engine in two months." He sighed. " Having come this far I'd like to see it through to the end. This place has become almost a part of me." He turned slowly and stared at the tailplane of the aircraft. " I'd like to see her flying."

I couldn't help him so I started the lathe again and he moved off along the bench and began work on an induction coil.

Half an hour later Saeton returned. He came and stood over me as I measured the diameter of the piston-head with a screw micrometer. Carter moved along the bench. "Well?" he asked, his voice hesitant.

"Oh, she agrees," Saeton said. His manner was offhand, but when I glanced at him I saw that he was pale as though he'd driven himself hard to get her agreement. "She'll bring lunch up to us here."

Carter stared at him almost unbelievingly. Then suddenly his eyes crinkled and his face fell into its natural mould of smiling good humour. "Well, I'm damned!" he said and went whistling down the bench back to his induction coil.

"I see you know how to handle a lathe," Saeton said to me. And then with sudden violence, "By God! I believe we'll do it in a couple of months."

And then the phone rang.

He started and the light died out of his face as though he were expecting this call. He went slowly down the bench and lifted the receiver. His face gradually darkened as he bent over the instrument and then he shouted, "You're selling out on me? Don't be a fool, Dick . . . Of course, I understand . . . But wait a minute. Listen, damn you! I've got another man up here. Two months, that's all I'm asking . . . Well, six weeks then . . . No, of course I can't guarantee anything. But you've got to hang on a bit longer. In a couple of months we'll have it in the air . . . Surely you can hang on a couple of months? . . . All right, if that's the way you feel. But come down and see me first . . . Yes. A thing like this needs talking over . . . To-morrow, then. All right."

He replaced the receiver slowly. "Was that Dick?" Carter asked.

Saeton nodded. "Yes. He's had an offer for the aircraft and all the equipment here. He's threatening to sell us up." He picked up a stool and sent it spinning across the hangar. "God damn him, why can't he understand we're on the verge of success at last?"

Carter said nothing. I returned to my lathe. Saeton hesitated and then seized hold of the folder of specifications. For a moment he held it in his hands as though about to tear it across. His face was dark with passion. Then he flung it down and went over to the engine standing on its blocks against the wall. He pressed a switch and the thing roared into life, a shattering, earsplitting din that drowned all sound of my lathe. And he stood watching it, caressing it with his eyes as though all his world was concentrated in the live, dinning roar of it.


# CHAPTER TWO

As I worked at the lathe and the day wore on, it slowly dawned on me what an incredible stroke of luck I had had. It was as though I had been given another chance. And this was legal. I might not have taken Saeton's word for it, but the presence of Tubby Carter proved there was nothing wrong with the set-up. He was so unquestionably honest. With him working beside me the whole thing became ordinary, matter-of-fact.

Saeton was different. It wasn't that I didn't trust the man. But he was a human dynamo, full of nervous, violent energy. The mercurial emotionalism of the Celt seemed mixed with a Saxon stolidity and singleness of purpose and I felt he was capable of anything. He was a born leader with that vital spark that can kindle enthusiasm in others, the type that can whip the dull heart of the mob into thundering passion. His strength was that he didn't need the support of others. It was all there inside him. He showed that when he switched off the thundering din of that one engine and turned with a grim concentration to the job of winding the armature of a starter motor. The structure of his life was crumbling about him. His partner was selling him up. But he didn't discuss it. He threw himself into the work that littered the bench with the silent preoccupation of a man who can see the finished article in his mind's eye.

Something of his drive and purpose seemed to enter into the two of us as we worked beside him. And the fascination of seeing a part of a complicated machine take shape under my hands so engrossed me that I lost all sense of time. I didn't notice Carter's wife bring in our lunch. Saeton pushed a mug of tea and some sandwiches along the bench to me and I ate whilst I worked. He and Carter did the same.

The only interruption was just after we'd switched on the light plant, shortly after four. There was a banging on the door. Saeton shouted to know who it was and a voice answered, " The police." I looked up at him from the lathe, my heart suddenly in my mouth. I had so completely lost myself in the work that the reminder that the authorities were searching for me came as a shock.

Saeton tossed me a flash-mask. " Put that on," he ordered crisply. " The oxy-acetylene equipment is at the end of the bench there." I saw Carter looking at me curiously. Then I had the mask on and was hurrying across to the oxygen cylinders.

By the time Saeton came back with a police inspector and a sergeant I had the flame going and was cutting across a piece of scrap metal. " Just routine," the Inspector said as he asked for our identity cards. He glanced at them idly, talking to Saeton all the time. " Thought we'd take a look round Membury before we packed it in. But he'll be out of the district by now. Probably out of the country in some private plane. Still, we'll just take a look round—in case. Quite a handy place, an old aerodrome, for a man to lie up." He handed back our cards. " No fear of his pinching your plane, anyway, sir. Can't fly a plane with two of its engines missing, can you?"

" No," Saeton answered and he didn't join in the Inspector's good-humoured laughter.

They left then and I put the flash-mask aside and got back to my lathe with a feeling that the last hurdle had been over-come. I was safe now. So long as I remained at Membury I was safe.

But as we worked on in the evening I was conscious of Carter watching me periodically from the other end of the bench. We knocked off at about eight. I was pretty tired by then and I might have felt depressed, but Saeton clapped his hand on my shoulder. " You're a better acquisition than I'd dared to hope," he said, and that word of praise lifted me above physical tiredness. " It's a pity though," he added.

" What's a pity?" Carter asked.

" That Dick Randall doesn't know anything about engineering," he answered. " If he could understand just how

much we've achieved in one single day with the three of us
working without interruption for meal-getting, then he'd realise
how close we are to success."

It was cold outside the hangar and the biting north wind
made the cut on my forehead ache as though the bone had
been smashed. Back at the quarters there was a smell of
roasting chicken. We cleaned ourselves up and then gathered
in the front room. The trestle table had been covered. It
was only an old curtain, but it gave it a more friendly air.
The table was laid for four. Saeton crossed to a cupboard and
brought out glasses and a bottle of whisky. "I thought you
were broke," Carter said.

Saeton laughed. "Only bankrupts can afford to be spend-
thrifts." But though he laughed, there was no laughter in his
eyes. "No point in hoarding when Randall may sell us out
to-morrow."

The click of high-heeled shoes sounded on the concrete of
the passage outside and Saeton sprang to open the door.

Diana Carter was such a contrast to her husband that she
produced in me a sense almost of shock. She was a product
of the war, a hard, experienced-looking woman with a wide,
over-thick mouth and hennaed hair. There was nothing homely
about her. She swept in, a flash of red dirndl skirt and tawny
hair with eyes that matched the green of her jersey and a
motion of the body that was quite uninhibited. Her glance
went straight to Saeton and then fell to the bottle. "What are
we celebrating, Bill?" Her voice was deep and throaty with
just the trace of an American accent.

"The fact that we're broke," Saeton answered, handing
her a glass. "Randall's selling us up to-morrow. Then you
and Tubby can go and raise a family in peace."

She made a face at him and raised her glass. "You'll talk
him out of it," she said. "But I'll need some curtains, table-
cloths, bed-linen and china. I'm not going to live in a pig-sty.
And we're short of beds." Her gaze had fastened on me. It
was a curiously personal stare and her green eyes were a little
too narrow, a little too close.

Saeton introduced us. Her eyes strayed to the adhesive
tape across my forehead. But all she said was, "Where is he
going to sleep?"

"I'll fix him up," Saeton answered.

She nodded, her gaze concentrated on him. "Two months,

you said, didn't you, Bill?" There was a sort of breathlessness about her that contrasted pleasantly with the essentially masculine atmosphere of the hangar. And the gleam of excitement in her eyes made me think she found it more interesting keeping house for three men on this lonely airfield than sharing a flat in London with a girl-friend. "Who's the girl that comes with the milk and eggs in the morning?" she asked.

"Oh, she works at the farm," Saeton answered carelessly. "Her name is Else."

"She behaved more like a camp-follower than a land-girl." She was looking at her husband as she said this, but then she switched her gaze back to Saeton. "Yours?"

"Really, Diana!" Saeton picked up the bottle and refilled her glass. "Have you managed to make the room opposite habitable?"

"After nearly a day's work—yes. Was she cook here before I came?"

"She came in and did things for us in the evening sometimes," Saeton admitted. "By arrangement with the farm."

"I thought she looked at me like a cat that sees the cream whipped away from under her nose." It wasn't said banteringly. Her tone was hard and her eyes searched her husband's face. "I guess I dug in my heels just in time." There was a bitter clutching in her voice. She was the sort of woman who would always be wanting the thing that had just been put out of her reach. Slowly she turned and faced Saeton again. "Is she foreign? She has a queer way of talking."

Saeton nodded. "Yes, she's German. A D.P. Her name is Else Langen." He seemed reluctant to talk about her. "Suppose we have some food now, Diana?"

She nodded and finished her drink. As she turned to go, she paused. "So long as I'm here tell her to confine her activities to outside help."

Saeton laughed. "I'll tell her." And he went on chuckling quietly to himself after Diana had left the room, as though at some private joke.

To my surprise Diana proved to be a good cook. The meal was excellent, but before it was over the warmth of the oil stove and the whisky had made me drowsy. I'd had a long day and not much sleep the night before and as they were planning to start work again at seven, I decided to go straight to bed. Saeton fixed me up with a camp bed in one of the

B

back rooms. But for a long time I lay awake, hearing the
murmur of their voices. It wasn't so much the cold that
seeped up through the canvas of the bed that kept me awake
as the fact that so much had happened since I had arrived
at Membury. My mind was chock-full of half-digested impressions, all of them slightly fantastic, like a dream.

But the thing that stood out in my mind was that this was
the beginning of a new life for me. I was safe up here at
Membury. Whatever the future of Saeton's outfit, it served
my purpose. I'd stay here for a time and then, when the
hunt had died down, I'd leave and get a job. I wouldn't
bother about flying. I'd go back to engineering. My day's
work had taught me that I was still an engineer, and there
was no shortage of jobs for engineers.

The only thing that worried me as I drifted off to sleep
was that Saeton's company would pack up before it was safe
for me to venture again into the outside world. All that
seemed to stand between it and failure was the personality
of the man. And yet, somehow, that seemed sufficient.

We breakfasted next morning at six-thirty. Diana got the
meal for us, an old blue dressing-gown over her nightdress,
her face freshly made-up. We ate in silence by the light of an
oil lamp, the threat of foreclosure hanging bleakly over the
table, like the reluctant daylight. Diana's eyes kept straying
to Saeton's face as though searching for something there that
she needed. He didn't once look up. He ate with the fierce
concentration of a man to whom the act of feeding is a necessary interruption to the day's work. Tubby Carter, on the
other hand, ate with a leisurely enjoyment.

As I went down the passage after breakfast to get my overalls, I passed an open door and paused at the sight of a bed
made up on the floor in the far corner. Hanging on the wall
was the jacket Saeton had worn the previous night. The man
had given me his own camp bed. I don't know whether this
had any direct bearing on my actions later, but I know that
at the time it made me feel part of a team and that from that
moment I wanted Saeton to win out and get his plane on to the
airlift.

There was no hesitation when we reached the hangar, no
discussion. We went straight on with the jobs we had left
the night before. But as we worked I was conscious of a
mounting tension. Several times Saeton paused and glanced

impatiently at his watch. A nerve twitched at the skin of his temple. But he worked steadily, unhurriedly, as though the day stretched ahead with absolute security.

Diana brought coffee shortly after eleven. She tossed the morning paper to me with a little secret smile and then turned to Saeton. " Well, he's here."

" Randall?"

" Yes."

" Then why the devil didn't you bring him up here with you?"

" I told him to wait. He's talking to that girl from the farm. I thought you'd like to know he's got someone with him."

" Someone with him?" He jerked round towards her. " A man?"

" Yes."

" What sort of a man?"

" Short, slightly bald, with glasses and——"

" I don't want to know what he looks like. What's his business?"

" I haven't asked him." She seemed to enjoy baiting him with the mystery.

" Well, what's he look as though he does?" he asked angrily.

" He's dressed in a dark suit and a Homburg. I guess he might be something in the City—a lawyer maybe."

" A lawyer! My God! Don't say he's brought his solicitor with him. Go and tell them to wait. I'll be down right away. And get rid of that girl." He was scrambling out of his overalls, cursing softly to himself, as her heels click-clacked across to the door of the hangar. When he had his jacket on, he picked up a mug of coffee and drank it slowly as though steadying himself, controlling the violence that seemed on the verge of erupting from him. At length he turned to Carter. " We've got to convince him, Tubby," he said in a tight, controlled voice.

The other nodded. " But don't lose your temper, Bill, like you did last time. It only makes him stutter. If he was an engineer——"

" Well, he's not an engineer," Saeton snapped. " He's just a jerk that's been left fifty thousand by an adoring aunt." He thrust his hands into his pockets. " All right. I won't lose my temper—provided he shows some sense." He turned then and walked quickly out of the hangar as though he were going to something unpleasant and wanted to get it over.

Carter watched him go and then shrugged his shoulders. "Trouble is, every time he meets Randall he acts as though he's a steam hammer driving sense into a block of pig iron."

"What's Randall like?" I asked. I wasn't really interested. This was none of my business. I had picked up the paper and was searching through it for a follow-up to the "Callahan" story of the previous day.

"Oh, he's not a bad fellow really. Got more money than sense, that's all."

I had found what I wanted now, a paragraph on an inside page stating that the police believed "Callahan" had left the country. I folded the paper and laid it on the bench. There was nothing for me to worry about. I looked across at Carter. "Why does Randall want to sell up?" I asked.

Carter shrugged. "Bored, I suppose. He's not really interested in aircraft. Horse racing is what he lives for. Besides, three years is a long time."

I glanced at the plane and then back again to Carter. There was something here I didn't understand. It had been at the back of my mind and now that I didn't have to worry about myself any more it came to the fore. "It doesn't take three years to get a plane into the air," I said.

Carter looked up at me guardedly. "Hasn't Saeton told you anything about these engines? I thought you were an old friend of his?"

I didn't pursue the matter, but turned back to the lathe.

It must have been about half an hour later that Saeton came in, his face dark with anger. With him was a tall, erect-looking man with a brushed-up ginger moustache and rather prominent eyes. He wore tweed trousers and a cloth cap and the open neck of his sheepskin jacket was filled with a brilliant blue and gold silk scarf. Behind them trotted a soft, plump little man with a brief-case.

Saeton went straight over to Carter. "You can pack up work on that induction coil, Tubby. We're through." His voice was hard and vicious.

Carter sat back on his stool, still holding the coil in his hands as though he didn't want to let it go, and stared at Randall unbelievingly. "Doesn't he understand we only need two more months?" he asked Saeton. "With Fraser here——"

" I've told him all that," Saeton cut in. " But we're not dealing with Randall. We're dealing with Mr. Reinbaum here." He nodded to the plump little man whose white fingers were fidgeting with the lock of his brief-case. " He holds the mortgages."

" I don't understand," Carter said slowly. " Those mortgages were given to Dick as security for money he advanced to the company. How does this fellow Reinbaum come into it?"

Randall cleared his throat awkwardly. " I borrowed money on the mortgages," he said.

" Well, surely if you repay the money——"

" We've been over all this," Saeton cut in impatiently. " Randall has lost heavily—betting." The word came out with an explosive violence. " Reinbaum has received an offer for the plane and all our tools and equipment and Randall has agreed to close."

" It is out of the question that we should receive a better offer," Reinbaum said. He had a soft, slightly foreign voice.

" The offer," Saeton said harshly, " is twenty-five thousand for the whole box of tricks. That's just two thousand more than the mortgages."

" But that means winding up the company," Carter said. " Randall can't do that unless one of us agrees. Together we out-vote him. Under the articles of the company——"

" Please, Mr. Carter," Reinbaum interrupted. " It is not a question of voluntary liquidation."

" You mean you're going to force us into liquidation?" Carter asked and there was an obstinate note in his voice that made me suddenly respect him.

" The damnable part of it is," Saeton said angrily, " that when Randall advanced us that last five thousand his solicitor insisted that since it was for material for building the engines, the engines themselves must be included in the mortgage." He swung round on Randall. " By God!" he said. " If it wasn't that I'd swing for it, I'd——" He turned quickly and started to pace up and down, his hands clenched as he fought down the fury that mottled his features. He stopped as he came face to face with the completed engine. Then he reached up to the wall and pressed the starter switch. The engine turned, coughed twice and roared into life. The hangar shook to the thundering din of it. He turned to Randall. " Come here, Dick," he shouted. "Look at it! Feel the power of it! That engine is ready for installation." He waved his thick hand at the bench. "The second is already taking shape. In a month it will be finished. In six weeks we'll be on test. And on the 25th January, we'll be on the airlift. In two months you'll be director of a company owning the most talked-of plane in the world. Think of it! Saeton Aircraft freighter slashes fuel costs! My God, man, haven't you any ambition? We'll make a fortune, and all I'm asking you for is two months. You've carried the company for nearly three years. Another two months isn't much to ask."

So that was it! Saeton had something new in engine design, something that would reduce fuel consumption. His wasn't the first company that had come to grief trying to pursue this particular mirage, and yet the vibrance in his voice, the sheer gripping enthusiasm of the man carried conviction. I stared at Randall. Surely he would give Saeton those two months? I wanted to see those engines finished now. I wanted to see them in the air, to see them tested. If Saeton succeeded. . . .

But Randall was shaking his head. "I'm s-sorry, Bill." He was stuttering now in his embarrassment. "I'm p-pretty well cleaned out, you know."

"You mean you've lost so heavily you can't buy those mortgages back?" Saeton was staring at him hard.

Randall nodded.

"But what about your horses, your car, that house down at Hatfield?"

The other stared at him. "But dash it," he exclaimed. "I can't sell the house. It's been in the family for generations. And I won't sell my horses." His face was flushed and there was an obstinate look in his eyes. "I'm sorry, Bill," he said again. "But you've had all the money you're going to get out of me. My solicitor warned me against——"

"Oh, damn your solicitor!" Saeton shouted. "Can't you understand that in two months' time——" He didn't finish. He had seen the obstinate look in Randall's eyes and he turned away in disgust. His hand reached out and switched off the engine. The din gradually died away. Saeton's hand tightened on the boss where the propellor would be fitted as he turned slowly and faced Reinbaum. "So it comes to this— we're dealing direct with you, Mr. Reinbaum. Is that correct?" His voice was quiet and controlled.

Reinbaum beamed and bowed slightly.

"What are your terms for allowing us to continue with the fitting out of the plane?"

Reinbaum shook his head. "I'm sorry, Mr. Saeton. I do not speculate."

"I've given you some idea of what we're doing here," Saeton said. "Surely we can come to some arrangement?"

"The offer I have for your plane and the equipment here is conditional on acceptance within forty-eight hours." Reinbaum spread his hands in a little apologetic gesture. "Unless you can pay what is due on the mortgages I must foreclose."

"You know damn well we can't pay. In two months——"

"I want the money now, Mr. Saeton." The softness was leaving Reinbaum's voice.

"But if you wait two months . . ." Saeton's voice was desperate. "Two months isn't long. In two months' time I'll have all the backing——"

"I repeat, if you cannot pay what is due, then——" Reinbaum shrugged his shoulders.

Saeton turned away and in the light from the high windows I caught a glint of tears in his eyes. He went slowly over to the bench and stood there, fiddling with the armature he'd spent so many laborious hours winding, his back towards us.

"Well, I think that is settled then," Reinbaum said, glancing up at Randall, whose face was stiff and wooden. "We had better go now, Major."

In a flash I saw my refuge up here on this aerodrome disappearing. But it wasn't only that. I believed in Saeton. I wanted to see these engines in the air. The money I had made ferrying planes and on currency deals wasn't honest money. I didn't care what happened to it. Probably it would be better if I threw it away and I might as well throw it away on this. "Just a moment," I said as Reinbaum and Randall were turning away. "Is it one of the mortgages that has fallen due?"

Randall shook his head. "No. It's the interest on them."

"The interest on them?" I exclaimed. "How much?"

"Eleven hundred and fifty," Randall murmured.

I turned to Saeton. "Can't you raise that?" I said. "You could sell something."

He shook his head. "There's nothing here that isn't essential," he said dully. "If we sold any part of the equipment we couldn't go on. Besides, it's all mortgaged. Everything in this hangar is mortgaged."

"But surely you've got some money of your own?" I persisted.

"Blast you!" he shouted, swinging round on me. "You don't have to hammer the truth of this home to me. I don't possess any money at all. For the past month we've lived on credit. My bank account is overdrawn to the tune of more than a hundred pounds. Carter is in the same boat. And don't for God's sake start asking me if I haven't any friends. I haven't any friends to the tune of eleven hundred quid." He turned to Randall and Reinbaum. "Now get the hell out of here, the pair of you. Take what action you like."

They turned to go.

"Just a minute," I called to them. "The amount is eleven hundred and fifty?"

It was Reinbaum who answered. "The exact amount is eleven hundred and fifty-two pounds four shillings and sevenpence."

"Then perhaps you would make me out a receipt," I said. I had got my wallet out and was extracting my cheque book.

He stood there staring at me as though a pit had suddenly opened at his feet. "A receipt, please, Mr. Reinbaum," I repeated.

He came slowly towards me. "How do I know that your cheque will be honoured? I do not give a receipt——"

"You have the law to protect you in a case like that," I said. "Can I see the documents proving that you are the legal possessor of these mortgages?" I was enjoying myself, enjoying the sudden surprised silence that descended on the hangar. Nobody spoke, and Reinbaum stared at me with baffled eyes. For some reason he didn't want to be paid. I thought of how I had got that money and I was suddenly glad I'd ferried those planes. Somehow this made the racket worth while.

Saeton was the first to come to life. "Just a minute, Fraser. Apart from the fact that I can't allow you to do this, it won't help you know. We owe money. Also we've got to be carried for two months."

"I realise that," I said. "What's the absolute minimum that will carry you to the flying stage?"

He hesitated. "About another thousand." His voice suddenly took on new life. "You see, we've got the metal and the castings. We've got everything. All we need is to cover some of the bills that'll come in and our living——" His sudden excitement faded and his words stopped. "To carry us and pay the interest on these mortgages you've got to have nearly two thousand five hundred."

I sat down and wrote out Reinbaum's cheque. "Who shall I make it out to?" I asked him.

"Weiner, Reinbaum and Company," he answered sullenly.

As I entered the amount on the cheque counterfoil Saeton touched my shoulder. "Have you really got two thousand five hundred in your account?" he asked almost unbelievingly.

"Not in my account," I answered. "But with my life policy I'm good for that much."

He didn't say anything, but his hand gripped my shoulder for a moment.

I checked the documents Reinbaum reluctantly produced from his brief-case. Then I gave him the cheque and got his receipt. All this time Saeton had been standing over us and as the little man straightened up, he said, "It was the engines you wanted, wasn't it, Reinbaum?" There was a dangerous quietness about his voice.

"I do not want anything," Reinbaum answered him. "Only the moneys." But I don't think he expected Saeton to believe him, for he added quickly, "My clients are interested in the charter business."

"And who exactly are your clients?" Saeton asked in the same quiet voice.

"I am sorry. I cannot tell you that."

Saeton took him gently by the collar. "It was the engines they wanted, wasn't it?" Somebody tipped them off that you held the mortgages." He turned to Randall. "Had you borrowed on these mortgages when you were down here last, in October?" he asked.

"I'm not sure," Randall answered unwillingly. "Possibly."

"Did you mention it to anyone—Else, for instance?"

Randall flushed. "I may have done. I can't remember. I——"

"You tell a stray D.P. and you don't tell me." Saeton's face was white with anger. "And you're a director of my company. My God!" He picked little Reinbaum up by his collar with his two hands and shook him. "Who are these clients of yours?" he shouted, and I thought he'd break the little man apart.

Reinbaum's spectacles fell to the ground. His plump white hand moved agitatedly with a flash of gold. "Please," he cried. " I will have the police——"

" Oh, no you won't." Saeton laughed through his clenched teeth. "You've no friends here. They'll swear I never laid a finger on you. Now, then. Who are your clients?" He shook the man till he screamed and then he flung him away like a discarded sack. Reinbaum stumbled, caught his foot against a stool and went sprawling on to the dusty concrete. " Well?" Saeton demanded, standing over him.

The man was fumbling blindly for his glasses. Saeton kicked them over to him and then picked up the brief-case, searching through it, strewing the papers he discarded over the floor. He found what he wanted in the end, holding it up, his eyes darkening with anger as he read it. " My God!" he exclaimed. " So that's it." He stuffed the letter into the pocket of his jacket and stared down at Reinbaum. " How did they discover I'd got the prototype?" he demanded. " How did they know that?" He turned away as Reinbaum shook his head obstinately. " All right. It doesn't matter." He tossed the brief-case and the rest of the papers on to the man's prostrate body. " Now, get out!"

Reinbaum seized hold of the case, bundled the documents into it and fled.

" Well, that's that," Saeton said. He was standing there in the centre of the hangar like a bull that has disposed of one matador and is glaring round in search of the next. His gaze fixed on Randall. " Do you realise what you've done? You bloody nearly——" His mouth clamped shut and he came steadily down the hanger. " You're not fit to be a director of a company." He stopped and Randall muttered inarticulate apologies. " Sit down," Saeton said, his voice shaking with anger. " Now write me out a letter of resignation."

" Suppose I refuse to resign?" Randall's face was pale and though his head was turned towards Saeton his eyes slid away from him.

" Refuse to resign!" There were white patches under Saeton's eyes. " Whilst we've been slaving our guts out up here to build something worth while, what have you been doing? Gambling. Gambling with the future of my company. Well, Carter and I aren't working twenty-four hours a day to make a fortune for a man who has never done a thing to help us, who——"

"That's not true," Randall answered. "Who brought the thing out of Germany in the first place? You'd never have got it back here unless I'd smuggled it out in one of my vehicles. Who's paid for all the development work? Every time you've asked for money——"

"It's all covered by those mortgages," Saeton cut in, his voice suddenly quiet. "You've never risked a penny, whilst Carter and I have sunk everything we had without security. The company owes you nothing, except a fee for smuggling the prototype out, and I'll see you're paid for that. As for the mortgages, it's not my fault you've borrowed on them and gambled away the proceeds." He paused for breath. "You've only yourself to blame, Dick," he added, almost gently. He pulled a pen out of his pocket and pushed it into Randall's hand. "I suggest ' pressure of other business.' "

Randall hesitated. But Saeton was standing over him and there was something compelling in the quietness of the man, the whiteness of his face. Randall glanced up once and then the pen was scratching at the paper Carter had thrust in front of him.

As soon as Randall had signed it, Saeton took it from him, glanced at it quickly and then slipped it into his pocket. "And now for God's sake get Reinbaum off the airfield before I murder the little bastard."

Randall stood up, hesitating as he faced us. I thought for a moment he was going to say something, but the hostile silence was too much for him. He turned away and we watched him go, heard the door click shut, and then we were alone in the hangar. Saeton pulled out his handkerchief and mopped his face. "Christ!" he said. "I didn't expect to come out of that with the company still intact." His gaze came round to me. "About the luckiest thing I ever did was to tell you you could stay on up here." He rubbed his hands and his voice was suddenly cheerful as he said, "Well, that leaves us short of the necessary three directors, Tubby. I suggest, therefore, as an acknowledgment of our gratitude to him for saving the company in its hours of need, we invite

Mr. Fraser to join the board." Relief had brought a hint of laughter to his voice. " Will you second that, Tubby?"

Carter glanced quickly across at me. I was conscious of a fractional hesitation, and then he said, " Yes. I second that."

Saeton came over and clapped me on the shoulder. " You're now a director of Saeton Aircraft Ltd., entitled to a yearly salary of £2,500." He gave a quick laugh. " It's never been paid yet." And then he added, " But some day—soon now——" He stopped. His voice had become serious. " Fraser, I can't thank you enough. God knows why you did it, but "—he gripped my hand—" I can't tell you——" His voice broke off as though the words he sought were inadequate and he just stood there, wringing my hand. " Why did you do it, eh? Why?" He was suddenly laughing. " I can't forget little Reinbaum's face when you asked him for that receipt." He laughed till the tears ran down his face. Then, with a quick change to brusqueness: " Well, why did you do it?"

" I don't quite know," I answered awkwardly. " I wanted to, that's all." I turned away, embarrassed by the sudden emotionalism in his voice.

There was a moment's silence, and then he said abruptly, " Well, let's get back to work." The sense of purpose was back in his eyes now and it gave me an odd feeling of closeness to him as I went over to my lathe and picked up the half-completed piston.

But somehow I couldn't concentrate. Randall's words came between me and my work. I'd been caught out in a racket once and I didn't want any more of it. If they were smuggling foreign patents. . . .

I switched off the lathe and went over to Saeton. He was seated on a stool, working on the armature again with the fierce concentration of a man who holds the future in his hands. He looked up at me as I stood over him. " Well, what is it?" he asked impatiently.

" I want all the cards on the table," I said. " I don't like working in the dark—not any more."

He stared at me, his jaw clamped shut, an angry frown creasing his forehead. I watched the thick hand resting on the bench slowly clench into a fist. His eyes had hardened and narrowed with the clenching of his hand. I was looking at the man who had hit me two nights ago in the woods on the edge of the airfield. " Well?"

I hesitated. But I had to know where I stood. The hours I had spent working at that lathe had given me a new sense of confidence in myself. " Come on, man, let's have it," he snapped. " What's on your mind?"

" This aero engine of yours "—I nodded to the gleaming bulk standing against the wall on its wooden chocks—" you didn't design it, did you."

" So that's it. You think I've filched somebody else's design, do you?"

" I didn't say that," I answered, feeling suddenly uncertain under the cold anger of his gaze. " I simply want to know whether you designed it?"

" Of course I didn't design it," he snapped. " You're not a fool. You know damn well I don't know enough about engineering to design an aero engine." He had risen slowly to his feet and was standing in what seemed to be a characteristic attitude, legs slightly straddled, head thrust forward. " I suppose, now you've bought your way into the thing, you think you're entitled to throw your weight about." The violence died out of him and in a milder tone he added, " If you must know, it's a bit of wartime loot. One day I'll tell you the whole story. But not now."

" Who owns the patent?" I asked.

" I do," he snapped. " The prototype was never completed. For a man in your position, you've a devilish sensitive conscience." He sat down abruptly. " For God's sake let's get on. We've wasted enough time already."

I had barely got back to my lathe when there was a knock at the door of the hangar. " See who it is, Fraser," Saeton said. " If it's Randall I won't talk to him."

But it wasn't Randall. It was Diana, and with her was a girl in a faded brown smock. I knew her at once. She was the girl who had been talking with Saeton in the hangar that first night I had come to Membury. She had recognised me, too, for she caught her breath and stared at me as though I were something unexpected, and her broad forehead contracted in a frown that gave her pleasant, quiet features a brooding look.

" She wants to see Bill," Diana said.

I pulled open the door and they came in, the girl hesitating over the sill as though she feared a trap. Then she was walking down the hangar, her head erect, her shoulders squared.

Saeton looked up, saw her and jumped to his feet. " What the devil are you doing here?" His thick eyebrows were dragged down, his body tense.

The girl didn't flinch. Her eyes roved quickly along the bench. They were wide, intelligent eyes, and they seemed to miss nothing. Finally they came to rest on the completed engine and their expression seemed to change, to soften.

" Did you bring her here, Diana?" Saeton's voice was harsh.

" Yes. She wanted to see you."

" I don't care who she wanted to see," he stormed. " Get her out of here." He got control of himself and turned to me. " Take her outside and find out what she wants. I won't have people walking in and out of this place as though it were a railway station." But almost immediately he changed his mind. " All right. I'll talk to her." He strode down the hangar. The girl hesitated, her eyes lingering a moment on the litter of the work bench, then she turned and followed him.

" That's a queer girl," Diana said to her husband. " When Randall was here she hung around the quarters like a cat on hot bricks. After a time she went out on to the airfield, and the next I saw of her she came flying through the woods, her face white and her eyes wet with tears. Had she been in a concentration camp or something?"

" Her father died in one," Carter answered. " That's all I know."

Saeton came back then, his face angry, the muscles at the side of his jaw swollen with the clenching of his teeth.

" What did she want?" Diana asked.

He didn't appear to hear her question. He strode straight past her and seated himself at the bench again. " Will you bring lunch for the three of us up here at one-thirty," he said.

Diana hesitated. But his manner didn't encourage questions. " All right," she said and left the hanger. I turned back to my lathe, but all the time I was trying to remember the scrap of conversation I'd overheard that night in the hangar.

Twice I glanced at Saeton, but each time his expression stopped me from putting the question that was on the tip of my tongue. At length I said, " Who is that girl?"

His head jerked up. " That was Else," he said.

" What was her father's work?"

His fist crashed down on the bench. " You ask too many damned questions," he shouted.

I felt the shock of his violence as though it was a physical blow and went quickly over to the lathe. But a moment later he was at my side. " I'm sorry, Neil," he said quietly. " Don't worry if I lose my temper now and then." His hand reached out and gripped my arm and he waved his free hand to the litter of parts on the bench. " I feel sometimes as though these were my organs and I was being slowly manufactured and pieced together. If anything happened to prevent the completion of the whole thing——" He didn't finish and the grip on my arm slowly relaxed. " I'm a bit tired, that's all. It'll be like this until we're in the air."


## CHAPTER THREE

TIME stood still for me on Membury aerodrome in the weeks that followed. November slid into December and I scarcely noticed it. We rose at six and started work at seven. There was coffee around eleven and we had our lunch and our tea at the work bench. Breakfast and dinner were the only meals we had back at the quarters, dinner anywhere between seven-thirty and nine according to how the work ran. Tempers were short and the working hours long, and though Diana Carter talked about Prince Charles and the fighting in Palestine and the opening of Tegel airport, it meant nothing to me, for I didn't read the papers. My life was the cold, grey cavern of the hangar ; I lived and dreamed engineering and the world outside Membury ceased to exist.

And yet through it all ran a thread of pure excitement. Saeton never gave me a briefing on the engines. He left me to find out for myself and as the Satan Mark II, which was what he called it, took shape under our hands, my sense of excitement mounted.

The difference lay mainly in the system of ignition and the method of fuel injection. High pressure injectors delivered filtered fuel to the combustion chambers. Injector timing replaced ignition timing and there was a complicated system for metering the fuel, the flow having to be adjusted constantly in relation to altitude. It was essentially a compression ignition motor and though it was a long way removed from the diesel design, it was soon clear to me that the man who had made the original design must have been a diesel expert.

It took us just over five weeks to build that second engine and all the time it was a race—our skill against my bank balance, with the airlift date looming ever nearer.

It was a queer life, the four of us alone up on that derelict airfield, held there by Saeton's tenacity and the gradual emergence of that second engine. I got to know Tubby Carter and his wife well, and they were as different as two people could be. Maybe that was why they had got married. I don't know. They were an oddly assorted pair.

Tubby was a stolid, unimaginative man, round of face and round of figure with rolls of fat across his stomach and sides that gave him the appearance of a man-sized cupid when stripped. His nature was happy and friendly. He was one of the nicest men I have ever met, and one of the most uninteresting. Outside of flying and engineering, he knew nothing of the world, accepting it and ignoring it so long as it let him get on with his job. What had caused this unenterprising son of a Lancashire poultry farmer to take to flying I never discovered. He had started in a blacksmith's shop and when that closed down he had got a job in a foundry producing farm equipment. He was one of those men who shift along on the tide of life and the tide had drifted him into a motor factory and so into the engineering side of the aircraft industry. That he had started to fly because he wanted to would have been quite out of character. I imagine it just happened that way and his stolidity would have made him an ideal flight engineer in any bomber crew.

When I think of Tubby, it is of a happy child, whistling gently between his teeth. He was like a fat, cheerful mongrel, something of a cross between airedale and pug. His eyes were brown and affectionate and if he'd had a tail it would have wagged every time anybody spoke to him. But when I think of him as a man, then it is only his hands I remember. His hands were long and slender, and quite hairless like the rest of him—very different from Saeton's hands. Give those hands a piece of metal and ask them to produce something out of it and he grew to man's stature in an instant, all his being concentrated in his fingers, his face wreathed in a smile that crinkled his eyes, and his short, fat lips pursed as he whistled endlessly at the work. He was a born engineer, and though he was a child in other respects, he had a streak of obstinacy that took the place of initiative. Once he had been persuaded on a course of action, nothing would deflect him. It was this tenacity that made one respect as well as like him.

His wife was so different it was almost unbelievable. Her father had been a railroad construction engineer. He had been killed when she was seventeen, crushed by a breakdown crane toppling on its side. In those seventeen years she had travelled most of America and had acquired a restless taste for movement and the atmosphere of the construction camps. Her mother, who had been half-Italian, had died in childbirth and Diana had been brought up in a masculine world. She had many of a man's qualities—a decisiveness, the need of a goal to aim for and a desire for strong leadership. She was also a woman, with a good deal of the hot passion of the Italian.

After her father's death she became a nurse. And when Pearl Harbour came she was one of the first to volunteer for overseas service. She had come to England as a Waac in 1943 and had been stationed at a B17 station near Exeter. That was where she had met Tubby. They had met again in France and had been married at Rouen in 1945. Later she had worked for a short time in the Malcolm Club Organisation, whilst Tubby was flying with Transport Command.

I have said that she was a hard, experienced-looking woman. Certainly that was my first impression. But then I had expected somebody altogether younger and softer. She was several years older than Tubby and her life had not been an easy one. Her brother had been working for the Opel people in Germany, and with no family and no friends, she had been very much on her own in the big hospital in New York. She would never talk about this period. She had endless stories to tell of the railroad camps and of her service life in Britain, France and Germany. But I never heard her talk of her life in that New York hospital.

Tubby she treated rather as a child. I learned later that she had had an operation that had made it impossible for her to have any children of her own. Whether this had anything to do with it, I don't know. But I do know this, that right from the start she was fascinated by Saeton. She breathed in the atmosphere of drive and urgency that he created as though it were life itself. I had a feeling that in him she found all the excitement of her girlhood again, as though he recreated for her the life she had led with her father on the railroads of America.

But though I got to know these two well, Saeton himself remained a mystery. What his background was I never discovered. It was as though he had sprung like a phoenix from the flames of war complete with his looted engine and the burning dream of a freighter fleet tramping the airways of the world. He'd talk and he'd conjure visions, but he never talked about himself. He had been a test pilot before the war. He knew South America, particularly Brazil, and he'd flown for an oil company in Venezuela. He'd done some gold prospecting in South Africa. But as to who his family were, what they did and where he'd been born and brought up, I still have no idea. Nor have I any knowledge of how he came to be a pilot.

He was the sort of person that you accept as a finished article. His personality was sufficient in itself. I felt no urge to rummage around the backstairs of his life. He seemed to have no existence outside of the engines. He even slept with them after that scene with Randall as though he were afraid an attempt might be made to steal them. When he had warned me that his temper would be short until we were in the air, it was no understatement. His moods were violent and when nervous or excited he used his tongue like a battering ram. I remember the day after I had promised to finance the company he came up to me as I was working at the lathe. " I think you agreed to cover us over the building period." His voice was angry, almost belligerent. " I want some money."

I began to apologise for not having settled the financial details with him before, but he cut me short: " I don't want your apologies. I want a cheque." The rudeness of his tone jolted me. But it was typical of the man, and if I expected deference on account of my financial standing in the company he made it clear I wasn't going to get it.

He wanted the money right away to meet some bills and I had to go back to the quarters for my cheque book. That was how I first came into real contact with Else, the fifth character in this extraordinary story. She was standing at the entrance to the quarters, calling for Diana.

" She's just taken coffee up to the hangar," I said.

The girl turned at the sound of my voice. She wore the same brown overall that she'd worn the previous day when Diana had brought her to the hangar and in her hands she

held four very still but sharp-eyed fowls. " I have bring these,"
she said, making a slight movement of her hands that caused
the one cockerel to beat his wings angrily.

" I didn't know we were having a feast to-night," I said.

" No, no. Mrs. Carter starts to keep chicken for you, I
think." The girl's voice, with its marked foreign accent, was
like a breath of the old life, a reminder of brief meetings in
bars and hotel bedrooms that is all in the way of memories
that most pilots take out of the cities where they touch down.

" She'll be back in a minute," I said. " If you and the
chickens can wait." I started to move through the door and
then stopped and we stood there for a moment smiling at each
other, not saying anything.

" You are partners with Mr. Saeton now?" she said at last.

" Yes."

She nodded and her gaze strayed to the trees that screened
us from the hangar. Her face was rather square, the cheekbones high, the skin pale and dappled with freckles. Her
nose tipped up slightly at the end as though she'd pressed it
too often against windows as a kid. She wore no make-up
and her eyebrows were thick and fair, like the untidy mop
of her hair that blew in the wind. She turned to me slowly
and her lips parted as though she were about to say something,
but she just stood there looking up at me with a frown as
though by staring at me she could resolve some riddle that
puzzled her. Her eyebrows were dragged down at the corners
and her eyes shifted from the adhesive tape on my forehead to
meet mine with a direct, level gaze. They were the colour of
mist in a mountain valley—a soft grey.

" What were you doing up at the hangar the other night?"
I had asked the question without thinking.

Her lips moved slightly at the corners. She had a very mobile
mouth. " Perhaps I ask you why you run away, eh?"

For an instant I thought she had connected me with the
police inquiries in the nighbourhood. But then she asked,
" Are you an engineer?" and I knew it was all right.

" Yes," I said.

" And you work on the engines with Mr. Saeton?"

I nodded.

" Then perhaps we meet again, yes?" She smiled and thrust
the birds into my hands. " Will you please give these to Mrs.
Carter." She half-turned to go and then hesitated. " When

you do not know what to do with yourself, perhaps you come and talk with me. It is very lonely up here sometimes." She turned then and walked across the clearing and as I watched her disappear amongst the trees I felt excitement singing through my blood.

The story of Else Langen was a jig-saw puzzle that I had to piece together, bit by bit. I asked Saeton about her that night, but all he'd say was that she was a German D.P. "Yes, but what's her story?" I persisted. "Tubby says her father died in a concentration camp."

He nodded.

"Well?" I asked.

His eyes narrowed. "Why are you so interested in her?" he demanded. "Have you been talking to the girl?"

"I had a few words with her this morning," I admitted.

"Well, keep clear of her."

"Why?"

"Because I tell you to," he growled. "I don't trust her."

"But you had her cooking here for you."

"That was——" He stopped and his jaw stiffened. "Have some sense," he added. "The girl's German and this engine we're working on was first designed in Germany."

"Is that why you're sleeping up at the hangar now?" I asked. "Are you suggesting that the girl——"

"I'm not suggesting anything," he snapped. "I'm just telling you to keep clear of her. Or is it too much to expect you to keep your hands off a woman for five weeks?"

The sneer in his voice brought me to my feet. "If you think——"

"Oh, for God's sake, Neil. Sit down. All I'm asking you to do is not to get talking to anyone outside of the four of us here. For your sake as well as mine," he added pointedly.

I might have taken his advice if the monotony of our life hadn't got on my nerves. Perhaps monotony is the wrong word. It was the tension really. The work itself was exciting enough. But we never relaxed. The four of us were cooped up together, never leaving the aerodrome, always in the same atmosphere of pressure, always in each other's company. Within a fortnight the strain was beginning to tell. Tubby ceased to whistle at the bench and his round, cheerful face became morose, almost sulky. Diana did her best, but her chatter was hard and brittle against the solid background of long hours in the hangar. Saeton became impossible—tense and moody, flying into a rage at the slightest provocation or at nothing at all.

The atmosphere got on my nerves. I had to find some relaxation, and automatically it seemed I began thinking of Else more and more often. *It is very lonely up here sometimes.* I could see the lift of her eyebrows, the smile in her eyes and the slight spread of the corners of her mouth. *When you do not know what to do with yourself. . . .* The invitation couldn't have been plainer. I brooded over it at my work, and particularly I brooded over Diana's suggestion that the girl had been a camp-follower. Saeton hadn't denied it. In the end I asked Tubby about it. " I wasn't interested in her, if that's what you mean," he answered. " I don't go for foreign women."

" What about Saeton?" I asked.

" Bill?" He shrugged his shoulders. " I wouldn't know." And then he added almost viciously, " They all fall for him. He's got something that appeals to women."

" And she fell for him?"

" She was always around before Diana came." He glanced up at me from the fuel pump he was assembling and his eyes crinkled. " The monastic life getting you down? Well, you shouldn't have much trouble with Else. Randall used to take her out in his car when he visited us up here."

It was a warm, soft night despite a clear sky and after dinner I said I'd take a stroll. Saeton looked across at me quickly, but he said nothing and a moment later I was striding through the still dampness of the woods, my heart suddenly light with the sense of relief at escaping at last from the atmosphere of the aerodrome. A track ran from the quarters down to the road and a little farther on I found the gates of the Manor. A light shone through the trees and the gentle putter of an electric light plant sounded across the silence of the lawns. An owl flapped like a giant moth to the shelter of the trees.

I went round to the side of the house, and through an uncurtained window saw Else standing over a table rubbing salt into a large ham. Her sleeves were rolled up and her face was flushed. She was a big, well-built girl with a full bosom and wide shoulders. She looked soft and pleasant, working there in that big kitchen and I found myself tingling with the desire to touch her, to feel the warm roundness of her body under my hands. I stood there for quite a while, watching her, liking the capable movements of her hands and the glowing concentration of her features. At length I moved to the door and knocked.

She smiled when she saw who it was. "So! You have become bored, eh?"

"I thought you might like to come for a walk," I said. "It's a warm night."

"A walk?" She looked up at me quickly. "Yes. Why not? Come into the kitchen whilst I go and dress myself in some clothes."

It was a big kitchen, warm and friendly, with bacon hanging from hooks in the ceiling and bunches of dried herbs and a smell of chicken. "You like cream?" She produced a bowl full of thick cream, a loaf of bread and some home-made jam. "Help yourself, please. I will be one minute, that is all."

I hadn't tasted cream in years and I was still eating when she returned. "You like to take some back with you? Mrs. Ellwood will not mind. She is a very 'ospitable woman."

"No. No thanks." I should have to explain to Saeton where it had come from.

She looked at me with a slight frown, but she made no comment. "Come. I take you to the pond. It is very funny there at night. The frogs croak and there are many wild things."

We went round behind the outbuildings, through the farmyard and out into a grass field. "There are mushrooms here in the autumn. What is your name?"

"Neil Fraser."

"Do you like working at the airfield?"

"Yes." I spoke without thinking, conscious only of her nearness and of the fact that she hadn't hesitated to come out with me.

"It is going well, I hope?"

"Yes. Very well."

"When will you have finished the engines?"

I took her hand. Her fingers were warm and soft in mine. She raised no objection.

"Well?"

"I'm sorry," I said. "What was it you asked?"

"When will you finish? When do you fly?"

"I don't know," I said. "In about a month."

"So soon?" She fell silent. We were in the woods again now on a path that ran downhill. The night air rustled gently among the tall, spear-like shafts of the osiers. I tightened my grip on her hand, but she didn't seem to notice, for she asked if I were a flier and then began to talk about her brother who had been in the *Luftwaffe*.

"Where is he now?" I asked.

She was silent for a moment, and then she said, "He is dead. He was shot down over England." She glanced up at me, her face serious. "Do you think we shall ever be at peace—Germany and England?"

"We're at peace now," I answered.

"Oh, now! Now you are the victors. You occupy us with your troops. But it is not peace. There is no treaty. Germany is not permitted to join any international organisation. We cannot trade. Everything is taken from us."

I didn't say anything. I wasn't interested in a political argument. I didn't want to be reminded that she was German. I just wanted her companionship, her warmth, the feel of her close to me. The screen of osiers parted and we were looking down a steep bank to a dew pond. It was fringed with reeds and the still surface in the centre was like a plate of burnished pewter reflecting the stars. "It is beautiful here, yes?" The cry of a night bird jarred the stillness and a frog croaked. The stillness and the wintry beauty of it brought the blood hammering to my throat. I reached out and caught her by the shoulder twisting her round so that her neck lay in the curve of my arm. Then I bent and kissed her.

For a moment she was limp in my arms, her lips soft and open against mine. Then her body became rigid and her mouth tightened. She fought me off with a sudden and intense fury. For a moment we struggled, but she was strong and my passion subsided with the obstinacy of her resistance and I let her go. "You—you——" She stood there speechless, panting with the effort she had made. "Because I am German and you are English you think I should lie on my back for you? *Verfluchter Kerl! Ich hasse Sie!*" She turned, tears of anger on her face, and fled up the path. In an instant the screen of osiers had swallowed her and I was alone by the pond with the protesting croak of the frogs.

Saeton was just leaving when I got back to the quarters. "What have you been up to?" he said, looking up at me from under his shaggy eyebrows. "That cut of yours has opened up again."

I put my hand to my forehead and my fingers came away sticky with blood. Else must have scratched the scab as she fought me off. "It's nothing," I said. "A branch of a tree caught me, that's all."

He grunted and went out into the night towards the hangar. As I passed the door of the Carters' home I heard Diana say, "All right. But any time I like the Malcolm Club will . . ." I was back in the tense atmosphere of our own little world and I'd destroyed my one chance of escape. I went to bed feeling depressed and angry with myself, for Else had been right—I had treated her as though she were a piece of occupied territory to be bought for a bar of chocolate.

The next day we had visitors. Diana rang through on the field telephone. "There's an R.A.F. officer here and a Mr. Garside of the Ministry of Civil Aviation. They want to speak to Bill." I had answered the phone and I passed on the message to Saeton. He jumped to his feet as though I'd cracked a stock whip. "Tell her they're not to come up here. I'll see them over at the quarters." He searched quickly along the bench, picking up odd parts that lay amongst the junk at the back. "Tubby. Take these out the back somewhere and hide them. Go over the whole bench and see that there's nothing left of the old engine here. I'll hold them at the quarters for five or ten minutes."

"They may only have come to check over the plane prior to airworthiness tests," Tubby said.

"Maybe. But I'm taking no chances. You'd better keep in the background, Neil."

He hurried out of the hangar and Tubby searched frantically along the bench, picking up parts and stuffing them into a canvas tool bag. I stood watching him, wondering whether my identity had been discovered.

Tubby had barely returned from hiding the bag when Saeton brought the two men into the hangar. "These are my two engineers," he said. "Carter and Fraser. Tubby, this is Wing-Commander Felton, R.A.F. Intelligence, and Garside, Civil Aviation. Well, now, what exactly do you want to look at?" Saeton was forcing himself to be genial, but I could see by the way his head was hunched into his shoulders that he was angry.

"Well, if you did take it, I don't imagine you'd be fool enough to leave the prototype lying about," the R.A.F. officer said. "We'd like to have a look at the design you're working on."

"I'm sorry," Saeton said. "That's the one thing I can't allow you to do. You can have a look at the finished engine, but the design remains secret until we're in the air."

"You're not being very helpful," the Intelligence Officer said.

"Why should I be?" Saeton demanded angrily. "A German company complains that an English concern is working on a pet project of their own and immediately they have the support of our own people and you come rushing up here to investigate."

"As far as I'm concerned the Germans can stew in their own juice," Felton replied. "But they've persuaded Control Commission the matter needs investigating. My instructions come from B.A.F.O. H.Q. Garside here is acting at the direct request of Control Commission."

"Have the Rauch Motoren sent over the plans of their prototype?" Saeton asked.

"No."

"Then how can you check from my plans whether I've lifted their design?"

The Intelligence Officer glanced at his companion. "According to my information," Garside said, "they claim that the plans were looted with the prototype."

"The plans can be withdrawn."

"The designer is dead. The fools arrested him in the middle of his work for alleged complicity in the July 20 bomb plot."

"Then they've only themselves to blame," Saeton said.

"How did you know that it was the Rauch Motoren who had lodged the complaint?" the R.A.F. officer asked.

"I've admitted already that it was seeing their prototype that gave me the idea," Saeton answered. His voice was quiet. He was keeping a tight hold of himself. "The same company has already made an effort to get control of my outfit through a gentleman called Reinbaum who now holds the mortgages on the plane and equipment here." He turned and faced the two of them. "What exactly are the authorities trying to do? Do they want a German company to produce a new type of aero engine in preference to a British concern? Carter and I have worked for nearly three years on this. If we'd pinched their prototype and it was so far advanced that they were ready to go into production with it, surely we'd have been in the air now, instead of mortgaged to the hilt and still working to produce a second engine?"

The two men glanced at each other. " So long as it can't be proved that you looted the thing . . ." The R.A.F. officer shrugged his shoulders. " The trouble with Control Commission is that they think in terms of supporting the Jerries. You don't have to worry as far as I'm concerned, Saeton. Three years ago I was bombing the beggars and if you'd looted the complete article . . ." He turned to his companion. " What's your view, Garside?"

The other looked helplessly round the hangar. " Even if it was looted," he said slowly, " it would be very difficult to prove it now." He turned to Saeton. " In any case, you've done three years' work on your engines. My advice is, get it patented as soon as possible. Doubtless the Patents Office will compare your design with the German company's, if they can produce one and if they put in a claim."

" I notified Headquarters at the time I saw the Rauch Motoren prototype," Saeton said.

The R.A.F. officer nodded. " Yes, I've looked over your report. Had the devil's own job digging it out of its pigeonhole in the Air Ministry. You acted perfectly correctly as far as the authorities were concerned. You don't have to worry about that. But as Garside says—get your patents. Every day you delay, German pressure is becoming more effective." He held out his hand to Saeton. " Well, good luck!"

" You'd better come and have some coffee before you drive back," Saeton suggested and he shepherded them out of the hangar.

" Well, what's all that about, Tubby?" I asked as the door of the hangar closed behind them.

" Just that our problems won't be over even when we get into the air," he answered and went back to the bench.

Saeton was looking pleased with himself when he came back. " What I didn't tell them," he said with a grin, " is that the designs are already with the Patents Office. If the German company want to put in a claim they'll have to get busy."

" Do you think Randall had anything to do with that visit?" Tubby asked.

"Randall? Of course not. If they got hold of Randall, then there would be trouble."

At dinner that night he announced that he was going to London. "I want to have a word with Dick," he said. "Also it's time I saw the patents people."

Diana paused, with her fork half-way to her mouth. "How long will you be gone, Bill?" Her voice was tense.

"A couple of days."

"Two days!"

It's strange how you can live with people and not notice what's happening right under your nose because it happens so gradually. Tubby glanced at his wife, his face pale, his body very still. The atmosphere had suddenly become electric. In the way she had spoken she had betrayed herself. She was in love with Saeton. And Tubby knew it. Saeton knew it, too, for he didn't look at her and answered too casually: "I shall be away one night. That's all."

It was queer. Nothing of any importance had been said, and yet it was as though Diana had shouted her infatuation from the middle of the runway. She had stripped herself naked with that too interested, too tense query and her repetition of the time as though it were eternity. Silence hung over the table like a storm that has revealed itself in one lightning stab but has still to break.

Tubby's hand had clenched into a fist and I waited for the moment when he'd fling the trestle table over and round on Saeton. I'd seen men break like that during the war, sane, solid men pushed over the edge by nerves strung too taut through danger, monotony and the confined space of a small mess.

But he had that essential stolidity, that Saxon aversion for the theatrical. The scrape of his chair as he thrust it back shattered the silence. "I'm going out for a breath of air." His voice trembled slightly. That was the only indication of the angry turmoil inside him—that and his eyes, which showed bright and angry in the creases of fat. His cheeks quivered slightly as he turned from the table. He shut the door quite softly behind him and his footsteps rang on the frozen earth outside and then died away into the woods.

The three of us sat there for a moment in a stunned silence. Then Saeton said, "You'd better go and talk to him, Diana.

I don't want him walking out on me. Without him, we'd be lost."

" Can't you think of anything but your engines?" The violence of her emotion showed in her voice and in her eyes. He looked at her then. There was something in his face I couldn't fathom—a sort of bitterness, a mixture of desire and frustration. " No," he said. The one word seemed drawn out of the depths of his being.

Diana leaned quickly forward. Her face was white, her eyes very wide and she was breathing as though she were making a last desperate effort in a race. " Bill. I can't go on like this. Don't you understand——"

" I didn't ask you to come here," his voice rasped. " I didn't want you here."

" Do you think I don't know that?" She seemed to have forgotten my presence entirely. Both of them had. Their eyes were at grips with each other, face to face with something inside them that had to come out. " But I'm here. And I can't go on like this. You dominate everything. You've dominated me. I don't care how long you're away. But I can't——" She stopped then and looked at me as though aware of my presence for the first time.

I started to get to my feet, but Saeton leaned quickly forward and gripped my arm. " You stay here, Neil," he said. I think he was scared to be left alone with her. Still gripping my arm as though clutching hold of something solid and reasonable, he turned and looked at her. " Go and find Tubby," he said. His voice was suddenly cold and unemotional. " He needs you. I don't."

She stared at him, her lips trembling. She wanted to fight him, to beat at his resistance till it was down. But I think the essential truth of his words struck home, for suddenly there were tears in her eyes, tears of anger, and she turned and fled from the room. We heard the door of her room slam and it muffled the sound of her sobs.

Saeton's fingers slowly released their grip of my wrist. " Damn all women to hell!" he muttered savagely.

" Do you want her?" I had put the question without thinking.

" Of course I do," he answered, his voice tight as a violin string and trembling with his passion. " And she knows it." He gave a growl of anger and got to his feet. " But it isn't

her I want. Any woman would do. She knows that, too—
now." He was pacing up and down and I saw him feel automatically in his pocket for a cigarette. " I've been lost to the
world up here too long. God! Here I am with the future
almost within my grasp, with everything I've dreamed of
coming to the verge of reality, and it can all be thrown in
jeopardy because a woman senses my primitive need."

" You could send her away?" I suggested.

" If she goes, Tubby goes, too. Tubby loves her more than
he loves himself or his future." He turned and looked at me.
" And Diana loves him, too. This is merely——" He hesitated.
And then almost bitterly, " You know, Neil, I don't think I'm
capable of love. It isn't a word I understand. Else knew
that. I thought she'd see me through this period of monasti-
cism. But when it came to the point, she wanted something I
wasn't prepared to give her." He laughed harshly. " Diana
is different. But she's got Tubby. She's driven by nothing
more than an urge for excitement. There's that in women,
too. The constant craving for novelty, conquest. Why the
hell can't she be satisfied with what she's got already?" His
hand gripped my shoulder. " Go and find Tubby, will you,
Neil. Tell him . . . Oh, tell him what you like. But for
Christ's sake smooth him down. I can't get this engine to
the flying stage. Nor can you. He's been in it from the beginning. The prototype didn't work, you know. For months I
studied engineering, made inquiries, picked other people's
brains. I produced a modified version, flew it in an old Hurricane and crashed it. Then I found Tubby and with his genius
for improvisation we built one that worked. Go and talk to
him. He's got to stay here, for another month at any rate. If
he doesn't, you've lost your money."

I found Tubby in the hangar and I think it was then that
I first really admired him. He was quietly working away,
truing up a bearing assembly that had been giving trouble.
He stopped me before I could say anything. " Bill sent you
to talk to me, didn't he?"

I nodded.

He put the bearing down. " Tell him that I understand."
And then, more to himself than to me: " It's not his fault.
It's something Diana wants that he's got. It was there inside
her before ever she came here—a restlessness, an urge for a
change. I thought by bringing her up here——" He moved his

hand in a helpless gesture. " It'll work itself out. She ought
to have had a child, but——" He sighed. " Tell Bill it's all
right. I won't blame him so long as he gives me no cause.
It'll work itself out," he repeated. And then added quietly :
" In time."

Saeton left next morning on the old motor bike which was
their sole form of transport. And it was only after he'd gone
that I realised how much the whole tempo of the place
depended on him. Without the driving enthusiasm of his personality it all seemed flat. Tubby worked with the concentration of a man trying hard to lose himself in what he was
making. But it was a negative drive. For myself I found the
time hang slowly on the hands of my watch and I determined
to go down to the farm that evening and make it up with Else.
Somehow I hadn't been able to get her out of my mind. I
think it was her presence in the hangar with Saeton that first
night that I'd arrived at Membury that intrigued me. The
obvious explanation I had proved to be wrong. Now, suddenly, I was filled with an urgent desire to get at the truth.
Also I was lonely. I suppose any girl would have done—then.
But she was the only one available and as soon as Tubby and
I knocked off I went down to the Manor.

The kitchen curtains were drawn and when I knocked at
the door it wasn't Else who opened it. A small, grey-haired
woman stood framed against the light, a swish of silk at her
feet and the scent of jasmine clinging on the air. " I was looking for Else Langen," I explained awkwardly.

She smiled. " Else is upstairs dressing. Are you from the
aerodrome? Then you must be Mr. Fraser. Won't you come
in? I am Mrs. Ellwood." She closed the door behind me.
" You must find it very cold up at the airfield now. I really
think Mr. Saeton should get some proper heating put in. I've
told him, any time he or his friends want a little home comfort
to come over and see us. But he's always so busy." We were
in the kitchen now and she went over to the Aga cooker and
stirred vigorously at the contents of a saucepan, holding her
dressing-gown close around the silk of her dress. " Have you
had dinner, Mr. Fraser?"

" No. We have it later——"

" Then why not stay and have some food with us? It's
only stew, but——" She hesitated. " I'm cook to-night. You
see, we're going to the Red Cross dance at Marlborough. It's

for Else, really. Poor child, she's hardly been anywhere since she came to us. Of course, she's what they call a D.P. and she's here as a domestic servant—why do they call them D.P.s? —it's so depressing. But whether she's a servant or not, I don't think it right to keep a young thing shut away here without any life. You people at the aerodrome are no help. We never see anything of you. And it is lonely up here. What do you think of Else? Don't you think she's pretty, Mr. Fraser?"

" I think she's very pretty," I murmured.

She cocked an eye at me. She was like a little grey-haired sparrow and I had a feeling that she missed nothing. " Are you doing anything to-night, Mr. Fraser?"

" No, I was just going to——"

" Then will you do something for me? Will you come to this dance with us? It would be a great kindness. You see, I had arranged for my son, who works with the railways at Swindon, to come over, but this afternoon he rang up to say he had to go to London. I wouldn't mind if it were an English girl. But you know what country places are. And after all "— she lowered her voice—" she is German. It would be a kindness."

" But I've no clothes," I murmured.

" Oh!" She waved the spoon at me like a little fairy god-mother changing me into evening clothes on the spot. " That's all right, I'm certain. You're just about my son's size. Come along and we'll see."

And of course the clothes fitted. It was that sort of a night. By the time I had changed the three of them were assembled in the big lounge hall. Colonel Ellwood was pouring drinks from a decanter that sparkled in the firelight. He was a tall, very erect man with grey hair and a long, serious face. His wife fluttered about with a rustle of silk. And Else sat in a big winged-chair staring into the fire. She was dressed in very deep blue and her face and shoulders were like marble. She looked lonely and a little frightened. She didn't look up as I came in. She seemed remote, shut away in a world of her own. Only when Mrs. Ellwood called to her did she turn her head. " I think you know Mr. Fraser." She saw me then and her eyes widened. For an awful moment I thought she was going to run from the room, but then she said, " Good-evening," in a cold, distant voice and turned back to the fire.

She hardly said a word all through dinner and when we

were together in the back of the car she drew away from me and sat huddled in her corner, her face a white blur in the reflected light of the headlights. Not until we were dancing together in the warmth of the ballroom did she break that frigid silence and then I think it was only her sense of loneliness in that alien gathering that made her say, " Why did you come?"

" I was lonely," I said.

" Lonely?" She looked up at me then. " You have your—friends."

" I happen to work there—that's all," I said.

" But they are your friends."

" Three weeks ago I had never met any of them."

She stared at me. " But you are a partner. You put up money." She hesitated. " Why do you come here if you do not know them?"

" It's a long story," I answered and holding her close in the swing of the music I suddenly found myself wanting to tell her. But instead I said, " Else. I want to apologise for the other night. I thought——" I didn't know how to put it, so I said, " That first night I came to Membury—why were you in the hangar with Saeton?"

Her grey eyes lifted to my face and then to the cut on my forehead. " That also is a long story," she said slowly. And then in a more friendly tone: " You are a strange person."

" Why did Saeton think I was a friend of yours that night?" I asked. " Why did he call to me in German?"

She didn't answer for a moment and I thought she was going to ignore the question. But at length she said, " Perhaps I tell you some day." We danced in silence for a time. I have said that she was a big girl, but she was incredibly light on her feet. She was like thistledown in my arms and yet I could feel the warm strength of her under my hand. The warmth and the music were going to my head, banishing loneliness and the tension of the past weeks. " Why did you come to the farm to-night?" she asked suddenly.

" To see you," I answered.

" To apologise?" She was smiling for the first time. " You did not have to."

" I told you—I was lonely."

" Lonely!" Her face seemed to harden. " You do not know what that word means. Please, I would like a drink." The music had stopped and I took her over to the bar. "Well, here is to the success of those engines!" Her tone was light, but as she drank her eyes were watching me and they did not smile. "Why do you not drink? You are not so crazy about those engines as Mr. Saeton, eh?" She used the word crazy in its real sense.

"No," I said.

She nodded. "Of course not. For him they are a part of his nature now—a great millstone round his neck." She hesitated and then said, "Everyone makes for himself on this earth some particular hell of his own. With Saeton it is these engines, *ja*?" She looked up into my face again. "When are they finished—when do you fly them?"

I hesitated, but there was no reason why she shouldn't know. Living so close at the Manor she would see us in the air. "With luck we'll be in the air by Christmas. Airworthiness tests are fixed for the first week in January."

"So!" A sudden mood of excitement showed in her eyes. "Then you go on to the air bridge. I hope your friend Saeton is happy then." Her voice trembled slightly. She was suddenly tense and the excitement in her eyes had changed to bitterness.

"Why are you so interested in Saeton?" I asked her.

"Interested—in Saeton?" She seemed surprised, almost shocked.

"Are you in love with him?" I asked.

Her face hardened and she bit at her lower lip. "What has he been saying?"

"Nothing," I answered.

"Then why do you ask me if I am in love with him? How can I be in love with a man I hate, a man who has——" She stopped short, staring at me angrily. "Oh!" she exclaimed. "You are so stupid. You do not understand nothing—nothing." Her fingers were white against the stem of the glass as she sought for words.

"Why do you say you hate him?" I asked.

"Why? Because I offer him the only thing I have left to offer—because I crawl to him like a dog——" Her face was suddenly white with anger. "He only laugh. He laugh in my face, I tell you, as though I am a common—*nutte*." She spat the word out as though she were hating herself as well as Saeton. "And then that Carter woman comes. He is a

C

devil," she whispered and then turned quickly away from me and stared miserably at the crowded bar. "You talk of loneliness! That is what it is to be lonely. Here, with all these people. To be away from one's own people, a stranger in a——"

"You think I don't understand," I said gently. "I was eighteen months in a prison camp in Germany."

"That is not the same thing. There you are still with your own peoples."

"Not after I escaped. For three weeks I was alone in Germany, on the run."

She stared up at me and gave a little sigh. "Then perhaps you do understand. But you are not alone here."

I hesitated, and then I said, "More alone than I have ever been."

"More alone than——" She stopped and gazed at me unbelievingly. "But why is that?"

I took her arm and guided her to a seat. I had to tell her now. I had to tell someone and she was a German, alone in England—my story was safe with her. I told her the whole thing, sitting there in an alcove near a roaring fire with the sound of dance music in my ears. When I had finished she put her hand on mine. "Why did you tell me?"

I shrugged my shoulders. I didn't know myself. "Let's dance," I said.

We didn't talk much after that. We just seemed to lose ourselves in the music. And then Mrs. Ellwood came and said we must go as her husband had to start work early the next morning. In the car going back Else didn't talk, but she no longer shrank into her corner of the seat. Her shoulder leant against mine and when I closed my hand over hers she didn't withdraw. "Why are you so silent?" I asked.

"I am thinking of Germany and what fun we could have had there—in the old days. Do you know Weisbaden?"

"Only from the air," I answered and then wished I had not said that as I saw her lips tighten.

"Yes, of course—from the air." She took her hand away and seemed to withdraw into herself. She didn't speak again until the car was climbing the hill to Membury, and then she said very quietly, "Do not come to see me again, Neil."

"Of course I shall," I said.

"No." She said it almost violently, her eyes staring at me

out of the darkness. Her hand gripped mine. "Please try to understand. We are like two people who have caught sight of each other for a moment through a crack in the wall that separates us. Whatever the S.S. do to my father, I am still a German. I must hold fast to that, because it is all I have left now. I am German, you are English, and also you are work- ing——" She stopped and her grip on my hand tightened. "I like you too much. Do not to come again, please. It is better so."

I didn't know what to say. And then the car stopped. We were at the track leading up to the quarters. "You can return the clothes in the morning," Mrs. Ellwood said. I got out and thanked them for the evening. As I was about to shut the car door, Else leaned forward. "In England do you not kiss your partners good-night?" Her face was a pale circle in the darkness, her eyes wide. I bent to kiss her cheek, but found her lips instead. "Good-bye," she whispered.

The Ellwoods were chuckling happily as they drove off. I stood watching until the red tail-light had turned into the Manor drive and then I went up the track to the quarters, wondering about Else.

It was to be nearly three weeks before I saw Else again, for Saeton returned the following evening with the news that the Air Ministry now wanted the plane on the airlift by the 10th January, and airworthiness tests had been fixed for 1st January.

In the days that followed I plumbed the depths of physical exhaustion. I had neither the time nor the energy for any- thing else. And it went on, day after day, one week dragging into the next with no let-up, no pause. Saeton didn't drive. He led. He did as long as we did at the bench, then he went back to the hangar, typing letters far into the night, ordering things, staving off creditors, running the whole of the business side of the company. My admiration for the man was bound- less, but somehow I had no sympathy for him. I could admire him, but I couldn't like him. He was inhuman, as impersonal as the mechanism we pieced together. He drove us with the sure touch of a coachman who knew just how to get the last ounce out of his horses, but didn't care a damn what happened to them in the end so long as he made the next stage on time.

But it was exciting. And it was that sense of excitement that carried me through to Christmas. The airfield hardened to iron as the cold gripped it. The runways gleamed white with frost in the sunshine on fine days. But mostly it was grey and cold with the ploughed-up earth black and ringing hard and metallic like solidified lava. There was no heating in the hangar. It had the chill dank smell of a tomb. Only the work kept us warm as we lathered ourselves daily into a sweat of exhaustion.

Saeton was working for engine completion on December 20, installation by December 23 and first test on Christmas Day. It was a tight schedule, but he wanted a clear week for tests. But though we worked far on into the night, we were behind schedule all the time and it was not until Christmas Eve that we completed that second engine.

The final adjustments were made at eight-thirty in the evening. We were dead beat and we stood in front of the gleaming mass of metal in a sort of daze. None of us said a word. We just stood back and looked at it. I produced a packet of cigarettes and tossed one to Saeton. He lit it and drew the smoke into his lungs as though smoke alone could ease the tension of his nerves. "All right, fill her up with oil, Tubby, and switch on the juice. I'll get Diana. She'd like to be in on this." He went over to the phone and rang the quarters. I helped fill up with oil. We checked that there was petrol in the wall tank, tightened the unit of the petrol feed and switched on.

There was a tense silence as we waited for Diana. Five weeks' work stood before us and a touch of the starter button would tell us whether we'd made a job of it. It wasn't like an engine coming out of a works. There everything moves with an inevitable progression from the foundry and the lathes and the electrical shop to the assembly and the final running in. This was different. Everything had been made by hand. One tiny slip in any of the precision work . . . I thought of how tired we were. It seemed incredible that everything would work smoothly.

A knock on the door of the hangar sounded incredibly loud in the silence. Tubby went to the door and let his wife in. "Well, there it is, Diana," Saeton said, pointing to the thing His voice trembled slightly. "Thought you'd like to see what your cooking has given birth to." Our laughter was uneasy, forced. "Okay, Tubby. Let her go." He turned away with a quick nervous twist of his shoulders and walked down to the far end of the bench. He wasn't going to touch that starter switch himself. He wasn't even going to watch. He stood with his back towards us, puffing at his cigarette, his hands playing aimlessly with the pieces of metal lying on the bench.

Tubby watched him, hesitating.

" Go on—start it." Saeton's voice was a rasp.

Tubby glanced at me, swallowed nervously and crossed to the starter motor which was already connected up. He pressed the switch. It groaned, overloaded with the stiffness of the metal. The groaning sound went on and on. He switched off and went over to the engine, his practised eye running over it, checking. Then he went back to the starter motor. The groaning sound was faster now, moving to a hum. There was a sharp explosion. The engine rocked. The hum of the starter took over again and then suddenly the stillness of the hangar was shattered by a roar as the motor picked up. The whole building seemed to shake. Tubby switched off, hurried to the engine and adjusted the controls. When he started it again, the roar settled to a steady, glorious hum of power, smooth and even like the dynamos of a power station.

Saeton ground out his cigarette and came back along the bench. His face was shining with sweat. " She's okay," he shouted above the din. It was part statement, part question. Tubby looked up from the controls and his fat, friendly face was creased in a happy grin and he nodded. " Carburation wants a bit of adjustment and the timing on that——"

" To hell with the adjustments," Saeton shouted. " We'll do those to-morrow. All I care about at the moment is that she goes. Now switch the damned thing off and let's go and have a drink. My God, we've earned it."

The roar died away as Tubby cut off the juice. The hangar was suddenly still again. But there was no tension in the stillness now. We were all grinning and slapping each other on the back. Tubby caught hold of his wife and hugged her. She had caught our mood of relief. Her eyes were shining and she just didn't seem able to contain her excitement. " Anybody else like a kiss?" I was nearest to her and she reached up and touched her lips to mine. Then she turned and caught hold of Saeton. She pressed her lips to his, her hands tightening on his overalls. He caught hold of her shoulders and pushed her away almost roughly. " Come on. Let's get a drink." His voice was hoarse.

Saeton had kept a bottle of whisky for this moment. "Here's to the airlift!" he said.

" To the airlift!" we echoed.

We drank it neat, talking excitedly of how we'd manage the installation, what the first test flight would show, how the plane would behave on two engines. Saeton planned to use the outboard engines for take-off only. With the extra power developed by the Satan Mark II all flying would be done on the two engines. We bridged in our excitement all the immediate problems and talked instead of how we should develop the company, what planes we should buy, what routes we should operate, whose works we should take over for mass production. In a flash the bottle was empty. Saeton wrung the last drop out of it and smashed it on the concrete floor. " That's the best bottle of Scotch I've ever had and I won't have it lying on any damned rubbish heap," he shouted. His eyes were dilated with the drink and his own excitement.

Our glasses suddenly empty, we stood around looking at them in silence. It seemed a pity to end the evening like this. Saeton apparently felt the same. " Look, Tubby," he said. " Suppose you nip on the old bike and run down into Ramsbury. Bring back a couple of bottles. Doesn't matter what it costs." He glanced at me. " Okay, Neil? It's your money." And as I nodded, he clapped my arm. " You won't regret having backed us. If you live to be as old as Methuselah you'll never make a better investment than this. More Scotch, Tubby!" He waved his arm expansively. " Get on your charger, boy, and ride like hell. This bloody dump is out of Scotch. Come on. We'll hold your stirrups for you and we'll be out to cheer you as you ride back, bottles clanking in your saddle-bags."

We were all laughing and shouting as we trooped out to the store-room where the bike was housed. Tubby roared off, his face beaming, his hand whacking at the rear of the bike as he flogged through the gears. His tail-light disappeared through the trees and we fell suddenly silent. Saeton passed his hand across his eyes. " Let's go in," he said moodily and I saw that the nerves at the corners of his eyes were twitching. He was near to breaking point. We all were. A good drunk would do us good and I suddenly thought of Else. "What about making it a party," I said. "I'll go down and see the Ellwoods." I knew they wouldn't come, but I thought Else might. Saeton tried to stop me, but I was already hurrying down the track and I ignored him.

A light was on over the front door of the farm. It looked friendly and welcoming.

Mrs. Ellwood answered my ring. "It's you, Mr. Fraser." She sounded surprised. "We thought you must have left."

"We've been very busy," I murmured.

"Come in, won't you?"

"No, thank you. I just came down to say we're having a party. I wondered if you and Colonel Ellwood could come up for a drink. And Else," I added.

Her eyes twinkled. "It's Else you're wanting, isn't it? What a pity! We've been expecting you all this time and now you come to-night. Else has had to go to London. Something about her passage. She's going back to Germany, you know."

"To Germany?"

"Yes. Oh, dear, it's all very sudden. And what we shall do without her I don't know. She's been such a help."

"When is she going?" I asked.

"In a few days' time I imagine. It was all very unexpected. Just after that dance. She got a letter to say her brother was very ill. And now there is some trouble about her papers. Do come and see her before she goes."

"Yes," I murmured. "Yes, I'll come down one evening." I backed away trying to remember if Else had said she had a second brother. "Good-night, Mrs. Ellwood. Sorry you won't join us." I heard the door close as I started back down the drive. Hell! The evening suddenly seemed flat. A feeling of violent anger swept through me. Damn the girl. Why for God's sake, couldn't she be home this evening of all evenings?

I took a short cut through the woods. I was just in sight of the quarters when I heard the snap of a twig behind me. I glanced over my shoulder and saw the figure of a man emerging out of the darkness. "Who's that?" he asked. The voice was Tubby's.

"Neil," I said. "Did you get the Scotch?"

For answer I heard the clank of bottle against bottle. "Bloody bike ran out of petrol just up the road." His voice was thick. He'd either had several at the pub or he'd opened one of the bottles. "What are you doing, looking for fairies?"

"I've just been down to the farm," I said.

"Else, eh?" He laughed and slipped his arm through mine.

We went on in silence. A lighted window showed through the trees like a homing beacon. We came out of the woods and there was the interior of the dining-room. Saeton and Diana were there, standing very close together, a bottle on the table and drinks in their hands. "I wonder where they got that?" Tubby murmured. "Come on. We'll give them a surprise."

We had almost reached the window when Diana moved. She put down her drink and moved closer to Saeton. Her hand touched his. She was talking. I could hear the murmur of her voice through the glass of the window. Tubby had stopped. Saeton took his hand away and turned towards the door. She caught hold of him, swinging him round, her head thrown back, laughing at him. The tinkle of her laughter came out to us in the cold of the night air.

Tubby moved forward. He was like a man in a dream, compelled to go to the window as though drawn there by some magnetic influence. Saeton was standing quite still, looking down at Diana, his hard, leathery face unsoftened, a muscle twitching at the corner of his mouth. Standing there in the darkness facing that lighted window it was like watching a puppet show. "All right. If you want it that way." Saeton's voice was harsh. It came to us muffled, but clear. He knocked back his drink, set down the glass and seized hold of her by the arms. She lay back in his grip, her hair hanging loose, her face turned up to him in complete abandon.

Saeton hesitated. There was a bitter set about his mouth. Then he drew her to him. Her arms closed round his neck. Her passion was to me something frightening. I was so conscious all the time of Tubby standing there beside me. It was like watching a scene from a play, feeling it through the senses of a character who had yet to come on. Saeton was fumbling at her dress, his face flushed with drink and quite violent. Then suddenly he stiffened. His hands came away from her. "That's enough, Diana," he said. "Get me another drink."

"No, Bill. It's me you want, not drink. You know you do. Why don't you——"

But he took hold of her hands and tore them from his neck. "I said get me another drink."

"Oh God! Don't you understand, darling." Her hand touched his face, stroking it, smoothing out the deep-etched lines on either side of the mouth. "You want me. You know you do."

Tubby didn't move. And I stood there, transfixed by his immobility.

Saeton's hands slowly reached out for Diana, closed on her and then gripped hold of her and hurled her from him. She hit the edge of the table and clutched at it. He took two steps forward, standing over her, his head thrust slightly forward. "You little fool!" he said. "Can't you understand you mean nothing to me. Nothing, do you hear? You're trying to come between me and something that is bigger than both of us. Well, I'm not going to have everything wrecked."

"Go on," she cried. "I know I don't rate as high as that bloody engine of yours. But you can't go to bed with an engine. And you can with me. Why don't you forget it for the moment? You know you want me. You know your whole body's crying out for——"

"Shut up!"

But she couldn't shut up. She was laughing at him, goading him. "You never were cut out for a monk. You lie awake at nights thinking about me. Don't you? And I lie awake thinking about you. Oh, Bill, why don't you——"

"Shut up!" His voice shook with violence and the veins were standing out on his forehead, hard and knotted.

Her voice dropped to a low murmur of invitation. I could no longer hear the words. But the sense was there in her face, in the way she looked at him. His hands came slowly out, searching for her. Then suddenly he straightened up. His hand opened out and he slapped her across the face—twice, once on each cheek. "I said—shut up! Now get out of here."

She had staggered back, her hand to her mouth, her face white. She looked as though she were going to cry. Saeton reached out for the bottle. "If you'd had any sense you'd have given me that drink." His voice was no longer hard. "Next time, pick somebody your own size." He tucked the bottle under his arm and turned to go. But he hesitated at the door, looking back at her. I think he was going to say something conciliatory. But when he saw the blazing fury in her eyes, his face suddenly hardened again. "If you start any trouble between me and Tubby," he said slowly, "I'll break

your neck. Do you understand?" He wrenched open the door
and disappeared.

A moment later the outer door of the quarters opened and
we were spotlighted in the sudden shaft of light. Saeton
stopped. " How long have you two been——" He slammed
the door. " I hope you enjoyed your rubbernecking. I'm going
over to the hangar." His footsteps rang on the iron-hard earth
as his figure merged into the darkness of the woods.

Neither of us moved for a moment. Utter stillness surrounded us, broken only by the muffled sound of Diana's sobs
where she lay across the table, her head buried in her hands
amongst the litter of glasses. I felt the chill glass of the bottles
as Tubby thrust them into my hands. " Take these over to the
hangar," he said in a strangled voice.

I watched him as he opened the door of the quarters and
went inside, walking slowly, almost unwillingly. I didn't move
for a moment. I seemed rooted to the spot. Then the door
of the dining-room opened and I saw him enter. I'd no desire
to stand in as audience on another painful scene. I turned
quickly and hurried through the woods after Saeton.

When I entered the hangar, Saeton was sitting on the work
bench staring at the new engine and drinking out of the bottle.
" Come in, Neil." He waved the bottle at me. " Have a
drink." His voice was slurred, almost unrecognisable. God
knows how much he'd drunk in the short time it had taken me
to get to the hangar.

I took the bottle from him. It was brandy and more than
half-empty. The liquid ran like fire down my throat and I
gasped.

" You saw the whole thing, I suppose?" he asked.

I nodded.

He laughed, a wild, unnatural sound. " What will Tubby
do?"

" I don't know," I said.

He got off the bench and began pacing up and down. " Why
did he ever let her come here? It was no place for her. She
likes plenty going on—lots of people, excitement, plenty of
noise and movement. Why don't men learn to understand
their wives? Let's forget about it." He waved his arm angrily.
" What have you got there—Scotch?" He came over and
picked up one of the bottles from the bench where I'd placed

it. " Thank God we've got some liquor, anyway." He glanced at the bottle of brandy which I still held. " Queer, a woman hiding away a bottle like that." He unscrewed the top of a whisky bottle.

" Haven't you had enough?" I suggested.

He gave me a glassy stare. " It's Christmas Eve, isn't it? And the engine is finished. I could drink a bloody vat." He raised the bottle to his lips and drank, rocking slightly back on to his heels and then forward on to his toes. " Funny, isn't it?" he muttered hoarsely, wiping his lips with the back of his hand. " You start out with the idea of celebrating and before you know where you are you're trying to drown your sorrows. Neil, old man." His free hand reached out and fastened around my shoulders. " Tell me something. Be honest with me now. I want an honest reply. Do you like me?"

I hesitated. If I'd been as drunk as he was it wouldn't have mattered. But I was comparatively sober and he knew it.

His arm slipped away from my shoulders and he staggered away from me towards the engine. He stood in front of it and addressed it. " You bastard!" he said. Then he lurched round towards me. " I haven't a friend in the world," he said and there was a frightful bitterness in his voice which caught on a sob of self-pity. " Not a friend in the whole wide world," he repeated. " Diana was right. An engine is something you create, not a living being. God damn it! I don't care. Do you hear me—I don't care. I don't give a damn for the whole human race. If they don't like me, why should I care? I don't need anything from them. I'm building something of my own. And that's all I care about, do you hear? I don't give a damn——" He turned suddenly at the sound of the hangar door opening.

It was Tubby. He came slowly down the hangar. " Give me a drink," he said.

Saeton handed him the bottle. Tubby raised it to his lips and gulped, Saeton watching him, his body tense. " Well?" he asked. And then as Tubby didn't answer he added, " For God's sake say something, can't you. What happened?"

Tubby raised his eyes and looked at Saeton. But I don't think he saw him. His hand strayed to the leather belt that supported his trousers. " I thrashed her," he said in the same flat tone. " She's packing now."

"Packing?" Saeton's voice was suddenly hard and crisp. In that moment he seemed to shake off all the effects of the drink.

"I've telephoned for a taxi."

Saeton strode over to him and caught hold of him by his jacket. "You can't walk out on me now, Tubby. In a few days we'll be making our first test flight. After all this time."

"Can't you forget about your engine for just one night?" Tubby's voice was tired. There was a sort of hopelessness about it. "I want some money, Saeton. That's what I came up to see you about."

Saeton laughed suddenly. "There isn't any money. You know that. Not until we're on the airlift." The sudden sense of domination was back in his voice and I knew that he had seen how he could keep Carter with us.

"How much do you want, Tubby?" I asked, feeling for my wallet.

Saeton rounded on me, his face heavy with anger. "If you think the two of us can get the plane into the air, you're crazy," he said. "For one thing the margin of time is too small. For another there may be alterations to make. Neither you nor I——" He turned away with a quick, angry shrug.

"How much do you want?" I asked again.

"A fiver." He came across to me and I gave him the notes. "I hate to do this, Neil, but . . ." His voice tailed away.

"Forget it," I said. "Are you sure that will be enough?"

He nodded. "It's only to get Diana to London. She'll stay with her friends. She's got a job waiting for her. It's just to see her through for a few days. She's going back to the Malcolm Club. She worked for them during the war and they've been wanting her back ever since the airlift got under way." He stuffed the money into his pocket. "She'll pay you back."

He turned to leave the hangar, but Saeton stopped him. "They employ girls at the Malcolm Club, not engineers. What are you going to do?"

Tubby looked at him. "I'm staying here," he said. "I promised I'd see you into the air and I'll keep my promise. After that——"

But Saeton wasn't listening. He came across the hangar like a man who has been reprieved. His eyes were alight with excitement, his whole face transfigured. "Then it's okay.

You're not walking out on me." He caught hold of Tubby's hand and wrung it. " Then everything's all right."

" Yes," Tubby answered, withdrawing his hand. "Everything's all right, Bill." But as he turned away I saw there were tears in his eyes.

Saeton stood for a moment, watching him go. Then he turned to me. " Come on, Neil. Let's have a drink." He seized hold of the opened bottle of Scotch. " Here's to the test flight!"

There was only room for one thing in the man's mind. With a sick feeling I turned away. " I'm going to bed," I said.

## CHAPTER FOUR

IT WASN'T until the following day that I realised how much Diana had been doing for us. It wasn't only that she'd cooked our food, made our beds, kept the place clean and neat and done all the little odd jobs that are so boring and yet are an essential part of the act of living. She'd done more than that. By her brightness, her cheerfulness—her mere presence—she had cushioned the tense exhaustion of our effort. She had provided a background for us in which we could momentarily relax and gather strength for another day's sustained effort. The place seemed flat without her.

I cooked the breakfast that morning. Tubby hadn't got back until the early hours of the morning. He looked all in when I called him. His round, friendly face was hollow and drained of all its natural cheerfulness. And Saeton looked like death when he came across from the hangar. His face was grey and the corners of his eyes twitched nervously. He was suffering from a hangover. But I think it was more than that. He was hating himself that morning. There was something inside of him that drove him on. It wasn't exactly ambition. It was something more urgent, more essentially a part of his nature—a frustrated creative urge that goaded him, and I think he'd been fighting it through the long, drunken hours of the night. He wasn't a normal human being. He was a cold, single-purposed machine. And I think that part of him was at war with his Celtic blood.

It was the grimmest Christmas I have ever had. We spent

the day in bench tests on the new engine and in getting the first engine in position in the nascelle. The hangar was equipped with overhead gear for this purpose. It had been a maintenance hangar in the days when the Americans had had the aerodrome. Without that gear I don't know how we should have done it. But no doubt Saeton had thought of that when he decided to rent the hangar. I was looking after the commissariat and though it was all canned food that I served it took time. I was thankful that we were so near the end of our work.

It wasn't only the fact that Diana had gone. There was Tubby. No set-back ever discouraged him and his cheery grin had seen me through many bad moments. But now his end of the bench was silent. He didn't whistle any more and there was no friendly grin to cheer me. He worked with stolid, urgent drive as though the work itself as well as Saeton stood between him and his wife. It was only then that I realised how much I had leaned on his good-natured optimism. He had never asked me any questions. To this day I don't know how much he knew about me. He had just accepted me and in his acceptance and in his solid ordinariness he had created an atmosphere that had made the aerodrome reality and the past somehow remote.

That was all gone now. A sense of impermanence crept into the hangar as though we were on the fringe of the outside world and I began to worry about the future, wondering whether, when we flew out of Membury, the police would get on my trail again. I suddenly found myself in dread of the outside world.

That first day after Diana's departure was hell. A tenseness brooded over us in the din of the hangar where the new engine was being run in on the bench. But on the following day Saeton had recovered from his hangover. He came down at six-thirty and got our breakfast. He didn't talk much but a quiet, steadying confidence radiated from him. I never admired him more than I did then. The following day would see the work of installation completed. He was face-to-face with the first test flight. Three years of work were concentrated on the results of that one day. The previous flying tests had resulted in the plane crashing and the man's nerves must have been stretched to the uttermost. But he never showed it. He set out to instil confidence in us and renew our interest and enthusiasm. A forced cheerfulness would have been fatal. He didn't make that mistake. He did it by the force of his personality, by implanting in us his own feelings. The mood sprang from deep within him and was natural and real. I felt as though he had stretched out his hand to lift me up to his own pitch of excitement. And Tubby felt it, too. It didn't start him whistling again at his work and there was no good-natured grin, but as we heaved on the pulley chains to jockey the second engine into position for lowering into its nascelle I suddenly realised that his heart was in it again.

We didn't knock off that night till past ten. By then the two engines were in position. All we had to do the next day was connect them up, fix the airscrews and prepare the plane for the first test. "Think she'll make it, Tubby?" Saeton asked.

"She'd better." Tubby spoke through his teeth and there was a gleam in his eyes as he stared up at the plane as though already he saw her winging into Gatow on those two engines we had sweated blood to produce.

I knew then that everything was all right. In one day Saeton had quietly and unobtrusively overlaid Tubby's bitterness with enthusiasm for the plane and an overwhelming interest in the outcome of the flight.

December 28—a Tuesday—was the last day of preparation. As the light faded out of the sky we slid back the doors of the hangar and started up the two motors. The work bench whitened under a film of cement dust kicked up by the backlash of the two props. Nobody cared. Tubby and I stood in the dust and grinned at each other as Saeton revved the motors and the whole fuselage quivered against the grip of the brakes. As the noise died down and the props slowly jerked to a standstill, Tubby gripped my arm. "By God!" he said. "They work. It's good to see something you've made running as smoothly as that. I've never built an engine from scratch before," he added.

We were building castles in the air that night as we sat over the remaining bottle of Scotch. The airlift was only our springboard. Between us we swept past the work-out into the airways of the world. Saeton's imagination knew no common bounds. He drew a picture for us of planes tramping the globe, able to cut steamer rates as well as steamer schedules, of a huge assembly line turning out freighters, of a gigantic organisation running freight to the ultimate ends of the earth. "The future

of the passenger plane lies in jets," he said. "But freight will
go to any company that can offer the lowest rates." He was
standing over us and he leaned down, his eyes shining, and
gripped the two of us by the shoulder. "It's queer. Here we
are, just three ordinary types—broke to the wide and living
on credit—and to-morrow, in the air over this derelict airfield, we shall fly the first plane of the biggest freight organisation the world has ever seen. We're going to be the most
talked-of people in the world in a few months' time. It's been
tough going up here." He grinned. "But not half as tough as
it's going to be. You'll look back on this period as a holiday
when we start to get organised."

And then, with one of those abrupt changes of mood, he sat
down. "Well, now, let's get to-morrow sorted out. To begin with
I'd rather not taxi out of the hangar. You never know, something may go wrong and she may swing. Neil. You know
the Ellwoods. Suppose you go down and arrange for them to
send one of their tractors up here. I'd like it here by eight."
He turned to Tubby. "Ground tests will take most of the
morning I expect. But I'd like to be in the air by midday.
How are we fixed for petrol? Are all the tanks full?"

Tubby shook his head. "No. Only the main tanks. They're
about two-thirds full."

"That'll do."

"What about checking over the controls?" Tubby asked.
"I'd like to run over the plane itself."

"We did it after she was flown in," Saeton said.

"Yes, I know, but I feel——"

"We haven't time, Tubby. She came in all right and we
went over her before we finally closed the purchase. If she
was all right then, she's all right now. Neil, go and fix that
tractor, will you? The sooner we get to bed the better. I want
everyone to be fresh to-morrow." He jerked back his chair
and got to his feet. "A lot depends on it." He pushed his
hand through his thick hair and grinned. "Not that I shall get
much sleep. I'm too darned excited. I haven't felt so excited
since I did my first solo. If we pull this off——" He laughed
nervously as though he were asking too much of the gods.
"Good-night." He turned quickly and went out.

I glanced at Tubby. He was tying endless knots in a piece
of string and humming a little tune. He was nervous, too.
So was I. It wasn't only the test flight. For me there was

the future. Membury had been a refuge, and now the outside world was crowding in on us. I pushed back my chair. " I'll go and arrange about the tractor," I said, but I was thinking of Else. I needed to feel that there was somebody, just one person in the world that cared what happened to me.

The Manor seemed in darkness, but I could hear the sound of the light plant and when I rang Else opened the door to me. " I was afraid you might have gone already," I said.

" I leave on Monday," she said. " You wish to come in?" She held the door open for me and I went through into the lounge where a great log blazed in the open hearth. " Colonel and Mrs. Ellwood have gone out for this evening." She turned quickly towards me. " Why have you come?"

" I wanted to arrange with Colonel Ellwood for a tractor to-morrow."

" To bring the airplane out of the hangar?"

I nodded. " We're flying tests to-morrow."

" *Das ist gut.* It will be good to see those engines in the air." Her tone was excited. " But——" She hesitated and the excitement died out of her, leaving her face blank and miserable. " But he will not be here to see." She turned back to the fire and almost automatically took a cigarette from the box on a side table and lit it. She didn't speak for a long time, just standing there, drawing the smoke into her lungs and staring into the fire. Something told me not to say anything. Silence hung between us in the flickering firelight, but there was nothing awkward about it. It was a live, warm silence. And when at length she spoke, the intimacy wasn't broken. " It has been such a long time." The words were whispered to the fire. She was not in the room. She was somewhere far away in the reaches of her memory. She turned slowly and saw me again. " Sit down, please," she said and offered me a cigarette. " You remember I ask you not to come here again?"

I nodded.

" I say that a wall separates us." She pushed back her hair with a quick, nervous gesture. " I was afraid I will talk to you because I am too much alone. Now you are here and——" She shrugged her shoulders and stared into the fire again. " Have you ever wished for something so much that nothing else matter?" She didn't seem to expect a reply and after a moment she went on. " I grew up in Berlin, in a flat in the

Fassenenstrasse. My mother was a cold, rather nervous person with a passion for music and pretty clothes. My brother Walther, was her life. She lived through him. It was as though she had no other existence. My father and his work did not mean anything to her. She knew nothing about engineering." She shifted her gaze from the fire and stared at me with a bitter smile. "I think I was never intended to be born. It just happened. My father never spoke about it, but that I think is what happen, for I was born eight years after my brother when my mother was almost forty." Her smile ceased suddenly. "I think perhaps it was a painful birth. I grew up in a world that was cold and unfriendly. I seldom saw my father. He was always working at some factory outside Berlin. When I left school I took a secretarial course and became a typist in the Klockner-Humboldt-Deutz A.G. There I fell in love with my boss." She gave a bitter laugh. "It was not difficult for him. I had not had much love. He took me away to Austria for the ski-ing and for a few months we shared a little apartment—just a bedroom really. Then he got bored and I cried myself into a nervous breakdown. That was when I first really met my father. My mother did not wish to be bothered with me, so she sent me to stay with him in Wiesbaden. This was in 1937."

Her gaze had gone back to the fire. "My father was wonderful," she went on, speaking slowly. "He had never had anyone to help him before. I looked after the flat and did all his typing. We made excursions down the Rhine and took long walks in the Black Forest. His hair was white even then, but he was still like a boy. And for my part, I became engrossed in his work. It fascinated me. I was not interested in men. I could not even bear for a man to touch me any more. I lived and breathed engineering, enjoying the exactness of it. It was something that had substance, that I could believe in. I think my father was very impressed. It was the first time he discover that women also have brains. He sent me to the University at Frankfurt where I took my engineering *staatsexamen*. After that I return to Wiesbaden to work as my father's assistant in the engine works there. That was in 1941. We were at war then and my father is engaged on something new, something revolutionary. We work on it together for three years. For us nothing else matters. Oh, I know that my father does not like the régime, that he is in touch with old friends who believe that Germany is doomed under Hitler. But apart from the air raids, it is quiet at Wiesbaden and we work at the designing board and at the bench, always on the same thing."

She threw her cigarette into the fire. Her face was very pale, her eyes almost luminous in the firelight as she turned to me. "They came when we were working in the engine shop—two officers of Himmler's S.S. They arrested him there in the middle of our work. They said he was something to do with the attempt on Hitler's life. It was a lie. He had nothing to do with the conspiracy. But he had been in contact with some of the people who were involved, so they took him away. They would not even wait for me to get him some clothes. That was on the 27th July, 1944. They took him to Dachau and I never saw him again." Her lips trembled and she turned away, stretching her hand down for another cigarette.

"What did you do?" I asked.

"Nothing. There was nothing I could do. I try to see him, of course. But it is hopeless. I can do nothing. Suddenly we have no friends. Even the company for whom he has worked for so long can do nothing. The *Herr Direktor* is very sympathetic, but he has instructions not to employ me any more. So, I go back to Berlin, and a few days later we hear my father is dead. It means little to my mother, everything to me. My world has ceased. Within a month Walther also is dead, shot down over England. They give him the Iron Cross and my mother has a breakdown and I have to nurse her. Her world also is gone. Her son, the pretty clothes, the music and the chatter all have disappeared and the Russians take Berlin. I do not think she wished to live any longer after Walther's death. She never leave her bed until she died in October of last year."

"And you looked after her all that time?" I asked, since she seemed to expect some comment.

She nodded. "I have never been so miserable. And then, when she is dead, I begin to think again about my father and his work. I go to Wiesbaden. But the designs, the experimental work is all disappeared. There is nothing left. However, the Rauch Motoren is still in business and they are willing for me to try to——" Her voice died away as though she could not find the right words.

"To try and recover the engines?" I suggested.

"*Ja.*"

"And that is why you are here at Membury?" It was so obvious now she had told me about her father, and I couldn't help but admire her pluck and tenacity.

She nodded.

"Why have you told me all this?" I asked.

She shrugged her shoulders and kicked at the big oak log, sending a shower of sparks up the chimney. "I do not know." Then she suddenly flung up her head and looked straight at me almost defiantly. "Because I am alone. Because I have always been alone since they took him away. Because you are English and do not matter to me." She was like an animal that is cornered and has turned at bay. "You had better go now. I have told you, we are on two sides of a wall."

I got slowly to my feet and went towards her. "You're very bitter, aren't you?" I said.

"Bitter?" Her eyes stared at me angrily. "Of course I am bitter. I live for one thing now. I live for the day when my father's work will be recognised, when he will be known as one of the greatest of Germany's engineers." The fire suddenly died out of her and she turned away from me. "What else have I to live for?" Her voice sounded desperately unhappy.

I reached out and put my hand on her shoulder, but she shook me off. "Leave me alone. Do not touch me." Her voice was sharp, almost hysterical. And then in a moment her mood changed and she turned towards me. "I am sorry. You cannot help. I should not have talked like this. Will you go now, please?"

I hesitated. "All right," I said. Then I held out my hand. "Good-bye, Else."

"Good-bye?" Her fingers touched mine. They were very cold despite the warmth of the fire. "Yes. I suppose it is good-bye."

"Will you give my message to Colonel Ellwood? We would like his heaviest tractor at the airfield at eight o'clock."

"I will tell him." She lifted her eyes to mine. "And you fly the test to-morrow?" Her fingers tightened on my hand. "*Alles gute!*" Her eyes were suddenly alive, almost excited. "I will watch. It will be good to see those engines in the air—even if no one knows it is his work." The last few words were little more than a whisper.

She came with me to the door then and as she stood there framed in the soft light of the lounge, she said, "Neil!" She had a funny way of saying it, almost achieving the impossible and pronouncing the vowels individually. " If you come to Berlin sometimes I live at Number Fifty-Two, Fassenenstrasse. That is near the Kurfurstendamm. Ask for—Fraulein Meyer."

" Meyer?"

" *Ja*. Else Meyer. That is my real name. To come here I have to have the papers of some other girl. You see—I am a Nazi. I belong to the *Hitlerjugend* before—before they kill my father." Her lips twitched painfully. " Good-bye," she said quickly. Her fingers touched mine and then the door closed and I was alone in the dark cold of the night. I didn't move for a moment and as I stood there I thought I heard the sound of sobbing, but it may only have been the wind.

It was a long time before I got to sleep that night. It was such a pitiful story, and yet I couldn't blame Saeton. I was English—she was German. The wall between us was high indeed.

Next morning the memory of her story was swamped in the urgent haste of preparations for tests. It was a cold, grey day and it was raining. A low curtain of cloud swept across the airfield. But nobody seemed to mind. Our thoughts were on the plane. Apparently Else had delivered my message, for promptly at eight o'clock a big caterpillar tractor came trundling across the tarmac apron leaving a trail of clay and chalk clods on the wet, shining surface of the asphalt. We slid the hangar doors back and hitched the tractor to the plane's undercarriage.

It gave me a sense of pride to see that gleaming Tudor nose slowly out of the hangar. It no longer had the toothless grin that had greeted me every morning for the past five weeks. It was a complete aircraft, a purposeful, solid-looking machine, fully engined and ready to go. The tractor dragged it to the main runway and then left us.

" Well, let's get moving," Saeton said and swung himself up into the fuselage. I followed him. Tubby wheeled out the batteries and connected up. First one engine and then another roared into life. Saeton's hand reached up to the four throttle levers set high up in the centre of the windshield. The engine revs died down as he trimmed the motors. Tubby came in through the cockpit door and closed it. " What about parachutes?" he asked.

Saeton grinned. " They're back in the fuselage, you old

Jonah. And they're okay. I packed them myself last night."

The engines roared, the fuselage shivering violently as the plane bucked against the wheel brakes. I was in the second pilot's seat, checking the dials with Saeton. Tubby was between us. Fuel, oil pressure and temperature gauges, coolant temperature, rev meters—everything was registering correctly. " Okay," Saeton said. " Ground tests." He released the brakes and we began to move forward down the shining surface of the runway. Left rudder, right rudder—the tail swung in response. Landing flaps okay. Tail controls okay. Brakes okay. For an hour we roared up and down the runways, circling the perimeter track, watching fuel consumption, oil indicators, the behaviour of the plane with four motors running and then with the two new inboard engines only. Tubby stood in the well between the two pilots' seats, listening, watching the dials and scribbling notes on a pad.

At length Saeton brought the plane back to the apron opposite the hangar and cut the engines. " Well?" he asked, looking down at Tubby. His voice seemed very loud in the sudden silence.

For answer Tubby raised his thumb and grinned. " Just one or two things. I'd like to check over the injection timing on that starboard motor and I want to have a look at the fuel filters. We got a slight drop in revs and she sounded a bit rough."

Saeton nodded and we climbed out. As we did so I saw a movement in the trees that screened the quarters. It was Else. Saeton had seen her, too. " What's that girl doing up here?" he muttered angrily. Then he turned quickly to me. " Did you tell her we were flying tests this morning?"

" Yes," I said.

" I thought I warned you to keep away from her." He glared at me as though I were responsible for her presence there on the edge of the airfield. Then he switched his gaze to the fringe of trees. Else had disappeared. " It's about time the authorities took some action about her."

" How do you mean?" I asked.

" She's here on false papers. Her name isn't really Langen."

" I know that—now," I said. And then suddenly I understood what he was driving at. " Do you mean to say you've reported her to the authorities?"

"Of course. Do you think I want her, snooping around the place, sending reports to the Rauch Motoren. They'd no right to let her into the country."

"Haven't you done that girl enough harm?" I said angrily.

"Harm?" He glanced at me quickly. "How much do you know of her story?" he asked.

"I know that it was her father who designed these engines," I said. "She worked on them with him." I caught hold of his arm. "Why don't you come to terms with her?" I said. "All she really wants is recognition for her father."

He flung my hand off. "So she's got round you, as she got round Randall—as she nearly got round me. She's just a little tart trading her body for the glorification of the fatherland."

I felt a sudden urge to hit him. "Don't you understand anybody?" I exclaimed through clenched teeth. "She loved her father. Can't you understand that all she wants is recognition for his work."

"Recognition!" He gave a sneering laugh. "It's Germany she loves. They killed her father, but still it is Germany she thinks of. She offered to be my mistress if I'd allow the Rauch Motoren to manufacture the engines. My engines! The engines Tubby and I had worked on all these years! She traded on my weakness, on the fact that I was alone up here, and if Diana hadn't come——" He half-shrugged his shoulders as though shaking off something he didn't like. "Her father has got about as much to do with these engines as you have."

"Nevertheless," I said, "it was his prototype you stole——"

"Stole! Damn it, man, a country that has gone through what we have on account of the blasted Germans has a right to take what it wants. If Professor Meyer had completed the development of those engines——" He stopped and stared at me angrily. "You bloody fool, Neil. Why waste your sympathy on the girl or her father? She was a good little Nazi till the S.S. took Meyer to Dachau. And Meyer was a Nazi too." His lips spread in a thin, bitter smile. "Perhaps you're not aware that Professor Meyer was one of the men who developed the diesel engine for use in bombers. London is in his debt to the tune of many hundreds of tons of bombs. My mother was killed in the blitz of 1940." He turned away, his shoulders hunched, his hands thrust deep into his pockets, and walked across the tarmac to the hangar. I followed slowly, thinking of the tangled pattern of motive that surrounded these engines.

For over an hour Tubby worked on the engine. Then he checked over the others. It was just on one o'clock when he climbed down and pulled the gantry away. " Okay," he said. " There's nothing more I can do."

" All right," Saeton said. " Let's have a bit of food." His voice was over-loud as though by speaking like that he could convince us of his confidence. I glanced at the plane. The rain clouds had broken up and she was caught in a gleam of watery sunlight. It was one thing doing ground tests, quite another to commit ourselves to the take-off. But she looked just like any other Tudor. It was difficult to realise, seeing her standing there on the tarmac, that this wasn't to be a routine flight.

Saeton had brought a loaf and some cheese and butter up from the quarters. We ate it in the hangar, none of us talking, all of us, I think, very conscious of the emptiness of the place and of the aircraft standing out there on the apron waiting for us. As soon as we'd finished we got into our flying kit and went out to the plane. Saeton insisted we wear our parachutes.

Once more we sat in the cockpit—Saeton and I in the pilots' seats, Tubby in the well between us—the engines ticking over. Saeton's hand reached out for the throttle levers. The engines revved and we moved away across the apron, along the perimeter track and swung on to the runway end, the concrete stretching ahead of us, a broad white path shining wet in the sunlight. " Okay?" Saeton looked at us. His jaw had broadened with the clenching of the muscles. His features looked hard and unsmiling. Only his eyes mirrored the excitement that held him in its grip.

" Okay," Tubby said. I nodded. Again Saeton's hand reached up for the throttle levers, pressing them slowly down with his palm. The four motors roared in unison. The fuselage shuddered violently as the thrust of the props fought the brakes.

Then he released the brakes and we started forward.

I won't pretend I wasn't nervous—even a little scared. But it was overlaid by the sense of excitement. At the same time it was difficult to realise fully the danger. Viewed from the cockpit all the engines looked ordinary standard models. There was nothing to bring home to us the fact that those inboard engines were the work of our own hands—only the memory, now distant, of the countless hours we'd worked at them in the hangar. In a sense it was nothing more than I'd done hundreds of times before—a routine take-off.

I tried to concentrate on the dials, but as we gathered speed my eyes strayed to the concrete streaming beneath us, faster and faster, and from thence to the ploughed verge of the runway and to the woods beyond. I caught a glimpse of the quarters through a gap in the trees. It suddenly seemed like home. Would we ever again sit at that trestle table drinking Scotch in celebration of success? Would we again lounge in those hard, uncomfortable chairs talking of a huge freighter fleet and our plans for a constant stream of aircraft tramping the globe? And as these questions appeared in my mind, my stomach suddenly became an empty void as panic hit me. Suppose those pistons I'd worked on when I first arrived were not quite true? Suppose . . . A whole stream of ugly possibilities flooded through my mind. And what about the engine that had been completed before I arrived? My hands tightened automatically on the control coloumn as I felt the tail lift.

I glanced at Saeton. His face was tense, his eyes fixed unblinkingly ahead, one hand on the throttles, the other on the control column. I saw his left foot kick at the rudder to counter a sudden swing of the tail. The end of the runway was in sight now. It ran slightly downhill and a bunch of oaks was rushing to meet us. No chance now of pulling up. We were committed to the take-off. The new starboard engine was still running a little rough. The tail swung. Left rudder again. I held my breath. God! He was leaving it late. I should have been watching the rev counters and the airspeed indicator. But instead my eyes were fixed on the trees ahead. They seemed to fill all my vision.

Then the control column eased back under my tense, clutched hands. The wheels bumped wildly on a torn-up piece of concrete. The starboard motor still sounded rough, the tail swung and the engine notes changed to a quieter drone. We were riding air, smooth, steady, the seat lifting me upwards as the trees slid away below us. Through the side window I saw Membury dropping away to a black circle of plough crisscrossed by the white pattern of runways and circled by the darker line of the perimeter track, the hangars small rectangles that looked like toys. We were airborne and climbing steeply, the full thrust of the motors taking us up in a steady, circling climb.

I glanced at Saeton. His body had relaxed into the shape of his seat. That was the only sign he gave of relief. "Check undercarriage up," he shouted to me as he levelled out. I glanced out of the side window. The starboard wheel was up inside the wing casing and I nodded. His eyes remained hard and alert, scanning the instrument panel. Tubby was jotting down notes as he read the dials. Oil Pressure 83— Oil Temp. 68—Coolant Temp. 90—Revs 2300, with the exception of the inboard starboard engine, which read 2270— Vacuum Pressure 4½ ins.—Height 1,500. We cruised around for a bit, checking everything, then we began to climb. Oil Presssure 88—Oil Temp. 77—Coolant Temp. 99—Revs 2850 plus 9—Vacuum Pressure 4½. I glanced at my watch. Rate of climb 1,050 feet a minute.

At 6,000 Saeton levelled out. "Okay to cut out the other motors?" He glanced down at Tubby, who nodded, his face unsmiling, his eyes almost lost in their creases of fat as he screwed them up against the sun which drove straight in through the windshield. At the same moment I saw the outboard engine slow. The individual blades of the prop became visible as it began to feather. The noise in the cockpit had lessened, so had the vibration. We were flying on our own motors only. Airspeed 175. Height 6,300. Still climbing. Swindon lay below us as we turned east, banking sharply.

The two motors hummed quietly. Saeton pulled back the control column. The nose of the plane lifted. We were climbing on the two engines only. Six thousand five hundred. Seven thousand. Eight thousand. Rate of climb 400 feet per minute. Half a dozen banking turns, then a long dive to 4,000 and up again. The motors hummed happily. The starboard engine was a shade rough perhaps, and engine revs were a little below those of the port motor. But there was plenty of power there.

Saeton levelled out. "I could do with a cigarette." He was grinning happily now, all tension smoothed out of his face. "From now on we can forget all the hours we've slaved at those engines. They're there. They exist. We've done what we set out to do."

Tubby was smiling, too, his face wreathed in a happy grin. He hummed a little tune.

We swung south over White Horse Hill. The racing gallops at Lambourne showed like age-old tracks along the downs. Climb, turn, dive—for two hours we flew the circuit of the Marlborough downs. Then at last Saeton said, " Okay. Let's go back and get some tea. To-morrow we'll do take-off and landing tests. Then we'll try her under full load and check petrol consumption."

" I want that starboard motor back on bench tests first," Tubby shouted.

Saeton nodded vaguely. For him it was all settled. He'd proved the motors. It only remained to get them to the highest pitch of efficiency. " Okay," he answered. " We've plenty of time. I'll fix airworthiness tests for the latter part of next week." He eased the control column forward and we slid down towards the rounded brown humps of the downs. Ramsbury airfield slid away beneath us, the Kennet showing like a twisting ribbon of steel in the cold light of the sinking sun. Membury opened out on the hill ahead of us. The two outboard motors started into life.

" Ready to land?"

We nodded.

Saeton looked down through the side window. " There's a bottle of whisky down there." He grinned as we peered down at the felted roof of our quarters. " Pity Diana isn't here to see this." He said it without thinking. I glanced at Tubby. His face gave no sign that he'd heard. " Better get your undercarriage down," Tubby said.

Saeton laughed. " If you think I'm going to prang the thing now, you're wrong." His hand reached down and found the undercarriage release switch automatically. He pulled it up and glanced out of his side window. Then he turned quickly, peered down at the lever and jerked at it. In the tenseness of his face I read sudden panic. I turned to my own side window and craning forward, peered back at the line of the wing. " The starboard wheel is down," I reported.

Saeton was flicking at the switch. " It's the port wheel," he said, staring out of his window. " The bloody thing's jammed." I don't think he was frightened for himself. The panic that showed in his face was for all our achievement that could be set at nought by a crash landing.

" I told you we ought to check over the plane," Tubby shouted back, peering forward over the lever.

" That's a hell of a lot of use now," Saeton's voice rasped through his clenched teeth. " Neil. Take over. Climb to 7,000 whilst we try and sort this bastard out. Tubby, see if she'll come down on the hand gear."

I felt the control column go slack under my hands as he eased himself out of his seat. I took hold of it, at the same time reaching out for the throttle levers. The engines responded to my touch and Membury dropped away from us as I pulled the control column back and climbed under full power, banking steadily. Saeton and Tubby were trying to wind the port wheel down, but the handle seemed to be alternately jamming and running free.

At 7,000 feet I levelled out. They had the floorboards up and Tubby was head down in the gap. A steady blast of bitterly cold air roared into the cockpit. For an hour I stooged round and round over Membury. And at the end of that hour Tubby straightened up, his face blue with cold and stood there blowing on his fingers. " Well?" Saeton demanded.

Tubby shook his head. " Nothing we can do," he said. " The connecting rod is snapped. A fault probably. Anyway, it's snapped and there's no way of lowering the port side undercarriage."

Saeton didn't speak for a moment. His face was grey and haggard. " The best we can hope for then is to make a decent pancake landing." His voice was a flat monotone as though all the weariness of the last few weeks had crowded in on him at this moment. " You're absolutely sure there's nothing we can do?" he asked Tubby.

The other shook his head. " Nothing. The connecting rod has snapped and——"

" All right. You said that once. I'm not that dense." He had pulled a packet of cigarettes out of his pocket. He handed it to me. I took one and he lit it for me. It was a measure of his acceptance of the facts of the situation. He would never have smoked in the cockpit unless he had abandoned all hope.

" The light's fading," I said. " And we haven't much gas left."

He nodded, drawing in a lungful of smoke.

" Better make for Upavon," Tubby shouted. It was an R.A.F. Station and I knew what was in his mind. There would be crash squads there and ambulances.

" No. We'll go back to Membury," Saeton answered. " You

two get aft. Have the door of the fuselage open. I'll take you over the airfield at 3,000 ft. Wind's easterly, about Force 2. Jump just before I cross the edge of the field." He climbed back into his seat. " All right, Neil. I'll take over now." I felt the pressure of his hands as he gripped the other control column and I let go of mine. Tubby started to protest, but Saeton rounded on him. " For God's sake do as you're told. Jump at the edge of the field. No point in more than one of us getting hurt. And as you so tactfully point out, it's my fault. Of course we should have checked the plane." Out of the tail of my eye I saw the starboard wheel folding into the wing again.

" I'm sorry, Bill," Tubby said. " I didn't mean——"

" Don't argue. Get aft. You, too, Fraser." His voice was almost vicious in his wretchedness. And then with that quick change of mood: " Good luck, both of you."

I had hesitated, half-out of my seat. His face was set in a grim mask as he stared straight ahead of him, thrusting the control column forward, dipping the nose to a long glide towards the airfield. Tubby jerked his head for me to follow him and disappeared through the door that communicated with the fuselage. " Good luck!" I murmured.

Saeton's eyes flicked towards me and he gave a bitter laugh. " I've had all the good luck I need," he snarled. I knew what he meant. Whether he came out of the plane alive or dead, he was finished. For a moment I still hesitated. I had a crazy idea that he might intend to crash the plane straight into the ground.

" What the hell are you waiting for?"

" I think I'd better stay," I said. If I stayed he'd be forced to make an attempt to land.

He must have sensed what was at the back of my mind, for he suddenly laughed. " You don't know very much about me, do you, Neil?" The snarl had gone out of his voice. But his eyes remained hard and bitter. " Go on. Get back aft with Tubby, and don't be a fool. I don't like heroics." And then suddenly shouting at me: " Get aft, man. Do you hear? Or have I got to come down there myself and throw you out." His eyes narrowed. " Ever jumped before?"

" Once," I answered, my mind mirroring the memory of that night landing in the woods of Westphalia, hanging in the straps with my parachute caught in a tree and my arm broken.

"Scared, eh?" The sneer was intentional. I knew that. He was goading me to jump. And yet I reacted. I reacted as he wanted me to because I was scared. I'd always been scared of having to bale out after that one experience. "Of course I'm not scared," I snapped and turned and moved awkwardly to the fuselage, the weight of my parachute bouncing against my buttocks.

Tubby already had the door of the fuselage open. The rush of air made it bitterly cold. The plane was turning now over the hangars, losing height rapidly. He didn't say anything. You haven't room for anything else in your mind when you are faced with a jump. We caught a glimpse of the quarters, looking very neat and snug in its little patch of trees. I could even make out the hen-run at the back with the white dots of two or three fowl. Then we were banking for the run-in. The trees slid away under us. I saw the snaking line of the road coming up from Ramsbury. Then, over Tubby's shoulder, I made out the edge of the airfield. He glanced at me with a quick, nervous grin, gripped my arm tightly and then, still looking at me, fell outwards into space.

I watched his body turn over and over. Saw his hand pull at the release of his parachute. The canopy of nylon blossomed like a flower and his body steadied, swinging rythmically.

We were right over the airfield now. My limbs felt cold and stiff. The sweat stood out on my forehead. I heard Saeton scream at me to jump, saw him clambering out of the pilot's seat. He was going to leave the controls, come aft and throw me out. I closed my eyes quickly, gripped the cold metal of the release lever and fell forward into the howl of the slipstream. My legs swung over the back of my neck. Opening my eyes I saw the sky, the sun, the horizon coming up the wrong way as though I were in a loop, the airfield rolling under me. Then I jerked at the release; jerked at it again and again in desperate fear that it wouldn't work.

Suddenly my shoulders were wrenched from their sockets, the inside of my legs cut by the hard pull of the straps. My legs fell into place. Sky and earth sorted themselves out. I was dangling in space, no wind, no sound—only the fading roar of the plane as it climbed, a black dot over the far side of the airfield. Above me the white cloud of the parachute swung gently, beautifully, the air-hole showing a dark patch of sky. Twisting my head I saw Tubby touch the ground, roll over and over in a perfect drill landing. Then he was scrambling to his feet, pulling in his parachute, legs braced against the drag of it, emptying the air till it lay in an inert white fold at his feet.

Travelling with the light wind the air was quite still. It was as though I were suspended there over the airfield for all eternity. There seemed to be no movement. Time and space stood still as I dangled like a daylight firework. The drone of the plane had died away. It had vanished as though it had never been. The stillness was all pervading, pleasant, yet rather frightening.

Though the movement was imperceptible my position gradually altered in relation to the ground. I was gliding steadily along the line of the east-west runway. I tried to work out my angle of drop in relation to the trees bordering the airfield near the quarters. But it was quite impossible to gauge the rate of fall. All I know is that one moment I was dangling up there, apparently motionless, and the next the concrete end of the runway was rushing up to meet me.

I hit the concrete with my legs too firmly braced for the shock. I hit it as though I'd jumped from a building into the street. The jar of the touchdown ran up my spine and hammered at my head and then all was confusion as my parachute harness jerked me forward. I had the sense to throw up my arms and duck my head into the protection of my shoulder as I hit the concrete. I remember being pitched forward and over and then there was a stunning blow on the front of my head and I lost consciousness.

I couldn't have been out for long because I came round to find myself being slowly dragged along the concrete by my shoulders. I dug my hands and feet in, anchoring myself for a moment. Blood ran down my face and dripped into a crack in the concrete. Somebody shouted to me and I caught hold of the strings of the parachute, struggling to fold it as I'd been taught to do. But I hadn't the strength. I dropped back, half-unconscious, a feeling of terrible lassitude running along my muscles.

The pull of my shoulders slackened. Somebody stooped over me and fingers worked at the harness buckles. " Neil! Are you all right? Please."

I looked up then. It was Else. " What—are you doing here?" I asked. I had some difficulty in getting my breath.

"I came to see the test. What has happened? Why have you jumped?"

"The undercarriage," I said.

"The undercarriage? Then it is not the engines? The engines are all right?"

"Yes, the engines are all right. It's the undercarriage. Won't come down." I looked up at her and saw that she was staring up into the sky, her eyes alight with some emotion that I couldn't understand. "Why are you so excited?" I asked her.

"Because——" She looked down at me quickly, her mouth clamped shut. "Come. I help you up now." She placed her hands under my arms. The world spun as I found my feet and leaned heavily against her, waiting for the aerodrome to stop spinning. Blood trickled into my mouth and I put my hand to my forehead. It was the old cut that had reopened and I thought: *This is where I came in.* "What about Tubby? Is he all right?"

"Yes. He is coming here now."

I shook the blood out of my eyes. A small dot was running down the runway. He shouted something. I didn't understand at first. Then I remembered Saeton and the aircraft. Ambulance! Of course. The quarters were not five hundred yards away. "Quick, Else. I must get to the phone." A muscle in one of my legs seemed to have been wrenched. It was hell running. But I made it in the end and seized hold of the telephone. My voice when I spoke to the operator was a breathless sob. She put me through to the Swindon hospital and then to the fire brigade. Tubby came in as I finished phoning. "Ambulance and fire brigade coming," I said.

"Good! You'd better lie down, Neil. Your head looks bad."

"I'm all right," I said. "What about the plane?" The need for action had given me strength.

"Saeton's stooging round over the field at about 5,000 feet using up his remaining gas." He turned to Else. "You'd better get some water on to heat. He may be a bit of a mess when we get him in." She nodded quickly and hurried out to the kitchen. "What's that girl doing here?" he asked me. But he didn't seem to expect an answer, for he went straight out to the airfield. I followed him.

Looking up into the sun brought a blinding pain to my eyes, but by screwing them up I could see the glint of the plane as it banked. The air was very still in the shelter of the woods and the sound of the engines seemed quite loud. Time passed slowly. We stood there in silence, waiting for the inevitable moment when the plane would cease its interminable circling and dive away over the horizon for the final approach. My legs began to feel weak and I sat down on the ground. "Why don't you go and lie down?" Tubby asked. His voice sounded irritable.

"I'll stay here," I said. I wasn't thinking of Saeton then. I was thinking of the plane. There it was, flying perfectly. Only that damned undercarriage stood between us and success. It seemed a hard twist of fate.

"I have arrange plenty of hot water." It was Else. She had a steaming bowl with her and she plumped down beside me. "Now we fix that cut, eh?" I winced as the hot water touched the open cut across my forehead. The water smelt strongly of disinfectant. Then she bandaged my head and it felt better. "That is finished. Now you look like you are a wounded man."

"So I am," I said. Her face hung over me, framed by the darkening blue of the sky. She looked young and soft and rather maternal. My head was in her lap. I could feel the softness of her limbs against the back of my skull. We should have been lying like that in a hay field in May. The distant drone of the aircraft was like the sound of bees. I caught the gleam of its wings just beyond her hair.

"Where the devil's the ambulance?" Tubby demanded. "He's coming in now."

I glanced at my watch. It was twenty minutes since I'd phoned. "They'll be here in about ten minutes," I told him. He grunted a curse. "They'll be here too late then."

I could see the plane gliding over Ramsbury, a black dot against the sunset. I thought of the engine we had laboured to complete all these weeks, of Saeton alone up there at the controls. The pain of my head was nothing then. My eyes were strained on the sky over Ramsbury and every fibre of my being was concentrated on the plane, which was banking sharply as it disappeared behind the trees, turning for the final approach.

It seemed an age before it appeared again. Then suddenly it was there over the end of the runway, hanging like a great, clumsy bird over the trees, dropping towards the concrete, its

D

landing flaps down, the props turning slowly. I scrambled to
my feet and began to run. Tubby was running, too. Saeton
levelled out for the touchdown and as the gap between plane
and concrete lessened, the aircraft seemed to gather speed till
it was rushing towards us.

Then the belly hit the concrete. Pieces of metal were flung
wide. There was a horrible scraping. But when the sound
reached me the plane had bounced several feet above the runway. It came down then with a splintering crash, swivelling
round, the fuselage breaking up as the tail disintegrated, grinding the concrete to puffs of powder, the metal sheeting stripping from her belly like tinplate. She slewed broadside, tipping
crazily, righted herself, straightened up and broke in half. The
appalling grinding sound went on for a second after she had
stopped. Then there was a sudden, frightening silence. The
plane lay there, a crumpled wreck, unnaturally still. Nothing
moved. The sunset was just as red, the trees just as black,
nothing had changed as though the aerodrome had taken no
interest in the accident. Somebody had pranged a plane. It
had happened here countless times during the war. Life went
on.

Tubby was running towards the machine. For a second I
stood rooted to the spot, my stomach quivering in expectation
of the sudden blossoming of the wreck into a blazing fury of
fire. But it just lay there, inert and lifeless, and I, too, started
to run.

We got Saeton out. There was a lot of blood, but it was
from his nose. He was unconscious when we laid him on the
concrete, his hand badly cut and a livid bruise across his forehead. But his pulse beat was quite strong. Tubby loosened
his collar and almost immediately his eyes opened, staring
up at us blankly. Then suddenly there was life behind them
and he sat up with a jerk that brought a groan from his lips.
" How's the plane? Is she——" His voice stopped as his eyes
took in the wreck. " Oh, God!" he murmured. He began to
swear then—a string of obscene oaths that ignored Else's presence and were directed solely at the plane.

" The engines are all right," Tubby said consolingly.

" What's the good of engines without a plane?" Saeton
snarled. " I got the tail too low." He began swearing again.

" You better lie back," Tubby said. " There's nothing you

can do about the plane. Just relax now. The ambulance will be here in a minute."

"Ambulance?" He glared at us. "What damn' fool phoned for an ambulance?" He got out his handkerchief and wiped some of the blood from his face. "Get down to the main road and stop them," he ordered Tubby hoarsely. "Tell them it's all right. Tell them there wasn't any crash after all—anything, so long as you get them away from here without them coming on to the airfield."

"But even if you're all right, there's Neil here needing treatment," Tubby said.

"Then take him with you and pack him off to hospital. But I don't want them on the field. I don't want them to know we've crashed."

"But why?" Tubby asked.

"Why?" Saeton passed his hand across his eyes and spat blood on to the concrete. "I don't know why. I just don't want anyone to know about this. Now for God's sake stop arguing and get down to the road."

Tubby hesitated. "That nose of yours looks as though it's broken," he said. "And there may be something else——"

"There's nothing else broken," Saeton snarled. "If there is I'll get to a doctor under my own steam. Now get going."

Tubby glanced at me. "I'm all right," I said. He nodded and started at a steady trot across the field towards the quarters. Saeton struggled to his feet and stood there, swaying weakly, staring at the wreckage, bitter, black despair in his eyes. Then, as he turned away, he caught sight of Else and his thick hands clenched with sudden violence of purpose. "I thought you were going back to Germany," he said hoarsely.

"I go on Monday." Her eyes were wide and she looked frightened.

"Wanted to be in at the death, eh? You timed it nicely."

"I do not understand."

"You do not understand, eh?" he mimicked her crudely. "I suppose you don't understand what happened up there?" He was moving towards her, staggering slightly, the sweat standing out in great drops on his forehead and running down into his eyes. "Well, the connecting rod was snapped. We couldn't lower the undercarriage. That surprises you, eh? You didn't know the connecting rod was broken."

The expression on his face held me rooted to the spot. It was a bloody mask of hatred. Else stood quite still, her eyes wide, her mouth slightly open. And then suddenly she was talking, talking fast, the words tumbling out of her as though in themselves they could form a barrier between herself and what was moving so inevitably upon her. " I do not touch your plane. I have nothing to do with what has happened. Please. You must believe me. Why should I do this thing? These are my father's engines—my father's and mine. I wish them to fly. I wish to see them in the air. It is all I have left of him. It is the work we do together. He was happy then, and I was happy also. I want them to fly. I want them——"

" Your father's engines!" The contempt in his voice stopped her like a slap in the face. " They're my engines. Mine. Your father's engine wouldn't work. It crashed. I broke my leg trying to fly the bloody thing. It was no good. We had to start again. All over again. A new design."

She flung up her head then, facing him like a tigress defending her young. " It is not a new design. It is different, but it is the same principle. Those engines belong to him. They are——"

He laughed. It was a wild, violent sound. " You've smashed what I've lived for for three years. You're happy now, aren't you? You think now that Germany will get control of them again. But she won't." He was very close to her now. " You tried to kill us. Well, now I'm going to——"

" That's a lie!" she cried. " I have nothing to do with it. Nobody has touched the airplane."

" Then why are you here—on the spot, gloating——"

" Oh, will you never understand?" she cried furiously. " I come to see them up there in the air. They are my father's work. Do you think it is no excitement for me to see them fly? Please, I have nothing to do with the crash." His hands had reached out to her and gripped her shoulders. She was suddenly pleading. " I have done nothing—nothing. You must believe what I say."

But he didn't seem to hear her. " You tried to kill us," he whispered hoarsely. " You tried to smash everything I have worked for. First you try to bribe me with your body. Then you try to get control of my company. When you don't succeed you try to destroy what I've worked for. If you can't get what you want you must destroy it. That is the German in you. Everything you touch, you destroy. And always you work for Germany."

" Not for Germany," she cried. " Only for my father. Everything I do, I do for my father. Why could you not give him the credit for what he do?"

" You're a part of the Germany I've hated since I was a kid," he went on, his voice thick as though clotted with blood, his hands gripping her violently, fumbling blindly for her throat. " My father in one war, my mother in another. All you can do is smash and break things. And now I'm going to break you—break you in little pieces."

Her eyes started wildly as his blunt fingers dug into her neck. Then she began to struggle, and in that instant I came to life and moved forward. But I needn't have bothered. His hands clawed at her clothes and his body slowly sagged against her, his knees giving under him and pitching him forward on to his face.

Saeton had fainted.

Else stared down at him, fear and horror stamped on her face. I think she thought he was dead. " I didn't do anything to the airplane." The words were a strangled sob. " Neil! " She glanced wildly at me. " Nobody touched the airplane. You must believe that."

Saeton moved suddenly, his fingers digging into the earth, scrabbling at it as he tried to rise, and when he had pushed himself up on to his knees, she broke and ran.

Tubby came back and we got Saeton to the quarters and put him to bed. His ribs were badly bruised, but nothing seemed to be broken. It was more shock than anything else. Still half-dazed he ordered us to get one of Ellwood's tractors and have the wreckage dragged into the hangar. He wanted it done that night. He seemed to have an unreasoned, instinctive urge to get the evidence of failure under cover as quickly as possible. It was as though he felt none of his own injuries, only the hurts of the aircraft and wanted to let it crawl away into the dark like a dog to lick its wounds.

By ten o'clock that night it was done and all trace of the crash landing was concealed behind the closed doors of the hangar. The plane was a hell of a mess. The tractor took it in in two pieces, the tail having ripped off completely as soon as we began to drag the wreck along the concrete. Saeton himself came out to the runway to make sure there was no trace of the accident left.

Whether the plan had formed in his mind then, I can't be certain. Personally, I don't think so. It was a matter of instinct rather than planning. If nobody knew we had crashed there might still be a chance. At any rate, if the idea was in his mind, it didn't show that evening as we sat over a drink and tried to sort out the future.

Tubby was through. That was clear from the start. "I'm going back to flying," he said. His tone was obstinate and quite final. "You know Francis Harcourt? He's got two Tudors on the tanking lift, and he's back in England now negotiating the purchase of two more. Just before Christmas he wrote asking me to join him as a flight engineer."

"And you've accepted?" Saeton asked.

For answer Tubby produced an envelope from his pocket. It was already stamped and sealed.

"We've still a month before we're due on the airlift—if we hold the Air Ministry to their first date," Saeton said quietly.

"A month!" Tubby grunted. "Six months wouldn't see that kite ready to fly—six months and a lot of money." He leaned forward and caught Saeton by the arm. "Listen, Bill. I've worked with you for nothing for just on two years. I haven't got a bean out of it. If you think I can go on any longer, you're crazy. Anyway, where the hell would you get the money from? You've cleaned me out. You've just about cleaned Neil out. We owe money all over the place. The company is broke—finished." His voice softened as he saw the bitter set of Saeton's mouth below the bandages. "I'm sorry, chum. I know what this means to you. But you've got to face the facts. We can't go on."

"Can't we? Well, I say we can. I don't know how—yet. But I'll find a way. You'll see me on the airlift next month. I'll do it somehow." His voice was trembling, but it had no conviction, only violence. His fist beat at the table. "If you think I'm going to let a little bitch of a German destroy everything I've worked for, you're wrong. I don't care what it costs me, I'll get those engines into the air."

"How do you know she was responsible for what happened?" I asked.

"Of course she was," he snarled. "Either her or one of the Rauch Motoren agents."

"You can't be certain," I said.

"Can't be certain! Damn it, man, how else could it have happened? She tracked me down to this airfield. How she did it I don't know. But suddenly she arrived at the Manor and because we were short-handed I got her to come up and cook and clean for us in the evenings. I thought she was just a D.P. It never occurred to me she was Professor Meyer's daughter."

"When did you discover who she really was?" I asked.

"That night you arrived and found us together in the hangar." He suddenly clicked his fingers. "She must have done it then. It's the only time she's ever been alone in the hangar."

"Are you seriously suggesting the girl filed through the undercarriage connecting rod?" Tubby asked.

"She an engineer, isn't she? And she had about half an hour up there on her own. She couldn't be sure the plan to buy up the outfit through Randall's mortgages would succeed. Anyway, what's it matter?" he added, his tone suddenly rising. "Finding out whether it was German thoroughness or a natural break won't put the crate back into the air. We'll sort it out to-morrow." He spoke through clenched teeth and his hands trembled as he thrust back his chair. I think he was in the grip of a bitter, raging anger, on the verge of tears. The man was dead beat anyway and his nerves must have been just about stretched to the edge of screaming hysteria. He had risen to his feet and he stood, staring at Tubby. "Are you going to post that letter?"

"Yes," Tubby answered.

"All right." The veins on Saeton's forehead seemed to swell. "But remember this ; join Harcourt's outfit and you're through with this company. Understand?"

"I understand," Tubby said in a level tone.

"You bloody fool!" Saeton said, and went out, slamming the door.

I was pretty tired and my head ached. I followed him out and was asleep almost before my head touched the pillow.

I awoke in a mood of despair. My job was gone and I was broke. The future was bleak. I longed to be back at the bench, driven beyond physical endurance to complete something that I believed in.

It was a chill, grey morning, frost riming the windows and the wind moaning round the building. Tubby produced tea and bacon and eggs in a mood of contrition for deserting us. Breakfast did nothing to lift us out of our gloom. We ate in silence and went out to the hangar. I suppose in the five weeks I had been there I had gradually come to identify my future with the plane. Seeing it lying there in the drab light, its metal all broken and twisted, the tail completely severed and lying like a piece of discarded junk gave me a sense of sudden loneliness. This was the end of our work together. We were no longer a team, but three individuals going our own separate ways. It was this, I think, that made me feel so wretched. I'd felt safe here and complete. I'd been doing something I'd come to believe in and there had been a goal to work for. Now there was nothing.

We cleared the torn metal away from the fuselage, working to reach the undercarriage and find out what had gone wrong. It was a useless investigation. Whatever we discovered, it wouldn't help us. We worked slowly, almost unwillingly, and in silence. Shortly before eleven the phone rang. It was Harcourt asking for Tubby. Saeton and I stood listening. " Yes . . . Yes, I'll be there. Diana is already in Germany . . . Well, maybe she'll fix it to get to the Gatow canteen . . . Fine. I'll meet you there." Tubby's eyes gleamed excitedly and he was whistling happily to himself as he replaced the receiver.

" Well, when do you leave?" Saeton barked in the hard, impersonal tone he used when he wished to hide his own feelings.

" He wants me down at Northolt at ten o'clock to-morrow," Tubby answered.

" Then you'd better get moving," Saeton said abruptly.

" It's all right. I'll get a train this evening. I don't want to leave without knowing what the trouble was."

" Hell, man! What difference does it make?"

" I'd like to know all the same," Tubby answered woodenly.

Saeton turned away with a shrug of his shoulders. "Well, let's get on with the post-mortem."

It was useless for him to pretend that he didn't care what had caused the break. He did care. He was looking for something to fight. He was that sort. But when we got to the connecting rod it showed a clean break and unmistakable signs of faulty casting.

"So it wasn't Else after all," I said.

"No." He threw the broken rod on to the concrete and turned away. "Better see if you can fix Fraser up with a job on the airlift," he said to Tubby over his shoulder, and he slammed out of the hangar.

Tubby left that afternoon and with his departure a tense, brooding gloom settled on the quarters. Saeton was impossible. It wasn't only that he wouldn't talk. He prowled up and down, constantly, irritably on the move, lost in his own morose thoughts. He was racking his brains for a means of getting on the airlift with the engines by 25th January. Once he turned to me, his eyes wild, his face looking grey and slightly crazy with the nose covered with adhesive plaster. "I'm desperate," he said. "I'd do anything to get hold of a plane. Anything, do you hear?"

At that moment I was prepared to believe he'd commit murder if he were sure of getting another aircraft as a result of it. The man was desperate. It showed in his eyes, in the way he talked. He hadn't given up hope. I think that was what made the atmosphere so frightening. He wasn't quite sane. A sane man would see that the thing was impossible. But he wouldn't. He was still thinking in terms of getting those engines into the air. It was incredible—incredible and frightening. No man should be driven by such violent singleness of purpose. "You're crazy," I said.

"Crazy?" He laughed and his laugh was pitched a shade too high. Then he suddenly smiled in an odd, secretive way. "Yes, perhaps you're right. Perhaps I am crazy. All pioneers are crazy. But believe me, I'll get into the air if I have to steal a plane." He stopped then and stared at me fixedly in an odd sort of way. Then he smiled again. "Yes," he said slowly, reflectively. "I'll get on to the airlift somehow." He went out then and I heard his feet dragging slowly down the frost-bound path until the sound lost itself in the noise of the wind blowing through the trees.

I went down to the Manor to see Else. I wanted to tell her that we knew she had had nothing to do with the failure of the undercarriage, that it was in fact an accident. But she had already gone. She had taken the afternoon train to London because she had to be at Harwich early the following morning to catch the boat. I returned to the quarters feeling that my last link with the past few weeks had gone.

The next two days were hell. I just drifted, clinging desperately to Membury, to the hangar and the quarters. I just couldn't nerve myself to face the outside world. I was afraid of it ; afraid of the fact that I had no job and only a few pounds left in my account. The memory of Else haunted me. God knows why. I wasn't in love with her. I told myself that a hundred times. But it made no difference. I needed a woman, someone to attach myself to. I was as rudderless as the wreck lying in the hangar.

To give me something to do Saeton had told me to get to work with the oxy-acetylene cutter and clean up the mess. It was like operating on the broken body of a friend. We lifted our two engines out of her and she looked like a toothless old hag waiting for the inevitable end. I could have wept for what might have been. A thousand times I remembered those supreme moments up in the air over Membury when we had climbed, superbly, majestically, on the power of the engines we'd made. I had felt then as though all the world lay within my grasp. And now I was cleaning up the wreck, cutting out the sections that had been torn to strips of tin by the concrete of the runway.

Saeton didn't even pretend that we were working to repair the plane. And yet he wasn't morose any more. There was a sort of jauntiness in the way he walked and every now and then I'd catch him watching me with a soft, secretive smile. His manner wasn't natural and I found myself wishing that he'd begin cursing again, wishing he'd make up my mind for me by throwing me off the place.

Well, I had my wish in the end. He made up my mind for me. But it wasn't at all the way I had expected it. It was the third evening after Tubby's departure. We were back in the quarters and the phone rang. Saeton leapt up eagerly and went into the office, the room that Tubby and Diana had had as a bedroom. I heard the murmur of his voice and then the sound of the bell as he replaced the receiver. There was a pause before his footsteps came slowly across the passage and the door of the mess room opened.

He didn't close it immediately, but stood there, framed in the doorway, staring at me, his head sunk into his shoulders, his chin thrust slightly out, a queer glint of excitement in his eyes. "That was Tubby," he said slowly. "He's found you a job."

"A job?" I felt a tingle of apprehension run along my nerves. "What sort of a job?"

"Flying for the Harcourt Charter Company." He came in and shut the door. His movements were oddly slow and deliberate. He reminded me of a big cat. He sat himself down on the trestle table. His thick, powerful body seemed to tower above me. "You're to pilot one of Harcourt's new Tudors. I got on to Tubby two days ago about it and he's fixed it."

I began to stammer my thanks. My voice sounded odd and far away from me, as though it were somebody else speaking. I was in a panic. I didn't want to leave Membury. I didn't want to lose that illusion of security the place had given me.

"You're to meet Harcourt at Northolt for lunch to-morrow," Saeton went on. "One o'clock at the canteen. Tubby will be there to introduce you. It's an incredible piece of luck." The excitement had spread from his eyes to his voice now. "The pilot he had engaged has gone down with pneumonia." He stopped and stared at me, his face faintly flushed as though he had been drinking, his eyes sparkling like a kid that sees the thing he's dreamed of come true at last. "How much do these engines we've built mean to you, Neil?" he asked suddenly.

I didn't know quite what to say. But apparently he didn't expect an answer, for he added quickly, "Listen. Those engines are okay. You've seen that for yourself. You've got to take my word for it about the saving in fuel consumption. It's about 50 per cent. Tubby and I proved that in the bench tests on the first engine. Now, suppose we got into the air as planned on January 10——"

"But we can't," I cried. "You know very well——"

"The engines are all right, aren't they? All we need is a new plane." He was leaning down over me now, his eyes fixed on mine as though trying to mesmerise me. "We've still got a chance, Neil. Harcourt's planes are Tudors. In a few days' time you'll be at Wunstorf and flying into Berlin. Suppose something went wrong with the engines over the Russian Zone?" He paused, watching for my reaction. But I didn't say anything. I suddenly felt ice-cold inside. "All you've got to do is to order your crew to bale out," he went on, speaking slowly as though talking to a child. "It's as easy as that. A little play-acting, a little organised panic and you'll be alone in the cockpit of a Tudor. All you've got to do then is to make straight for Membury."

I stared at him foolishly. "You *are* crazy," I heard myself say. "You'd never get away with it. There'd be an inquiry. The plane would be recognised when they saw it again. Harcourt's not a fool. Besides——"

He stopped me with a wave of his hand. "You're wrong. To begin with an inquiry would show nothing. The crew would say the plane had made a forced landing in the Russian Zone. The Russians would deny it. Nobody would believe them. As for the plane being recognised, why should it? Nobody knows we've crashed our machine here. At least they don't know how badly. All that happens is that a plane disappears on the Berlin Airlift and on January 10 another flies in to take its place. Harcourt's all right—he gets his insurance. The country's all right, for the number of Tudors remains the same. God, man—it sticks out a mile. You'll make a fortune. We'll both of us make a fortune."

"You'd never get away with it," I repeated obstinately.

"Of course I'll get away with it. Why should they ever suspect anything? And if they did, what then? Look. Part numbers and engine numbers can be altered to those of our wrecked Tudor. Our own two engines will be in her. As for our own plane, we'll cut it up into small bits. You've already started on that work. In a few days we could have the whole plane in fragments. A load of those fragments can be strewn over Russian territory. The rest we'll dump in that pond over on the far side of the airfield. God! It's too easy. All I need is for you to fly Harcourt's plane back here."

"Well, I won't do it," I said angrily.

"Do you want the Germans to be the first to produce these engines?" His hand came out and gripped my shoulder. "Just think before you refuse. Damn it, haven't you a spark of adventure in you? A slight risk and this country can have the biggest fleet of freighters in the world—a global monopoly." His eyes were blazing and I suddenly felt scared. The man was a fanatic.

"I won't do it," I repeated stubbornly.

"When you've flown the plane in here all we have to do is drop you just inside the British Zone," he went on. "You report back to Wunstorf with the story that you made a forced landing in the Russian Zone and got back under your own steam across the frontier. It's child's play."

" I won't do it."

He gave an ugly laugh. " Scared, eh?"

I hesitated, trying to sort out in my mind whether it was because I was scared or whether my refusal was on moral grounds. I couldn't sort it out. All I knew was that I didn't want to be mixed up in anything like this. I wanted to forget that sense of being hunted. I didn't want ever again to have anything on my conscience, to have to run and hide—I didn't want to be afraid of the world any more.

He suddenly let go my arm. " All right," he said, and I didn't like the softness in his voice and the way he smiled down at me. " All right, if that's the way you feel." He paused, watching me with an odd expression in his eyes. " Do you remember the other evening I said I'd do anything to get hold of a plane?"

I nodded.

" Well, I meant that. I meant every word of it. I said I was desperate. I am desperate. If one man's life stood between me and getting into the air, I'd kill that man. I'd brush him out of my way without a thought. Bigger things than a single life are involved. It's not just my own future I'm thinking of. Don't think that. I happen to believe in my country. And I believe that these engines are the greatest contribution I can make to my country. There's nothing I won't do to see these engines are operated by a British concern. Nothing. Nothing." His voice had risen and there was a wild look in his eyes. " Forget about yourself. Forget about me. Won't you do this for your country?"

" No," I said.

" God, man! You fought for your country in war. You risked your life. Have some imagination. Can't you fight for her in peacetime? I'm not asking you to risk your life. All I'm asking you to do is to fly that plane back here. What's the trouble? You're not damaging Harcourt. Or is it the risk you're afraid of? I tell you, there isn't any risk. Do it the way I've planned it and you're as safe as houses. You've nothing to be afraid of."

" I'm not afraid," I answered hotly.

" What's the trouble then?"

" I just don't like it and I won't do it."

He sighed and eased himself off the edge of the table. " All right. If that's the way you want it——" He stood for a moment, looking down at me. The room was suddenly very silent. I felt my nerves tightening so that I wanted to shout at him, to do anything to relieve the tension. At length he said, " If you don't do what I want you to I'll turn you over to the police." He spoke quite flatly and my inside seemed to curl up into a tight ball. " You were in a prison camp, weren't you? You know what it's like then. Three years in prison is quite a slice out of a man's life. Do you think you could stand it? You'd go mad, wouldn't you? You were on the edge of hysteria when you came here. You're all right now, but in prison——"

" You bastard!" I screamed at him, suddenly finding my voice. I called him a lot of other names. I had got to my feet and I was trembling all over, the sweat breaking out in prickling patches across my scalp and trickling down my forehead. I was cold with fear and anger. And he just stood there, watching me, his shoulders hunched a little forward as though expecting me to charge him, a quiet, confident smile on his lips.

" Well?" he said as I paused for breath. " Which is it to be?"

" You're crazy," I cried. " And you're trying to drive me crazy, too. I won't do it. Suppose one of the crew were killed? Suppose they did discover what had happened? And if I did it—then I'd have something on you. You wouldn't stand for that. Somehow you'd get rid of me. You're not doing this for your country. You're doing it for yourself. Your love of power is driving you—driving you over the edge of reason. You can't get away with a thing like——"

" Which is it to be?" he cut in, his lips tightening and his voice suddenly cold and metallic. " Do you take this job with Harcourt or do I telephone the police? I'll give you half an hour to make up your mind." He hesitated and then said slowly, " Just remember what it's like to be locked away in a cell, seeing the sun through iron bars, with no hope—and no future when you get out. I'm offering you a flying job—and a future. Now sit down and make up your mind." He turned abruptly then and went out.

With the closing of the door the room seemed suddenly empty and silent. The key grated in the lock. It was like the turning of the key in the solitary confinement cells—only there the door had been of metal and had clanged. Stalag Luft I, with its lines of huts, the barbed wire, the endless march of the guards, the searchlights at night, the deadly monotony, was there in my mind, as vivid as though I had only just escaped. Surely to God I'd had enough of life behind bars. Surely to God. . . .

## CHAPTER FIVE

I WON'T attempt to defend my decision. Saeton had asked me to steal a plane and I agreed to do it. I must take full responsibility, therefore, for all that happened afterwards as a result of that decision.

We went down to Ramsbury and in the smoky warmth of the pub that faces the old oak, he went over the plan in detail. I know it sounds incredible—to steal a plane off such a highly organised operation as the Berlin Airlift and then, after replacing two of the engines, to fly it back to Germany and operate it from the same airfield from which it had been stolen. But he had it all worked out. And when he had gone over all the details, it didn't seem incredible any more.

The devil of it was the man's enthusiasm was infectious. I can see him now, talking softly in the hubbub of the bar, his eyes glittering with excitement, smoking cigarette after cigarette, his voice vibrant as he reached out into my mind to give me the sense of adventure that he felt himself. The essence of his personality was that he could make others believe what he believed. In any project, he gave himself to it so completely that it was impossible not to follow him. He was a born leader. From being an unwilling participant, I became a willing one. Out of apparent failure he conjured the hope of success, and he gave me something positive to work for. I think it was the daring of the plan that attracted me more than anything else. And, of course, I was up to the hilt in the thing financially. I may have thought it was money better thrown away considering how I'd got it, but no one likes to be broke when he is shown a way to make a fortune. The only thing he didn't allow for was the human factor.

As we left the pub he said, " You'll be seeing Tubby tomorrow. Don't tell him anything about this. You understand?

He's not to know. His family were Methodists." He grinned at me as though that explained everything that constituted Tubby Carter's make-up.

Early the following morning Saeton drove me to Hungerford Station. Riding behind him on the old motor bike through the white of the frozen Kennet valley I felt a wild sense of exhilaration. For over five weeks I hadn't been more than a few miles from Membury aerodrome. Now I was going back into the world. Twenty-four hours ago I should have been scared at the prospect, afraid that I might be picked up by the police. Now I didn't think about it. I was bound for Germany, riding a mood of adventure that left no room in my mind for the routine activities of the law.

Tubby met me at Northolt. " Glad to see you, Neil," he said, beaming all over his face, his hand gripping my arm. " Bit of luck Morgan goin, sick. Not that I wish the poor chap any harm, but it just happened right for you. Harcourt leaves for Wunstorf with one of the Tudors this evening. You're flying a test with him this afternoon in our plane."

I glanced at him quickly. " Our plane?"

He nodded, grinning. " That's right. You're skipper. I'm engineer. A youngster called Harry Westrop is radio operator and the navigator is a fellow named Field. Come on up to the canteen and meet them. They're all here."

I could have wished that Tubby wasn't to be a member of the crew. I immediately wanted to tell him the whole thing. Maybe it would have been better if I had. But I remembered what Saeton had said, and seeing Tubby's honest, friendly features, I knew Saeton was right. It was out of the question. Duty, not adventure, was his business in life. But it was going to make it that bit more difficult when I ordered the crew to bale out.

I began to feel nervous then. It was a long time since I'd flown operationally, a long time since I'd skippered an air crew. We went into the bar, and Tubby introduced me to the rest of the crew. Westrop was tall and rather shy with fair, crinkly hair. He was little more than a kid. Field was much older, a small, sour-looking man with sharp eyes and a sharper nose. " What are you having, skipper?" Field asked. The word " skipper " brought back memories of almost-forgotten nights of bombing. I ordered a Scotch.

"Field is just out of the R.A.F.," Tubby said. "He's been flying the airlift since the early days at Wunstorf."

"Why did you pack up your commission?" I asked him.

He shrugged his shoulders. "I got bored. Besides, there's more money in civil flying." He looked at me narrowly out of his small, unsmiling eyes. "I hear you were in 101 Squadron. Do you remember——" That started the reminiscences. And then suddenly he said: "You got a gong for that escape of yours, didn't you?"

I nodded.

He looked at the ceiling and pursed his thin lips. I could see the man's mind thinking back. "I remember now. Longest tunnel escape of the war and then three weeks on the run before——" He hesitated and then snapped his fingers. "Of course. You were the bloke that flew a Jerry plane out, weren't you?"

"Yes," I said. I was feeling suddenly tight inside. Any moment he'd ask me what I'd been doing since then.

"By jove! That's wizard!" Westrop's voice was boyish and eager. "What happened? How did you get the plane?"

"I'd rather not talk about it," I said awkwardly.

"Oh, but dash it. I mean——"

"I tell you, I don't want to talk about it." Damn it! Suppose his parachute didn't open? I didn't want any hero-worship. I must keep apart from the crew until after the first night flight.

"I only thought——"

"Shut up!" My voice sounded harsh and violent.

"Here's your drink," Tubby said quietly, pushing the glass towards me. Then he turned to Westrop. "Better go and check over your radar equipment, Harry."

"But I've just checked it."

"Then check it again," Tubby said in the same quiet voice. Westrop hesitated, glancing from Tubby to me. Then he turned away with a crestfallen look. "He's only a kid," Tubby said and picked up his drink. "Well, here's to the airlift!" *Here's to the airlift!* I wondered whether he remembered the four of us drinking that toast in the mess room at Membury. It all seemed a long time ago. I turned to Field. "What planes were you navigating on the lift?" I asked him.

"Yorks," he replied. "Wunstorf to Gatow with food for

the bloody Jerry." He knocked back his drink. "Queer, isn't it? Just over three years ago I was navigating bombers to Berlin loaded with five hundred pounders. Now, for the last four months I've been delivering flour to them—flour that's paid for by Britain and America. Do you think they'd have done that for us?" He gave a bitter laugh. "Well, here's to the Ruskies, God rot 'em! But for them we could have been a lot tougher."

" You don't like the Germans?" I asked, glad of the change in conversation.

He gave me a thin-lipped smile. "You should know about them. You've been inside one of their camps. They give me the creeps. They're a grim, humourless lot of bastards. As for Democracy, they think it's the biggest joke since Hitler wiped out Lidice. Ever read Milton's *Paradise Lost*? Well, that's Germany. Don't let's talk about it. Do you know Wunstorf?"

" I bombed it once in the early days," I said.

" It's changed a bit since then. So has Gatow. We've enlarged them a bit. I think you'll be quite impressed. And the run in to Gatow is like nothing you've ever done before. You just go in like a bus service, and you keep rolling after touchdown because you know damn well there's either another kite coming down or taking off right on your tail. But they'll give you a full briefing at Wunstorf. It's reduced to a system so that it's almost automatic. Trouble is it's bloody boring— two flights a day, eight hours of duty, whatever the weather. I tried for B.O.A.C., but they didn't want any navigators. So here I am, back on the airlift, blast it!" His gaze swung to the entrance. " Ah, here's the governor," he said.

Harcourt was one of those men born for organisation, not leadership. He was very short with a small, neat moustache and sandy hair. He had tight, rather orderly features and a clipped manner of speech that finished sentences abruptly like an adding machine. His method of approach was impersonal—a few short questions, punctuated by sharp little nods, and then silence while shrewd grey eyes stared at me unblinkingly. Lunch was an awkward affair carried chiefly by Tubby. Harcourt had an aura of quiet efficiency about him, but it wasn't friendly efficiency. He was the sort of man who knows precisely what he wants and uses his fellow creatures much as a carpenter uses his tools. It made it a lot easier from my point of view.

Nevertheless, I found the test flight something of an ordeal. It was the machine that was supposed to be on test. He'd only just taken delivery. But I knew as we walked out to the plane that it was really I who was being tested. He sat in the second pilot's seat and I was conscious all through the take-off of his cold gaze fixed on my face and not on the instrument panel.

Once in the air, however, my confidence returned. She handled very easily and the fact that she was so like the one we'd flown only a few days before made it easier. Apparently I satisfied him, for as we walked across the airfield to the B.E.A. offices, he said, " Get all the details cleared up, Fraser, and leave to-morrow lunchtime. That'll give you a daylight flight. I'll see you in Wunstorf."

We left Northolt the following day in cold, brittle sunshine that turned to cloud as we crossed the North Sea. Field was right about Wunstorf. It had changed a lot since I'd been briefed for that raid nearly eight years ago. I came out of the cloud at about a thousand feet and there it was straight ahead of me through the windshield, an enormous flat field with a broad runway like an autobahn running across it and a huge tarmac apron littered with Yorks. There were excavations marking new work in progress and a railway line had been pushed out right to the edge of the field. Beyond it stretched the Westphalian plain, grim and desolate, with a line of fir-clad hills marching back along the horizon.

I came in to land through a thick downpour of rain. The runway was a cold, shining ribbon of grey, half-obscured by a haze of driven rain. I went in steeply, pulled back the stick and touched down like silk. I was glad about that landing. Somehow it seemed an omen. I kicked the rudder and swung on to the perimeter track, the rain beating up from the concrete and sweeping across the field so that the litter of planes became no more than a vague shadow in the murk.

" Dear old Wunstorf!" Field's voice crackled over the inter-com. " What a dump! It was raining when I left. Probably been raining ever since."

A truck came out to meet us. We dumped our kit in it and it drove us to the airport buildings. They were a drab olive green ; bleak utilitarian blocks of concrete. The Operations

Room was on the ground floor. I reported to the squadron leader in charge. " If you care to go up to the mess they'll fix you up." Then he saw Field. " Good God! You back already, Bob?"

" A fortnight's leave, that's all I got out of getting demobilised," Field answered.

" And a rise in pay I'll bet." The squadron leader turned to me. " He'll get things sorted out for you. Report here in the morning and we'll let you know what your timings are."

The station commander came in as he finished speaking, a big blond Alsatian at his heels. " Any news of that Skymaster yet?" he asked.

" Not yet, sir," replied the squadron leader. " Celle have just been on again. They're getting worried. It's twenty minutes overdue. There's been a hell of a storm over the Russian Zone."

" What about the other bases?"

" Lubeck, Fuhlsbuttel, Fassberg—they've all made negative reports, sir. It looks as though it's force-landed somewhere. Berlin are in touch with the Russians, but so far Safety Centre hasn't reported anything."

" Next wave goes out at seventeen hundred, doesn't it? If the plane hasn't been located by then have all pilots briefed to keep a lookout for it, will you?" He turned to go and then stopped as he saw us. " Back in civvies, eh, Field? I must say it doesn't make you look any smarter." He smiled and then his eyes met mine. " You must be Fraser." He held out his hand to me. " Glad to have you with us. Harcourt's up at the mess now. He's expecting you." He turned to the squadron leader. " Give the mess a ring and tell Wing-Commander Harcourt that his other Tudor has arrived."

" Very good, sir."

" We'll have a drink sometime, Fraser." The station commander nodded and hurried out with his dog.

" I'll get you a car," the squadron leader said. He went out and his shout of "*Fahrer!*" echoed in the stone corridor.

The mess was a huge building; block on block of grey concrete, large enough to house a division. When I gave my name to the German at the desk he ran his finger down a long list. " Block C, sir—rooms 231 and 235. Just place your baggage there, please. I will arrange for it. And come this way, gentlemen. Wing-Commander Harcourt is wishing to speak with you." So Harcourt retained his Air Force title out here! We followed the clerk into the lounge. It had a dreary waiting-room atmosphere. Harcourt came straight over. "Good trip?" he asked.

"Pretty fair," I said.

"What's visibility now?"

"Ceiling's about a thousand," I told him. "We ran into it over the Dutch coast."

He nodded. "Well, now we've got six planes here." There was a touch of pride in the way he said it and this was reflected in the momentary gleam in his pale eyes. He'd every reason to be proud. There was only one other company doing this sort of work. How he'd managed to finance it, I don't know. He'd only started on the airlift three months ago. He'd had one plane then. Now he had six. It was something of an achievement and I remember thinking: *This man is doing what Saeton is so desperately wanting to do.* I tried to compare their personalities. But there was no point of similarity between the two men. Harcourt was quiet, efficient, withdrawn inside himself. Saeton was ruthless, genial—an extrovert and a gambler.

"Fraser!"

Harcourt's voice jerked me out of my thought. "Yes?"

"I asked you whether you're okay to start on the wave scheduled for 10.00 hours to-morrow?"

He nodded. "Good. We've only two relief crews at the moment so you'll be worked pretty hard. But I expect you can stand it for a day or two." His eyes crinkled at the corners. "Overtime rates are provided for in your contracts." He glanced at his watch. "Time I was moving. There's a wave due to leave at seventeen hundred. Field knows his way around."

He left us then and we went in search of our rooms. It was a queer place, the Wunstorf Mess. You couldn't really call it a mess—aircrews' quarters would be a more apt description. It reminded me of an enormous jail. Long concrete corridors echoed to ribald laughter and the splash of water from communal washrooms. The rooms were like cells, small dormitories with two or three beds. One room we went into by mistake was in darkness with the blackout blinds drawn. The occupants were asleep and they cursed us as we switched on the light. Through the open doors of other rooms we saw men playing cards, reading, talking, going to bed, getting up. All the life of Wunstorf was here in these electrically-lit, echoing corridors. In the washrooms men in uniform were washing next to men in pyjamas quietly shaving as though it were early morning. These billets brought home to me more than anything the fact that the airlift was a military operation, a round-the-clock service running on into infinity.

We found our rooms. There were two beds in each. Carter and I took one room ; Westrop and Field the other. Field wandered in and gave us a drink from a flask. "It's going to be pretty tough operating six planes with only two relief crews," he said. "It means damn nearly twelve hours duty a day."

"Suits me," I replied.

Carter straightened up from the case he was unpacking. "Glad to be back in the flying business, eh?" He smiled.

I nodded.

"It won't last long," Field said.

"What won't?" I asked.

"Your enthusiasm. This isn't like it was in wartime." He dived across the corridor to his room and returned with a folder. "Take a look at this." He held a sheet out to me. It was divided into squares—each square a month and each month black with little ticks. "Every one of these ticks represents a trip to Berlin and back, around two hours' flying. It goes on and on, the same routine. Wet or fine, thick mist or blowing half a gale, they send you up regular as clock-work. No let-up at all. Gets you down in the end." He shrugged his shoulders and tucked the folder under his arm. "Oh, well, got to earn a living, I suppose. But it's a bloody grind, believe you me."

After tea I walked down to the airfield. I wanted to be alone. The rain had stopped, but the wind still lashed at the pine trees. The loading apron was almost empty, a huge, desolate stretch of tarmac shining wet and black in the grey light. Only planes undergoing repairs and maintenance were left, their wings quivering soundlessly under the stress of the weather. It was as though all the rest had been spirited away. The runways were deserted. The place looked almost as empty as Membury.

I turned back through the pines and struck away to the left, to the railway sidings that had been built out to the very edge of the landing field. A long line of fuel wagons was being shunted in, fuel that we would carry to Berlin. The place was bleak and desolate. The country beyond rolled away into the distance, an endless vista of agriculture, without hedges or trees. Something of the character of the people seemed inherent in that landscape—inevitable, ruthless and without surprise. I turned, and across the railway sidings I caught a glimpse of the wings of a four-engined freighter—symbol of the British occupation of Germany. It seemed suddenly insignificant against the immensity of that rolling plain.

We were briefed by the officer in charge of Operations at nine o'clock the following morning. By ten we were out on the perimeter track waiting in a long queue of planes, waiting our turn with engines switched off to save petrol. Harcourt had been very insistent about that. " It's all right for the R.A.F.," he had said. " The taxpayer foots their petrol bill. We're under charter at so much per flight. Fly on two engines whenever possible. Cut your engines out when waiting for take-off." It made me realise how much Saeton had to gain by the extra thrust of those two engines and their lower fuel consumption.

The thought of Saeton reminded me of the thing I'd promised to do. I wished it could have been this first flight. I wanted to get it over. But it had to be a night flight. I glanced at Tubby. He was sitting in the second pilot's seat, the earphones of his flying helmet making his face seem broader, his eyes fixed on the instrument panel. If only I could have had a different engineer. It wasn't going to be easy to convince him.

The last plane ahead of us swung into position, engines revving. As it roared off up the runway the voice of Control crackled in my earphones. " *Okay, Two-five-two. You're clear to line up now. Take off right away.*" Perhaps it was as well to fly in daylight first, I thought, as I taxied to the runway end and swung the machine into position.

We took off dead on time at 10.18. For almost three-quarters of an hour we flew north-east making for the entry to the northern approach corridor for Berlin. " *Corridor beacon coming up now,*" Field told me over the inter-com. " *Turn on to 100 degrees. Time 11.01. We're minus thirty seconds.*" That meant we were thirty seconds behind schedule. The whole thing was worked on split-second timing. Landing

margin was only ninety seconds either side of touch-down
timing. If you didn't make it inside the margin you just had
to overshoot and return to base. The schedule was fixed by
timings over radar beacons at the start and finish of the air
corridor that spanned the Russian Zone. Fixed heights ensured
that there were no accidents in the air. We were flying Angels
three-five—height 3,500 feet. Twenty miles from Frohnau
beacon Westrop reported to Gatow Airway.

As we approached Berlin I began to have a sense of excitement. I hadn't been over Berlin since 1945. I'd been on night
raids then. I wondered what it would look like in daylight. Tubby seemed to feel it, too. He kept on looking
down through his side window and moving restlessly in his
seat. I pushed my helmet back and shouted to him. " Have
you seen Berlin from the air since the war?"

He nodded abstractedly. " I was on transport work."

" Then what are you so excited about?" I asked.

He hesitated. Then he smiled—it was an eager, boyish smile.
" Diana's at Gatow. She's working in the Malcolm Club there.
She doesn't know I'm on the airlift." He grinned. " I'm going
to surprise her."

Westrop's voice sounded in my earphones, reporting to
Gatow Airway that we were over Frohnau beacon. We
switched to contact with Traffic Control, Gatow. " *Okay,
Two-five-two. Report again at Lancaster House.*" So Diana
was at Gatow. It suddenly made the place seem friendly,
almost ordinary. It would be nice to see Diana again. And
then I was looking out of my side window at a bomb-pocked
countryside that merged into miles of roofless, shattered buildings. There were great flat gaps in the city, but mostly the
streets were still visible, bordered by the empty shells of buildings. From the air it seemed as though hardly a house had a
roof. We were passing over the area that the Russians had
fought through. Nothing seemed to have been done about it.
It might have happened yesterday instead of four years ago.

Over the centre of the city Field gave me my new course and
Westrop reported to Gatow Tower, who answered, " *Okay,
Two-five-two. Report at two miles. You're Number Three in
the pattern.*"

There was less damage here. I caught a glimpse of the
Olympic stadium and then the pine trees of the Grunewald

district were coming up to meet me as I descended steeply. Havel Lake opened out, the flat sheet of water across which the last survivors from the Fuehrer Bunker had tried to escape, and Westrop reported again. *"Clear to land. Two-five-two,"* came the voice of Gatow Control. *"Keep rolling after touchdown. There's a York close behind you."*

I lowered undercarriage and landing flaps. We skimmed the trees and then we were over a cleared strip of woods dotted with the posts of the night landing beacons with the whole circle of Gatow Airport opening up and the pierced steel runway rising to meet us. I levelled out at the edge of the field. The wheels bumped once, then we were on the ground, the machine jolting over the runway sections. I kept rolling to the runway end, braked and swung left to the off-loading platform.

Gatow was a disappointment after Wunstorf. It seemed much smaller and much less active. There were only five aircraft on the apron. Yet this field handled more traffic than either Tempelhof in the American Sector or Tegel in the French. As I taxied across the apron I saw the York behind me land and two Army lorries manned by a German labour team, still in their field grey, nosed out to meet it. I went on, past the line of Nissen huts that bordered the apron, towards the hangars. Two Tudor tankers were already at Piccadilly Circus, the circular standing for fuel off-loading. I swung into position by a vacant pipe. By the time we had switched off and got out of our seats the fuselage door was open and a British soldier was connecting a pipeline to our fuel tanks.

"Where's the Malcolm Club?" Tubby asked Field. His voice trembled slightly.

"It's one of those Nissen huts over there," Field answered, pointing to the off-loading apron. He turned to me. "Know what the Army call this?" He waved his hands towards the circular standing. "Remember they called the cross-Channel pipeline PLUTO? Well, this one's called PLUME—Pipeline-under-mother-earth. Not bad, eh? It runs the fuel down to Havel where it's shipped into Berlin by barge. Saves fuel on transport."

We were crossing the edge of the apron now, walking along the line of Nissen huts. The first two were full of Germans. "Jerry labour organisation," Field explained.

" What about the tower?" I asked. Above the third Nissen hut was a high scaffolding with a lookout. It was like a workman's hut on stilts.

" That's the control tower for the off-loading platform. All this is run by the Army—it's what they call a FASO. Forward Airfield Supply Organisation. Here's the Malcolm Club." A blue board with R.A.F. roundel faced us. " Better hurry if you want some coffee."

Tubby hesitated. " She may not be on duty," he murmured.

" We'll soon see," I said and took his arm.

Inside the hut the air was warm and smelt of fresh-made cakes. A fire glowed red in an Army-type stove. The place was full of smoke and the sound of voices. There were about four aircrews there, in a huddle by the counter. I saw Diana immediately. She was in the middle of the group, her hand on the arm of an American Control officer, laughing happily, her face turned up to his.

I felt Tubby check and was reminded suddenly of that night at Membury when he and I had stood outside the window of our mess. Then Diana turned and saw us. Her eyes lit up and she rushed over, seizing hold of Tubby, hugging him. Then she turned to me and kissed me, too. " Harry! Harry!" She was calling excitedly across the room. " Here's Tubby just flown in." She swung back to her husband. " Darling—remember I told you my brother Harry was in Berlin. Well, here he is."

I saw the stiffness leave Tubby's face. He was suddenly grinning happily, shaking the big American's hand up and down, saying, " My God! Harry. I should have recognised you from your photograph. Instead, I thought you were some boyfriend of Diana's." He didn't even bother to hide his relief, and Diana never seemed to notice that anything had been wrong. She was taken too much by surprise. " Why didn't you tell me you were flying in?" she cried. " You devil, you. Come on. Let's get you some coffee. They only give you a few minutes here."

I stood and watched her hustling him to the bun counter, wondering whether he had told her what had happened at Membury, wondering what she'd say if she knew I was going to ditch him in the Russian Zone.

" You must be Fraser." Her brother was at my elbow. " I've heard a lot about you from Di. My name's Harry Culyer, by the way." He had Diana's eyes, but that was all they had in common. He had none of her restlessness. He was the sort of man you trust on sight; big, slow-spoken, friendly. "Yes, I've heard a lot about you and a crazy devil called Saeton. Is that really his name?" He gave a fat chuckle. "Seems apt from what Di told me."

I wondered how much she had told him. "Are you connected with the airlift?" I asked him.

He shook his head. "No, I'm attached to the Control Office of the U.S. Military Government. I used to work for the Opel outfit before the war so they figured I'd have to stay on in some sort of uniform and keep an eye on vehicle production in the Zone. Right now I guess you could do with some coffee, eh?"

The coffee was thick and sweet. With it was a potted meat sandwich and a highly-coloured cake full of synthetic cream. "Cigarettes?" I said, offering him a packet.

"Well, thanks. That's one of the troubles here in Berlin. Cigarettes are damned hard to come by. And it's worse for your boys. They're down to about fifteen a day. Well, what do you think of Gatow?" He laughed when I told him I was disappointed. "You expected to find it littered with aircraft, eh? Well, that's organisation. Tempelhof is the same. They've got it so that these German labour teams turn the planes round in about fifteen minutes."

"What brings you out to Gatow?" I asked him. "Just paying Diana a visit?"

"Sort of. But I got a good excuse," he added with a grin. "I had to interview a German girl who has just got a job out here as a checker in your German Labour Organisation. Some trouble about her papers and we urgently need her down at Frankfurt. That's why I came up to Berlin."

"You're not stationed here then?" I asked.

"No. I'm normally in the Zone. It's nice and quiet down there—by comparison. I just been talking to your SIB major over there. The stories that man can tell!"

"What's he doing up at Gatow?" I asked.

"Oh, there's been some trouble with the Russians. This is your first trip, isn't it? Well, you see those trees on the other side of the airfield?" He nodded through the windows. "That's the frontier over there."

"The Russian Sector?"

"No. The Russian Zone. Last night Red Army guards opened up on a German car just after it had been allowed through the frontier barrier into the British Sector. Then their troops crossed the frontier and pushed the car back into their Zone under the nose of the R.A.F. Regiment. Your boys are pretty sore about it."

"You mean the car was shot up in British territory?" I asked.

He laughed. Seems that sort of thing is happening every day in this crazy town. If they want somebody, they just drive into the Western Sectors and kidnap them." The corners of his eyes crinkled. "From what I hear our boys do the same in the Eastern Sector."

An R.A.F. orderly called to me from the door. "Two-five-two ready, sir."

"Well, I guess that's your call. Glad to have met you, Fraser."

"Neil!" Diana caught hold of my arm. "Tubby has just told me—about the crash." She glanced quickly at Tubby who was saying good-bye to her brother. "What's Bill doing now?" she asked in a quick whisper. I didn't know what to say so I kept my mouth shut. "Oh, don't be silly. I've got over that. But I know how it must have hit him. Where is he now?"

"He's still at Membury," I said. And then added, "He's sticking the plane together with sealing wax."

"You don't mean to say he's still going on with it?"

"Look—I've got to go now," I said. "Good-bye, Diana."

She was staring at me with a puzzled frown. "Good-bye," she said automatically.

Outside it was still raining. We climbed into the plane and taxied out to the runway. "*You're clear to line up now, Two-five-two. Two-six-O a-concrete—angels three-five.*" We flew out along the single exit corridor and were back in Wunstorf in good time for lunch. A letter was waiting for me at the mess. The address was typed and the envelope was postmarked "Baydon." *Dear Neil. Just to let you know I have almost completed the break-up. I have a flare path now. All you have to do is buzz once and I'll light you in. Good luck. Bill Saeton.* As I folded the letter Tubby came into the room. "Message from Harcourt. We're not on the 1530 wave. He's switched us to 2200. Says the other boys need a night's sleep."

So it had come. I had a sudden sick feeling.

He peered at me anxiously. " You feeling all right, Neil?"

" Yes. Why?"

" You look pretty pale. Not nervous, are you? Damn it, you've no reason to be. You had enough experience of night-flying during the war." His gaze fell to the letter in my hand, but he didn't say anything and I tore it into small pieces and stuffed them into my pocket.

" Better turn in then if we're going to fly all night," I said.

But I knew I shouldn't sleep. Hell! Why did I have to agree to this damn-fool scheme? I was scared now. Not scared of the danger. I don't think it was that. But what had seemed straightforward and simple over a drink in the pub at Ramsbury seemed much more difficult now that I was actually a part of the airlift. It seemed utterly crazy to try and fly a plane out of this organised bus service of supply delivery. And I had to convince a crew that included Tubby Carter that they had got to bale out over the Russian Zone. The menace of the Zone had already gripped me. I lay and sweated on my bed, listening to the 1530 wave taking off, knowing that mine was the next wave, scared that I should bungle it.

At tea I could eat nothing, but drank several cups, smoking cigarette after cigarette, conscious all the time of Tubby watching me with a puzzled, worried expression. Afterwards I walked down to the field in the gathering dusk and watched the planes pile in, a constant stream of aircraft glimmering like giant moths along the line of the landing lights. I saw my own plane, Two-five-two, come in, watched it swing into position on the loading apron and the crew pile out, and I hung on, waiting for the maintenance crew to finish servicing it. At last it stood deserted, a black shape against the wet tarmac that glistened with the reflection of the lights. I climbed on board.

Saeton and I had discussed this problem of simulating engine failure at great length. The easiest method would have been simply to cut off the juice. But the fuel cocks were on the starboard side, controlled from the flight engineer's seat. We had finally agreed that the only convincing method was to tamper with the ignition. I went forward to the cockpit and got to work on the wiring behind the instrument panel. I had tools with me and six lengths of insulated wire terminating in small metal clips. What I did was to fix two wires to the back of three of the ignition switches. These wires I led along the back of the instrument-panel and brought out at the extreme left on my own side. All I had to do when I wished to simulate engine failure was to clip each pair of wires together and so short out the ignition switches. That would close the ignition circuit and stop the plugs sparking.

It took me the better part of an hour to fix the wires. I was just finishing when a lorry drove up. There was the clatter of metal and the drag of a pipe as they connected the fuel lorry to the tanks in the port hand wing. The lorry's engine droned as it began refuelling.

I waited, conscious already of a fugitive, guilty feeling. Footsteps moved round the plane. Rather than be caught crouched nervously in the cockpit of my own machine, I went aft down the fuselage, climbing round the three big elliptical tanks and dropping on to the asphalt. I started to walk away from the plane, but the beam of a torch picked me out and a voice said, " Who's that?"

" Squadron-Leader Fraser," I answered, reverting automatically to my service title. " I've just been checking over something."

" Very good, sir. Good-night."

" Good-night," I answered and went hurriedly across to the terminal building and along the road to the mess. I went up to my room and lay on my bed, trying to read. But I couldn't concentrate. My hands were trembling. Time dragged by as I lay there chain-smoking. Shortly after seven-thirty the door opened and Westrop poked his head into the room. " You coming down to dinner, sir?"

" May as well," I said.

As we went down the echoing corridors and along the cinder paths to the mess, Westrop chattered away incessantly. I wasn't listening until something he said caught my attention. " What's that about a crash?" I asked.

" Remember when we arrived here yesterday—the station commander was talking about a Skymaster that was missing?" he said. " Well, they made a forced landing in Russian territory. I got it from a flight lieutenant who's just come off duty at Ops. One of our crews sighted the wreck this afternoon. The Russians have apparently denied all knowledge of it. What do you think happens to crews who get landed in the Russian Zone?"

" I don't know," I said shortly.

" The flight lieutenant said they were probably being held for interrogation. He didn't seem worried about them. But they might be injured. Do you think the Russians would give them medical treatment, sir? I mean "—he hesitated—" well, I wouldn't like to have a Russian surgeon operate on me, would you?"

" No."

" What do you think they hope to gain by this sort of thing? Everybody seems convinced they're not prepared to go to war yet. They've stopped buzzing our planes. That seems to prove it. They got scared when they crashed that York. I was talking to an R.E. major this afternoon. He said the trouble was their lines of communication. Their roads are bad and their railways from Russia to Eastern Germany are only single track. But I think it's more than that, don't you, sir? I mean, they can't possibly be as good as us technically. They could never have organised a thing as complicated as the airlift, for instance. And then their planes—they're still operating machines based on the B 29's they got hold of during the war." He went on and on about the Russians until at length I couldn't stand it any more. " Oh, for God's sake," I said. " I'm sick and tired of the Russians."

" Sorry, sir, but——" He paused uncertainly. " It's just— well, this is my first operational night flight."

It was only then that I realised he'd been talking because he was nervous. I thought: *My God! The poor kid's scared stiff of the Russians and in a few hours' time I'm going to order him to jump.* It made me feel sick inside. Why wasn't my crew composed entirely of Fields. I didn't care about Field. I'd have ordered him to jump over wartime Berlin and not cared a damn. But Tubby and this child. . . .

I forced myself to eat and listened to Westrop's chatter all through the meal. He had a live, inquiring mind. He already knew that we had to cover seventy miles of the Russian Zone in flying down the Berlin approach corridor. He knew, too, all about Russian interrogation methods—the round-the-clock interrogation under lights, the solitary confinement, the building up of fear in the mind of the victim. " They're no better than the Nazis, are they?" he said. " Only they don't seem to go as far as physical torture—not against service personnel." He paused and then said, " I wish we wore uniform. I'm certain,

if anything like that happened, we'd be better off if we were
in R.A.F. uniform."

"You'll be all right," I answered without thinking.

"Oh, I know we shan't have to make a forced landing," he
said quickly, mistaking what had been in my mind. "Our
servicing is much better than the Yanks and——"

"I wouldn't be too sure of that," I cut in. "Have a cigarette
and for God's sake stop talking about forced landings."

"I'm sorry, sir. It was only——" He took the cigarette.
"You must think me an awful funk. But it's odd—I always
like to know exactly what I'm facing. It makes it easier,
somehow."

Damn the kid! I'd always felt just like that myself. "I'll
see you at the plane at 21.46," I said and got quickly to my
feet. As I went out of the dining-hall I glanced at my watch.
Still an hour to go! I left the mess and walked down to the
airfield. The night was cold and frosty, the sky studded with
stars. The apron was full of the huddled shapes of aircraft,
looking clumsy and unbeautiful on the ground. Trucks were
coming and going as the RASO teams worked to load them
for the next wave. I leaned on the boundary fence and watched
them. I could see my own plane. It was the left-hand one of
a line of Tudors. Fuel loading and maintenance crews had
completed their work. The planes stood deserted and silent.
The minutes dragged slowly by as I stood, chilled to the
marrow, trying to brace myself for what I had to do.

The odd thing is I never thought of refusing to carry out
my part of the plan. I could have raised technical difficulties
and put it off until gradually Saeton lost heart. Many times
since I have asked myself why I didn't do this, and I still
don't really know the answer. I like to think that Saeton's
threat of exposing my identity to the police had nothing to
do with it. Certainly the audacity of the thing had appealed
to me. Also I believed in Saeton and his engines and the airlift
had only served to increase their importance in my eyes. Moreover, my own future was involved. I suppose the truth is that
my attitude was a combination of all these things. At any rate,
as I stood there on the edge of Wunstorf airfield waiting for
zero hour, it never occurred to me not to do it.

At last my watch told me it was nine-fifteen. I went slowly
back to the mess. Tubby came in as I was getting into my
flying kit. "Well, thank God the weather's cleared," he said

cheerfully. "I wouldn't want to be talked down by GCA the first time we went in by night." GCA is Ground Control Approach, a means of blind landing where the plane lands on instructions from an officer operating radar gear at the edge of the runway.

By nine-fifty we were climbing into the plane. Our take-off time was 22.36 and as I lifted the heavy plane into the starlit night my hands and stomach felt as cold as ice. Tubby was checking the trim of the engines, his hand on the throttle levers. I groped down and found one of my three pairs of wires and touched the ends of them together. The inboard port motor checked. It worked all right. I glanced quickly at Tubby. He had taken his hand from the throttles and was listening, his head on one side. Then he turned to me. "Did you hear that engine falter?" he shouted.

I nodded. "Sounded like dirt in the fuel," I called back.

He stayed in the same position for a moment, listening. Then his hand went back to the throttles. I glanced at the airspeed indicator and then at my watch. Three-quarters of an hour to Restorf beacon at the entrance of the air corridor.

The time dragged. The only sound was the steady drone of the engines. Twice I half-cut the same motor out. On the second occasion I did it when Tubby had gone aft to speak to Field. I held the wires together until the motor had cut out completely. Tubby suddenly appeared at my elbow as I allowed it to pick up again. "I don't like the sound of that engine," he shouted.

"Nor do I," I said.

He stood quite still, listening. "Sounded like ignition. I'll get it checked at Gatow."

I glanced at my watch. It was eleven-sixteen. Any minute now. Then Field's voice crackled in my ears. "We're over the corridor beacon now. Right on to 100 degrees. We're minus ten seconds." I felt ice cold, but calm, as I banked. My stomach didn't flutter any more. I leaned a little forward, feeling for the metal clips. One by one I fastened them together in their pairs. And one by one the engines died, all except the inboard starboard motor. The plane was suddenly very quiet. I heard Tubby's muttered curse quite distinctly. "Check ignition!" I shouted to him. "Check fuel!" I made my voice sound scared. The airspeed indicator was dropping, the luminous pointer swinging back through 150, falling back

E

towards the 100 mark. The altimeter needle was dropping, too, as the nose tilted earthwards. "We're going down at about 800 a minute," I shouted.

"Ignition okay," he reported, his hand on the switches. "Fuel okay." His eyes were frantically scanning the instrument panel. "It's an electrical fault—ignition, I think. The bastards must have overlooked some loose wiring."

"Anything we can do?" I asked. "We're down to three thousand already."

"Doubt it. Not much time."

"If you think there's anything we can do, say so. Otherwise I'm going to order the crew to bale out." I had kept my intercom mouthpiece close to my lips so that Field and Westrop could hear what we were saying.

Tubby straightened up. "Okay. We'd better bale out." His face looked stiff and strained in the light of the instrument panel.

"Get your parachutes on," I ordered over the inter-com. "Field. You go aft and get the fuselage door open. We may have to ditch her." Out of the tail of my eye I saw the two of them struggling with their parachutes. Field shouted something to Westrop and a moment later the bags containing the other two parachutes were slid on to the floor of the cockpit. "Get back to the fuselage door," I told Westrop. "I'll send Carter aft when I want you to jump." I glanced at the altimeter dial. "Height two-six," I called to Tubby.

He straightened up. "Nothing I can do," he said. "It's in the wiring somewhere."

"Okay," I said. "Get aft and tell the others to jump. Give me a shout when you're jumping."

He stood there, hesitating for a moment. "Okay." His hand gripped my arm. "See you in the Russian Zone." But he still didn't move and his hand remained gripping my arm. "Would you like me to take her while you jump?" he asked.

I realised suddenly that he was remembering the last time I'd jumped, over Membury. He thought my nerve might have gone. I swallowed quickly. Why did he have to be so bloody decent about it? "Of course not," I said sharply. "Get aft and look after yourself and the others."

His eyes remained fixed on mine—brown, intelligent eyes that seemed to read my mind. "Good luck!" He turned and dived quickly through towards the fuselage. Leaning out of my seat, I looked back and watched him climbing round the fuel tanks. I could just see the others at the open door of the fuselage. Tubby joined them. Westrop went first, then Field. Tubby shouted to me. " Jump!" I called to him. The plane skidded slightly and I turned back to the controls, steadying her.

When I looked back down the length of the fuselage there was no one there. I was alone in the plane. I settled myself in my seat. Height one thousand six hundred. Airspeed ninety-five. I'd take her down to a thousand feet. That should put her below the horizon of the three who had jumped. Through the windshield I saw a small point of light moving across the sky—the tail-light of one of the airlift planes holding steadily to its course. I wondered if those behind could see me. In case, I banked away and at the same time broke one of the wire contacts. The outboard port engine started immediately as I unfeathered the prop.

As I banked out of the traffic stream a voice called to me— " You bloody fool, Neil. You haven't even got your parachute on." I felt sudden panic grip me as I turned to find Tubby coming back into the cockpit.

" Why the hell haven't you jumped?"

" Plenty of time now," he said calmly. " Perhaps the other engines will pick up. I was worried about you, that's why I came back."

" I can look after myself," I snapped. " Get back to that door and jump."

I think he saw the panic in my eyes and misunderstood it. His gaze dropped to my parachute still in its canvas bag. " I'll take over whilst you get into your parachute. With two engines we might still make Gatow."

He was already sliding into the second pilot's seat now and I felt his hands take over on the controls. " Now get your 'chute on, Neil," he said quietly.

We sat there, staring at each other. I didn't know what the hell to do. I glanced at the altimeter. The needle was steady at the thousand mark. His eyes followed the direction of my gaze and then he looked at me again and his forehead was wrinkled in a puzzled frown. " You weren't going to jump, were you?" he said slowly.

I sat there, staring at him. And then I knew he'd got to come back to Membury with me. " No," I said. And with sudden violence, "Why the hell couldn't you have jumped when I told you?"

"I knew you didn't like jumping," he said. "What were you going to do—try and crash land?"

I hesitated. I'd have one more shot at getting him to jump. I edged my left hand down the side of my seat until I found the wires that connected to the ignition switch of that outboard port motor. I clipped them together and the motor died. "It's gone again," I shouted to him. I switched over to the automatic pilot. "Come on," I said. "We're getting out." I slid out of my seat and gripped him by the arm. "Quick!" I said, half-pulling him towards the exit door.

I think I'd have done it that time, but he glanced back, and then suddenly he wrenched himself free of my grip. I saw him reach over the pilot's seat, saw him tearing at the wires, and as he unfeathered the props the motors picked up in a thrumming roar. He slid into his own seat, took over from the automatic pilot and as I stood there, dazed with the shock of discovery, I saw the altimeter needle begin to climb through the luminous figures of its dial.

Then I was clambering into my seat, struggling to get control of the plane from him. He shouted something to me. I don't remember what it was. I kicked at the rudder bar and swung the heavy plane into a wide banking turn. "We're going back to Membury," I yelled at him.

"Membury!" He stared at me. "So that's it! It was you who fixed those wires. You made those boys jump——" The words seemed to choke him. "You must be crazy. What's the idea?"

I heard myself laughing wildly. I was excited and my nerves were tense. "Better ask Saeton," I said, still laughing.

"Saeton!" He caught hold of my arm. "You crazy fools! You can't get away with this."

"Of course we can," I cried. "We have. Nobody will ever know." I was so elated I didn't notice him settling more firmly into his seat. I was thinking I'd succeeded. I'd done the impossible—I'd taken an aircraft off the Berlin airlift. I wanted to sing, shout, do something to express the thrill it gave me.

Then the controls moved under my hands. He was dragging the plane round, heading it for Berlin. For a moment I fought the controls, struggling to get the ship round. The compass wavered uncertainly. But he held on grimly. He had great strength. At length I let go and watched the compass swing back on to the lubber lines of our original course.

All the elation I had felt died out of me. " For God's sake, Tubby," I said. " Try to understand what this means. Nobody's going to lose over this. Harcourt will get the insurance. As for the airlift, in a few weeks the plane will be back on the job. Only then it will have our engines in it. We'll have succeeded. Doesn't success mean anything to you?" Automatically I was using Saeton's arguments over again.

But all he said was, " You've dropped those boys into Russian territory."

" Well, what of it?" I demanded hotly. " They'll be all right. So will Harcourt. And so will we."

He looked at me then, his face a white mask, the little lines at the corners of his eyes no longer crinkled by laughter. He looked solid, unemotional—like a block of granite. " I should have known the sort of person you were when you turned up at Membury like that. Saeton's a fanatic. I can forgive him. But you're just a dirty little crook who has——"

He shouldn't have said that. It made me mad—part fear, part anger. Damn his bloody high and mighty principles! Was he prepared to die for them? I reached down for the wires. My fingers were trembling and numb with the cold blast of the air that came in through the open doorway aft, but I managed to fasten the clips. The engines died away. The cabin was suddenly silent, a ghostly place of soft-lit dials and our reflections in the windshield. We seemed suddenly cut off from the rest of the world. A white pin-point of light slid over us like a start—our one contact with reality, a plane bound for Berlin.

" Don't be a fool, Fraser!" Tubby's voice was unnaturally loud in the stillness.

I laughed. It wasn't a pleasant sound. My nerves were keyed to the pitch of desperation. " Either we fly to Membury," I said, " or we crash." My teeth were clenched. It might have been a stranger's voice. " You can jump if you want to," I added, nodding towards the rear of the cockpit where the wind whistled.

" Unfasten those wires!" he shouted. And when I made no move he said. " Get them unfastened and start the motors or I'll hurt you."

He was fumbling in the pocket beside his seat and his hand

came out holding a heavy spanner. He let go the controls then. The plane dipped and slid away to port. Automatically I grasped the control column and righted her. At the same time he rose in his seat, the spanner lifted in his hand.

I flung myself sideways, lunging out at him. The spanner caught me across the shoulder and my left arm went numb. But I had hold of his flying suit now and was pulling him towards me. He had no room to use the spanner again. And at the same moment the plane dropped sickeningly. We were flung into the aisle and fetched up against the fuel tanks in the fuselage.

For a moment we stood there, locked together, and then he fought to get clear of me, to get back to start the motors again. I was determined he shouldn't. I'd take him down into the ground rather than fly on to Gatow to be accused of having attempted to take a plane off the airlift. I clutched hold of him, pinning his arms, bracing myself against the tanks. The plane lurched and we were flung between the tanks into the main body of the fuselage where the wind roared in through the open doorway. That lurch flung us against the door to the toilet, breaking us clear of each other. He raised the spanner to strike at me again and I hit him with my fist. The spanner descended, striking my shoulder again. I lashed out again. My fist caught his jaw and his head jerked back against the metal of the fuselage. At the same moment the plane seemed to fall away. We were both flung sideways. Tubby hit the side of the open doorway. I saw his head jerk back as his forehead caught a protruding section of the metal frame. Blood gleamed red in a long gash and his jaw fell slack. Slowly his legs gave under him.

As he fell I started forward. He was falling into the black rectangle of the doorway. I clutched at him, but the plane swung, jerking me back against the toilet door. And in that instant Tubby slid to the floor, his legs slowly disappearing into the black void of the slip-stream. For an instant his thick torso lay along the floor, held there by the wind and the tilt of the plane. I could do nothing. I was pinned by the tilt of the plane, forced to stand there and watch as his body began to slide outwards, slowly, like a sack, the outstretched hands making no attempt to hold him. For a second he was there, sliding slowly out across the floor, and then the slip-stream whisked him away and I was alone in the body of the plane

with only the gaping doorway and a thin trickle of blood on
the steel flooring to show what had happened.

I shook myself, dazed with the horror of it. Then I closed
the door and went for'ard. Almost automatically my brain
registered the altimeter dial. Height 700. I slipped into the
pilot's seat and with trembling fingers forced the wires apart.
The engines roared. I gripped the control column and my feet
found the rudder bar. I banked and climbed steeply. The
lights of a town showed below me and the snaking course of
a river. I felt sick at the thought of what had happened to
Tubby. Height two-four. Course eight-five degrees. I must
find out what had happened to Tubby.

I made a tight, diving turn and levelled out at five hundred
feet. I had to find out what had happened to him. If he'd
regained consciousness and had been able to pull his parachute release . . . Surely the cold air would have revived him.
*God! Don't let him die.* I was sobbing my prayer aloud. I
went back along the course of the river, over the lights of the
town. A road ran out of it, straight like a piece of tape and
white in the moonlight. Then I shut down the engines and
put down the flaps. This was the spot where Tubby had fallen.
I searched desperately through the windshield. But all I saw
was a deserted airfield bordered by pine woods and a huddle
of buildings that were no more than empty shells. No sign
of a parachute, no comforting mushroom patch of white.

I went back and forth over the area a dozen times. The aerodrome and the woods and the bomb-shattered buildings stood
out clear in the moonlight, but never a sign of the white silk
of a parachute.

Tubby was dead and I had killed him.

Dazed and frightened I banked away from the white grave-
yard scene of the shattered buildings. I took the plane up to
10,000 feet and fled westward across the moon-filled night.
Away to the right I could see the lines of planes coming in
along the corridor, red and green navigation lights stretching
back towards Lübeck. But in a moment they were gone and
I was alone, riding the sky, with only the reflection of my face
in the windshield for company—nothing of earth but the flat
expanse of the Westphalian plain, white like a salt-pan below
me.

# CHAPTER SIX

THERE was no problem of navigation to distract my mind on the homeward run. The earth lay like a white map below me. I found the North Sea at Flushing, crossed the southern extremity of it, flying automatically, and just as automatically picked up the Thames estuary, following the curves of the river till it met the Kennet. And all the time I was remembering every detail of what had happened. It seemed such waste that he shoud die like that. And all because he'd called me a crook. My face, ghostly in the windshield, seemed to reflect the bitterness of my thoughts.

I had three hours in which to sort the thing out and face it. But I didn't face it. I know that now. I began that flight hating myself. I ended it by hating Saeton. It was he who had forced me into it. It was he, not I, who was responsible for Tubby's death. By the time I was over the Kennet I had almost convinced myself of that.

I dropped to a thousand feet in a mood of cold fury, picked up Ramsbury and swung north-east. The trees of Baydon Hill were a dark line and there, suddenly, were the hangars of Membury and, as I swept low over the field, I caught a glimpse of the quarters nestled snugly in their clearing in the woods. All just as I had left it. Nothing changed. Only a man dead and the moon bathing everything in a white unreal light.

I had no need of any flares. I skidded in a tight, vicious turn, dropped flaps and undercarriage, and slammed the machine down on to the runway not caring whether I smashed it up in the violence of my anger.

Saeton was at the hangar and came running out to meet me as I cut the engines. He was waiting for me as I stepped out on to the concrete, his face alive with excitement. " Well done, Neil! Magnificent!" He seized my hand and wrung it.

I flung him off. I couldn't say anything. The words choked in my throat. He was gazing at the plane, caressing it with his eyes, like a father who has been presented with another son to replace one that has died. My hands clenched with the desire to hit out, to smash the eagerness of his face.

Then he turned and met my gaze. "What's the trouble?" His hand reached out and caught my arm in a hard, unyielding grip. His voice was urgent, his mood tuned to mine.

I faced him then, my guts screwed up in a tight little knot in my belly and my teeth clenched. "Tubby's dead," I said.

"Dead?" His fingers dug into the muscles of my arm and he stared at me hard. Then his grip relaxed. "What happened?" he asked, in a flat tone.

I told him what had happened—how Tubby's body had slumped unconscious through the fuselage door, how I'd searched the area and found no sign of a parachute. When I had finished he turned and stared at the plane. Then he shook himself. "All right. Let's get the plane into the hangar."

"The plane!" I heard myself laugh. "I tell you, Tubby's dead."

"All right," he said angrily. "So he's dead. There's nothing you or I can do about it."

"Diana was at Gatow," I told him. "She's working at the Malcolm Club there. I saw her yesterday." I was remembering the sudden radiance of her face as she turned and found Tubby standing beside me.

"What's Diana got to do with it?" he asked angrily. "She'll get over it. Now give me a hand with the hangar doors. We've got to get this plane under cover right away."

Anger burst like a torrent inside me. "My God! You callous bastard! You don't care who's killed so long as you get your bloody engines into the air. Nothing else matters to you. Can't you understand what's happened? He was unconscious when he fell through the door. And now he's lying out there beside a disused airfield in the Russian Zone. He's dead, and you killed him," I screamed. "And all you can think about is the plane. You haven't the decency even to say you're sorry. He was straight and honest and decent, and you wipe his memory off your mind as though he were no more than——"

He hit me then, across the face with the flat of his hand. "Shut your mouth!" His voice trembled, but it was without anger or violence. "It doesn't occur to you, I suppose, that I was fond of Tubby? He was the nearest I ever had to a friend in my life." He said that slowly as though he were explaining something to himself. Then he turned away, his shoulders hunched, his hands thrust into his trouser pockets as though he didn't trust them in the open. " Now come and help me get the hangar doors opened."

I followed him dully, tears stinging the back of my eyeballs, blurring the white naked brilliance of the scene. He opened the wicket door, undid the bolts of the main doors and between us we slid them back. Moonlight flooded into the hangar, showing it strangely empty. The crashed Tudor was gone. All that remained of it was a jumbled heap of broken metal piled along each side of the hangar walls. And at the far end the bench with its lathes and machine tools stood deserted and silent. The whole place reeked of Tubby. I could see him beside me at that bench, whistling his flat, unending tunes, a grin crinkling his cheerful, sweaty face.

The engines of the plane roared. The vague outline of Saeton's head showed behind the glass of the windshield as he turned it and taxied into the hangar. Between us we got the doors closed again. " We'll go back to the quarters now," he said. " You need a drink." His hand gripped my shoulder. " I'm sorry, Neil. I should have let you blow off steam. You've had a hell of a night."

" I can't get the memory of Tubby out of my mind," I said, more to myself than to him.

We walked through the woods in silence and went into the mess room. Nothing had changed—the same trestle table, the four chairs and the cupboard in the corner. But there were just the two of us now. I stood there, feeling cold and numb. " Sit down," he said, " and I'll get you a drink." He returned in a few minutes with two tumblers of whisky and a bundle of maps. " Knock that back," he said gently. " You'll feel better then."

As I drank he shuffled through the maps, picked out one and spread it flat on the table. " Now then, where exactly did it happen?"

" I'd rather not talk about it," I said dully.

He nodded. " I understand how you feel. But I must get it pin-pointed whilst it's still vivid in your mind. Now. Here's Restorf at the entrance to the corridor. How soon did you cut out the engines?"

" About three minutes after Field had reported that we'd passed the entrance beacon," I answered.

" Field was your navigator?"

" Yes."

" Speed?"

" About one-sixty knots." I put down my tumbler. " What are you going to do?"

" I don't know yet."

" Tubby's dead," I said bitterly. " He was unconscious when he went through the door. I searched the whole area. There wasn't any sign of a parachute. There's nothing we can do." I looked at him, the beginnings of a decision forming in my mind. " I must give myself up."

" What good do you think that will do?" he demanded harshly.

I shook my head. " None." My voice was bitter. " But I can't go on like this. Do you know what he called me? He called me a dirty little crook. That's what started it all." I stared down at my drink. " He was right, too. That's what hurt. First the ' Callahan ' business. Now, this. Saeton, I can't go on with it. It'd drive me crazy. All the time I'd be thinking——"

" Stop thinking about yourself," he snapped. The vein on the side of his forehead was beginning to throb.

" We killed him," I said dully. " Between us, we killed him."

" We did nothing of the sort," he replied angrily. " It was an accident."

" He tried to stop me taking the plane. In the eyes of the law it would be——"

" Damn the law! So you told him what you were doing?"

" I had to. He came back after the others had jumped." I wiped my hand across my eyes. " I've made up my mind," I said. " I can't go on——"

" Oh, for God's sake!" he cried. And then he leaned towards me, his eyes fixed on mine. " You think I'm callous about Tubby's death, don't you?" His gaze dropped slowly to the map and he shrugged his shoulders. " Maybe it's happened too often before—men going out and not coming back. I had nearly a year in command of a bomber station out in France. I lost fifty-five in that year—just boys I knew who passed through my life and were gone. Maybe I got hardened to it." His eyes lifted and fastened on me again. " But Tubby wasn't just a boy I knew. Damn it, we worked together for two years, side-by-side on the same project with the same end in view. When you told me he was dead, I could have killed you. You've bungled it, and through your bungling you've killed the one man I was really fond of. And now you have the bloody nerve to say you won't go through with the rest of the plan. Get this into your head, Neil. If you don't go through with it, you make Tubby's death utterly pointless. If it was necessary for him to die that a British company should get a world lead in air-freight transport, well and good. But if you're now going to——"

"I must tell the police the whole thing," I repeated obstinately.

"Why? Telling the police won't help. You say Tubby is dead. All right then. He's dead. But for the love of God let's see to it that his death was to some purpose." He slewed the map round towards me. "Now then. You dropped Field and the other fellow about there—correct? What happened then?"

"I banked away out of the traffic stream," I answered, my voice trembling. "Then Tubby came back to the cockpit. He knew I was scared of jumps. He came back to make sure I got out. We were at about a thousand feet——"

"And then?"

"Christ!" I said. "Don't you see? It was because he was so bloody decent. That was why he died. Because he was so bloody decent. He was afraid I wouldn't jump. He was going to take the controls . . ." I was almost sobbing.

Saeton pushed the tumbler into my hand. "Drink up," he said. The drink produced a little oasis of warmth in the cold pit of my stomach. "You're at a thousand feet. What happened then?"

I swallowed another mouthful. "I was on two motors then. I cut one. I nearly convinced him. He was just going aft again when he saw the clips. He took control then and turned the machine back into the corridor."

"I see. And you tried to persuade him to make for Membury. That's when you told him our plan?"

"That's right. But he wouldn't. His Methodist upbringing. You told me about that. You warned me . . ." My mind was confused now. I felt damnably tired.

He shook my shoulder. "Then you had a fight. That's what you told me."

"Yes. He called me a dirty little crook. That made me mad. I cut the engine out then. I told him either we crashed or he let me take over. That's when he came at me with a spanner.

The rest you know." My eyelids felt heavy. I couldn't keep them open. "What are you going to do?" I mumbled.

"How long between his returning to the cockpit and the fight?"

"Five minutes—ten minutes. I don't know."

"What height were you when Tubby went out through the fuselage door?"

"I don't know. Yes. Wait a minute. About seven hundred. I climbed to over two thousand and then went down to five hundred again to search for him."

"You mentioned a disused airfield."

"Yes." My head nodded forward uncontrollably and I felt him shaking me. "There was a small town. There was a river, too, and a road ran north, quite straight, past the edge of the airfield." I stared at him dully. He was peering at the map, marking off distances with a rule. "Can you find it?" I asked.

He nodded. "Yes. Hollmind. No doubt of it."

"What are you going to do?" I asked again.

"Nothing much we can do," he said. "But an old friend of mine is at Lübeck, flying Daks. I'll cable him and have him search the area as he flies over in daylight."

I nodded vaguely. I couldn't keep my eyes open.

"You're dead beat, Neil. Better get some sleep." His voice sounded miles away. I felt his hands under my arm. "Come on, old chap."

I think Saeton must have put something in my drink, for I don't remember anything more until I woke to sunlight streaming into the familiar, comfortless little room. It had never done that before and when I glanced at my watch I found it was past two. I was still in my clothes and I had slept for nearly twelve hours. I fumbled for a cigarette, lit it and lay back.

The events of the night before came back to me then, like some nightmare half forgotten in waking. Tubby's death was no longer vivid in my memory. The whole thing had an unreal quality, until I went across to the hangar and saw the plane with Saeton already at work on the inboard engines.

"Feeling better," he asked. "I left some food out for you. Did you find it?"

"No." I walked round to the front of the machine and saw that he had already got the starboard engine out. The single-purposed drive of the man was incredible.

" I'm having difficulty with the securing nuts of this engine,"
he said. " Can you come up and give me a hand?"

I didn't move. I stood there, staring at the shining sweep of
the wings—hating the plane, hating Saeton, and hating myself
worst of all. Slowly my eyes travelled from the plane to the
litter of the hangar. God, how the man must have worked
whilst I'd been at Wunstorf! He'd cut the old machine to
pieces with an oxy-acetylene cutter ; wings, tail, fuselage were
a jumble of unrecognisable fragments piled along the walls.
Only the engines were left intact.

He climbed down from the wheeled gantry. " Snap out of
it, Neil!" His voice was hard, almost violent. " Put your
overalls on and get to work on that engine." His face, close
to, looked grey and haggard, his eyes shadowed with sleeplessness. He looked old. " I'm going to get some sleep." He
cleared a space for himself on the bench and lay down. He
kept his eyes open until I'd climbed the gantry and started
work. After that he didn't stir until I switched the light plant
on.

He brought some food over then and we worked on together
until we had the port engine lowered on to the concrete floor.
It was then eight forty-five. " Nearly news time," I said and
lit a cigarette, my hands trembling.

We got the news on the plane's radio. There was nothing
in the summary. With the earphones clamped to my ears the
announcer's voice seemed to be there in my head, telling me
of political wrangles, strikes, a depression over Iceland, anything but what I wanted to hear. Right at the end, however,
he paused. There was a rustle of paper and then his voice was
back in my ears and I gripped the edge of the seat.

*News has just come in that the Tudor aircraft, missing on the
airlift since last night, has crashed in the Russian Zone of
Germany. Two members of the crew, who baled out, crossed
the frontier into the British Zone this morning. They are R. E.
Field, navigator, and H. L. Westrop, radio operator. According to their report, the plane's engines failed shortly after it
had turned into the northern approach corridor to Berlin and
the captain ordered the crew to bale out. Still missing are
N. L. Fraser, pilot, and R. C. Carter, flight engineer. The pilot
of one of the planes following the missing Tudor has reported
seeing a single parachute open at about a thousand feet. It
was clearly visible in brilliant moonlight. As Field and West-*

*rop came down together, it is thought that this parachute may
belong to one of the other two members of the crew. So far
the Russians have denied that any plane crashed in their territory or that they hold any of our aircrews. The plane was a
Tudor tanker belonging to the Harcourt Charter Company.
Squadron Leader Neil Fraser, escaped from Germany during
the war by flying out a Messerschmitt after——*

I switched it off and removed my headphones. *A single
parachute!* " Do you think he's alive? " The sudden relief of
hope made my voice unsteady. Saeton made no answer. He
was staring down the fuselage at nothing in particular. " A
single parachute! That must be Tubby. The others went out
together. They came down together. The news said so."

" We'll see what the papers say to-morrow." Saeton got to
his feet.

I caught hold of his arm as he passed me. " What's the
matter? Aren't you glad? "

He looked down at me, his eyes grey like slate. " Of course,
I'm glad." There was no enthusiasm in his voice.

His reaction left me with a sense of depression. The report
was third or fourth hand. The pilot might have been seeing
two parachutes as one. It might mean nothing—or everything. I got out on to the floor of the hangar and stood, staring
at the plane. If only Saeton hadn't taken the inboard engines
out. If the machine had been left as I had brought it in, we
could have gone over, landed on that disused airfield and
searched the area. It was a crazy idea, but it stuck in my mind.

And as though Saeton had also thought of that, he pressed
straight on with the installation of the first of our own engines.
We finished it at three in the morning. But even then I couldn't
sleep. My mind kept on seeing that single parachute, a white
mushroom of silk in the moonlight, picturing Tubby forced
to consciousness by the rush of cold air, tugging at the release.
Pray God the papers carried more detail.

I was up at eight. The quarters were silent. There was no
sign of Saeton. I thought he must be over at the hangar until
I found a note on the mess table to say he'd gone into Baydon
for the papers. By the time I'd cooked the bacon he was
back. I saw at once he had some news. There was a gleam
of excitement in his eyes and his face looked younger as though
all the sleeplessness had been wiped away. " What is it? " I
asked breathlessly. " Have they found him? "

" No."

" What then?"

" Take a look at that." He handed me a teleprint.

*Your plane urgently required Wunstorf to replace Tudor tanker missing stop Ministry Civil Aviation agree rush C of A stop Report Wunstorf soonest possible notifying your E.T.A. Signed Aylmer B.E.A.*

I handed it back to him. " I suppose you didn't bother to see what the papers say about the crew of the plane?"

" Can't you get your mind off what's happened?" he demanded irritably.

" No," I said. " I can't. Have you got the papers?"

" Here you are." He handed me a whole bundle of newspapers. " They tell us nothing that we didn't know last night."

I glanced quickly through them as he went past me to get his breakfast. All the reports were the same. It was obviously a hand-out. The only difference was that in two cases the position at which the pilot had seen that single parachute was given. The position was two miles north of Hollmind.

When I entered the mess room again Saeton was already there, the teleprint beside his plane. He was making notes whilst he ate. I thrust the paper in front of him. " Have you seen that?" I asked.

He nodded, looking up at me, his mouth full.

" It means Tubby is alive," I cried. " He must have come to and pulled the release."

" I hope you're right," was all he said.

" What else could it mean?" I demanded.

" You remember I said I'd cable a friend of mine at Lübeck? I phoned it through that morning. This morning I got his reply. I'll read it to you." He pulled a second teleprint out of his pocket and read it out to me. " *Regret no trace of Carter or Fraser stop All aircraft ordered from dawn third to keep sharp lookout Hollmind area stop Routes staggered to cover limits of Corridor stop Visibility perfect stop Two parachutes reported near frontier belonging Westrop Field stop No wreckage, parachute or signal reported target area stop Sorry signed Manning.*" He pushed it into my hand. " Read it yourself."

" It doesn't prove anything," I said. " He may have been hurt."

"If he were he would have made some signal—smoke or something." He turned back to his breakfast.

"He may not have been able to. He may have been unconscious."

"Then his parachute would have been seen."

"Not necessarily. Hollmind airfield is surrounded by a belt of pine woods. His parachute could easily have been invisible from the air if he'd come down in the woods."

"If he'd landed in the woods his parachute would have been caught in the trees. It would be clearly visible."

"Then maybe he was seen coming down and picked up by a Russian patrol or some Germans." I felt suddenly desperate. Tubby had to be alive. My mind clung desperately to the slender hope of this report of a parachute near Hollmind.

Saeton looked up at me again then. "What time did Tubby drop?"

"I don't know. It must have been just near eleven-thirty."

"On the evening of the second?"

I nodded.

"Within a few hours all pilots had been ordered to keep a sharp lookout. That means that from dawn onwards there was a constant stream of aircrews overhead searching the area. Do you seriously suggest that in the intervening seven hours of darkness Tubby would have been picked up?"

"There was a moon," I said desperately.

"All right—five hours of moonlight. If Tubby pulled his parachute release, then he would still have been there on the ground at dawn. If he were hurt, then he wouldn't have been able to do anything about his parachute and it would have been clearly visible from above. And if he wasn't injured, then he'd have been able to signal." He hesitated. "On the other hand, if he never regained consciousness——"

"My God!" I said. "I believe you want him dead."

He didn't say anything, ignoring me as I stood over him with my hands clenched. "I've got to know what happened," I cried. I caught hold of his shoulder. "Can't you understand? I can't go through life thinking myself a murderer. I've got to go out there and find him."

"Find him?" He looked at me as though I were crazy.

"Yes, find him," I cried. "I believe he's alive. I've got to believe that. If I didn't believe that——" I moved my hand uncertainly. Couldn't the man see how I felt about it? "If he's dead, then I killed him. That's murder, isn't it? I'm a murderer then. He's got to be alive." I added desperately, "He's got to be."

"Better get on with your breakfast." The gentleness was back in his voice. Damn him! I didn't want kindness. I wanted something to fight. I wanted action. "When will the plane be ready?" I demanded thickly.

"Sometime to-morrow," he answered. "Why?"

"That's too late," I said. "It's got to be to-night."

"Impossible," he answered. "We'll barely have got the second motor installed by this evening. Then there's the tests, refuelling, loading the remains of the old Tudor, fixing the——"

"The remains of the old Tudor?" I stared at him. "You mean you're going through with the plan? You'll leave Tubby out there another whole day just because——"

"Tubby's dead," he said, getting to his feet. "The sooner you realise that, the better. He's dead and there's nothing you can do about it."

"That's what you want to believe, isn't it?" I sneered. "You want him dead because if he isn't dead, he'd give the whole game away."

"I told you how I feel about Tubby." His face was white and his tone dangerously quiet. "Now shut up and get on with your breakfast."

"If Tubby's dead," I said, "I'll do exactly what he would have done if he'd been alive. I'll go straight to the authorities——"

"Just what is it you want me to do, Fraser?"

"Fly over there," I said. "It's no good a bunch of bored aircrews peering down at those woods from a height of three thousand or more. I want to fly over the area at nought feet. And if that doesn't produce any result, then I want to land at Hollmind airfield and search those woods on foot."

He stood looking at me for a moment. "All right," he said.

"When?" I asked.

"When?" He hesitated. "It's Tuesday to-day. We'll have the second engine installed this evening. To-morrow I'll fly down for the C of A. Could be Friday night."

"Friday night!" I stared at him aghast. "But good God!" I exclaimed. "You're not going to leave Tubby out there whilst you get a certificate of airworthiness? You can't do that. We must go to-night, as soon as we've——"

"We'll go as soon as I've got the C of A." His tone was final.

"But——"

"Don't be a fool, Neil." He leaned towards me across the table. "I'm not leaving without a C of A. When I leave it's going to be for good. I'll be flying direct to Wunstorf. We'll call at Hollmind on the way. You must remember, I don't share your optimism. And now get some breakfast inside you. We've got a lot to do."

"But I must get there to-night," I insisted. "You don't understand. I feel——"

"I know very well how you feel," he said sharply. "Anybody would feel the same if he'd caused the death of a good man like Tubby. But I'm not leaving without a C of A and that's final."

"But the C of A might take a week," I said. "Often it takes longer—two weeks."

"We'll have to chance that. Aylmer of B.E.A. has said the Civil Aviation inspectors will rush it through. All right. I'm banking on it taking two days. If it takes longer, that's just too bad. Now get some breakfast inside you. The sooner we get to work, the sooner you'll be at Hollmind."

There was nothing I could do. I got up slowly and fetched my bacon.

"Another thing," he said as I sat down again. "I'm not landing at Hollmind except in moonlight. If it's a pitch black night, you'll have to jump."

I felt my stomach go cold at the thought of another jump. "Why not go over in daylight?"

"Because it's Russian territory."

"You mean because those engines are more important——"

"For God's sake stop it, Neil." His voice was suddenly violent. "I've made a bargain with you. To land there at night will be dangerous enough. But I'm willing to do it—for the sake of your peace of mind."

"But not for Tubby?"

He didn't answer. I knew what he was thinking. He was thinking that if I'd described the scene accurately Tubby couldn't be alive. But at least he had agreed to look for him now and I held on to that.

The urge to find him drove me to work as I'd never worked the whole time I'd been at Membury. I worked with a concentrated frenzy that narrowed my world down to bolts and petrol unions and the complicated details of electrical wiring. Yet I was conscious at the same time of Saeton's divergent interest. The clack of his typewriter as he cleared up the company's business, the phone calls instructing the men he'd picked as a crew to report to R.A.F. Transport Command for priority flights to Buckeburg for Wunstorf—all reminded me that, whatever had happened, his driving purpose was still to get his engines on to the Berlin airlift. And I hated him for his callousness.

It was past midnight when the second engine was in and everything connected up. Saeton left at dawn the next morning. The pipes were all frozen and we got water by breaking the ice on the rainwater butt. Membury was a frozen white world and the sun was hazed in mist so that it was a dull red ball as it came up over the downs. The mist swallowed the Tudor almost immediately. I turned back to the quarters, feeling shut in and wretched.

The next two days were the longest I ever remember. To keep me occupied Saeton had asked me to proceed with the cutting up of the old aircraft into smaller fragments. It occupied my hands. Nothing more. It was an automatic type of work that left my mind free to think. I couldn't leave the airfield. I couldn't go anywhere or see anybody. Saeton had been very insistent on that. If I showed my face anywhere and was recognised then he wouldn't go near Hollmind. It meant I couldn't even visit the Ellwoods. I was utterly alone and by Friday morning I was peering out of the hangar every few minutes searching the sky, listening for the drone of the returning Tudor.

It was Saturday afternoon that Saeton got in. He had got his C of A. His crew were on their way to Wunstorf. " If it's clear we'll go over to-night," he said. And we got straight on with the work of preparing for our final departure. We tanked up and he insisted on filling the fuselage of the plane with pieces of the old Tudor. He was still intent on going through with his plan. He kept on talking about the airworthiness tests. " The inspectors were pretty puzzled by the engines," he said. " But I managed to avoid any check on petrol consumption. They know they're a new design. But they don't know their value—not yet." The bastard could think of nothing else.

Dusk was falling as we finished loading. The interior of the hangar was still littered with debris, but Saeton made no attempt to dispose of it. We went back to the quarters. Night had fallen and I had seen the last of Membury. When the moon rose I should be in Germany. I lay in my blankets, barely conscious of the gripping cold, my thoughts clinging almost desperately to my memory of the place.

Saeton called me at ten-thirty. He had made tea and cooked some bacon. As soon as he had finished his meal he went out to the hangar. I lingered over a cigarette, unwilling to leave the warmth of the oil stove, thinking of what lay ahead of me. At length Saeton returned. He was wearing his heavy, fleece-lined flying jacket. "Ready?"

"Yes, I'm ready," I said and got slowly to my feet.

Outside it was freezing hard, the night crystal clear and filled with stars. Saeton carried the oil stove with him. At the edge of the woods he paused for a moment, staring at the dark bulk of the hangar with the ghostly shape of the plane waiting for us on the apron. "A pity," he said gruffly. "I've got fond of this place." When we reached the plane he ordered me to get the engines warmed up and went on to the hangar. He was gone about five minutes. When he climbed into the cockpit he was breathing heavily as though he had been running. His clothes smelt faintly of petrol. "Okay. Let's get going." He slid into the pilot's seat and his hand reached for the throttle levers. But instead of taxi-ing out to the runway, he slewed the plane round so that we faced the hangar. The wicket door was still open and a dull light glowed inside. We sat there, the screws turning, the air frame juddering. "What are we waiting for?" I asked.

"Just burning my boats behind me," he said.

The rectangular opening of the hangar door flared red and I knew then what he had wanted the oil stove for. There was a muffled explosion and flames shot out of the gap. The whole interior of the hangar was ablaze, a roaring inferno which almost drowned the sound of our engines.

"Well, that's that," Saeton said. He was grinning like a child who has set fire to something for fun, but his eyes as he looked at me reflected a more desperate mood. Another explosion shook the hangar and flames licked out of the shattered windows at the side. Saeton reached up to the throttle levers, the engines roared and we swung away to the runway end.

A moment later we turned our backs on the hangar and took off into the frosted night. At about a thousand feet Saeton banked slightly for one last glimpse of the field. It was a great dark circle splashed with an orange flare at the far end. As I peered forward across Saeton's body the hangar seemed to disintegrate into a flaming skeleton of steel. At that distance it looked no bigger than a Guy Fawkes bonfire.

We turned east then, setting course for Germany. I stared at Saeton, seeing the hard inflexible set of the jaw in the light of the instrument panel. There was nothing behind him now. The past to him was forgotten, actively erased by fire. There would be nothing at Membury but molten scraps of metal and the congealed lumps of the engines. As though he knew what I was thinking he said. "Whilst you were sleeping this evening I went over this machine erasing old numbers and stamping in our own." There was a tight-lipped smile on his face as he said this. He was warning me that there would be no proof, that I would not be believed if I tried to accuse him of flying Harcourt's plane.

The moon rose as we crossed the Dutch coast, a flattened orange in the east. The Scheldt glimmered below us and then the snaking line of water gave place to frosted earth. "We're in Germany now," Saeton shouted, and there was a note of triumph in his voice. In Germany! This was the future for him—the bright, brilliant future to replace the dead past. But for me . . . I felt cold and alone. There was nothing here for me but the memory of Tubby's unconscious body slumping through the floor of this very machine—and farther back, tucked away in the dark corners of my mind, the feel of branches tearing at my arm, the sight of the barbed wire and the sense of being hunted.

My brain seemed numb. I couldn't think and I flew across the British Zone of Germany in a kind of mental vacuum. Then the lights of the airlift planes were below us and we were in the corridor, flying at five thousand feet. Saeton put the nose of the machine down, swinging east to clear the traffic stream and then south-west at less than a thousand with all the ground laid bare in brilliant moonlight, a white world of unending, hedgeless fields and black, impenetrable woods.

We found Hollmind, turned north and in an instant we were

over the airfield. Saeton pressed the mouthpiece of his helmet to his lips. "Get aft and open the fuselage door." His voice crackled in my ears. "You can start shovelling the bits out just as soon as you like. I'll stooge around to the north of the airfield." I hesitated and he looked across at me. "You want me to land down there, don't you?" he said. "Well, this machine's heavily overloaded. And that runway hasn't been used for four years. It's probably badly broken up by frost and I'm not landing till the weight's out of the fuselage. Now get aft and kick the load out of her."

There was no point in arguing with him. I turned and went through the door to the fuselage. The dark bulk of the fuel tanks loomed in front of me. I climbed round them and then I was squeezing my way through the litter of the old Tudor that was piled to the roof. Jagged pieces of metal caught at my flying suit. The fuselage was like an old junk shop and it rattled tinnily. I found the fuselage door, flung it back and a rush of cold air filled the plane. We were flying at about two thousand now, the countryside, sliding below us, clearly mapped in the white moonlight. The wings dipped and quivered as Saeton began to bank the plane. Above me the lights of a plane showed driving south-east towards Berlin with its load of freight; below, the snaking line of a river gleamed for an instant, a road running straight to the north, the black welt of a wood, and then the white weave of ploughed earth.

The engines throttled back and I felt the plane check as Saeton applied the air brakes. I caught hold of the nearest piece of metal, dragged it to the wind-filled gap and pushed it out. It went sailing into the void, a gleam of tin twisting and falling through the slip-stream. Soon a whole string of metal was falling away behind us like pieces of silver paper. It was like the phosphorescent gleam of the log line of a ship marking the curve of our flight as we banked.

By the time I'd pitched the last fragment out and the floor of the fuselage was clear, I was sweating hard. I leaned for a moment against the side of the fuselage, panting with the effort. The sweat on me went cold and clammy and I began to shiver. I pulled the door to and went for'ard. "It's all out now," I told Saeton.

He nodded. "Good! I'm going down now. I'll take the perimeter of Hollmind airfield as my mark and fly in widening circles from that. Okay?" He thrust the nose down and the airfield rose to meet us through the windshield. The concrete runways gleamed white, a huge cross. Then we were skimming the field, the starboard wing-tip down as we banked in a right turn. He was taking it clockwise so that I had a clear, easy view of the ground through my side window. " Keep your eyes skinned," he shouted. " I'll look after the navigation."

Round and round we circled, the airfield sliding away till it was lost behind the trees. There was nothing but woods visible through my window, an unending stream of moon-white Christmas trees sliding away below me. My eyes grew dizzy with staring at them, watching their spiky tops and the dark shadows rushing by. The leading edge of the wing seemed to be cutting through them we were so low. Here and there they thinned out, vanishing into patches of plough or the gleam of water. The pattern repeated itself like flaws in a wheel as we droned steadily on that widening circle.

At last the woods had all receded and there was nothing below us but plough. Saeton straightened the plane out then and climbed away to the north. " Well?" he shouted.

But I'd seen nothing—not the glimmer of a light, no fire, no sign of the torn remains of parachute silk—nothing but the fir trees and the open plough. I felt numb and dead inside. Somewhere amongst those woods Tubby had fallen—somewhere deep in the dark shadows his body lap crumpled and broken. I put the mouthpiece of my helmet to my lips. " I'll have to search those woods on foot," I said.

" All right," Saeton's voice crackled back. " I'll take you down now. Hold tight. It's going to be a bumpy touchdown."

We banked again and the airfield reappeared, showing as a flat clearing in the woods straight ahead of us. Flaps and undercarriage came down as we dropped steeply over the firs. The concrete came to meet us, cracked and covered with the dead stalks of weeds. Then our wheels touched down and the machine was jolting crazily over the uneven surface. We came to rest within a stone's throw of the woods, the nose of the machine facing west. Saeton followed me out on to the concrete. No light showed in all the huge, flat expanse of the field. Nobody came to challenge us. The place was as derelict and lonely as Membury. Saeton thrust a paper package into my hand. " Bread and cheese," he said. " And here's a flask. You may need it."

" Aren't you coming with me?" I asked.

He shook his head. " I'm due at Wunstorf at 04.00. Besides what's the use? We've stooged the area for nearly an hour. We've seen nothing. To search it thoroughly on foot would take days. It doesn't look much from the air, but from the ground——" He shook his head again. "Take a look at the size of this airfield. Just to walk straight across it would take you half an hour."

I stood there, staring at the dark line of the woods, the panic of loneliness creeping up on me. " I won't be long," I said. " Surely you can wait an hour for me—two hours perhaps?" The plane was suddenly important to me, my link with people I knew, with people who spoke my own language. Without it, I'd be alone in Germany again—in the Russian Zone.

His hand touched my arm. " You don't seem to understand, Neil," he said gently. " You're not part of my crew—not yet. You're the pilot of a plane that crashed just north of here. I couldn't take you on to Wunstorf even if you wanted to come. When you've finished your search, make for Berlin. It's about thirty-five miles to the south-east. You ought to be able to slip across into the British Sector there."

I stared at him. " You mean you're leaving me here?" I swallowed quickly, fighting off the sudden panic of fear.

" The arrangement was that I should fly you back to Germany and drop you there. As far as I'm concerned that plan still holds. All that's different is that I've landed you and so saved you a jump."

Anger burst through my fear, anger at the thought of him not caring a damn about Tubby, thinking only of his plans to fly his engines on the airlift. " You're not leaving me here Saeton," I cried. " But I must know whether he's alive or dead."

" We know that already," he said quietly.

" He's not dead," I cried. " He's only dead in your mind —because you want him dead. He's not dead, really. He can't be."

" Have it your own way." He shrugged his shoulders and turned away towards the plane.

I caught him by the shoulder and jerked him round. " All right, he's dead," I shouted. " If that's the way you want it. He's dead, and you've killed him. The one friend you ever had! Well, you've killed your one friend—killed him, just as you'd killed anyone who stood between you and what you want."

He looked me over, measuring my mood, and then his eyes were cold and hard. "I don't think you've quite grasped the situation," he said slowly. "I didn't kill Tubby. You killed him."

"Me?" I laughed. "I suppose it wasn't your idea that I should pinch Harcourt's Tudor? I suppose that's your own machine standing there? You blackmailed me into doing what you wanted. My God! I'll see the world knows the truth. I don't care about myself any more. What happened to Tubby has brought me to my senses. You're mad—that's what you are. Mad. You've lost your reason, all sense of proportion. You don't care what you do so long as your dreams come true. You'll sacrifice everything, anyone. Well, I'll see you don't get away with it. I'll tell them the truth when I get back. If you'd got a gun you'd shoot me now, wouldn't you? Or are you only willing to murder by proxy? Well, you haven't got a gun and I'll get back to Berlin somehow. I'll tell them the truth then. I'll——"

I paused for breath and he said, "Telling the truth won't help Tubby now—and it won't help you either. Try to get the thing clear in your mind, Fraser. Tubby's dead. And since you killed him, it's up to you to see that his death is to some purpose."

"I didn't kill him," I shouted. "You killed him."

He laughed. "Do you think anybody will believe you?"

"They will when they know the facts. When the police have searched Membury, when they have examined that plane and they've interrogated——"

"You've nothing to support your story," he said quietly. "The remains of Harcourt's plane are strewn over the country-side just north of here. Field and Westrop will say that you ordered them to bale out, that the engines had packed up. You yourself will be reporting back from the area of the crash. As for Membury, there's nothing left of the hangar now except a blackened ruin."

I felt suddenly exhausted. "So you knew what I'd do. You knew what I was going to do back there at Membury. You fooled me into pushing out that load of scrap. By God——"

"Don't start using your fists," he cut in sharply. "I may

be older than you, but I'm heavier—and tougher." His feet
were straddled and his head was trust forward, his hands
down at his sides ready for me.

I put my hands slowly to my head. "Oh, God!" I felt so
weak, so impotent.

"Get some sense into your head before I see you again,"
he said. "You can still be in this thing with me—as my partner. It all depends on your attitude when you reach Berlin."

For answer I turned away and walked slowly towards the
woods.

Once I glanced back. Saeton was still standing there, watching me. Then, as I entered the darkness of the trees, I heard
the engines roar. Through needle-covered branches I watched
the machine turn and taxi to the runway end. And then it
went roaring across the airfield, climbing, a single white light,
like a faded comet, dwindling into the moonlit night, merging
into the stars. Then there was silence and the still shadows
of the woods closed round me. I was alone—in the Russian
Zone of Germany.


## CHAPTER SEVEN

For a long time after the plane had disappeared I stood there
on the fringe of the woods gazing at the empty expanse of the
airfield. A small wind whispered in the upper branches of the
fir trees and every few minutes there was the distant drone of
a plane—airlift pilots flying down the corridor to Berlin. Those
were the only sounds. The cold seeped through my flying suit,
stiffening my limbs, and at length I turned and walked into
the woods. A few steps and I had lost the airfield. The trees
closed round me and I was in a world apart. It was very still
there in the woods, even the sound of my footsteps was muffled
by the carpet of pine needles. I could still hear the planes, but
I couldn't see them. The branches of the trees cut me off from
the sky and only a ghostly radiance told me that the moon
still filled the world with its white light.

I found a path and followed it to the earth mound of an
old dispersal point. The frost-cracked concrete was a white
blaze in the moonlight, cutting through the dark ranks of the
trees to the open plain of the airfield. I stopped there to con-

sider what I should do. My mind went back to the scene in the plane. We had been flying almost due south when Tubby's body slid through the open doorway. I had gone straight back to the cockpit and then I had looked through my side window and seen Hollmind airfield below me. That meant that Tubby had gone out north and slightly west of the field.

I followed the line of the concrete till I came out on to the edge of the airfield and turned left, walking in the shadow of the woods till I reached the north-west extremity of the field. Buildings began there, shapeless heaps of broken rubble. I skirted these and entered the woods again, following a path that ran in the direction I wanted to go.

It was four o'clock when I began my search. I remember thinking that Saeton would be at Wunstorf. The plane would be parked on the loading apron in the row of Tudors where it had stood before. Only the crew would be different—and the numbers and the engines. He'd be reporting to Ops and checking in at the mess, finding a bed in the echoing concrete corridors of that labyrinth that housed the human force of the airlift. He'd be one of them now, getting up when the world was asleep, going to bed when others were shaving. In a few hours perhaps it would be his plane I'd hear droning over on its way to Berlin. He'd be up there, with success ahead of him, whilst I was down in these grim, dark woods, searching for the body of the man who'd given two years to help him build those engines. Damn it, it wasn't even his plane. It was my plane. Nothing was really his. Even the design of the engines he'd pinched from Else's father.

Blind anger drove everything else out of my head for a moment. Then I steadied myself, forcing my mind to concentrate on the thing I'd set myself to do. I decided to walk east and west, backwards and forwards on a two mile front working gradually northwards. The impossibility of complete coverage was apparent from the start. I had a small pocket compass, that was all. The trees, fortunately, were well spaced out, but they were all alike. There was nothing to guide me. It was obvious that at some points I should be covering the same ground twice, maybe three times, whilst at other times I should be leaving large gaps uncovered. But it was the only course open to me and with a feeling of hopelessness I turned west on my first beat. It was past five when I came to the western fringe of the woods and looked across the dreary flatness of the Mecklenberg plain with the moon dipping over it towards the horizon. And in that time I had stopped a hundred times to investigate a deeper shadow, a dead branch that looked like an arm or a patch of white where a beam of direct moonlight shone on the bark of a pine trunk.

Dawn found me at the end of the eastward beat. The daylight penetrated slowly into the woods, a slight lightening of the deeper shadows, a paling of the moon's whiteness. I didn't really see it until I was in a clearing that showed me the bomb-battered ruins of the hangars that lay along the north fringe of Hollmind airfield. It was a grey dawn, still, but pitilessly cold, with great cloud banks rolling in from the north and the feel of snow in the air.

I ate two sandwiches and took a nip from the flask Saeton had given me. There was rum in that flask and I could feel the warmth of it trickling into my stomach. But as I turned westward again on my third beat I was already tired. There was no breath of wind. The woods seemed frozen into silence. The only sound was the drone of aircraft. That sound had been with me all the time. It was monotonous, unending. But God, how glad I was of it! That sound was my one link with the world, with reality. And as the daylight increased, I began to look for the planes in the gaps in the trees. At last I saw one. It was flying across my line of march at about three thousand feet, the thick belly unmistakable—a York. That meant that it had come from Wunstorf. The men in that plane would have breakfasted before dawn with the electric lights on and the mess warm with the smell of hot radiators and food. They had hot food in their bellies and hot coffee.

I stood there in the clearing, watching the plane till it was out of sight, the smell of coffee stronger than the smell of the pines, remembering a shop I'd known as a kid that had a big grinder always working in the window, spilling its fragrance into the street. As the plane disappeared over the tops of the trees another came into sight, exactly the same, flying the same route, flying the same height. I watched another and another. All Yorks. All exactly the same. It was as though they were on an endless belt going behind the trees, like those little white clay airgun targets you find at fairs.

The smell of coffee lingered with me as I went on into the sombre gloom of the woods.

Shortly after midday it began to snow, the flakes drifting

gently down out of the leaden sky, dark, widely-spaced specks until they landed and were transformed to little splashes of virgin white. It was less cold after the snow began to fall. But by then I was feeling sleepy, exhausted and hungry. There were two sandwiches left and half a flask of rum. I saved them for the night and stumbled on.

On my eighth beat I found a crumpled piece of metal. It was lodged in the branches of a tree—a piece of the tailplane of the Tudor Saeton that had pranged at Membury. It didn't seem possible that it was less than twelve hours since I'd slung that fragment out of the open door of the fuselage with these woods flashing by below me.

An hour later I nearly walked into a Russian patrol. I was almost on top of them before I heard the low murmur of their voices. They were in a group, short men with round, sallow faces, black boots and brown tunics buttoned to the neck. The soldiers leaned on their rifles while two officers bent over a piece of metal that gleamed dully.

I wondered what they'd make of these scraps of metal scattered through the woods as I slipped past them and continued eastward. The snow thickened and the sky darkened. Patches of white showed in the gaps between the trees and these I had to avoid for fear of leaving footprints. In the gathering darkness and my growing weakness every shadow became a Russian soldier. My progress became wretchedly slow. Finally it was too dark to go on and I dug a hole for myself close under the low-sweeping branches of a large fir and lay down in it, covering myself with pine needles.

I finished the two sandwiches and drank the rest of the rum. But within an hour the warmth of the rum had completely evaporated; the cold of the night moved in on me, gripping my limbs like a steel sheet. Sleep was impossible. I lay and shivered, my mind a blank, my body in a coma of misery. The cold covered everything. The snow became hard and powdery, the trees cracked.

By midnight I was so frozen that I got to my feet and stamped and swung my arms. My breath hung like smoke in front of my face. The snow clouds had passed. Stars shone frosty-clear above my head and the moon had risen showing me a beautiful, fairy-white world of Christmas trees.

I started moving westward, walking blindly, not really caring where I went so long as I got some warmth into my limbs. And that was how I found Tubby's flying helmet. I just stumbeld on it lying on a patch of snow. I suppose what had happened was that it had been caught on one of the branches of a tree and when the snow weighed the branch down it had slipped to the ground.

I don't remember feeling any excitement. I think I was too numbed with cold to have any feelings at all. And I had no sense of surprise either. I had been so determined to find him that it hadn't occurred to me that I should fail. I have always believed that if you go out for a thing hard enough, you get it in the end, and I didn't bother to consider the virtual impossibility of the task I had set myself. But though I had found his helmet I could find no trace of Tubby himself. There was just the helmet. Nothing else.

After a thorough search of the area I returned to the spot where the helmet had lain. The trees were very thick and in the darkness of the shadows it was impossible to see whether there was anything lodged in the branches. In the end I climbed to the top of the tree that overhung the spot. With my head thrust above the snow-laden branches I looked over a plain of white spikes that glistened in the moonlight. By shaking the tree I got rid of most of the snow. The needle foliage looked very green, but there was no sign of anything that would prove that this was the spot where Tubby had fallen.

I was half-way down the tree, back in the world of half-light and shadows, when my hand slid from the gritty surface of the bark to something softer. My fingers closed on it, feeling the smoothness of light material. I didn't need to look at it to know that this was nylon. I pulled at it and my hand came away with a torn strip of parachute silk about the length of a scarf.

I was excited then. That strip of nylon silk showed that Tubby had pulled his parachute release before he hit the ground and I went tumbling down the tree, oblivious of the snow that fell on my neck and trickled in icy streams down my back, oblivious of everything but that single fact—Tubby wasn't dead. He might have hurt himself, but he'd regained consciousness, he'd pulled the release and his parachute had opened. And I realised then how the fear of finding him, a mangled, blood-stained heap of broken bones and torn flesh, had haunted me. In a frenzy I searched the area again, trampling the snow in my haste to find out what had happened to him after he'd cashed through the trees.

But the snow hid all trace.

At length, utterly exhausted, I sat down on a dry patch of ground with my back against the bole of a tree and lit one of my last cigarettes. I had searched the area in a circle extending about fifty yards from the spot where I had come upon the helmet. I had found no trace of him. Clearly one of two things had happened—either he had been all right and had left the area on foot or else he had been injured and some woodman had found him and got him away. Or perhaps it had been the Russians who'd found him. Maybe the patrol I'd seen in the afternoon had come upon him and carted him off to Hollmind. The possibility that he might be dead was nagging at me again. I had to be sure that he was alive.

I got to my feet again. I would have to widen my search, radiate out until I found some trace. I began walking again, circling out from the spot where the helmet had lain. The snow helped me here, for all I had to do was walk outside the footprints I'd made on my previous circuit. The moon was high overhead now and it was much lighter under the trees. At four o'clock in the morning, after walking for over two hours in a widening circle, I stumbled upon a broad track running through the woods. One side of the track was sheltered by the trees and was clear of snow and there I found the marks of a farm cart. I traced it back to a spot where it had stood for some time. The tracks did not continue. They finished there and I knew then that Tubby was either dead or injured. Cold and wretched, I turned westward and followed the track till it left the shelter of the woods and ran out into the bitter flatness of ploughed land that was all white under the moon.

The wheel tracks were lost under the snow now, but the track was still visible—two deep ruts swinging south-west towards a Christmas card huddle of steep-roofed farm buildings. As I approached I saw the yellow glow of a light. It came from the half-open door of a barn. Inside the barn a man was filling sacks with potatoes from a deep, square hole in the floor. Wooden boards heavy with earth were stacked against the heaped-up straw and earth had been piled near the door.

The man must have sensed my presence, for he suddenly paused in his work and looked straight at me where I stood in the gaping doorway. He was short and wiry with a broad forehead and his eyes looked startled and afraid. *"Wer sind Sie? Was wollen Sie?"*

"I am an English flier," I replied in German. "I am looking for a friend of mine who may be injured."

He put down his fork and came towards me, his dark, frightened eyes peering first at my face, then at my clothes. "Come in then and close the door please. The wind blow it open I think." He fixed the latch with trembling fingers. "I was afraid it was the Russians." He laughed nervously. "They want everything—all my crops. For the East, you know." His speech was jerky. "To feed our pigs we must keep something." He held the lantern close to me, still examining me uncertainly. Apparently he was finally satisfied, for he lowered the lantern and said, "You look tired. You walk far, yes."

"What has happened to my friend?" I asked. "He was brought here, wasn't he? Is he—is he dead?" I waited, dreading his answer.

He shook his head slowly. *"Nein.* He is not dead. But he injure himself very much when he land in the trees. Now you lie down in the straw there. I must finish my work before it is light. Then I get you something to eat, eh?"

But I wasn't listening. "Thank God!" I breathed it aloud. Tubby was alive. He was alive and I'd found him. I hadn't killed him after all. I felt suddenly light-headed. I wanted to laugh. But once I started to laugh I felt I should never stop. I held my breath, fighting to control myself. Then I stumbled into the straw, sinking into it, relaxing, knowing I had done everything I could and that God had been with me. I had found Tubby and he wasn't dead. "When did you find him?" I asked.

"Four days ago," the man answered. He had returned to his work.

"And you have not handed him over to the Russians?"

He paused with a forkful of potatoes. "No, we do not hand him to the Russians. You have to thank my wife for that. Our daughter is in Berlin. She live in the French Sector with her husband who work on the railways there. But for the air bridge, she would be like us—she would be under the Russians."

I mumbled my thanks. My head kept nodding. It was very warm and comfortable there in the straw. "Is he badly hurt?"

"*Ja.* He is not so good. Several ribs are broken and his arm and he has concussion. But he is conscious. You can speak with him."

"He should have a doctor." My voice sounded very far away. I couldn't keep my eyes open.

"You do not have to worry. Our doctor is coming here to see him every day. He is a good doctor and he do not love the Russians because they take him to the East for a year to work with our prisoners. Once he meet my son. My son, Hans, is a prisoner of the Russians since 1945. Before that he is in North Africa and Italy and then on the Eastern front. I do not see him now for almost six years. But soon I hope he will come home. We have had two letters . . ."

His voice droned pleasantly and my eyelids closed. I dreamt I was back in Stalag Luft I, but the guards all wore tight-necked brown tunics and black knee-length boots, and there was always snow and no hope of release or escape—only the hope of death. They kept on interrogating me, trying to get me to admit that I'd killed Tubby—there were intensely bright lights and they kept on shaking me . . . I woke to find the farmer bending over me, shaking my shoulder. "Wake up, Herr Fraser." He pronounced the "s" sharply and not as a "z." "It is seven o'clock. We will have some food now and then you can talk with your friend."

"You know my name?" I murmured sleepily. And then I felt in my breast pocket. My papers were still there. He must have put them back after examining them. I clambered stiffly to my feet. I was cold and very tired.

"I think perhaps we put your flying clothes under the straw, eh? I do not wish my men to know I have a British flier here. By talking, one of them might be given my farm. That is something they learn from the Nazis." He said the word "Nazis" unemotionally as one might talk of an avalanche or some other act of God.

When I had hidden my flying suit he took me across the farmyard to the house. It was a cold, bleak dawn, heavy with leaden cloud that promised more snow. Overhead I heard the drone of the planes flying in to Berlin, but I couldn't see them, for the ceiling was not much more than a thousand.

My memory of the Kleffmann's house is vague; a memory of warmth and the smell of bacon, of a big kitchen with a great, clumsy, glowing stove and a bright-eyed, friendly little woman with wisps of greying hair and the slow, sure movements of one who lives close to the earth and whose routine never changes. I also remember the little bedroom high up under the roof where Tubby lay, his fat cheeks strangely hollow, his face flushed with fever and his eyes unnaturally bright. The ugly, patterned wallpaper with butterflies flying up vertical strips was littered with photographs of Hans Kleffmann who would some day come back from Russia and meet his mother and father again for the first time in six years. There were photographs of him as a baby, as a boy at the school in Hollmind, in the uniform of the Nazi Youth Organisation and finally in the uniform of the Wehrmacht—against the background of the Hradcany Palace in Prague, in a Polish village, with the Eiffel Tower behind him, in the Desert leaning on a tank, in Rome with St. Peter's Dome over his left shoulder. And there were a few less formal snaps—Hans in bathing shorts on the Italian Riviera, Hans with a dark-haired girl in Naples, Hans ski-ing in the Dolomites. Hans filled that room with the nostalgia of a boy's life leading inevitably, irrevocably to the Russian prison camp. They showed me a letter. It was four lines long—*I am well and the Russians treat me very kindly. The food is good and I am happy. Love, Hans.*

Tubby, lying in that small, neatly austere bed, was an intruder.

He was asleep when I went in. The Kleffmanns left me sitting by his bed whilst they got on with the business of the farm. Tubby's breath came jerkily and painfully, but he slept on and I had a long time in which to become familiar with Hans. It's almost as though I had met him, I got to know him so well from those faded photographs—arrogant and fanatical in victory, hard-faced and bitter in defeat. There in that room I was face to face with the Germany of the future, the Germany that was being hammered out on the vulcan forge of British, American and Soviet policy. I found my eyes turning back repeatedly to the grim, relentless face in the photograph taken at Lwow in the autumn of 1944 and comparing it with the smiling carefree kid in knickerbockers taken outside the Hollmind school.

Then Tubby opened his eyes and stared at me. At first I thought he wasn't going to recognise me. We stared at each other for a moment and then he smiled. He smiled at me with his eyes, his lips, a tight line constricted by pain. " Neil! How did you get here?"

I told him, and when I'd finished he said, " You came back. That was kind of you." He had difficulty in speaking and his voice was very weak.

" Are they looking after you all right?" I asked awkwardly.

He nodded slowly. " The old woman is very kind. She treats me as though I were her son. And the doctor does his best."

" You ought to be in hospital," I said.

He nodded again. " But it's better than being in the hands of the Russians."

" Thank God you're alive anyway," I said. " I thought——" I hesitated and then said, " I was afraid I'd killed you. You were unconscious when you went out through the door. I didn't mean it, Tubby. Please believe that."

" Forget it," he said. " I understand. It was good of you to come back." He winced as he took a breath. " Did you take the plane back to Saeton?"

" Yes," I said. " It's got our engines in now and Saeton's at Wunstorf. They ordered him over immediately to replace Harcourt's Tudor."

His mouth opened to the beginning of a laugh and then he jerked rigid at the pain it caused him.

" You ought to be in hospital," I said again. " Listen," I added. " Do you think you could stand another journey in that cart, up to Hollmind airfield?"

I saw him clench his teeth at the memory.

" Could you stand it if you knew at the end there would be a hospital and everything in the way of treatment you need?"

The sweat shone on his forehead. " Yes," he breathed, so quietly that I could hardly hear him. " Yes, I'd face it again if I knew that. Maybe the doc here would fix me up with a shot of morphia. But they've so little in the way of drugs. They've been very kind, but they're Germans, and they haven't the facilities for . . ." His voice trailed away.

I was afraid he was going to fade into unconsciousness and I said quickly, " I'm going now, Tubby. To-night I'll start out for Berlin. I'll make it just as quickly as I can. Then, within a few hours, I'll be back with a plane and we'll evacuate you from Hollmind. Okay?"

He nodded.

"Good-bye then for the moment. I'll get through somehow and then we'll get you to a hospital. Hold on to that. You'll be all right."

The corners of his lips twitched in a tight smile. "Good luck!" he whispered. And then as I rose from the bed, his hand came out from beneath the sheets and closed on mine. "Neil!" I had to bend down to hear him. "I want you to know—I won't say anything. I'll leave things as I find them. The plane crashed. Engine failure—ignition." His voice died away and his eyes closed.

Bending close to him I could hear the sob of his breathing. I reached under his pillow for his handkerchief to wipe the sweat from his forehead. The handkerchief was dark with blood. I knew then that his lung was punctured. I wiped his forehead with my own handkerchief and then went quietly out of Hans's little bedroom and down the dark stairs to the kitchen.

They gave me a bed and I slept until it was dark. Then, after a huge meal by the warmth of the kitchen stove, I said good-bye to the Kleffmanns. "In a night or two," I told them, "I will be back with a plane and we'll get him away."

"Gut! Gut!" The farmer nodded. "It is better so. He is very bad, I think. Also it is dangerous for us having him here in the farm."

Frau Kleffmann came towards me. She had a bulky package in her hand. "Here is food for your journey, Herr Fraser—some chicken and some bread and butter and apples." She hesitated. "If anything happens, do not worry about your friend. He is safe here. We will look after him. There has been war between us, but my Hans is in Russia. I will care for your friend as I would have others care for Hans if he is sick. *Auf wiedersehen!*" Her gnarled hand touched my arm and her eyes filled with tears. She turned quickly to the stove.

The farmer accompanied me to the door. "I try to arrange for you to ride in a lorry who go once a week to Berlin with potatoes. But "—he spread his hands hopelessly—" the driver is sick. He do not go to-night. If you go three miles beyond Hollmind there is a café there for motor drivers. I think you will perhaps get a ride there." He gave me instructions how to by-pass Hollmind and then shook my hands. "*Viel Glück,*

*Herr Fraser.* Come soon, please, for your friend. I fear he is very sick."

More snow had fallen during the day, but now the clouds had been swept away by a bitter east wind and the night was cold and clear. The moon had not yet risen, but the stars were so brilliant that I had no difficulty in seeing my way as soon as my eyes became accustomed to the darkness. High above me the airlift planes droned at regular three-minute intervals—I could see their navigation lights every now and then, green and red dots moving steadily through the litter of stars and the drift of the Milky Way. The white pin-point of their tail-lights pointed the way to Berlin for me. I had only to follow them through the night sky and I should arrive at Gatow. For them Gatow was twenty minutes flying time. But for me. . . .

I turned south on the hard straight road that led to the town of Hollmind, wondering how long the journey would take me. The snow was deep and crisp under my feet. Kleffmann had given me an old field-grey Wehrmacht greatcoat and a Wehrmacht forage cap; Hans's cast-off clothing. For the first time since I'd landed in Germany I felt warm and well-fed.

Nothing stirred on the road. The snow seemed to have driven all transport off it. My footsteps were muffled and I walked in a deep silence. The only sound was the drone of the planes overhead and the hum of the wind in the telegraph wires. I reached the fork where the road branched off that I was to take in order to by-pass Hollmind. There was a signboard there—Berlin 54 km.

Fifty-four kilometres isn't far; not much more than thirty miles. A day's march. But though I had had a good rest, I was still tired and very stiff. I was wearing shoes and my feet were blister-sore. And there was the cold. For a time the warmth of exercise kept it out, but, as I tired, the sweat broke out on my body and chilled into a clammy, ice-cold film, and then the wind cut through my clothing and into my flesh, seeming to blow straight on to my spine. God, it was cold! For miles, it seemed, I walked along by-roads through unmarked snow and there was no traffic. I must have missed the turning back on to the Berlin road, for it was almost midnight when I finally found it again and I saw no transport café —only dark woods and the illimitable miles of white agricultural land, flat and wind-swept.

Several times I tried to thumb a lift. But each time the heavy, long-nosed German trucks ignored me, thundering by in a shower of snow that spattered icily on my face. However the fourth truck I waved to stopped and a voice called out, *"Wohin, Freund?"*

"Berlin," I shouted.

There was a pause and then a Red Army soldier clambered down from the cabin. He was sleepy and he'd left his rifle in the truck. That was the only thing that saved me. He asked me in vile German for my papers. Fortunately the edge of the road was wooded. I dived into the dark shelter of the pines, ignoring the branches that lashed at my face, running until I was exhausted.

Dawn found me trudging through powdery snow along a narrow side road flanked with trees, following blindly the drone of the airlift planes. It was a blood-red dawn, wild and violent and full of cold. The sun was a misty red disc above the pines. I staggered into the shelter of the woods, ate Frau Kleffmann's chicken and bread, wrapped myself in pine needles and slept.

All that day I slept, if you can call it sleep. It was more like a bone-chilled coma. I suppose I was suffering from mental as well as physical exhaustion. At all events I found the present and the past inextricably mixed in my mind, so that the urge to reach Berlin became confused with the urge to get out of Germany and I was back on those cold, wretched starved weeks of escape.

Night came at last, cold and black. There were no stars. I stumbled to the road and headed south-east, the drone of the planes my only guide. I passed through a small town, not bothering to note its name, joined a broader road where the snow had been churned up by traffic, and the first truck that came along stopped beside me. In the headlights I saw that the country bordering the road was flat. If there had been woods I should almost certainly have dived into them. But it was bare, open plain. *"Wo wollen Sie hin, mein Lieber?"* the driver called.

"Berlin," I heard myself answer in a cracked, trembling voice. Any moment I expected the brown, tunic-clad figure of a Red Army man to jump out and face me. But all that happened was that the driver called, *"Kommen Sie rauf, Kamerad. Ich fahre auch nach Berlin."*

It was almost too good to be true. I hauled myself up into the cabin. The driver was alone. There was no mate with him. The gears ground and the old vehicle lurched forward, wheels spinning in the snow. The cabin was hot and stuffy and smelt comfortingly of exhaust fumes. "*Was wollen Sie in Berlin?*" the driver asked.

"Work," I answered him gruffly in German.

"Out of Russia into the Western Sectors, eh?" He grinned at me. He was a small, hard-bitten little man with ferrety eyes. "Well, I don't blame you. If I thought there was a trucking job for me in the Western Sectors I'd be across the border in no time. But I have a wife and family up in Lübeck. Every night I come down this same road. Sometimes I wish I was up there flying the air bridge. I was in the *Luftwaffe*, you know. Radio operator. Had a little radio business before the war. But now, of course, it is finished. There are so few radio sets. It is better to drive a truck. But those bastards up there get to Berlin a lot quicker than I do. My wife always tells me . . ."

He went on and on about himself and the drone of his voice merged with the engine and the eternal distant hum of aircraft throbbing through the clouds. My head nodded, sleepy with the sudden, unaccustomed warmth of the cabin. His voice lost itself in the engine. I slept fitfully, conscious of the lights of a town, of a signboard caught in the headlights that said Berlin 27 km., of the unending dirty yellow of hard-packed snow slipping away beneath us.

And then finally he was shaking me. "*Aufwachen! Aufwachen! Berlin!*"

I opened my eyes blearily and surveyed unlit, slush-filled streets flanked by the empty, blasted shells of buildings which had not been touched since we'd smashed them to rubble five years ago. So this was Berlin! "Where are you making for?" I asked him.

"Potsdam." He peered at me out of the corners of his eyes. "That's in the Russian Zone. Don't imagine you'll be wanting to go there." He laughed mirthlessly, his breath whistling through broken front teeth.

"Where are we?" I asked.

"Oranienburg." He was still looking at me out of the corners of his eyes. "You are a Pole, no? You are not German. Not with that accent."

I didn't say anything and he shrugged his shoulders. "*Na*

*was, schadet es schon?"* He eased his foot on the accelerator pedal. " Well, where do you wish to go, eh? In a few moments I turn right. I have to keep inside the Russian Zone. But if you follow this road it will lead you to Frohnau. Frohnau is in the French Sector."

Frohnau! Frohnau beacon! Frohnau meant Berlin to every airlift pilot. But the warmth of the truck held me tight in my seat. Frohnau was many miles from Gatow. I should have to walk right across Berlin, more than twenty kilometres. " Where do you go when you turn right?" I asked.

" Velten, Schonewald Airfield, Falkensee, Staaken Airfield, past Gatow and then into Potsdam. Choose which you like. It's all the same to me."

" You're going near Gatow?" I asked him.

His eyes narrowed. " What do you want Gatow for, eh?" His voice was harsher. He braked violently and the lorry skidded as he swung right off the main Oranienburg-Berlin road. " Why Gatow?" he repeated. And when I didn't say anything, he added slowly, " Gatow is in the British Sector. It's owned by *Die verdammten Tommies.* Night after night they come. *Die verfluchten Kerle!* I have send my family to my parents in Hamburg. Night after night the English come. They flatten Hamburg and the *Schweinehunde* kill both the kids—the boy was nine and the girl five. They were crushed when the building they shelter in collapses." He stopped talking and stared at me. " Why do you want Gatow, eh?"

" I have a job to go to in the British Sector," I answered.

" What sort of a job?"

I thought desperately. Remembering the crowded Nissen huts at the edge of the off-loading apron at Gatow, I said, " Labour corps. I have a friend who is a checker at Gatow, unloading the airlift planes."

His lips tightened. " You say airlift, when we always say air bridge. Why do you say airlift?" I shrugged my shoulders. " Only *Die verdammten* English and Americans call it airlift." For a long time there was a tense silence in the cabin. We were entering Falkensee now. Staaken aerodrome lay ahead, and then Gatow. " Please, your papers. I wish to see your papers."

I hesitated. " I have no papers," I said. I felt empty and cold inside.

" So! No papers, eh?" He peered through the windshield,

searching the road ahead with his eyes. There were few lights.
Falkensee was asleep. Then, far ahead in the gleam of the
headlights, I saw two figures in the grey of the German police.
The driver's foot checked on the accelerator and his eyes swung
nervously to me. I knew what he was going to do then. I
could see him working it out in his mind. There was only one
thing for me to do. I felt with my hand for the handle of the
door and pushed. It swung back violently and a stream of
bitter air struck my face. I heard the door clang against the
tin of the cabin, saw the rutted, slushy snow spraying up from
the wheels, heard the driver shout as he leaned across to grip
my arm—and I jumped.

I hit the snow with my feet and was flung down, striking
the side of the lorry with my head. A sudden blackness enve-
loped me as the snow closed over my face. I could not have
been out for more than a few seconds, for the lorry was still
screeching to a halt, its horn blaring excitedly, as I lifted my
head from the cold, gritty filth of the snow. I pressed myself
upwards with my hands, feeling suddenly sick at the sight of
my blood scarlet against the yellow, gravel-covered surface of
the snow. Then I was on my feet and running for the shelter
of a side-street, shouts echoing after me.

As I turned out of the main street, I looked over my shoulder
and saw that the two German policemen were level with the
stationary truck now and running towards me. Whistles
shrilled. The side-street was narrow and flanked with the
rubble ruins of shattered buildings. I scrambled over a pile
of bricks and mortar and half staggered, half fell into a cleared
space that had been the cellars of houses in the next street.
An open doorway gaped black and I slid into the welcoming
darkness and leaned panting against the wall almost oblivious
in my fear of the nauseating smell of human excreta.

More whistles shrilled and voices shouted in the darkness
outside. Boots climbed the mound of rubble up which I had
scrambled. Mortar dust streamed down in a choking cloud
in the open doorway. " *Hier, Kurt. Hierlang ist er gelaufen.*"
The voice was heavy and menacing. The man was standing
right above my hide-out. There was a clatter of dislodged
bricks higher up the crumbling rubble and a voice answered
faintly, " *Nein. Komm hierlang. Hier kann er zur Friedrich-
strasse durenkommen.*" The chase went thudding and slithering over my head and gradually faded into the distance.

All the time I had been standing there rigid. Now my muscles relaxed. I wiped the sweat from my forehead. My hand was gritty and I winced with the pain of the grit on raw flesh. It was the old cut in my forehead that had opened up. My hand came away, wet and sticky with my own blood. The moon was shining opaquely through low cloud and the faint, ghostly light of the doorless gap showed my hand all red and dripping. The blood was trickling down my face, getting into my eyes and into the corner of my mouth the way it had done that first time I'd come to Membury. Only there was grit in my mouth now, sharp and hard, setting my teeth on edge as I clenched them.

I wiped my hands on the inside of my clothes and then tied my handkerchief over the cut. For a long time I just stood there, trying to stop the trembling of my limbs. It was very cold. It seemed as though my body had no warmth and the wind cut like a knife through the gaping doorway—nervous reaction and the shock of my fall from the moving lorry! I wished to God I had some liquor with me, something to warm the frozen guts of my belly.

I moved at last and went out of the nauseous cell. I was facing a cleared strip where demolition gangs had been working. There was a railway and a line of loaded tip trucks. The snow was a thin layer of powder that had deepened into windy little drifts in the corners of still-standing masonry. Behind rose a hill of brick and rubble over which the gaunt finger of a building pointed a broken chimney at the pale, luminous clouds. There was no sound except the distant rumble of the airlift rolling into Gatow. The pursuit had moved on and lost me.

I stood for a moment, getting my bearings. This was Falkensee, a western suburb of Berlin. The sound of the planes landing and taking off from Gatow drew me as something familiar, friendly and homelike. I could almost smell the coffee and cakes in the Malcolm Club. But if I went direct to Gatow I should all the time be in the Russian Zone. To the east lay the British Sector and I knew it couldn't be far away. I faced into the wind and began to walk.

My left leg was very stiff and painful when I moved. I had grazed my knee-cap when I fell and had strained a muscle somewhere in the groin. But I didn't care about that. My one thought was to get out of the Russian Zone and into the British

Sector. The sight of another human being sent me scuttling into the doorway or into the shadows of the broken buildings that flanked the streets. And yet, not more than two or three miles away in the same sort of streets I should be able to stop the first person I met and demand his help.

I twisted and turned through narrow, broken streets, always keeping the sound of Gatow over my right shoulder. At length I came out on to a broad highway that led almost due east. It was Falkenhagener Chaussee and it ran straight like a ruled line towards Spandau—and Spandau I knew was in the British Sector.

It was three o'clock in the morning and the Falkenhagener Chaussee seemed dead. Nothing stirred. The snow-powdered thoroughfare was deserted. The crumbling masses of the buildings were white mounds in the darkness marked occasionally by a still-standing wall, tottering skyward like some two thousand-year-old tomb seen along the Appian Way. Somewhere in Berlin a train whistled like an owl in a forest of dead oaks. There were no lights, no people—no suggestion even that anything lived here. It was all devastation and slow, timeless ruin.

For an hour or more I limped along that arrow-straight road without seeing a living soul, with only the constant drone of Gatow to remind me I was still in a living world and to give me hope. Then at last, when I was tottering with weakness, I saw the distant gleam of lights shining on a road barrier. I was nearing the limits of the Russian Zone. That knowledge gave me fresh strength. I walked to within five hundred yards of the barrier and then turned down a side-street.

At a crossing a small truck slipped quietly eastward without lights. I followed it on to a quiet, rubble-packed track that ran close beside the railway. A goods train clanked noisily, a rattle of buffers that seemed to split the night it was so loud in the utter stillness.

For half an hour I walked eastward, searching the track ahead, trembling and scuttling into the shadows at every sign of movement. But always it was nothing but my eyes playing me tricks. And at the end of half an hour I knew I must have passed over into the British Sector. A blockade-running German lorry had shown me the way through the road checks.

I followed the railway right into Spandau and there a German railway worker going on duty at five in the morning directed me to a British Army M.T. Section. I must have looked a pretty sight, for all the time he was talking to me the German kept looking nervously about him and when he had given the directions I wanted he was almost running in his hurry to get away from me.

I found the place without difficulty. It was an R.A.O.C. Depot and a big board directed me into the sidings of what had once been a huge factory. I was trembling with fatigue and feeling sick with relief when I faced the German orderly who seemed to be the only person awake in the depot. At first he refused to do anything about me. His eyes were coldly contemptuous. I began to curse him in English, all the filthy words I could think of spewed off my tongue as I consigned the whole German race to perdition with tears of frustration hot on my eyeballs. Still he didn't move, and then I saw hanging on a peg a web belt complete with holster and revolver. I dived towards it, pulled the revolver out and thumbed forward the safety catch with trembling fingers. " Now, get the duty officer," I shouted. " Quick! Or I shoot."

The man hesitated and then hurried out, returning a few minutes later with a tall, lanky youth who had an officer's greatcoat wrapped over his pyjamas, a solitary pip gleaming on its shoulder. " What's the trouble?" he asked sleepily, rubbing at his eyes.

" My name's Fraser," I said. " Squadron Leader Fraser. I've just got out of the Russian Zone. I've got to get to Gatow at once."

He was staring at the weapon in my hand. " Do you usually go about threatening people with revolvers." He came across to me and took the revolver out of my hands. " This is an Army revolver. Is it yours?"

" No," I said. " I got it there." And I nodded to the belt hanging on the hook.

The lieutenant swung round on the orderly. " What's that equipment doing there, Heinrich?"

They began a long discussion as to why an officer had left it in the orderly room. At length I shouted at him, " For Christ's sake!"

He turned and stared at me blankly. " Heinrich here says you threatened him with this revolver," he said accusingly.

" Look!" I couldn't keep my hands still, I was so angry. " Can't you understand what I'm trying to tell you? I'm an

R.A.F. officer. I'm a pilot on the airlift and my plane crashed at Hollmind. I've just got out of the Russian Zone. I must get to Gatow quickly. I want transport. Do you understand? Some transport. I've got to get to Gatow." I was talking wildly. I knew that. I knew I must seem like a lunatic, but there was nothing I could do about it. My nerves were all to pieces.

" May I have a look at your papers, please?"

I fumbled for my wallet, dropping the papers on the floor in my nervous haste. The German orderly picked them up for me and handed them back with a click of the heels. His eyes were no longer contemptuous.

The lieutenant glanced through them. " You say you crashed at Hollmind?"

I nodded.

" When?"

When? Was it the night before last or—no I mustn't say that. It was the original night he wanted, the night when Tubby had gone out through the door. My mind searched desperately for a date, but I'd lost all sense of time. " Several days ago," I mumbled. " What's it matter when I crashed?"

" What's your base?"

" Wunstorf."

" You were flying a York?"

" No. A Tudor tanker."

" A Tudor. His face suddenly cleared and he gave me a sheepish grin. " I say, I'm awfully sorry, sir. Of course, I know who you are now. You're the chap who flew that Messerschmitt out of Germany during the war. I mean—well, there's been a lot about it in the papers. Nobody could find any trace of the plane and you and Carter were missing." He looked at me, hesitating awkwardly. " You look as though you've had a rough trip, sir. Are you all right? I mean, oughtn't I to run you down to a first-aid post?"

" I must get to Gatow," I said.

" Yes, of course. I'll drive you myself. I'll just put some things on. Won't be a jiffy." He hesitated in the doorway. " Would you like a cup of char? And you'd probably like to get cleaned up a bit. That's an awfully nasty cut you've got."

He took me through to the washroom. The water was icy cold. However, I cleaned off some of the dirt and he produced a proper bandage from a first-aid kit. Then the German orderly appeared with a steaming tin mug of dark, sweet tea. Ten minutes later we were in an Army fifteen hundredweight roaring along the Wilhelmstrasse.

We turned left on to the Gatower Damm. I knew I was home then, for planes were thundering low overhead with their flaps down and the underbelly of the low cloud was illumined by the brilliant fire-glow of the sodium lights and high intensity cross bars that marked the approach to Gatow.

We were stopped at the barrier to Gatow Airport and a corporal of the R.A.F. Police came out and peered at the car, a gleam of white-blancoed webbing against the blue of his battledress. Then he asked for our papers. " Squadron Leader Fraser is just out of the Russian Zone," my lieutenant explained quickly. " He's the pilot of that Tudor that crashed."

The corporal handed my papers back without looking at them. " Glad you're safe, sir." He drew himself up stiffly and saluted. The truck ground forward. " Where do you want to go?" the lieutenant asked. " Terminal building?"

All the time I'd been getting closer to Gatow I'd been wondering about what I should do when I got there. There was Diana. That was the first thing I had to do—tell Diana that Tubby was alive and safe. And I wanted to get hold of Saeton. Now that I was back in the organised life of Occupied Berlin I had a feeling that there might be difficulties raised about landing an R.A.F. plane in the Russian Zone. Officially it would be embarrassing. If the plane were captured by a Russian patrol the diplomatic repercussions would be endless and far-reaching. But if Saeton would land there unofficially . . . He had the nerve to do it. He wouldn't be hide-bound by regulations and diplomatic dangers. Saeton was the person I had to see. " Will you take me straight to the Malcolm Club, please," I said.

" Malcolm Club? That's down by FASO, isn't it?"

" That's right."

" Sure you don't want to report in to Ops. first?" he asked.

" No. The Malcolm Club, please."

" Okay."

The truck slipped down through the trees, past the lighted entrance of the mess and then suddenly there were the yellow and purple runway and perimeter lights of Gatow with the concrete square box of the terminal building to the right, rising to the tall, lighted windows of the control tower. The truck turned left through the white-painted boundary fence, skirted a B.E.A. Skymaster and hummed across the tarmac which was streaked with a white, wind-driven powder of snow. The hangars were dark, rectangular shadows to our left and ahead the lights of Piccadilly Circus shone yellow, showing the PLUME standing empty of aircraft. Planes moved along the perimeter track, engines roaring, drowning the thinner sound of planes streaming in along the runway. Everything was normal, familiar. I might never have been outside the organised bus-service of the airlift.

We skirted Piccadilly Circus, tyres jolting rhythmically on the joints of the concrete, and then we were on the FASO apron where big arc lamps blazed and there was the bustle of planes and lorries and German off-loading teams. The control tower shack on its scaffold stilts stood high and dark above the line of Nissen huts.

"Shall I wait for you?" the lieutenant asked as he drew up at the roundel signboard of the Malcolm Club.

"No, thanks," I said. "I'll be all right now. And thank you very much for running me out."

"Not at all. He got down and opened the door for me, his hand steadying me as though he thought I were too weak to climb out on my own. "Good-bye, sir. And good luck!" He gave me a parade ground salute.

I hesitated at the entrance of the club and stood watching him get back into his truck, turn and drive off. The red tail-light dwindled and was lost amongst the litter of lights. I stared at the planes coming in. They were Daks from Lübeck with coal. There was a line of them standing in the slush of the apron. I stared at them dully. A girl checker with the nearest German labour team looked up from her manifest and stared at me. She was big and fair-haired with high cheek bones. She reminded me of Else, except that she was covered in coal dust. I turned towards the entrance to the Malcolm Club, still hesitating, reluctant to go in. If Diana were there it would be all right. But if she weren't . . . I'd have to explain myself and the filthy state I was in and I should be surrounded by a barrage of questions as air crew after air crew came in and wanted to know the story of the crash.

A group of R.A.F. boys tumbled out of the hut, laughing and talking, bringing with them through the open doorway that familiar smell of coffee and cakes. There was no point in putting it off any longer—besides, the smell of the place had made me realise how hungry I was. I brushed quickly at my filthy clothing and pushed open the door.

It was hot inside, the stove roaring red and the place full of smoke and cheerful chatter. I crossed the long room, pushing my way towards the counter, conscious of the gradual fall of conversation as eyes fastened on my scarecrow figure. " Is Mrs. Carter here?" I asked the girl behind the counter. I had spoken quietly, but even so my voice sounded loud in the silence that had developed.

The girl looked nervously to the mute groups behind me. " No," she said. " She doesn't come on until seven."

I glanced at my watch. It was half-past six. " I'll wait," I said. " Can I have some coffee and a plate of sandwiches, please?"

The girl hesitated. " All right," she said.

A hand touched my shoulder. I spun round and found myself facing a big blond man with a wide moustache. "Who are you?" he asked. The silent circle of eyes echoed his question.

" My name's Fraser," I answered.

" Fraser." He turned the name over in his mouth as though searching for it in his memory. And then he suddenly boomed out. " Fraser! You mean the pilot of that Tudor?"

" That's right," I said.

" Fraser! Good Christ Almighty!" He seized hold of my hand. " Don't know you from Adam, old man. But allow me to do the honours and welcome you back. You look about all in. Here, Joan—the coffee and sandwiches are on me. What happened? Come on, tell us all about it. We've got to go in a minute. What happened?" The circle of faces closed in like a pack of wolves, avid for news. Their eyes shone with excitement. Questions were hurled at me from all directions.

" There's nothing to tell," I murmured awkwardly. " The engines failed. The plane crashed near Hollmind."

" And you've just got out of the Russian Zone?"

" Yes." The girl thrust a cup of coffee and a plate of sandwiches into my hand. " If you don't mind—I'd rather not talk about it." The heat of the room was making my legs shake under me. " I'm very tired. You must excuse me. I must sit down."

Hands gripped my arms at the elbows and half-lifted me to
one of the easy-chairs by the stove. "You sit there and drink
your coffee, old man. We'll have you fixed up in no time."

"I must speak to Mrs. Carter," I insisted.

"All right. We'll get her for you."

They left me then and I grasped the coffee cup in my hands,
feeling the warmth of it spread up my arms, savouring the
glorious, reviving smell of it. I could hear them talking about
me in the background. Fresh air crews came in to replace
others that went out to their planes. The word was passed on
and they took up the story, talking about me in whispers.

Somebody came and squatted down on his haunches beside
me. "Glad to know you're back, Fraser," he said. "You must
be the greatest escape merchant alive. All the boys back at
Wunstorf will be glad as hell to know you're back. We thought
you'd had it."

"Wunstorf?" I stared at him. His face seemed vaguely
familiar.

"That's right. Remember me? I'm the guy that was sitting
right next to you at dinner that night you crashed. You were
growling at Westrop for talking too much about the Russians.
Seems he had second sight or something. I'll see that the
station commander knows you're back."

"Is the Wunstorf wave coming in now?" I asked.

"Yes. Just started to come in."

"Is a man called Saeton flying a Tudor tanker on the lift
yet?"

"Is he flying the lift!" The kid laughed. "I'll say he is.
Been flying for two days now and he's got the development
section puzzled as hell. Flies on his two inboard engines all
the time, except on take-off, and his fuel consumption is knocking holes the size of a hangar door in all the aero engine boys'
ideas. He said you worked on the motors with him at one
time. Boy, he's certainly got them guessing. Boffins from
Farnborough are flying out to-morrow with the C.T.O. of the
Ministry of Civil Aviation and a big pot from the Ministry of
Supply. Saeton will be in shortly."

"How soon?" I asked.

"About quarter of an hour. The Tudors aren't far behind
us."

An R.A.F. corporal pushed forward. He had a big web
satchel with a red cross on it. "I've got an ambulance outside,

sir. Do you think you can walk to it or shall I get a stretcher in for you?"

"You can send your bloody ambulance away," I said angrily. Why the devil couldn't they leave me alone? "I'm not leaving here until I've seen Mrs. Carter."

The fellow hesitated. "Very good, sir. I'll be back in a minute and then we'll get you patched up. Nasty cut you got there. Sure you're all right, sir?"

"Of course I'm all right," I snapped. "I've walked nearly twenty miles already to-night."

"Very good, sir." He went to the door and opened it, and at that moment Diana came in.

Her face, devoid of make-up, looked quite haggard. At sight of me she stopped as though she couldn't believe that I was really sitting there in an easy-chair beside the stove. "So it *is* you." She said it almost accusingly. Then she came slowly towards me. "What happened? What have you done with Tubby? Why didn't you let him jump with the others?" Her voice trembled and there was a look of dull pain in her eyes.

"You needn't worry," I said. "He's safe."

She stared at me. "You're lying." Her voice was suddenly hard. "You know he's dead."

"Tubby's all right," I repeated. "He's alive."

"I don't understand." Her voice had faded to a whisper. "It can't be true. If you're alive, then it's Tubby whose body——" Her words died away in a choking sob.

"Tubby's alive," I said again. I reached out and caught hold of her hand. Her fingers were cold and slack in mine. "Diana. I want your help. He's alive, but he's injured and we've got to get him out. You've got to persuade Saeton to fly there and get him out."

"What are you saying?" Her voice was flat and toneless.

I didn't understand her attitude. "I thought you'd be glad," I said. "I came straight here to tell you."

"Glad that you're alive?" She turned away. "Of course I'm glad only . . . I loved him," she suddenly burst out. "I loved him, I tell you."

Somebody bent over me, an officer in R.A.F. uniform with dark, boot-button eyes and a thin, aquiline nose. "You're Fraser, aren't you?" he said. "They just told me."

"For God's sake!" I pushed him away. "I'm trying to tell Mrs. Carter something."

"Yes. I heard. I think you'd better listen to me first. I'm the I.O. here. We know all about your plane. It crashed two miles north of Hollmind Airfield, dived straight into the ground."

I stared at him. "Who told you it crashed at Hollmind?" I demanded.

"The Russians."

"The Russians?"

"Yes. After denying the whole thing for days, they came through with a report yesterday. They've found the wreckage in the woods north of Hollmind." He leaned down and lowered his voice. "They also found the remains of one body. We didn't know whether it was yours or Carter's." His glance slid to Diana whose face was buried in her hands. "Now you're safe, of course, we know whose it was." He straightened up. "Soon as you're ready, we'll go up to my office and I'll get a statement from you. I'll have to have a report ready for the station commander."

I stared at him. Why should the Russians make such a report? It didn't make sense. I felt suddenly scared—scared that they wouldn't believe what I had to tell them.


## CHAPTER EIGHT

THE next quarter of an hour was a nightmare. I started by trying to convince the Intelligence Officer that the Russian report was nonsense. It was a mistake. He believed the information the Russians had given him. What's more, the lieutenant who had driven me to Gatow had reported to him after dropping me at the Malcolm Club. He knew that I'd held a German orderly up with a revolver. "You don't know what you're saying—or what you're doing, Fraser," he said. His voice was cold and practical. "Better come up to my office and then I'll take you along to the sick bay."

I thought of the little patrol of Red Army men in the woods near Hollmind. They knew damn well the plane hadn't dived into the ground. "Can I see this report?" I asked him.

"It's up at my office now."

"Does the report give any details?"

"Oh, yes. It's quite detailed. No question about it being

your plane. They've even got the number—Two-five-two." He turned to the medical orderly who had returned. "Take Mrs. Carter back to her quarters."

"Wait," I said. If I couldn't convince him, at least I might be able to convince Diana. I pulled myself out of my seat and went over to her, catching hold of her shoulders and shaking her in my desperate urge to get her to concentrate on what I had to tell her. "You've got to listen to me, Diana." She lifted her head and stared at me through tear-dimmed eyes. "I was with Tubby yesterday. He *is* alive."

The desire to believe me was there in her face. Hope showed for an instant in her eyes, but then it died and she clenched her teeth. "Take him away from me, please," she said in a whisper.

The I.O. pulled my hand away from her shoulder. "The Russians wouldn't say he was dead if he wasn't." He pushed me gently back into the chair. "Just take it easy. You're a bit upset—but it's no good raising Mrs. Carter's hopes. Carter's dead. No question of that. Now all I want from you——"

"He's not dead," I cut in angrily. "He's badly injured, but he's alive. He's at a farm——"

"Stop it, Neil!" Diana screamed at me. "For God's sake stop it! Why do you keep saying he's alive when you know he's dead? If it hadn't been for me," she added in a lifeless tone, "he'd never have taken the job. He'd still have been with Saeton. Bill wouldn't have crashed him. He'd have been all right with Bill. Oh, God!"

She was beside herself and I sat there staring at the misery which made her face look wild and wondering how the devil I could convince her that her husband was alive. I turned to the I.O. "I want to see the station commander," I said. "I want a plane put at my disposal to-night. Do you think he'd do that?"

"What do you want a plane for?" His tone was the sort you use to placate an excited child and I saw him exchange a quick glance with the medical orderly.

"I want to fly to Hollmind Airfield," I answered quickly. "If I can land at Hollmind I can get Carter out."

"Is that ambulance still here?" he asked the medical orderly.

"Yes, sir. Mr. Fraser told me to send it away, but I thought

I'd better——" He stared at me without finishing the sentence.

"Good! Come along, Fraser. You need a good, hot drink, warmth and a bed. We'll soon have you fixed up." His hand was on my arm, gently but firmly raising me from my seat.

I flung him off. "Can't you understand what I'm trying to tell you? Tubby Carter is alive. He didn't die in any crash." It was on the tip of my tongue to say there hadn't been any crash, but I knew he wouldn't believe that, not unless I told him the whole story and I wasn't going to do that until I had seen Saeton. "He's at a farm, being cared for by the local doctor. He's got a broken arm, several broken ribs and a pierced lung and he needs treatment."

"Now, be reasonable, Fraser." The I.O.'s hand was back on my arm. "We all understand how you feel. But it's no good pretending he's alive just because you're worried that you jumped when he was still in the plane. We'll get all that sorted out later. Now come on up to the sick bay."

So they were going to pin that on me! I felt the blood rush, hammering, to my head. Damn them! At least that wasn't the truth. I'd gone back for him, hadn't I? I felt a sense of utter frustration taking hold of me.

And then Diana's hand was on my arm. "Why do you keep on talking about a farm?" she asked. The desire to believe me was back in her face.

I told her about the Kleffmanns then and about their son Hans. "Tubby is lying in Hans's old room," I said. I half-closed my eyes, forcing to my mind the picture of that room. "The wallpaper has butterflies on it and it's littered with faded photographs of Hans. The bedstead is of iron and brass and the single dormer window looks out on to the roof of a barn." I seized hold of her shoulder again. "You've got to believe me, Diana. You've got to help me persuade Saeton to fly in to Hollmind to-night. Please—please, for God's sake believe what I'm trying to tell you."

She stared at me and then she nodded slowly, half-dazed. "I must believe you," she said half to herself. Her eyes searched my face. "You do know what you're saying, don't you? You aren't lying—just to protect yourself?"

"To protect myself?"

"Yes—so that we'd think you didn't leave him to——" She stopped and bit hold of her lip. "No. I can't believe you'd do that. I guess you mean what you say." She looked up quickly at the I.O. "Leave us a minute. Do you mind? I'd like to talk to him."

The I.O. hesitated and then turned away to the coffee counter.

"How did you know Bill was here?" She was leaning forward and the unexpectedness of her question nearly caught me off my guard. I was feeling wretchedly tired. The warmth of the stove was making me sleepy. I pushed my hand over my face. "One of the air crews, a fellow from Wunstorf, told me," I answered. I shook myself, trying to keep my mind clear. I mustn't tell her what really happened. If I did that Saeton wouldn't help me. "Can you find out when he'll be in?" I asked her. "I've got to speak to him. Once I get up there in the terminal building they'll start questioning me and then they'll push me off to hospital or something. Saeton must take me to Hollmind. Tubby's got to be flown out to-night."

"Why are you so set on Bill going?" she asked.

"He was a friend of Tubby's," I said. "It was Tubby who got those engines made for him, wasn't it? Damn it, he owes Tubby that?"

"There's no other reason?" She hesitated, staring at me hard. "You say you jumped, leaving Tubby in the plane?"

Again the quickness of her question almost caught me off my guard. "I said nothing of the sort. Don't try and pin anything like that on to me," I added angrily.

"Then why was he hurt and not you?"

"Because——" I dropped my head into my hand, pressing at the corners of my eyes with finger and thumb, trying to loosen the band of strain that was tightening across my forehead, "I don't know," I said wearily. "For God's sake stop asking me questions. All I want you to do is to get Saeton for me."

Diana caught hold of the lapels of my German greatcoat. "You're lying!" Her voice hissed between her clamped teeth. "You're lying, Neil. I know you are. You're hiding something. What is it? You must tell me what it is." She was shaking me violently. "What happened? What really happened?"

"Leave me alone, can't you?" I whispered. If only she'd leave me alone, let me think. "Get Saeton," I added. "I want to talk to Saeton."

"Something happened that night. Didn't it? Something

happened. Neil—what was it? Please tell me what it was?"
She was kneeling beside me now and her voice had risen hysterically. I could feel the sudden silence in the room, feel them staring at me—the regular air crew boys, men who knew nothing about my story, who would be judging me in the light of Diana clinging to my greatcoat and crying out, "*What happened? What happened that night?*"

"Wait till Saeton comes," I said wearily.

"What's Bill got to do with it? Was he the cause of it?"
She looked wildly round and then swung fiercely back on me.
"Will you talk if Bill is here? Will you tell me what really happened then?"

"Yes, if you'll get him to fly out to Hollmind to-night. He can land at the airfield and then we'll get Tubby out. Tubby will be all right then."

"Hollmind is a disused aerodrome. I checked that yesterday when I got the news. Are you sure he'll be able to land there?"

"He's done it once."

"What do you mean?"

I pressed my head into my hand. "Nothing," I said. If I didn't get some sleep soon I'd be saying the first thing that came into my mind. "I didn't mean anything," I murmured. "I don't know what I'm saying. I'm very tired, Diana. Get Saeton for me, will you; and stop asking me questions."

She hesitated as though on the brink of another question. But all she said was, "Bill isn't here yet."

The I.O. was back at my side now. "You want Saeton? He'll be here any minute now. The first Tudor has just come in. You worked with him on these engines of his, I understand?"

"Yes." I didn't want to talk any more. The idea that the authorities wouldn't help me was firmly fixed in my mind. Saeton was the only man who could help me. I sat there, stupid with the warmth of the stove and the fatigue of my body, feeling the blood drying in a crust on my temple, watching the door. Air crews moved in and out and as they passed they stared at us silently as though we were some queer tableau entirely divorced from the solid, everyday routine of flying in and out of Berlin.

Then at last the door was pushed open and Saeton came striding in followed by his crew. He was almost past us before he saw me. He checked, rocking back on his heels as though for an instant he had been caught off balance. Then his features set themselves into a smile of welcome. " Hallo, Neil!" He reached down and grasped my shoulder. " Glad you're safe." But I noticed that his eyes didn't light up with his face. They were hard as slate and withdrawn as though wrestling with the problem of my presence. He had a silk sweat rag knotted round his throat and his flying suit was un-zipped, making him appear more solid than ever. " Well, what happened? How did you get out?"

" I hitched a ride and walked the rest," I said.

There was an awkward silence. He seemed to want to put a question, but his eyes slid to the others and he remained silent. I knew suddenly that he was nervous. I hadn't thought of him as a man who could ever be nervous, but as he lit a cigarette his hands were trembling. " You've heard the news, have you? About the engines, I mean. They're proving even better than we expected—twenty per cent increase in power and a forty-five per cent reduction in fuel consumption. They're going to be——"

" Tubby is alive," I said.

" Alive?" The echo of my statement was jerked out of him as though I'd hit him below the belt. Then he recovered himself. " Are you sure? You're not——" He stopped, conscious of the silence of the others watching him. " Where is he?"

" In a farmhouse near Hollmind Airfield."

" I see." He took a long pull at his cigarette. The news had jolted him and I could see he didn't know what to do about it. He glanced at Diana and then at the I.O. who drew him on one side. I saw the man's lips frame the words " Russian report " and I could almost have laughed at the thought of an R.A.F. Intelligence Officer giving Saeton the details of what had happened to that plane when all the time it was sitting out there on the FASO apron unloading fuel.

At length Saeton said, " All right. I'll see if I can get some sense out of him. Mind if I talk to him alone?"

The I.O. agreed and led Diana away. Saeton came and stood over me. He was smiling. " For some reason the Russians have been very helpful," he said. He was quite sure of himself again now. " You've heard about this report, have you? They say they found the remains of one of the crew." I made no comment. His head was in silhouette against the light. It hung over me as it had done that first night at Membury. And he was smiling. "Well, how did you find him?" I told him about the search and when I had finished he said, "So he's injured. Badly?"

"Broken arm and ribs and a pierced lung," I said. "We've got to get him out. He needs hospital treatment."

"And if he doesn't get it?"

"I don't know," I answered. "There's a German doctor looking after him. But Tubby is pretty bad. I think he might die."

"I see." He ran his thumb along the blue line of his jaw. "What are you going to do about it?"

"I can't do anything. That bloody little Intelligence Officer doesn't believe me. I want you to tell them you believe what I'm saying—persuade them to give us a plane."

"Us?" He gave a quick laugh.

"Tubby won't talk," I said quickly. "He promised me."

"I'm on the very edge of success," he said and I realised that he had room for nothing else in that queer, urgent mind of his.

"Yes, I heard about that," I said. "Is it true officials are coming out from England?"

He nodded, his eyes lighting up. "Everything's gone marvellously. First trip my flight engineer was staggered by the performance of the engines. Within twenty-four hours it was all over the mess at Wunstorf and R.A.F. engineers were flying the airlift with me, checking for themselves. Now the Ministry of Civil Aviation and the Ministry of Supply are sending their experts out, including a boffin from Farnborough. By this afternoon——"

"What about Tubby?" I said. "You can't abandon him. You've got to get him out."

"You should have thought about him before you told me you were going to the authorities as soon as you got back here."

"I won't talk," I said hastily. "Nor will Tubby."

"It's too late to say that now." And then he added slowly, "As far as I'm concerned Tubby is dead."

He said it without any emotion and I stared up at him, seeing the hard line of his jaw, the cold slatiness of his eyes, unable to believe even then that he meant what he said.

"We've got to get him out," I insisted.

He shrugged his shoulders. "You know damn' well I can't accept your story. It would be fatal."

I didn't believe him at first. "You can't leave Tubby out there in the Russian Zone."

"I'll do nothing to betray the belief of the authorities in this Russian report," was his reply.

The full horror of what he was saying dawned on me slowly. "You mean——" The words choked in my throat.

"I mean I'll do nothing," he said.

All right. If he was as cold-blooded as that . . . "Do you remember how you blackmailed me into stealing that plane?" I asked.

He nodded slowly, that cold smile back on his lips.

"Well, I'm going to blackmail you now," I said. "Either you fly me into Hollmind to-night to pick up Tubby or I tell the I.O. here everything—how I pinched the plane, how I nearly killed Tubby, how you altered the numbers and we strewed the wreckage of our old Tudor through the Hollmind woods and how you set fire to the hangar at Membury so that there would be no trace."

"You think he'd believe you?" There was almost a sneer in his voice.

"Get him out, Saeton," I whispered urgently. "If you don't, I'll bust the whole game wide open. Understand?"

His eyes narrowed slightly. That was the only sign he gave that he took my threat seriously. "Don't think I haven't taken care of the possibility of your reaching Berlin," he said quietly. He glanced round at Diana and the I.O. and then in a louder voice: "No wonder you get scared when it comes to jumping. You're about the most imaginative flier I ever met." He turned and nodded to the I.O. "I'm sorry," he said. "I can't get any sense out of him." He drew the officer to one side. "I'm afraid he's pretty bad. Concussion or something. He keeps on talking about pinching a plane and having a fight with Carter. I think he's all mixed up in his mind with that escape he did from Germany in 1944." They began whispering together and I heard the I.O. mention the word "psychiatrist." Diana was staring at me dully, all hope gone from her eyes, her body slumped at the shoulders in an attitude of dejection. Saeton and the I.O. came back towards me and I heard Saeton saying, ". . . if we knew what happened when the plane crashed."

"You know damn' well it didn't crash," I jerked out. Sudden, overwhelming hatred of him swept me to my feet. "I know what it is. You want Tubby dead. You know damn' well the credit for those engines is his. You want him dead."

They stared at me like humans looking through bars at a caged animal. "I'll get him away," the I.O. whispered quickly to Saeton and Saeton nodded.

I turned to Diana then. She was the person I had to convince. She knew Saeton, knew the set-up—above all she was the only one of them that wanted to believe that Tubby was alive. "Diana, you must listen to me," I implored her. "You've got to believe me. Tubby isn't dead. I saw him yesterday afternoon." My head was swimming and I pressed my hands to my temples. "No, it wasn't yesterday. It was the day before. He was badly injured, but he could talk. I promised I'd come back for him. If you love him, Diana, you've got to help me. You've got to make the people here believe——"

A hand grasped my shoulder and spun me round. "Shut up!" Saeton's face was thrust close to mine. "Shut up, do you hear? Tubby's dead. You're just saying this to cover yourself. Can't you realise how Diana feels? Until you turned up there was a good chance he was alive. Everybody thought the body the Russians found in the plane must be yours. You were the skipper. But you turn up. So it's Tubby who is dead, and now you try to raise false hopes in an effort to——"

I flung his hand off. "You devil!" I said. "You're the cause of all this. It's your fault he's out there in the Russian Zone." I turned to Diana. "The plane didn't crash at all," I cried. "I flew it back to Membury. Saeton forced me to do it. Tubby tried to prevent me. There was a struggle and——" I could see they didn't believe me.

"Get him out of here," I heard Saeton say. "Get him out before he drives Mrs. Carter crazy." Hands closed on my arms and I was dragged across the room to the door. I screwed my head round and saw Saeton standing alone, his face grey and tired looking, and Diana was staring across at him, her lips trembling. Behind them the air crews stood in silence looking on. Then the door closed in my face and I was out in the grey dawn of Gatow Airfield with the roar of planes and the deliberate, operational movements of lorries and German labour teams.

I had a brief glimpse of the FASO apron, gleaming dully in its leaden mantle of slush. Close by a German labour team was hauling sacks of coal from the belly of a Dak and beyond it another Dak was swinging off the perimeter track and an R.A.F. corporal was signalling it into position. A lorry rolled past us to meet it. A sergeant of the R.A.F. Police had the ambulance doors open and I was bundled in. The Intelligence Officer climbed in beside me. The sergeant saluted stiffly and the doors closed, boxing us into a dark little world that shook with the roar of planes. A slight vibration of the stretcher bunk on which I had been sat told me the engine was running, and then we moved off, slithering on the wet surface as we swung round the fuel standing at Piccadilly Circus. " Where are we going?" I asked the I.O.

" Sick bay," he answered. " I rang up Squadron Leader Gentry from the Malcolm Club. He's the M.O. He's expecting you."

I was conscious of that sense of helplessness that comes to the individual when he is in process of being absorbed into the machine of an organised unit. Once I was in the M.O.'s clutches anything could happen—they'd regard any request as prejudicial to the patient's recovery. They might even drug me. " I want to see the station commander," I said.

The intelligence officer didn't answer. I repeated my request. " Take my advice, Fraser," he said coldly. " See the M.O. first."

I hesitated. Somehow his voice seemed to carry a note of warning. But I wasn't thinking about myself. I was thinking about Tubby. " I've got to see the station commander," I said.

" Well, you can't. I'm taking you to the M.O. Put your request to him if you want to." In the half-light I could see his eyes watching me. " I'm saying that for your own good."

" For my own good?" His eyes had turned away as though breaking off the conversation. All I could see was the pale outline of his face under the peaked cap. " I'm not worrying about myself," I said. " It's Carter I'm worried about."

" I should have thought that was a waste of time now."

The tone of his voice stung me. " Civil airlift pilots come under R.A.F. for administration and discipline, don't they?" I asked. The outline of his head nodded slowly. " Very well, then. Take me to the station commander's office. That's a formal request."

His eyes were back on my face again now. "Have it your own way," he said. "But if you're fit enough to see the station commander, you're fit enough to see Squadron Leader Pierce, R.A.F. Police." He turned and tapped on the partition separating us from the driver. A small hatch slid back. "Terminal building first," he ordered the driver.

"What did you mean about R.A.F. Police?" I asked.

"Pierce is very anxious to see you. Some question of an identity check."

Identity check! "What do you mean?" For a moment the thought of Tubby was thrust out of my mind. Identity check! Had Saeton talked about me? Was that what he meant when he had said he had taken care of the possibility of my reaching Berlin? Was this his attempt to discredit me? "Whose instructions is he acting on?" I asked.

"I know nothing about it," the I.O. answered in that same cold, deliberate voice.

Before I could question him further the ambulance had stopped and we were getting out. The terminal building was a lifeless hulk of concrete in the cloud-skimmed dawn. The tall windows of the control tower looked with dead eyes upon the runway where a single Tudor was lining up for take-off. There was no outward sign that this was the hub and heart of the world's busiest air traffic centre; beyond it the wings of a Dak widened against the dull cloud-scape over Berlin as it dropped towards the runway like a toy pulled by an unseen string. As we went through the swing doors the Tudor took off with a roar that split the dawn-cold stillness.

The I.O. took me up to the first floor. Little placards stood out from the doors of wood-partitioned offices; Flight Lieutenant Symes, Intelligence Officer—white on blue next to Public Relations. The I.O. pushed open the door. "Wait here, will you, Fraser. I'll go down and see if the station commander has come in yet. He usually shows up about this time. Likes to have a look around before breakfast." He turned to the medical orderly. "You wait here with Mr. Fraser, corporal." He glanced at me quickly, but his eyes slid away from mine and I went into his office, wondering whether he thought I was going to try and escape. The corporal shut the door as I stood there listening to the I.O.'s footsteps fading down the wide corridor.

The office was a big one with two windows looking out

across the standing and the hangars to the FASO apron still barely visible in the reluctant daylight of that bleak January morning. The arc lamps had been switched off, but runway and perimeter lights still burned, a complicated network of yellow and purple. The Dak was landing now and another Tudor was moving up the perimeter tracks towards the control tower. I could almost hear the pilot calling his number over the R/T, requesting permission from Traffic Control to taxi, and I wondered whether it was Saeton. Beyond the hangars lorries moved in a steady stream from the off-loading platform, moving slowly and positively towards Berlin with their loads of Ruhr coal.

" Fraser ! "

I turned. The door behind me had opened and the I.O. was standing there, holding it open for a short, burly man in a wing commander's uniform. "This is the station commander," the I.O. said, closing the door and switching on the light.

" Sit down, Fraser." The station commander nodded to a chair. " Glad you got back all right. But I'm sorry about Carter." His voice was quiet, impersonal. He placed his cap on the top of a steel filing cabinet and seated himself at the desk. In the naked lights I saw that the beaverboard walls of the office were covered with maps and charts, a kaleidoscope of colour—Russian tanks, Russian planes, survey maps of Berlin, Germany with the air corridors marked in white tape, a huge map of the British Zone dotted with flags bearing squadron numbers and a smaller map of Eastern Germany covered with chinograph on which had been scribbled in different colours the numbers of Russian units. The whole room was a litter of secret and semi-secret information, most of it relating one way and another to the Russians. " Understand you wanted to see me?" The slight rise of inflection in the station commander's voice at the end of the sentence was, I knew, my cue. But I hesitated, reluctant to commit myself to a line of approach. " Well?"

I gripped hold of the wooden arms of the chair. The walls of the room were beginning to move again. It seemed very hot in there and the lights were blinding. " I want a plane, sir. To-night. Carter's alive and I've got to get him out. We can land at Hollmind. He's at a farm about three miles from the airfield." The words came out in a rush, tumbling incoherently over each other, not a bit as I had intended. " It would only take a couple of hours. The airfield's quite deserted and the runway is sound."

"How do you know?"

I stared at him. It sounded like a trap, the way he barked the question at me. His face kept blurring so that I couldn't see his expression. "How do I know?" I moved my fingers back and forth along the dirt-caked lines of my forehead. "I just know," I heard myself mumble. "I just know. That's all." I straightened my body up. "Will you let me have a plane, sir—to-night?"

The door behind me opened and a squadron leader came over to the desk, a thin file in his hand. "Here's the report you wanted, sir." The man's eyes glanced curiously in my direction. "I've rung for the M.O. and Pierce is in my office now. Shall I let him come up?"

The station commander glanced quickly across at me and then nodded. "All right. Any further news about that threat of ack-ack practice in the exit corridor?"

"No more than we know already, sir. Air Safety Centre have lodged protests, but as far as we're concerned at the moment the Russians will be firing to 20,000 feet in the exit corridor. I don't think we're going to give way."

"I should damn well hope not. They're just bluffing. They know what it means if they start shooting our boys down." He gave a long sigh. "All right, Freddie. But let me know as soon as you get any news." The door closed and the station commander stared for a moment out through the windows to where another freighter was thundering down the runway. He watched it rise, watched it until it disappeared into the low cloud, a small speck carrying an air crew of four headed for base through the exit corridor. His eyes switched slowly to me. "Where were we? Oh, yes. You claim Carter is alive." He picked up the file his adjutant had brought in, opened it and handed me a slip of paper. "Read that, Fraser. It's the Russian report on your aircraft."

I took it and held it in my hands, the print blurring into solid, straight lines. I let my hand drop, not bothering to go through it. "I know about this," I said. "It's completely phoney. It didn't dive into the ground. And they didn't find the charred remains of a body. They don't know anything about the plane—they're just guessing. The wreckage is strewn for miles around."

"How do you mean?" The station commander's voice was sharp and practical.

I pressed my fingers to my temples. How was I going to make them understand what had really happened. It was quite clear to me—ordinary and straightforward. But as soon as I tried to put it into words I knew it would sound fantastic.

"I think we'd better do it by questions, sir." The I.O.'s voice seemed oddly remote, yet it rattled in my ears like the sharp, dry sound of a porcupine's quills. "He's just about dead beat."

"All right, Symes. Go ahead."

I wanted to tell the station commander to let me tell it in my own way, but before I could say anything the I.O.'s sharp, insistent voice was saying, "You claim Carter is alive, that he's lying injured at a farmhouse near Hollmind. Hollmind is thirty miles from the point where Westrop and Field jumped. That's almost ten minutes' flying time. What happened in those ten minutes? Didn't Carter jump with the others?"

"No."

"He stayed in the plane with you?"

"Yes. He knew I didn't like jumping——" I was determined now that they should have every detail of the thing. If I told them everything, kept nothing back, they must believe me. "We had to jump once before at Membury, when the under-carriage of Saeton's Tudor jammed; that's how he knew I was scared. He came back to see me out. Then I got the engines going and started to fly to Membury. He got angry then and——"

"You mean Gatow, don't you?"

"No, Membury." I stared at him, trying to force him to understand that I meant Membury. "I was taking the Tudor back to Membury. That's why I took the job with Harcourt. It was all planned. I was to steal a plane from the airlift and——" My voice trailed away as I saw the look of bewilderment on the station commander's face. If only they'd let me tell it my own way.

"I don't understand this sequence of events at all, Fraser." His voice was kindly, but there was an underlying impatience. "Go back to where you and Carter are alone in the plane. Westrop and Field had jumped. Who went out next?"

"Please——" I implored, "let me tell it my own way. When I reached Membury——"

"Just answer my questions, will you, Fraser?" The voice

was authoritative, commanding—it reminded me of Saeton's voice. " Who jumped next?"

All my muscles seemed rigid with the violence of my need to tell it to them as a straight story. But I couldn't fight him. I hadn't the energy. It was so much easier just to answer the questions. " Carter," I said in a dull voice.

" But I thought you said he came back to see you out?"

" I pushed him out."

" I see. You pushed him out." I could tell by the tone in which he repeated the phrase that he didn't believe me. " And then what happened?"

" I flew the plane back to Membury. It was moonlight all the way. I found the airfield quite easily and when I landed——"

" Please, Fraser . . . I want to get at what happened in that plane. Now try to help me. What happened after Carter went out. We know the plane dived into the ground. I want to know how——"

" It didn't dive into the ground," I said. " I told you what happened. I flew it back to Membury."

He got up and came over to me. " Now pull yourself together, please." His hand pressed gently on my shoulder. " We naturally want to know what happened. There's no question of the accuracy of the Russian report. They've even sent us a piece of the tailplane. The plane is yours all right. It has your flight number on it and it's unquestionably a Tudor. Now what caused it to crash?"

" It didn't crash," I said wearily. " I tell you, I flew it——"

" Then if it didn't crash, how the devil are the Russians able to send us a sample of the wreckage that clearly shows it to be your plane?"

" I tell you, we put it there," I replied desperately. " We loaded it into the plane and flew it there. Saeton stooged around whilst I pushed the bits out. Then he landed me at Hollmind. That was when he flew out to Wunstorf to join the airlift. I searched all that night and all the next day for some trace of Carter. Then I found his helmet. It was just after the snow had started. It was lying on the snow and——"

" I just can't follow what you're staying," the station commander interrupted. " Will you please stick to what happened in the plane."

But before I could answer, the door of the room opened.

" Come in, Pierce. You, too, Gentry." The station commander crossed over to the taller of the two men, drawing him aside and speaking to him in a low voice. I could see the two of them glancing covertly in my direction. Symes was beating an impatient tattoo on the edge of the desk with his long fingers, his dark eyes fixed curiously on my face.

I felt as though an invisible curtain was being lowered, separating me from contact with them and I pulled myself to my feet. " You don't understand," I said angrily. " I joined Harcourt's outfit in order to get hold of one of his planes. We'd crashed ours. It had to be replaced. We had to get hold of another plane in order to test the engines. Saeton was due on the airlift on the 25th. We had to have another plane. The only place we could get one was in Germany—off the airlift. It had to be a Tudor. That was why——" My voice trailed away as I saw them all staring at me as though I were crazy.

The man who was talking to the station commander said quietly, " It's obvious he's had a nasty shock. He's suffering from some sort of mental disturbance—he's all mixed up with that escape he did. I'll get him down to the sick bay."

The station commander stared at me and then nodded. " All right. But I wish to God I could find out what happened to that plane of yours."

" Nothing happened to it," I cried angrily. " There was nothing wrong with it at all. I flew it back to Membury. All the Russians have found——"

" Yes, yes," the station commander cut in impatiently. " We've heard all about that. All right, Gentry. Take him down to the sick bay. Only for God's sake get some reasonable statement out of him as soon as possible."

The M.O. nodded and started towards me. It was then that the other man stepped forward. " Mind if I have a word with him first, sir?"

The station commander shrugged his shoulders. " Just as you like, Pierce. I suppose you think in his present muddled state he's more likely to tell you the truth." He gave a quick laugh. " I hope you make better progress than we have." He crossed to the door and paused with his hand on the handle. " I'd like a word with you, Symes, after breakfast."

The I.O. rose to his feet. " Very good, sir."

The door closed behind the station commander and as I slid wearily back into my seat the policeman came and leaned

on the edge of the desk, his hard, slightly pitted features seeming to hang over me, a dark blur against the lights. " My
name's Pierce," he said. " R.A.F. Police. You're Fraser?"

I nodded hopelessly. All chance of a plane had vanished
with the departure of the station commander and I felt drained
and utterly exhausted. If only they'd let me tell my story the
way I'd wanted to. But I knew that even then they wouldn't
have believed me. Put into words it immediately became
fantastic.

" Christian names Neil Leyden?"

Again I nodded. It was stupid of him asking me my name
when everybody in the room knew damn' well who I was.

" I've been instructed to ask you a few questions." His voice
was quiet, almost gentle ; very different from his features. " Do
you remember the night of November 18th last year?"

I thought back. What an age it seemed. That was the night
I'd arrived at Membury. " Yes," I said. " I began working
with Saeton that night."

" At Membury?"

" Yes."

" How did you get there—by car?"

" Yes, by car. There's no train service to Membury."

" A car was found that night at the foot of Baydon Hill.
That was your car, wasn't it?"

I stared at him, struggling to understand the drift of his
questions. My hand reached up almost automatically to the
crust of blood where my forehead was cut. " I had a crash,"
I said.

He nodded. " You've another name, haven't you? Callahan."

I started involuntarily. So that was it. This was what
Saeton had meant. I stared up at him, meeting his steady
gaze, knowing they'd got me and thinking that I might just as
well have refused when Saeton had forced me to take that
job with Harcourt. But it didn't matter now. So much had
happened, nothing seemed to matter any more. It was as
though in some queer way I was now paying the price for
what I'd done to Tubby. " Yes," I said in a whisper. " I'm
Callahan." And then in the silence that gripped the room I
asked, " What happens now?"

He shrugged his shoulders. " It's nothing to do with me, old
man. I'll send back a report to England. In due course I
imagine you'll be flown back and they'll decide what they're

going to do about you. There's no warrant for your arrest or
anything like that at the moment." He coughed awkwardly.
" Sorry to have to put the questions so soon after your escape
from the Russian Zone. Now, I think you'd better go along
with Squadron Leader Gentry here. It's time you had that cut
cleaned up and you look as though you could do with a bit
of rest. I shan't be worrying you again—not for some time
anyway. So you can just relax."

I thought how reasonable and logical his questions had
been. If I could get him to do the questioning about what had
happened to Tubby—they'd believe me then. I pulled myself
to my feet again. He was already at the door. " Just a minute,"
I gasped, feeling the room reel. " I've got to tell you something." He had stopped in the doorway and was looking at
me with a slight frown. " You got this from Saeton, didn't
you? It was Saeton who told the authorities who I was. You
know why he did that? It was because he was afraid I'd talk.
I didn't want to pinch the plane. But he made me do it. He
said if I didn't he'd——" I closed my eyes trying to shut out
the blurred movement of the room. The engines of a plane
thundered on the perimeter track just outside the building.
The windows rattled, the sound merging with the din in my
ears. The sound was like the roar of a great fall; it went on
and on. " Don't you see?" I gasped. " He blackmailed
me——" My knees trembled and gave. Somebody called out
something and I felt myself slipping. Hands caught hold of
me as I fell, supporting me whilst my legs seemed to trickle
away like used-up water from the base of my body. Everything was remote and indistinct as I slipped into unconsciousness.

I suppose they gave me something for I don't remember
anything more till I woke up in bed with a nurse standing over
me. " Feeling better?" Her voice was gentle and soothing.

" Yes, thanks." I closed my eyes, searching in my mind for
what had happened, gradually piecing it together.

" Open your mouth, please. I want to take your temperature." I obeyed her automatically and she pushed a thermometer under my tongue. " You were a bit feverish when they
brought you in and you've been talking a lot."

" Delirious? What was I saying?"

" Keep your mouth closed now. All about your flight and
a friend of yours in the Russian Zone. Squadron Leader

Pierce was here for a time. They're flying you out to-morrow
—that is if the M.O. says you're fit enough."

"Flying me out to-morrow?" I thrust at the bed, forcing
myself up into a sitting position. If they flew me out to-morrow
nothing could ever be done about Tubby.

"Now don't get excited otherwise we shan't allow you to
go." Her hands touched my shoulders, pushing me gently back
against the pillows.

My eyes went past her, searching the room. At least I was
on my own. A single window rattled to the sound of planes
behind black curtains. "What's the time?" I mumbled the
question, my tongue still closed over the thermometer.

"Don't talk, please. It's nearly seven and if you're good
you can have some supper." She reached down and took the
thermometer out of my mouth, peering at it through her thick-
lensed glasses. "That's fine. We're back to normal now." She
shook it down with a neat, practised flick of the wrist. "I'll
get you some food. Are you hungry?"

I realised then what the faint feeling in the pit of my stomach
was. I couldn't remember when I'd last had a meal. "Very,"
I said.

She smiled in her efficient, impersonal way. "Just a minute,
nurse," I said as she was going out. "I'm still at Gatow, aren't
I?" She nodded. "Will you get a message to someone for
me? It's for Mrs. Carter. She works in the Malcolm Club.
I want her to come and see me—right away. It's urgent, tell
her."

"Mrs. Carter. Is she the wife of your friend?" She nodded.
"I'll see she gets the message."

She went out, closing the door, and I lay there staring at the
light which hurt my eyes, listening to the planes coming in and
taking off, and going over and over in my mind what I would
say to Diana when she came. There must be no mistake this
time. I had to convince her. She was my one hope. If they
flew me out in the morning I'd be able to do nothing more for
Tubby. And then I began to think about Saeton. I was angry
then and I wished to God I had never met the man.

The nurse wasn't away long and when she returned she had
a tray full of dishes. "I brought you extra big helpings of
everything," she said. "They told me you probably hadn't
had a proper meal for some time."

"What about Mrs. Carter?" I asked. "Is she coming?"

"I haven't been able to get your message to her yet."

"You must," I said desperately. "Please, sister. It's urgent."

"All right. Don't you fuss now. I'll see she gets your message. Now you eat that."

I thanked her for the food and she left me. For a time I could think of nothing but the joy of eating again. I ate until I was full and then I lay back replete and the thought of Tubby was nagging at my mind again. Perhaps if I put it all down on paper . . . The thought excited me. That was the answer. If they read it as a straightforward report . . . I would address it to Squadron Leader Pierce. He had a logical, reasonable mind. They couldn't ignore it if it was sent to them in the form of a factual report. I lay there planning how I'd write it until the nurse returned.

"You must have been hungry," she said as she saw the empty places. "You look better, too. The M.O. will be round later. I don't think you need be afraid he'll stop you from going out on the P 19 in the morning."

"What about Mrs. Carter. Did you get my message to her?" I asked.

"Yes. I went all the way down to the Malcolm Club myself. I'm sorry, Mr. Fraser, but she won't see you."

"Didn't you tell her it was urgent?" The sense of being boxed in with an invisible wall of disbelief was back with me again.

"Yes, I told her that. I even told her it might affect your recovery."

"What did she say?"

"She said there was no point in her seeing you."

I lay back and closed my eyes, feeling suddenly exhausted. What was the good of going on fighting? Then I remembered the report I was going to write. "Can I have a pencil and some paper, please?"

She smiled. "You want to write to your girl-friend?"

"Yes. Yes, that's it." I nodded. "Can I have them quickly, please. It's urgent. I must write now."

She laughed. I remember it was a pleasant laugh. "Everything is always urgent with you, isn't it?"

"I'd like a pen if possible," I added. It would be better if it was written in ink. Somehow it seemed to make it more formal, more definite than if I scribbled it in pencil. "Where are my clothes? There's a pen in my flying suit."

"They're in the cupboard just outside. I'll get it for you. I haven't any note-paper, I'm afraid. Will typing paper do?"

"Yes, anything. Only hurry, please. I've got a lot to write and I want to get it finished before the M.O. comes round."

But the M.O. didn't come round. Propped up in bed I set it all down right from the time of my arrival at Membury. I had no reason to hide anything now and my pen fairly flew over the paper. And when I was in the middle of it the door opened and Saeton walked in. He was dressed in his flying kit. "Feeling better?" he asked as he crossed the room.

"I thought you were flying tests," I said.

"So I am. But they can't spare tankers off the fuel run. The boffins are flying routine flights with me."

It was odd how matter-of-fact our conversation was and Saeton kept it that way. He came over and sat down on my bed. "Writing a report?"

"Yes."

He nodded. "I guessed you'd do that. It won't help you, you know, Neil—unless Tubby gets back to corroborate your statement." He glanced at his watch. "I've only got about five minutes so I'll say what I've got to say right away." He hesitated as though marshalling his thoughts. "You've put a lot of money and work into the company. I wouldn't want you to think I'm not grateful and I wouldn't want you to lose by it." I think he meant that. "You've seen Pierce?"

"Yes," I said.

"And you've guessed that it was I who put them on to you?"

I nodded.

"Well, you didn't give me much alternative, did you? I was convinced Tubby was dead and you made it quite clear that if you didn't find him you'd give yourself up to the police. I couldn't risk that. I had to discredit you in advance." He took a packet of cigarettes out of his pocket and tossed me one. His eyes were watching my face as he lit it for me. "I'm very near to success now, Neil. I'm so near success that the authorities would be most unwilling to believe any report that you made. The Rauch Motoren have got the Americans behind them. If your report were accepted, it would mean a trial and the whole thing would become public. In those circumstances the Americans would bring pressure to bear on our people and the engines might have to be handed back to the

Rauch Motoren. At best the design would become generally available for any company in any country. You see what I'm driving at?"

"You want me to keep my mouth shut?"

"Exactly. I want you to admit that the Russian report is correct." I started to say something, but he held up his hand. "I know it's tough on you. You'll go to jail for this Callahan business. But as an airlift pilot I don't imagine you'll get more than a year, perhaps less. After all, you've got a fine record. As for the fact that you came out of the crash alive, you could say it was Tubby, not you, who was scared of jumping."

"Aren't you forgetting one thing?" I said.

"What's that?"

"That Tubby is alive."

"I hadn't forgotten that." He leaned closer to me, his eyes still on my face. "I can cope with your evidence or Tubby's evidence, but not the two of you together."

"What do you mean?"

"If you do as I want you to, it doesn't matter to me if Tubby does get out alive. A fantastic story told by a man who has been badly injured, wouldn't carry much weight. Now as regards compensation for yourself. I'm prepared to offer you £10,000 and of course your position as a director of the firm would stand. And don't think I won't have the money to pay you. I'll have all the money I want in a few days' time."

"And you'll leave Tubby to rot in that farmhouse?"

He shrugged his shoulders. "I can't do anything about getting him out, if that's what you mean. If you admit the Russian report to be true, then I must accept it that he's dead."

"And if I send in this report?" I asked.

He glanced at his watch and then got to his feet. "Time I was going." He paused, looking down at me. "If you send in that report, nothing will come of it. That I can assure you. Without Tubby's corroborative evidence it will be disregarded. And I'll see to it that there is no corroborative evidence."

I stared at him. His tone was so easy and natural it was difficult to believe that there was any sort of a threat behind his words. "What do you mean by that?" I asked him.

"Think it out for yourself, Neil. But remember this. I haven't come all this way with those engines to be beaten now."

"And either way Tubby doesn't get brought back for hospital treatment?"

He nodded. "Either way Tubby remains where he is."

"By God, you're a callous bastard," I said. "I thought he was the only man you were ever fond of?"

That touched him on the raw and his face darkened with sudden passion. "Do you think I like the thought of him out there in the Russian Zone? But I can't help it. This thing is a lot bigger than the comfort of one man. I think I told you once that if one man stood between me and getting those engines into the air, I'd brush him aside. Well, that still holds good. As far as I'm concerned, Tubby is dead." He glanced at his watch again. "Well, think it over, Neil." His tone was once more even and friendly. "Either way you won't help Tubby, so you might just as well tear up that report." He hesitated and then he said gently, "We've come a long way together in a short time, Neil. I'd like to know that we were going on together. You've done all you could to help when the going was tough. Don't shut yourself out from the thing just as it's starting to go well. I'd like us to continue the partnership." He nodded cheerily and opened the door. A moment later it had closed on his thick, burly figure and I was alone again.

I lay there for a moment going over in my mind that incredible conversation, appalled at Saeton's complete lack of any moral sense. This was the third time in our short acquaintance that he had forced a desperate choice on me. But this time it never entered my head to agree to his terms. I didn't even consider them. I was thinking only of Tubby. Somehow I had got to get him out.

I don't know quite when I reached the decision to get out of the sick bay. It just seemed to come as a logical answer to my problem. So long as I remained there, I should be taken out on the P 19 flight in the morning and then there would be no chance of doing anything for Tubby. On the other hand, if I were clear of Gatow, free of the whole organisation, then there might still be a chance.

As soon as I had reached that decision I set to work again on the report. By ten-fifteen it was done. After that I lay back, shielding my eyes from the light, waiting. Shortly before eleven the nurse came in. "Lights not out yet?" She patted the pillows into place. " You're looking tired now. My! What a lot you have written to your girl-friend."

" It isn't to my girl-friend," I said rather sharply. " Where's the M.O.?"

" He's not coming to see you to-night. But don't worry. He'll be here first thing in the morning."

The morning was no good. This must be read to-night by somebody in authority. " Do you know Squadron Leader Pierce?" I asked.

" Of course."

" Will you do something for me? Will you get this to him to-night?" I folded the numbered sheets across and handed them to her. " Will you see that he gets it personally?"

" And I suppose it's urgent?" She smiled indulgently as she took the sheets from me. " All right. I'll see he gets it if you promise to be a good boy and go to sleep."

" I'll sleep if I know that that will reach Pierce to-night. Will you promise that, sister? When he's read it, he'll understand the urgency."

She nodded seriously, humouring me with an imitation of my own mood. " Now, you go to sleep. Good-night."

The room was suddenly in darkness as she switched out the light. I had to suppress an urge to leap out of bed and go with her to the mess. But it wouldn't help. She'd only think I was mad and she'd call the M.O. and between them they'd drug me into a coma until I was on that damned plane and out of Berlin. The door closed with a decisive click and I lay there suddenly aware that I was alone again and all that stood between Tubby and complete disbelief of his need for help were a few flimsy sheets of paper in the hands of a nurse who thought I was slightly nuts.

I waited for about half an hour and then I slipped out of bed and groped my way to the door. A blast of cold air swept past me as I opened it. A blue-painted bulb showed me the top of some stairs and a corridor. The concrete flooring was bitterly cold against the soles of my feet.

I found the cupboard. My clothes were still there and I bundled them over my arm and slipped back into the room. It took me some time to dress in the dark, fumbling awkwardly with the laces of my cold, wet shoes, tugging at the zip of my flying suit. Finally I struggled into the heavy German greatcoat and jammed the forage cap over the bandages that circled my head.

Thinking back on it now I suppose I was still a little dazed with the exhaustion of the last few days, for I had no plan and as far as I can remember my mind made no effort to grapple with the problem of what I intended to do. I just knew I had to get out of the clutches of the Gatow authorities before they flew me out and, like an automaton who can only manage one idea at a time, I worked towards that end without a thought to the future.

As soon as I was dressed I felt my way to the door and opened it. The single blue-painted light bulb threw a weird light on to the empty corridor and the deserted stair-head. There was no sound except the intermittent murmur of the planes. I closed the door and went boldly down the stairs. There were two flights, each with its blue light, and then I was in the entrance hall. The light was bright here and a man's figure lounged by the open doorway where a car was drawn up. I hesitated. But there was no point in skulking in the shadows. I crossed the hall and went quickly out through the door to the accompaniment of a murmured " *Gute Nacht* " from the German driver who stood there.

I replied " *Gute Nacht*," my heart hammering against my ribs. But he made no move to stop me and in a moment the night had swallowed me with its blackness and its murmuring of the wind in the firs. I kept to the road, walking quickly, the sound of the planes on the airfield over my left shoulder, and in a few minutes I came out on to the road which ran from the entrance gates down past the mess to the terminal building. I recognised it at once in the lights of a *Volkswagen* saloon that went careering past me. I waited until its lights had completely disappeared and then I crossed the road and slipped into the sheltering anonymity of the fir woods.

I had no difficulty getting out of Gatow unobserved. I simply pressed on through the woods, keeping the sound of the airfield at my back. I had occasional glimpses of the lights of buildings and the swift rush of cars' headlights. The rest was utter blackness with the branches clutching at my bandaged head and roots tripping at my feet. I met no one and in a comparatively short time I was brought up by a wire boundary fence. After that I was in the open with the lights of a lorry showing me the Kladowerdamm and the way to Berlin.

There was some advantage in wearing Hans's discarded greatcoat and cap, for I was able to stop the first lorry that came along. The truck was a Bedford, one of a continuous line that moved through the night from the FASO apron to Berlin. I suppose the driver took me for one of the German labour teams slogging my way home. I climbed in and lay back on piled-up bags of flour that tickled my nostrils with their fine dust as we clattered over the pot-holed road.

We went into Berlin by way of the An Der Heer Strasse with its glimpse of Havel Lake where the Sunderlands had landed through the summer. There were lights along the An Der Heer Strasse, for the power, like that of Gatow itself, came from the Russian Zone. But darkness closed in with the trees of the Grunewald and the broad, straight line of the Kaiserdamm was like a dark cleft in the waste of ruins dimly seen from the swaying back of the lorry.

At length the truck slowed and the driver shouted to me, " *Wo wollen Sie hin?*"

" Anywhere in the centre of Berlin will do," I answered in German.

" I drop you at the Gedachtniskirche."

The Gedachtniskirche I knew—the Kaiser Wilhelm memorial church, one of the most conspicuous buildings in Berlin. It had been pointed out to me more than once during operational briefings. " *Dankeschön*," I said.

A few minutes later the lorry stopped again. Leaning out I saw a gigantic, ruined tower rearing above us into the darkness. A train hooted eerily and clattered by, wheels rattling hollow on the rails of a viaduct. I climbed over the tail-board and dropped to the ground. " *Dankeschön*," I called to the driver. " *Gute Nacht.*"

" *Gute Nacht.*" His voice was almost drowned in the roar of the engine as the heavily-laden lorry rolled on with its load of flour. I watched it disappear round the bend of the platz and then I was alone in the darkness with the monstrous hulk of the Gedachtniskirche above me, its colossal tower so battered by bombs that it looked as though it must topple into the street.

I turned and walked slowly up the Kurfurstendamm. This had been the Piccadilly of Berlin. Now it was a broken, ruined thoroughfare, the shops ground-floor affairs of wood and plaster board whose flimsy construction seemed constantly threatened by the rubble of the upper stories. There was no lighting in the Kurfurstendamm; all allied Berlin was under drastic power-cut now that fuel had to be flown in. But it was possible to see as though the thousands who huddled behind the broken façades of the buildings emanated a sort of radiance.

It was past midnight now, but despite the cold there were still prostitutes on the sidewalks, wandering up and down past the deserted street cafés. There were cars, too—black-marketeers' cars and taxis with American Negroes trading currency. Prowlers moved in the shadows, pimps and currency dealers, men who brushed by with a muttered, "*Fünf Ost für eine West.*" Bundles of rags lay huddled in doorways or dragged slowly along with a clop of wooden shoes as they searched the dustbins in the rich heart of Berlin.

I drifted up the Kurfurstendamm, only half conscious of the dim, shadowy life around me, my mind suddenly face-to-face with the problem of what I was going to do now. Until that moment my only thought had been to escape from the organised world that centred around the airlift at Gatow and so avoid being flown out on the P 19 passenger service in the morning. But now, in the heart of occupied Berlin, dressed half as a British civilian flier and half as a German labourer with no German money and no one I knew, I felt suddenly lost and slightly foolish.

But I wasn't cold any more and I had food inside me. My head was painful, but my mind was clear as I grappled with the problem. A dim figure slid past me with its muttered, "*Ich tausche Ost gegen West.*" I stopped him. "Do you exchange English pounds?" I asked him in German.

"*Englische Pfunde?*"

"*Ja.*"

"You want Deutschmark or Bafs?"

"West Deutschmark," I answered. "What is the rate of exchange?"

"I give you thirty-two Deutschmark for one pound sterling." Gold teeth glittered with a drool of saliva as the lights of a car slid past. The man had a wide-brimmed black hat and his face was swarthy with greasy sideboards. The long semitic nose was thrust inquisitively into my face. A Greek or perhaps a Pole—certainly not a German.

I changed ten pounds with this shadow of the Berlin under-

world and with the Deutschmark forming a wad in the pocket
of my flying suit I felt that the first hurdle was past. But what
next? I stood on a corner by one of those circular poster
hoardings that look like overgrown pillar boxes and wondered
how I could get Tubby out of the Russian Zone. If I could
get Tubby out, then there'd be no doubt about my story.

But in all Berlin I had no friend to help me.

# CHAPTER NINE

To HAVE no friends, no sense of security, in a city occupied
by one's own people is not pleasant. There was no one I
could turn to. I thought of Diana's brother—Harry Culyer.
Maybe he was still in Berlin. But would he believe me when
my own people didn't? And to contact any of the Allied
headquarters and clubs would only be putting me back into
the situation from which I had just been at such pains to
escape.

I don't know what made me think of it. Maybe it was the
prostitute who murmured an English, " Hallo, darling," from
the shadowy gloom of the sidewalk. The soft warmth of her
voice came like the nuzzling of a friendly bitch. And when
I didn't turn away the dim shadow of her slunk to my side.
" You are American?" she asked. The power of the dollar
was strong on the Kurfurstendamm.

" No. English," I answered.

I saw her eyes, soft and hungry in the darkness, looking me
over and noting my clothes. Probably she thought I was a
deserter. Deserters would be bound to make for the Kurfurstendamm. But she asked no questions. All she said was,
" You come with me, honey? I have a room only two blocks
away and it is comfortable."

I didn't answer because her German accent had started a
train of thought in my mind.

" Please come." Her voice was suddenly desperate. " I have
been here all evening and I am hungry. You take me to a café.
I know somewhere is cheap, very cheap." Her hand reached
out and slid along my arm. " Please, honey. I sing for you,
too, perhaps. I was in opera once. I only do this when my
baby and I are hungry and nobody will pay to hear me sing.

My name is Helga. You like me? I give you love and music —you forget everything. Come on, honey." She dragged at my arm. " Please, honey."

" Where is the Fassenenstrasse?" I asked.

" It is just near here. You wish to go? I take you if you wish." The voice was harder now, desperately urgent. " Please. It is cold standing here. Please, honey."

" All right," I said. " Take me there."

" Okay."

We moved off together up the wide cleft of the Kurfursten-damm, her hand clutching my arm. She was tall and her hip was level with mine, pressing against it. She hummed a little aria, something from Verdi. " Where is this place you wish to go, honey?" she said, stopping at a corner. " Here is the Fassenenstrasse. It runs right across the Kurfurstendamm. Which part do you wish?"

" I want Number 52," I said. " It's near the Savoy Hotel."

" Ach. So! Das Savoy. It is this way."

She took me down a tram-lined street and underneath the iron girders of a railway bridge, and then we passed the Hotel Savoy and were at Number 52. She stared at the blank face of the closed door. " Why you bring me here?" she asked. " This is not a club. We cannot eat here. Why you bring me, eh?"

" I have a friend here," I said and tugged at the old-fashioned bell-pull. Then I pulled out my Deutschmark and gave her twenty. She stared at them. " Go and get something to eat," I said. " And thank you for showing me the way."

Her eyes looked up into my face unbelievingly. " You do not want me?" She evidently saw that I didn't for she made no protest. Instead she reached up and kissed me. " Danke-schön." She turned away quickly and as the sound of her high heels faded away into the darkness I wondered whether per-haps she really was an opera singer with a baby and no job.

There was the rattle of a chain from the other side of the heavy door and then it opened, just a crack, and a woman's voice, old and hoarse and rather frightened, asked me what I wanted.

" I am a friend of Fraulein Langen," I answered in German. " I wish to see her please."

" I do not know any Fraulein Langen."

The door was closing and I put my foot against it.

"Fraulein Meyer, then." And I added quickly, "I have come all the way from England to see her."

"*Aus England?*" There was a moment's pause. "You are English?" The old woman spoke the words slowly as though she had learned the language at school.

"Yes," I said. "I am an English flier. Neil Fraser, tell her." The door opened to the full extent of the securing chain. Beady eyes stared at me through the crack. "You do not look to be very English," she said suspiciously. "Where in England do you meet Fraulein Meyer?"

"At Membury," I answered. "I have had an accident. That's why I'm dressed like this."

"Membury! So! It is very late, but come in. *Kommen Sie herein.*" The door opened. She closed it hastily behind me and in the darkness I heard the rattle of bolts and chain. "We must be very careful. The Russians, you know. It is terrible. They come and take people away." An electric torch gleamed faintly. "Poor Fraulein Meyer. So pretty, so clever! And all this trouble over her papers." I followed the old woman's shapeless figure up the stairs. The sound of our footsteps on the bare boards was very loud in the stillness of the house. "I do not like to think what the Russians do to her if the English send her to the East Sector police. The Russians are brutes—*schweinehunde.* They rape everyone." A door opened as the torch finally gave out. A match spurted and rose in a steady flame as a candle was lit.

"*Was ist los, Anna?*" It was Else. Though I couldn't see her I recognised her voice.

"*Ein Mann aus England. Herr Fraser. Er sagt er kennt Sie von Membury her.*"

"Herr Fraser?" Else's tone was suspicious. The flame of the candle was lifted to my face. Through it I saw that she was peering at me with wide, frightened eyes, her dressing-gown clutched tightly round her. "Neil! It is you?" She began to laugh then. I think it was relief at finding it really was me. "You look so funny. Why are you in Berlin? And why do you dress yourself up in the uniform of the *Wehrmacht?*"

"It's a long story," I said.

She smiled. "Another long story? That is what you say before. Remember?"

"May I come in? I want to talk to you."

"Yes, of course. I have only a bedroom now, but——"

She glanced uncertainly at the old woman. " So many peoples in Berlin have no homes," she murmured. Then she glanced up at my face again and saw the bandages. " You have hurt yourself again also."

" I had an accident," I said.

" Come in then," she said and pushed open the door of her room. " Anna. Have we any of that coffee left?"

" *Ja*, but for two cups only," the old woman answered.

" It is so difficult now in Berlin. This blockade—it is worse than——" She shrugged her shoulders. " Let us have the coffee, Anna. When it is finish, it is finish."

" *Schön*." The old woman tapped her torch on the banisters and it flickered into doubtful life. As she hobbled off down the stairs Else led me into her room and shut the door. It was a big room, furnished as part bedroom and part sitting-room, with a couch under the window, a dressing-table covered with photographs and a big double bed in the corner. It had the fierce, penetrating cold of a room that has had no heat in it for a long time. " Is your head all right?" she asked. " Can I do anything for it?"

" No, it's all right," I said. " They fixed it for me at Gatow."

" Gatow! When do you arrive at Gatow?"

" This morning."

" So! It is you I see standing outside the Malcolm Club." I stared at her, remembering the girl checker with her face covered in coal dust. " Are you working with the German Labour Organisation?" I asked.

" *Ja*." She laughed. " It is what you peoples call a very small world, eh?"

" But why?" I asked.

She shrugged her shoulders. " I must work. Also I wish to be at Gatow to see if Mr. Saeton get on to the airlift. It is most important that I find this thing out."

" Well, he is. I've seen him to-day."

She nodded. " He make the first flight two days ago. And he has my father's engines. I know them by the sound. Tell me something, please. How does he manage to fly again so quickly? His own plane is crashed. It was finished. This cannot be the same airplane."

" It isn't," I said.

" But how does he get another? He have no money. You tell me so yourself. Did you get it for him?"

"Yes," I said. She stared at me angrily and I added, " Do you know what the word blackmail means?"

She nodded.

"Well, he blackmailed me into getting him another plane. I stole it off the airlift for him."

"You stole it? I do not understand."

I told her briefly what had happened then and when I had finished she stood there staring down at the flame of the candle. "He is mad, that one," she breathed. She turned to look at me and the corners of her mouth turned up momentarily in a smile. " I think perhaps you are a little mad also."

"Perhaps I was," I said. "You've no idea how glad I was to find that Tubby was alive."

She nodded slowly.

"The trouble is Saeton won't do anything to get him out. He can't think of anything but the engines."

She swung round on me. "He is crazy. He is crazy, I tell you. It is as though—as though when he steal my father's work he start somethings and now he cannot stop."

Her words were an echo of my own thoughts. My mind was on Tubby and I was wondering what Saeton would do when he discovered I had made a written report. He would brazen it out, say that I was suffering from delusions as a result of the crash, but all the time he would be thinking of Tubby out there in that farmhouse, the one man who by his mere existence threatened the whole future of what he was striving for. And as I thought about this, Saeton loomed in my mind as a sort of monster—a man who, as Else said, had started something that he could not stop. " I must get Tubby out," I said.

"Is that why you come to see me?"

I nodded, dimly aware that she wanted some other explanation of my visit. But I was too tired to pretend. Everything I had done since waking up in Gatow sick bay had been done because of Tubby. I was responsible for what had happened. I had to get him out. "You've got to help me," I said.

"Why should I?" Her voice was harder now. "His wife work at the Malcolm Club. Let her help him."

"But she thinks he's dead. I told you that."

"If his wife think he is dead, why should not I?"

I stepped forward and caught her by the shoulders. "You've got to help me, Else."

"Why?" She was staring up at me, her eyes wide, almost calculating.

Why? I dropped my hands to my side and turned away. Why should this German girl I had met two or three times help me? "I don't know why," I said.

There was a knock at the door and the old woman came in with the coffee on a tray and a small oil lamp. *"Hier ist Ihr Kaffe, Fraulein Else."*

"Do you keep some for yourself, Anna?" Else asked.

The old woman moved her head from side to side awkwardly. "Just a little. Just for one cup." Her beady eyes fastened on me. *"Soll ich aufbleiben um den Herrn hinauszulassen?"* Else spoke quickly to her in German and the old woman laughed. "So!" She stared at me as though I were some strange animal. "I do not meet one like that." And still laughing to herself she sidled out and closed the door.

"What was all that about?" I asked.

Else looked across at me. "She is worried for me, that is all. I tell her you are quite safe, but——" She turned away to hide her smile.

Her smile made me angry. "Why didn't you tell her what happened when you took me to listen to the frogs?" I demanded.

"If I tell her that," she said over her shoulder as she poured out the coffee, "then she will want to see you go. And you must sleep. You look tired. I also am tired. I have to be up at six to catch the lorry to Gatow."

I brushed my hand across my face. I was tired. "Can you really put me up for the night?"

"Of course. If you do not mind the couch there. It is hard, but it is all right. I have to sleep there myself several times. Now, drink this please while it is hot."

"But——" I stared at her. "You mean sleep here—in this room?"

She looked up at me quickly. "Have you some place in Berlin you can go then?"

"No," I said. "No, I've no place I can go now."

"Very well then. It is settled. You sleep on the couch and I go back to my bed." She went over to the bed and ripped off two of the blankets. "There. We share the bedclothes. All right?" She put them on the couch. "I am sorry I am not able to give you a room for yourself. Once we have the whole floor—seven rooms with bathroom, kitchen, everything. But part of the house is destroyed and there are many families homeless. So now, all I have is this one room." She shrugged her shoulders. " It is all right. But I do not like to share my kitchen with other peoples. Please, you will excuse me, but I am cold." She slipped into the bed and reached for her coffee cup. " Do you have a cigarette?"

I felt in my pocket. The nurse had given me a packet. " Yes, here we are." She took one and I lit it for her. Her eyes watched me over the flame and then she blew out a long streamer of smoke. " Oh, it is so good to have a cigarette. I do not have one since I leave England."

" Don't you get any at Gatow?" I asked.

" No. They do not give us any. I do not think there are very many for your own people."

" Is the work hard?"

" No. Just checking the manifest of the cargo, so that nothing is missing. But it is a long time I am there and it is very cold on the airfield."

I had sat down on the edge of the bed to drink my coffee. Perhaps it was the closeness—maybe it was just the strangeness of the circumstances, the two of us sharing that one room. At any rate that was the end of our small talk. There seemed nothing really to say and I sat there staring at her and absorbing the warmth of the coffee. Tired though I was I found the blood hammering in my veins. I suddenly found I wanted her. I wanted her more than I'd wanted anything in my life before. For the moment it seemed as though her competence and self-sufficiency was swept aside. She was just a rather pathetic, very attractive girl, sitting up in a double bed—and I wished to God she was sitting there waiting for me. But somehow I could do nothing about it. I didn't want to do anything to break the mood of that moment. If I had touched her I think she would have responded. But if that had happened then something would have gone that I desperately wanted. Instead of touching her, I said, " Else, you've got to help me."

She frowned and pulled her dressing-gown closer round her. " To find your friend Carter?" she asked with a queer lift of the eyebrows that gave her face a puzzled look.

I nodded. " I've got to get him out of the Russian Zone."

"It means so much to you?" The softness disappeared from her face. "What happens if we do not get your friend out?"

"He may die," I said.

"And if he die, what happens then?"

"There'll be no evidence to support my report of what happened."

"And Saeton will go on flying my father's engines?"

"Yes. He'll get away with the whole thing."

She nodded as though that were the answer she had expected. "All right. I will do what I can."

I started to thank her, but she cut me short. "I do not do this thing for you, Neil. I do it because I wish to destroy Saeton." Her hands were fastened tightly on the bedclothes, the cigarette burning unheeded in the saucer as she stared past me to the lamp. "He has taken everything that is left of my father—the work we do together. I hate him. I hate him, I tell you." She spat the words out through clenched teeth in the intensity of her feeling. "He has no soul. He is a monster. That night you come to Membury, I offer him—I offer him myself. I know he want me. I do not love him. But I think I will barter my body for the recognition I want of my father's work. Do you know what he do? He laugh in my face." She relaxed slowly and picked up her cigarette. "Then you come into the hangar. After that I telephone to Reinbaum to go ahead and smash his company." She gave a bitter little laugh. "But you save it for him. Then he crash and I think that is the end of him. But you save him again." She gave me a wry little smile. "And now you wish me to help you. That is very funny." She sat for a moment, quite still. Then with a quick movement of her fingers she stubbed out the cigarette. "Okay, Neil. I do what I can. Now we must get some sleep. If I find somebody to take us into the Russian Zone it will be at night because it will be for the black market—perhaps to-morrow night."

"You think you can find somebody?" I asked.

She nodded. "Ja. I think so. I have many friends among the drivers at Gatow. I will find someone who goes near Holl-mind. There are many trucks going from the Western sectors into the Russian Zone. The Russians do not mind because they get things they want that way. I shall find someone."

"I can't thank you enough," I began, but she stopped me. "You do not have to thank me. I do not do this for you. Good-night."

She snuggled down into the bedclothes. I had got to my feet and for a moment I stood there, hesitating, staring down at her. It seemed to me there were two Elses—the girl who excited me and was sweet and gentle, and the German who was revengeful and who would stop at nothing to do what she thought was right for her country and her father. "Good-night." I turned heavily away and blew the lamp out.

In the heavy curtained darkness of the room I undressed to my underclothes and curled myself up on the couch under the blankets. It was bitterly cold in that room. It ate right into my bones. But then I thought of Tubby alone out there in that German farmhouse, desperately hurt, and the cold didn't seem so bad. I prayed that Else would find some means of getting me there so that I could bring him back, so that I could prove that what I had said was true.

Neither the cold nor the constant racket of the airlift overhead kept me awake for long. I slept and in a moment it seemed the lamp was lit again and the old woman was in the room, talking to Else. I turned over and opened my eyes. Else was already up, brushing her hair. The old woman was standing by the door, a spluttering candle in her hand. "I hope you are not too cold, Herr Fraser?" she said in German. It may have been my fancy but I thought her gnarled features had an expression of contempt as she said something very rapidly to Else.

"What did she say?" I asked as the bundle of old clothes disappeared through the door.

Else was giggling to herself. "Nothing," she said.

"She made some crack," I said.

"You really wish to know?" She was smiling. "She say you are not much like our boys, that if you are typical English then she do not understand how you win the war. Did you sleep well?"

"I slept all right," I said curtly, wondering why the hell I hadn't shared Else's bed since that was apparently what had been expected of me.

"You were not cold?"

"It didn't stop me sleeping."

"Now you are sulking. You do not want to pay any attention to Anna. She is old-fashioned, that is all. Now, please will you turn the other way. I have to wash."

I turned over and faced the heavy curtains that covered the window. "What time is it?" I asked.

"A quarter past five."

"Good God!" I lay there feeling the cold numbing my body, thinking how tough Else must be. The room was icy and I could hear her splashing about with the water. "Is that hot water?" I asked, thinking I would feel a lot better if I could have a shave.

"Of course not. We cannot heat water. Our fuel is for cooking only. If you stay here long you will get used to it."

"Stay here long?" The problem of the future suddenly faced me. I was a fugitive in Berlin. I could not go back to my own people, not until Tubby was out of the Russian Zone. "You must find some transport going to Hollmind to-night," I said urgently. "If I don't get him out soon he may——" Without thinking I had turned towards her and then the future and Tubby was driven out of my mind by the sight of Else leaning over the basin washing herself. She was naked to the waist, and her firm breasts looked big and warm in the soft lamplight.

She turned her head, conscious of my stillness, and for a moment her hands were still, holding the flannel, as she met my gaze. Water ran from her neck down her breasts and poured from her nipples into the basin. "I thought I told you to turn the other way?" She laughed. It was an unselfconscious laugh. "Do not stare at me as though you are hungry. Have you never seen a girl washing herself before?" She dipped the flannel into the water and began washing the soap from her face. It might have been the most natural thing in the world for her to have a man in her room watching her as she washed.

"Has this happened before?" I asked thickly.

"What?" Her words were half-obscured by the flannel.

"I didn't mean that," I said quickly and turned to face the curtains again, the sight of her still a vivid picture on the retina of my brain.

She came and stood over me. I didn't hear her come across the room, for her feet were bare. I just sensed her standing there, looking down at me. Her fingers touched my hair.

Sometimes I think you are very young, Neil. You do not know much about life. Or perhaps it is because we live among the ruins and when you do that you have not many conventions left. Life is very primitive in Berlin—like when we are in a yacht or up in the mountains." She turned away with a little sigh. " You would have liked it here in Germany before the war."

She was dressed by the time the old woman brought breakfast up. " It is not much," Else said, as she handed me a plate of dark bread with a small piece of butter. " But you will become accustomed to that if you stay here long."

I hardly recognised her as the same person. She wore no make-up and she was padded out underneath a dirty raincoat so that she had no shape. Only her hair looked the same, golden silk in the soft glow of the lamp.

At ten to six she pulled on an old brown beret. " Now I must go to catch the truck in the Kurfurstendamm. I think it is best if you do not go out. You have no papers and your shoes do not go with your Wehrmacht coat. Our police are very suspicious." I held the door open for her, huddled against the cold in my borrowed greatcoat. " Do not worry. I will find some way to get your friend out."

I touched her hand. It was very cold. " Thank you," I said. " You've been very kind and understanding."

" I am not being kind," she said almost sharply. " I am doing this for myself. I would like to say differently, but——" She stared at me, her eyes very wide and troubled-looking. " But it is the truth." Her hand tightened on mine. " One thing I wish you to know, however, I am glad it is something you want also. I am glad we both want this." She said it quite fiercely as though she were angry with herself for what had gone before. Then she reached up and kissed me, pressing her lips to mine as though this alliance were something she had wanted badly. " Do not worry. I fix something."

" For to-night?" I asked.

" I hope so."

She smiled and slipped out through the door. " Do not go out—please." Her footsteps sounded, quick and light on the stairs, disappearing into the dark vault of the house. I heard the front door open and close. Then there was silence and I shut the door and went back into the lamplit room that was so full of the girl who had just left me.

For some time I wandered round it, conscious of the alien heaviness of the furniture, of the photographs and particularly of her things that lay strewn about—clothes, books, sewing, an empty silver cigarette box, hair brushes, washing things, old papers, the tumbled bedclothes, her nightdress and the slippers she'd worn, all the litter of things that were Else when she herself was not there.

It was the photographs that I returned to. They were mostly of a big man with a short pointed beard and a high, domed forehead curving back to a mane of white hair. It was her father and the quiet, serious features with the slight droop at the corners of the mouth, the rather blunt nose and the lines of thought that furrowed the broad forehead reminded me of Else when she was puzzled by something. There was the suggestion of a twinkle in the lines at the corners of the eyes. But the face had none of Else's fierceness and passion. That she had got from her mother. Professor Meyer was a deeper, more thoughtful person than his daughter. This was particularly noticeable in the photographs of the two of them together. These were holiday snaps taken whilst climbing or on skis. But though the photographs showed her faults more clearly, I was glad of the opportunity to study her father. It explained so much of her that had puzzled me and I could understand more clearly her passionate loyalty to the work that she and this old man who was now dead had done together.

Very conscious of Else's presence in that room I returned to the couch and for a long time lay huddled under the blankets thinking about her and the peculiar relationship that was developing between the two of us. I tried to analyse my feelings, but I couldn't and in the end I went to sleep.

I didn't get up until past midday. The sky was overcast, the battered buildings opposite black in the bitter cold. Overhead the airlift planes droned steadily, but I could not see them. The old woman brought me some food—bread and some soup that was chiefly potatoes. She didn't attempt to talk to me. There was a barrier between us that was something more than a question of race. I found the answer in an old photograph album tucked away in a bookshelf, a picture of a little girl and an attractive, middle-aged nurse; underneath was written in an awkward, childish hand—*Ich and Anna.*

By five o'clock the light was fading and I could no longer decipher the unaccustomed German print of the book I was reading. I began to pace the room, wondering whether Else would have found transport to take me into the Russian Zone. My mood was a queer mixture of impatience and fear. It was bitterly cold.

Just after six I heard the sound of footsteps on the stairs. I checked in my pacing and listened. This wasn't the clumsy sound of wooden clogs on bare boards. It was a man's tread and he wore shoes. He didn't belong to the building.

The footsteps stopped on the landing outside and the old woman's clogs shuffled to the bedroom door. " I do not know why she is not back already," she said in German. " But you can wait for her in her room."

" Will she be long?" the man asked. His German was too lazy, too soft. In a panic I looked round for some place to conceal myself. But I was still standing in the middle of the room when the door opened.

" She always return at five. I do not know what has happened." There was a knock at the door and the old woman opened it without waiting for permission. " The gentleman here speaks your language. Perhaps you can talk to him while you are waiting for Fraulein Meyer."

I had backed away towards the window. The old woman stood aside and Else's visitor came in. I saw his brown boots and the olive khaki of his trousers—an American. And then I looked at his face. " Good God!" I exclaimed. It was Harry Culyer—Diana's brother. " How did you know where I was?"

He stopped, staring at me. " What makes you think I did, Fraser?"

" Didn't Diana send you?" I asked.

" Diana? No, of course not."

" Why are you here then?"

" I might ask you the same question." His gaze travelled quickly over the room, missing nothing and finally coming to rest on the Wehrmacht greatcoat I was wearing. " So this is where you're hiding up. They told me at Gatow you'd disappeared from the sick bay."

" You've been to the airport—to-day?"

He nodded. " I've just come from there."

" Did you see Diana?"

" Yes. Why?"

" She knows the truth now, doesn't she?" There was a puzzled frown on his face and I added quickly, " She knows

Tubby is alive now. She knows that, doesn't she?" My hands were sweating and I was almost trembling as I put the question.

"Alive? You know as well as I do he's dead." He was leaning slightly forward, and his grey eyes were no longer friendly. "So it's true what they told me about you."

"What did they tell you?"

"Oh, just that you were a sick man. That's all." He had thrown his hat on to the couch and he lowered his long body down beside it. "When will the Meyer girl be back? I guess I must just have missed her at the airport."

"I don't know," I said. "Did you see Pierce or the I.O.?"

"Yes, I saw them both." He eyed me watchfully as though I was a strange dog that he was not quite sure of.

"I sent Pierce a report—a written report. Did he mention it?"

"No, he said nothing about a report."

"Did he mention me at all?"

He lifted his eyes to my face. "Suppose you stop asking questions, Fraser?" His tone was abrupt, almost angry.

"But I must know," I said. "I must know what he said about me."

"All right—if you want to know—he said you were—ill." He was watching me closely as he said this, like a doctor examining a patient for reaction.

I slumped down on to the farther end of the couch. "So he doesn't believe it even when he sees it in writing." I felt suddenly very weary. It would be so much easier just to say no more, give myself up and go back to England to stand trial. "I must get Tubby out," I murmured. "I must get him out." I was speaking to bolster my determination, but of course he stared at me as though I was mad. "You're waiting to see Else, are you?" I asked, and when he gave an abrupt nod, I added, "Well, since you've nothing to do whilst you wait you may as well hear what happened that night in the Corridor. I'd like to know whether you believe me."

"Why don't you rest?" he suggested impatiently. "You look just about all in."

"Can I have a cigarette? I've finished all mine."

He tossed me a packet. "You can keep those."

"Thanks." I lit one. "Just because you've been told I'm ill, it doesn't mean I can't remember what happened. The chief thing for you to know is this: Tubby is alive. And but for that bastard Saeton he'd be here in Berlin now. It's a pity your sister can't recognise the truth when she hears it."

I had his interest then and I went straight on to tell him the whole thing.

I was just finishing when footsteps sounded on the stairs outside—Else's footsteps. She looked damnably tired as she pushed open the door. "I've done it, Neil. We——" She stopped as she saw Culyer. "I'm so sorry, Mr. Culyer. Have you been waiting long?"

"It hasn't been long," Culyer answered, rising to his feet. "I've been talking to Fraser here—or rather, he's been talking to me."

Else glanced quickly from one to the other of us. "You know each other?"

"We met the other day—out at Gatow," Culyer answered. "I tried to catch you at the airport, Miss Meyer, but I guess you'd just gone." He glanced awkwardly at me. "Can we go somewhere and talk?" he asked her.

Else spread her hands in a quick gesture of despair. "I am afraid this is the only room I have. You will not mind, Neil, if we talk about our own business for a moment, will you?" She turned to Culyer. "Have the British agreed? Shall I be permitted to go to Frankfurt?"

Culyer glanced hesitantly at me. Then he said. "Yes, everything's fixed, Miss Meyer. As soon as your papers come through we'll fly you down to Frankfurt and then you can join Professor Hinkmann of the Rauch Motoren and get to work right away. Of course," he added, "you must realise Saeton is a jump or two ahead of us. His engines are flying right now."

"Of course," Else said. "What about patents?"

"That is still undecided," Culyer answered. "We're pressing hard for refusal of patent on the grounds that it's largely your father's work. Mind you, Saeton's developed them to the flying stage, but I think our case may be strong enough for the whole thing to be left to sort itself out in open competition. Anyway, what I wanted to tell you was that the British have agreed for you to come to Frankfurt. I thought you'd want to know that right away."

"Thank you—yes." She hesitated and then asked. "No questions about the papers I had in England?"

"No questions. They'll forget about that."

Else turned and pulled off her beret. She stood for a moment staring at the large photograph of her father that stood above the huge oak tallboy. " He would have been glad about this." She suddenly swung round to Culyer again. " It was Saeton who informed the British security officials about my papers, wasn't it?"

Culyer shrugged his shoulders. " I don't think we need concern ourselves with that, Miss Meyer."

" No, perhaps it is not important." She turned to me. " Saeton has requested the permission of the station commander to fly a plane to Hollmind."

" To Hollmind?" I stared at her, hardly able to believe my ears. " When?"

" To-night."

" Are you certain?" I asked urgently. " How do you know?"

She smiled. " I have friends at Gatow—a young officer of the R.A.S.C. tell me. Saeton is flying there to-night, just to make certain."

For a second I was filled with relief. Saeton had realised he had been inhuman. He was going to get Tubby out. And then Else's choice of words thrust themselves into my mind. *Just to make certain.* In an instant the monster I had built of Saeton was there again in my mind. " Just to make certain," I heard myself say aloud. " My God! It can't be that. It can't be."

" What's that you say?" Culyer asked uneasily.

But I was looking at Else, wondering whether she knew what was in my mind. " It must be to-night," I said.

" What must be to-night?" Culyer asked.

" Nothing," Else said quickly. " Please, Mr. Culyer. I am very tired and I have some things to do."

He looked uncertainly from one to the other of us and then picked up his hat. " Okay, Miss Meyer. I'll be getting along then. As soon as the formalities are through I'll contact you."

" Thank you." She held the door open for him.

He hesitated on the threshold and his gaze swung back to me. He was obviously puzzled.

Else touched his arm. " You will not say anything—about Mr. Fraser. Please."

He shrugged his shoulders. " I guess it's none of my business anyway."

But it was his business. He was Diana's brother. " Will you be seeing your sister again?" I asked him.

He nodded. " I'm going out to Gatow right now."

" Will you give her a message? Will you tell her Tubby will be all right—that it's true what I said in that report, every word of it?"

He glanced across at Else. " Do you know about this?"

Else nodded.

" And do you believe him? Do you believe Carter is still alive, the way he says he is?"

" Of course," Else said.

Culyer shook his head slowly. " I don't know what to think. But I'll give her your message, Fraser. Maybe if Saeton's flying out there——" He shrugged his shoulders. " Good-night, Miss Meyer. I hope we'll have this thing all tied up very shortly now. This project has great possibilities and my head-quarters . . ."

He was still talking as Else lighted him to the stairs, but I wasn't listening. I was thinking of Tubby out there in that farmhouse. Saeton was flying to Hollmind. That was the thing that was still in my mind. I turned to the window. I had to get out there right away. I had to get there somehow. The door of the room closed and I swung round. Else was stand-ing there, staring at me. " Are you all right, Neil?" she asked.

" Yes, of course I'm all right," I answered irritably. " When you came in to-night—you started to say something?"

" Oh, yes. I have found a truck that is going into the Russian Zone. It is all fixed."

" When for?" I asked. " It must be to-night. I must get there to-night."

She nodded. " Yes. It is to-night."

" Thank God!" I crossed the room and caught hold of her arms. " How did you manage it?" I asked.

" Oh, I find out about it from one of the drivers at Gatow. We have to be at the corner of Fassenenstrasse and the Kant-strasse at ten-thirty."

" Not before?" I thought of the short time it would take to fly. " What time is Saeton leaving, do you know?"

She shook her head. " That is something I cannot find out. But he will not dare to go till it is very late if he have to leave the plane on Hollmind airfield."

" That was true. " How long will it take in this truck of yours?"

She shrugged her shoulders. " We do not go the direct way.

There are things to be delivered, you understand. Two or three hours perhaps."

Two or three hours! I turned away. "Couldn't the driver be persuaded to go there first?"

"I do not think so," she replied. "But I will talk to him. Perhaps if you have money——"

"You know I've no money," I cut in. "A few marks——"

"Then we will see."

I stopped in my pacing and turned to her. "We?" I asked. "You don't mean you're coming into the Russian Zone?"

"But of course."

I started to dissuade her. But she was quite determined. "If I do not come the driver of the truck will not take you. It is a big risk for him. If we are stopped by the Red Army then there has to be some story that they can understand. It is better if you have a German girl with you." She turned to the bed. "Now please, I must rest. You also. I do not think you are too well."

Not too well! That phrase kept recurring to me as I lay sleepless on the couch.

Else was asleep the instant she had climbed into her bed. But I had been resting all day. There was no sleep left in me and all the time I lay there, feeling the cold even through my clothes and listening to the sound of the airlift planes overhead, I kept on turning her words over in my mind. Was she herself uncertain of my story? Was that why she was coming —to see whether it was the truth or only the hallucinations of a sick man? I remembered how Culyer had reacted.

I must have fallen asleep in the end, for I woke in a sweat of fear that Tubby was dead and that the authorities at Gatow had been right in believing the Russian report.

And then I saw that Else was dressing and everything seemed suddenly normal and reasonable. We were going out of Berlin in a black market truck and in a few hours we should be coming back with Tubby. I was glad then that she was coming. If Tubby were dead, or if he didn't survive the journey back, then she would be witness to the fact that he had been at the farmhouse at Hollmind, that he had been alive.

We had some food and by ten-thirty we were at the corner of the Fassenenstrasse and the Kantstrasse. The truck was late and it was very cold. By eleven o'clock I was becoming desperate, convinced that something had gone wrong with her arrangements and that it would not come. Else, however, seemed quite resigned to waiting. "It will come," she kept saying. "You see. It will come."

Three-quarters of an hour late it ground to a stop beside us, one of those ugly, long-nosed German vehicles driven by a youth who was introduced to me as Kurt and whose jaw bore the purple markings of a bad burn. An older man was with him in the cab. We bundled into the back, climbing over packing cases piled to the roof to a cramped and awkward space that had been left for us. The gear cogs fought for a hold on each other, oil fumes seeped up from the floor, the packing cases jolted around us as we crawled out of Berlin.

We were nearly three hours in the back of that truck. We were cold and we both suffered from waves of nausea owing to the fumes. Periodically the truck stopped, packing cases were off-loaded and their place was taken by carcases of meat or sacks of flour. I cursed these delays, and at each stop it seemed more and more urgent that I should reach the farmhouse before Saeton.

At last all the packing cases had been off-loaded. We made one more stop, for poultry—there must have been hundreds of dead birds—and then at last through a rent in the canvas cover I saw that we had turned south. Shortly afterwards the truck stopped and I was told to get out and sit with the driver to direct him. We were then on the outskirts of Hollmind.

It was difficult to get my bearings after being cooped up in the body of the truck so long. However, I knew I had to get to the north of Hollmind and after taking several wrong turnings I at last found myself on a stretch of road that I remembered. By then the driver was getting impatient and he drove down it so fast that I nearly missed the track up to the farm and we had to back. The track was narrow and rutted and when he saw it the driver refused to take the truck up it. Else got down and did her best to persuade him, but he resolutely shook his head. "If I go there," he told her, "I may get stuck. Also I do not know these people at the farm. The Red Army may be billeted there. Anything is possible. No. I wait for you here on the road. But hurry. I do not like to remain parked at the side of the road too long—it is very conspicuous."

H

So Else and I went up the track alone, the ice crackling under our feet, the mud of the ruts black and hard like iron. " How far?" she asked.

" About half a mile," I said. My teeth were chattering and there was an icy feeling down my spine.

The lane branched and I hesitated, trying to remember which track I had come down that night that seemed so long ago.

" You have been here before, haven't you, Neil?" Else asked and there was a note of uncertainty in her voice.

" Of course," I said and started up the left-hand fork. But it only led to a barn and we had to turn back and take the other fork. " We must hurry," Else whispered urgently. " Kurt is a nervous boy. I do not wish for him to drive away and leave us."

" Nor do I," I said, thinking of the nightmare journey I had had into Berlin.

We were right this time and soon the shape of the farm buildings was looming up ahead of us against the stars. " It's all right," I said as the silhouette of the outbuildings resolved itself into familiar lines. " This is the place."

" So! The farm does exist. Your friend is alive."

" Of course," I said. " I told you——"

" I am sorry, Neil." Her hand touched my arm.

" You mean you weren't sure?"

" You were hurt and you look so ill. I do not know what to think. All I know is that it is urgent for you to come and that I must come with you."

I could see the faint shape of her head. Her eyes looked very big in the darkness. I took hold of her hand. " Come on," I said. " I hope to God——" I stopped then, for we had turned the corner of a barn and I saw there was a lamp on in the kitchen of the farmhouse. It was nearly two, yet the Kleffmanns hadn't gone to bed. The shadow of a man crossed the drawn curtains. I hurried across the yard and tapped on the window.

It was Kleffmann himself who answered my tap. He came to the back door and peered nervously out into the night. " Herr Kleffmann!" I called softly. " It's me—Fraser. Can we come in?"

" Ja. Kommen Sie herein. Hurry please." As he stood back to let us through the door he turned his face towards the lamplight that came through from the kitchen. He looked startled, almost scared.

"Is he all right?" I asked.

"Your friend? Yes, he is all right. A little better, I think."

I breathed a sigh of relief. "We've got a truck waiting down on the road," I said. "This is Fraulein Meyer."

He shook hands with Else. "Come in. Come in, both of you." He shut the door quickly and led us through into the kitchen. "*Mutter*. Here is Herr Fraser back again."

Frau Kleffmann greeted me with a soft, eager smile, but her eyes strayed nervously to the stairs that led up from the kitchen. "I do not understand," she murmured uneasily in German. Then she turned to her husband and said, "Why do they both come?"

I started to explain Else's presence and then I stopped. That wasn't what she had meant. Lying across the back of a chair was a heavy, fleece-lined flying jacket. Else had seen it, too. I turned to the Kleffmanns. They were standing quite still, staring towards the dark line of the stairs. From above us out of the silence of the house, came the sound of footsteps. They were coming down the stairs.

Else gripped my arm. "What is it?" she whispered.

I couldn't answer her. My gaze was riveted to the stairs and all the muscles of my body seemed frozen in dread of the thing that was in my mind. The footsteps were heavy now on the bare boards of the landing. Then they were coming down the last flight. I saw the boots first and then the flying suit and followed the line of the zip to his face. "Saeton!" The name came from my lips in a whisper. God! I'll never forget the sight of his face. It was grey like putty and his eyes burned in their sockets. He stopped at the sight of us and stood staring at me. Eyes and face were devoid of expression. He was like a man walking in his sleep.

"How's Tubby?" My voice was hoarse and grating.

"He's all right," he answered, coming on down into the kitchen. "Why did you have to come here?" His voice was flat and lifeless and it carried with it a terrible note of sadness.

"I came to get him out," I said.

He shook his head slowly. "It's no use now."

"What do you mean?" I cried. "You said he was all right. What have you done to him?"

" Nothing. Nothing that wasn't necessary."

I started towards the stairs then, but he stopped me. " Don't go up," he said. And then slowly he added, " He's dead."

" Dead?" The shock of the word drove me to action. I thrust past him, but he caught me by the arm as I started up the stairs. " It's no good, Neil. He's dead, I tell you."

" But that is impossible!" Frau Kleffmann had retreated towards her chair by the fire. " Only this morning the doctor is here and he say he will be well again. Now you say he is dead."

Saeton pushed his hand across his eyes. " It—it must have been a stroke—heart or something," he muttered uncertainly.

" But only this evening he is laughing and joking with me," Frau Kleffmann insisted. " Is not that so, Frederick?" she asked her husband. " Just before you come. I take him his food and he is laughing and saying I make him so fat he live up to his name."

" Where is he?" Else whispered to me.

" Up at the top of the house. An attic. I'll go up and see what's happened."

I started up the stairs again, but Saeton blocked my way. " He's dead, I tell you. Dead. Going and looking at him won't help."

I stared at him. The blackness of the eyes, the smallness of the pupils—the man seemed curled up inside himself and through the windows of those eyes I looked in on fear and the bitter, driven urge of something that had stepped out of the world's bounds. In sudden panic I flung him aside and leaped up the stairs. There was a small lamp on the landing and I picked it up as I turned to climb to the attic.

The door of Tubby's room was ajar and as I went in the lamplight picked out the photographs of Hans lining the walls. My eyes swung to the bed in the corner and then I stopped. From the tumbled bedclothes Tubby stared at me with fixed and bloodshot eyes. His face had a bluish tinge even in the softness of the lamplight. There was a froth of blood on his puffed lips and his tongue had swollen so that it had forced itself between his teeth. He had struggled a great deal before he had died, for in the wreck of the bed his body lay in a twisted and unnatural attitude.

Avoiding the fixed gaze of his eyes, I crossed the room and

touched the hand that had reached clear of the bed and was hanging to the floor. The flesh was still warm.

Else came into the room then and stopped. " So! It is true." She looked across at me with a shudder. " How does it happen?"

" Perhaps it was a stroke. Perhaps——" My voice trailed away as I saw her eyes fasten on something that lay beside the bed.

" Look!" She shivered slightly, pointing to the pillow.

I bent and picked it up. It was damp and torn and bloody at the centre where Tubby had fought for air. The truth of how he had died was there in my hands.

" He did it," she whispered. " He killed him."

I nodded slowly. I think I had known it all along. Tubby's wasn't the face of a man who had died a natural death. Poor devil! Alive he had threatened the future of Saeton's engines. Because of that Saeton had come all the way from Berlin to kill him, to smother him as he lay helpless on the bed. The force that had been driving Saeton all along had taken him to the final and irrevocable step. He had killed the man without whom the engines could never have been made, the one man whom he'd thought of as a friend. *If one man stood between me and success, I'd brush him aside*. I could remember how he had stood in the centre of the mess room at Membury and said that—and now he had done it. He had brushed Tubby aside. I dropped the pillow back on to the floor with a feeling of revulsion.

" I think he is mad." Else's horrified whisper voiced my own thoughts. And at that moment I heard slow, heavy footsteps on the stairs. Saeton was coming back up to the attic. I wasn't prepared to face him yet. I reached for the door, closing it, my action unreasoned, automatic. I slid the bolt home and stood there, listening to the footsteps getting nearer.

" Come away from the door," Else whispered urgently.

I stepped back and as I looked at her I saw she was scared. The footsteps stopped outside the door and the handle turned. Then the thin deal boards bulged to the pressure of the man whose breathing I could hear. The room was very still as we waited. I think Else thought he would break the door down. I didn't know what I expected, all I knew was that I didn't want to talk to him. The silence in the room was heavy with suspense. Then his footsteps sounded on the stairs again as he went slowly down.

I opened the door and listened. There was the murmur of voices and then the side door closed with a bang. From the window I saw Saeton, looking big and squat in his flying jacket, cross the farmyard and go out through the gate by the barn. I felt relieved that he had left. It wasn't only that I didn't want to talk to him. I was scared of him. Perhaps Else's fear was infectious, but I think it would have come, anyway. The abnormal in its most violent form is a thing all sane men are afraid of. The initiative lies with the insane. It's that which is frightening.

I turned back to the door. "I'll get Kleffmann," I said. "We must get his body down to the truck and take it back to Berlin." Tubby's sightless eyes watched me in a fixed stare. I turned quickly and went down the stairs, conscious of Else's footsteps hurrying after me.

The kitchen looked just the same as when we had entered it. Frau Kleffmann sat huddled in her thick dressing-gown by the fire. Her husband paced nervously up and down. There was nothing in the warmth and friendliness of that room to indicate what had happened upstairs in the attic—only the tenseness. Frau Kleffmann looked up quickly as I entered. "Is it true?" she asked. "Is he dead?"

"Yes," I said. "He's dead."

"It is unbelievable," she murmured. "And he was such a nice, friendly man."

"Why did that other man—Herr Saeton—leave so quickly?" Kleffmann demanded.

I could see that he was suspicious, but there seemed no point in telling him what had happened. "He was worried about his plane," I said. "Will you help me get Carter's body down? We are taking it back to Berlin."

"Ja." He nodded. "Ja, I think that is best."

"Would you please find something for us to carry him on?" I asked Frau Kleffmann.

She nodded, rising slowly to her feet, a little dazed by what had happened.

"You stay here, Else," I said and followed Kleffmann up the stairs to the attic again. We covered Tubby with a blanket and got his body down the steep, narrow stairs. Back in the kitchen Else and Frau Kleffmann had fixed a blanket over

two broom handles. The improvised stretcher lay on the table
and we put Tubby's body on it. Frau Kleffmann began weep-
ing gently at the sight of his shrouded figure. I think she was
remembering her son out there in a Soviet labour camp.

Else stood quite still, staring down at the shape huddled
under the blanket.

"Will you help us to carry him down to the truck?" I asked
Kleffmann.

"*Ja*. It is better that you take him away from here." His
voice trembled slightly and the sweat shone on his forehead.
He had known as soon as he'd seen Tubby that the poor devil
hadn't died naturally and he wanted to get the body out of
his house, to be shot of the whole business. He hadn't said
anything, but he knew who had done it and he was scared.

We picked the stretcher up, he at one end, I at the other.
"Come on, Else," I said.

She didn't move and as I lifted the latch of the door she
said, "Wait!" Her voice was pitched high on a hysterical
note. "Do you think Saeton will let you go back to Berlin
with—with that." She came across the room, seizing hold of
my arm and shaking it in the extremity of her fear. "He cannot let either of us go back."

I stood still, staring at her, the truth of what she was saying
gradually sinking in.

"He is waiting for us—out there." She jerked her arm towards the window.

I could see in her eyes that she was still remembering the
sight of Tubby's face as he lay propped up in that bed. I lifted
the stretcher back to the table and went towards the window.
My hand was on the curtains to pull them back when Else
seized my arm. "Keep away from the window. Please, Neil."
I could feel the trembling of her body.

I turned irresolutely back into the room. Was he really waiting for us out there? The palms of my hands were damp with
sweat. Saeton had never turned back from anything he had
started. He wouldn't turn back now. Else and I were as fatal
to him as a hangman's rope. A desperate feeling of weariness
took hold of me so that my limbs felt heavy and my movements were slow. "What do we do then?"

Nobody answered my question. They were all staring at me,
waiting for me to make the first move. "Have you got a gun
here?" I asked Kleffmann.

He nodded slowly. " *Ja*. I have a shotgun."

" That will do," I said. " Can I have it, please?"

He went out of the room and returned a moment later with the gun. It looked about the equivalent of an English 16 bore. He gave it to me together with a handful of cartridges. " I'll go out by a window on the other side of the house," I said. " When I've gone, keep the doors bolted." I turned to Else. " I'll circle the house and then go down to the road and persuade Kurt to bring the truck up here."

She nodded, her lips compressed into a tight line.

" If I find it's all clear, I'll whistle a bit of the Meistersingers. Don't open up until you hear that." I turned to Kleffmann. " Have you got another gun?"

He nodded. " I have one I use for the rooks."

" Good. Keep it by you." I broke the gun I held in my hands and slipped a cartridge into each of the barrels. I felt like a man going out to finish off an animal that has run amok.

As I snapped the breech Else caught hold of my hand. " Be careful, Neil. Please. I—I do not know what I shall do if I lose you now."

I stared at her, surprised at the intensity of feeling in her voice. " I'll be all right," I said. And then I turned to Kleffmann and asked him to show me to the other side of the house.


CHAPTER TEN

I DROPPED out near some bushes and slid into their shadow. Overhead the stars still shone, bright and cold, but to the west the sky was black with cloud. The wind seemed warmer now. I pulled my coat round me and slid along the wall of the house, ran past the gate to the farmyard and crouched in the shadow of the barn. I stood there, quite still, the barrel of the gun cold on the palm of my left hand, listening to the sounds of the night. One by one I identified them—the wind tapping the branch of a tree against the wooden side of the barn, a cow moving in its stall, the grunt of a pig, the tinkle of ice knocked from some guttering by the flutter of an owl. And over all these sounds the solid thumping of my heart.

I tried to tell myself that I was a fool to be standing out there, scared of every shadow that seemed to move, waiting with a gun in my hand. But every time I nearly convinced myself that I was being a fool, the memory of Tubby's face came to remind me that Saeton was now a killer. For a long time I stood quite still with my back against the wood of the barn, hoping that somewhere in the darkness round me I should hear a sound, see a movement that would prove he was really there. I longed to know, to end the suspense of waiting. But nothing stirred.

It was out of the question for me to stand there doing nothing till dawn. Kurt was waiting down on the road and he would not wait much longer. The thing to do was to go down there and get the truck up. If he left without us ... The memory of that other journey into Berlin spurred me to action.

Moving warily I slid along the wall of the barn, past a piled-up heap of manure, through a litter of decaying farm machinery. A twig snapped under my feet. I stepped in a rut where the water was all frozen and the ice crunched under my weight. They were only little noises, but they sounded loud, and once away to the left, I thought I heard an answering movement. But when I stopped there was nothing but the sounds I had already identified.

I circled the farm without seeing any sign of Saeton. Then I started down the track to the road. I kept well clear of the ruts, moving slowly along the grass verge, brambles tearing at my trousers.

And then suddenly, out of the darkness ahead, a beam of a torch stabbed the night. As the dazzle of it touched my eyes I flung myself sideways. But I wasn't quick enough. There was a spurt of flame and the bullet thudded into my body, knocking me off my feet and sending me sprawling into the brambles that bordered the track. Boots crunched in the frozen ruts as the beam of the torch probed my shelter. I lifted the shotgun and fired at the torch. The kick of the gun wrenched me with pain, but the torch went out and above the sound of the shot I heard a cry. I fought my way through the thicket, the thorns tearing at my face and hands, all the right side of my body racked with pain. Behind the screen of brambles I crouched down and very gently ejected the spent shell and reloaded. My right hand had no strength in it. The fingers were stiff and clumsy and the cartridges sticky with blood. The click of the catch as I closed the breech seemed unnaturally loud in the stillness that had descended on the lane.

My eyes had been momentarily dazzled by the torch, but as they became accustomed to the darkness again I saw the line of the brambles bordering the track, and on either side of me and behind me the slope of the ground was visible against the stars. I was in a slight hollow. If he tried to circle me I should see him against the stars. The danger lay to my immediate front. The strange thing was that now I knew he was there and was at grips with him I was no longer afraid.

Away to my left on the main road the engine of a truck broke the silence, headlights cut a swathe through the night and began to move. Frightened by the shots Kurt was pulling out, leaving us to find our own way back to Berlin. I cursed under my breath as I listened to the sound of the engine dying away. Soon all that remained was a faint glow in the darkness to the south. Then that, too, was gone. The wind rustled in the brambles. A night bird cried its call. There was no other sound.

Then something moved in the bushes to my left. It moved again, nearer this time. I raised the gun to my shoulder. There was the sound of earth being dislodged and the rattle of dry bramble branches almost at my side. I fired at the sound. From behind me, echoing the sound of my own shot, the revolver smacked a bullet into the ground at my feet. I swung round, realising how he'd fooled me by throwing earth into the undergrowth. I saw his figure crouched against the stars and let off my second barrel at it. There was a grunt and a curse as something thudded to the ground. Desperately I broke my gun and fumbled in my pocket for the cartridges.

When the gun was loaded I started forward. I knew I had to finish it off now. If I didn't I should lose my nerve. I sensed that in the trembling of my hands. I had to finish it one way or the other. Crouched low I could see his body close to the ground as he waited for me. Whatever happened now I was close enough for the shotgun to be effective. I steeled myself to the jolt of a bullet hitting. I'd let him have both barrels. Wherever he got me I'd still have time to fire.

But I didn't have to. Even when I was so close I could have blown the top of his head off he did not move. He was crouched in an unnatural position, his head bent almost to the ground, his fingers dug deeply into the hard earth. Beside him his torch glimmered faintly in the starlight. The chromium was all wet and sticky as I picked it up and when I flicked it on I saw the metal was badly dented and filmed with blood. I turned him over on to his back and as I did so his service revolver slipped from between his fingers. His left arm was all bloody, the hand horribly pitted by the shot. There was a livid bruise above his left temple and the skin had split. But apart from this he didn't seem badly hurt and his breathing was quite natural. I think what had happened was that the main weight of my shot had struck the torch and flung it against the side of his head. There was no doubt that he'd been knocked clean out.

I picked up the revolver and slipped it into my pocket. I turned then and went back into the lane through a gap in the bramble hedge. It was fortunate that the torch hadn't been put out of action, because I was feeling dizzy and very faint as I staggered up the track and without its light I'm not at all sure I should have been able to find my way back to the farm.

I was pretty well all in by the time I reached the side door. I remember slumping against it, beating on it with my hands. But they had no strength and all I achieved was a faint scrabbling as I slid to the ground. Probably Else was listening for me. At any rate I never sang a bar of the Meistersingers, but when I came round I was in a chair by the kitchen fire and Else was cutting the blood-soaked clothes away from the wound in my shoulder. As she saw my eyes open her hand reached up and she pushed her fingers through my hair. " You are always in the wars, Neil." She smiled softly. " I think you need someone to look after you."

" Where's Kleffmann?" I asked her.

" *Hier.*" His big figure bent over me. "What is it?"

I gave him the revolver and told him to go down the lane and get Saeton. " If he's still there I don't think he'll give you much trouble," I said.

" What happened?" Else asked.

As I told her Frau Kleffmann came in with a bowl of hot water. Else began to bathe the wound and the warmth of the water took some of the numbness out of it. " I think the bullet is still there," Else said after peering at the torn flesh with the aid of a torch.

" Well, patch me up the best you can," I said. " I've got to fly."

" To fly?"

"Yes. The truck is gone. Kurt cleared off as soon as he heard our shots. Our only way out now is Saeton's plane."

"But the airfield is more than a mile from here," Else pointed out. "I do not think you will be able to walk so far."

"Perhaps not. We'll borrow a horse and cart from the Kleffmanns. I've no doubt they'll be only too glad to speed the parting guests." I tried to smile at my little joke, but I didn't seem able to make the effort. I felt sick and tired. As soon as Else had finished dressing my wound I got her and Frau Kleffmann to harness one of the farm horses. They had got Tubby's body on to the cart and I was sitting in it by the time Kleffmann returned with Saeton. It was lucky that the farmer was a big man, for Saeton was still unconscious. He carried him slung over his shoulders in a fireman's lift and when he reached the cart he dumped the body into the muck of the farmyard like a sack of potatoes.

"Ready?" he asked me.

"Yes, I'm ready," I said. I was anxious to be off. The plane was my only hope of getting back to Berlin. I knew the Kleffmanns wouldn't shelter us after what had happened, and every minute the plane stood out there in the airfield it ran the risk of being spotted by a Red Army patrol.

Else helped Kleffmann load Saeton's body on to the cart. Then he climbed up and clicked his tongue at the horse. Frau Kleffmann opened the gate for us. She spoke quickly and urgently to her husband. He nodded and the cart jolted over the frozen ruts into the lane. I called good-bye to her, but she did not answer. She just stood there, a frozen expression on her face, glad to see us go.

Kleffmann had returned the revolver to me and I kept my left hand on the butt as it lay in the pocket of my coat. My eyes were on Saeton's unconscious body as we jolted towards the woods. Rain clouds were spreading across the night sky and when we entered the woods it was as dark as pitch. Nobody spoke and the only sound was the creaking of the cart and an occasional snort from the horse. I kept my foot against Saeton's body. The cart jolted in the ruts and each jolt was like a knife stabbing at the blade of my shoulder. Else had seated herself so that I could lean against her and she seemed conscious of my pain, for when it was very bad she would slip her hand over my left arm.

We must have been about half-way through the woods when

Saeton stirred. He lay groaning for a moment and then he sat up. I could see his face, a pale oval in the darkness. My hand tightened automatically on the gun in my pocket . " Don't move," I told him. " I've got a gun. If you move I'll shoot."

There was a long silence. Then he said, " That's you is it, Neil?"

" Yes," I told him.

He was sitting up now and he gave a little cry of pain as he shifted his position. " What happened?"

I didn't say anything. He could think it out for himself. The silence became heavy as the memory of Tubby's death came to all of us. " Where's Tubby?" he asked at length. " Did you—bury him?"

" No. His body is beside you in the cart."

He said, " My God! Why couldn't you leave him there." And then silence descended on us again. I tried not to think of what Tubby looked like there under the blanket. The pain helped. It wrenched at my mind and made it difficult to think. I clung to the gun. If he made any move I'd use it. Maybe he sensed that, for he stayed quite still all the way through the woods.

At last we were out of the trees and dragging slowly across the flat expanse of the airfield. It was very dark. Isolated drops of rain began to fall. " Where did you leave the plane?" I asked Saeton.

He didn't answer. Maybe he thought if he said nothing we might fail to find it. I peered anxiously into the darkness ahead. The cart jolted endlessly in the black void. Maybe the horse could see when we couldn't. At any rate the plane was suddenly there right in front of us, a shadowy, insubstantial shape. Kleffmann reined in the horse and turned to me. " I think it is better if one of us goes and has a look round there."

" I will go," Else said. She eased herself gently away from me and dropped to the ground. In a moment the darkness had swallowed her. I waited, my nerves tense for the challenge of a Russian sentry. But no sound broke the stillness, only the soft whisper of the rain falling. Then Else was back. " It is okay," she whispered and we started forward again. Else was at the horse's head and she backed the cart against the door of the fuselage.

It was queer to think that that plane was the bridge between us and Berlin. Standing there, it was just an inert piece of metal. And yet with a pilot's direction it would set us down at Gatow. It seemed to me symbolic of the whole airlift, symbolic of the ingenuity of man to do the impossible, to jump in a few minutes from alien to friendly ground. But it required the direction of a pilot and my body cringed at the thought that it was I who had got to bridge that gap—in a night of black darkness, without a navigator and with a bullet wound in my shoulder. At least it was a Dakota. I don't think I could have handled a four-engined job.

Else helped Kleffmann to get Tubby's body into the fuselage. Saeton and I were alone in the cart. I saw him shift his position. "Keep still!" I ordered him.

"What are you going to do?" he asked.

"Fly your plane back to Gatow."

"What about me?"

"You're coming, too."

There was a pause and then he said, "You're wounded, aren't you?"

"Yes," I said. "But don't worry. I'll make it."

"And if you don't?"

"If I don't you'll be able to take over and fly where you like." It wasn't subtlety on my part that made me say that. But looking back on it I think that was why he didn't make a break for it there on Hollmind airfield. Maybe he was too weak. He had been out for a hell of a long time. But if he'd jumped from the cart right then he'd have had a chance.

Else and Kleffmann appeared at the fuselage door again. "Get in!" I told Saeton. I had the gun in my hand now. "And don't try anything," I said. "I'm quite willing to fire."

He got up without a word. His movements were slow, but that was the only indication he gave that he had been hurt. I followed him, feeling sick and a little giddy as I moved my cramped limbs. Kleffmann dropped into the cart and picked up the reins, clicking his tongue to the horse. I called my thanks to him from the door of the fuselage, but he didn't answer. Where horse and cart had been there was nothing but the blackness of the airfield and only the faint creaking of the cart told me that a moment before it had stood there beside the plane.

"Herr Kleffmann is glad to go, I think," Else said in a strained voice.

I couldn't blame him, but I wished I could have done something to compensate him for what had happened. He and his wife had been very good to Tubby. " All right, get the door closed," I said. I switched the lights on and for the first time I saw Saeton's face. It was streaked with mud and blood and the skin was quite white. His left arm hung limp at his side and blood trickled from his shot-pitted hand. " Sit down," I said.

He began to move towards the long line of seats that flanked the fuselage. Then he stopped and faced me again. " Neil. Can't we come to an arrangement?"

" No," I said. " You know damn well we can't."

" Because of Tubby?"

" Yes."

He grunted and pushed his hand across his face, smearing the blood. " It was necessary," he said heavily. " You made it necessary."

" It was cold-blooded murder," I said.

He shrugged his shoulders. " You left me no alternative. It's a pity you can't see the wider issues. What's one man's life against what we planned?"

" The man was your friend," I said.

" Do you think I enjoyed doing what I had to?" he said with a trace of anger. And then, almost to himself: " He took time to die and he knew what I was going to do as I pulled the pillow from under his head. I hated doing it. And I hated you for making me do it." My hand clenched round the butt of the revolver at his sudden violence. " Now it's done," he added, " why not leave it at that? Why make his death pointless?"

It was the same argument that he'd used before when he had been trying to stop me making that report. The man could see things only from the standpoint of his own ambition. " Sit down!" I said again and turned to Else. " You'll have to watch him. Do you know how to use one of these?"

She took the gun from me and examined it. " Is the safety catch on now or is it off?"

" It's off," I told her.

She nodded. " That is all I have to know. I understand how to use it."

Saeton had sat down now. " Sit over there," I told her. " And keep well away from him. If he moves from that seat, you're to shoot. You understand? Are you capable of firing just because a man moves?"

She glanced at Saeton. " You do not have to worry. I know how to shoot." Her hand had closed over the gun and she had the muzzle of it pointing towards Saeton. Her eyes were steady and her hand did not tremble. I knew she would fire if Saeton moved and I started forward towards the cockpit. But she put out her hand. " Are you all right, Neil? Do you need some help?"

" I'll be all right," I said.

She smiled and pressed my sound arm. " Good luck!" she whispered.

But I wasn't so sure I would be all right. When I had struggled into the pilot's seat a wave of dizziness came over me and I had to fight it off. The engines started without difficulty and I left them running to warm up whilst I went back to the navigator's table and worked out my course. It would be easy enough getting back to Berlin once I had got the plane into the air. What worried me was the airlift. I could go in above the lift-stream, but when I was over Berlin I should have to come down to the line of flight of the other planes. Somehow I'd have to fit myself into the pattern and with the weather closing in I might have to do this in cloud. There would be a big risk of collision then.

For a moment I sat there, fighting a growing weakness and the frightened emptiness of my belly. I needn't go in to Berlin. I could make for one of the base airfields—Wunstorf, or Celle, which was nearer, or I could fly north to Lübeck, which was nearer still. But I had no navigator and I was very conscious of the fact that I was in no fit state to pilot a plane. Lübeck was the better part of 150 miles away, nearly an hour's flying, whereas I could be in Gatow in twenty minutes.

I reached up to the throttle levers and revved the engines. It would have to be Gatow. I switched on the twin spotlights, released the brakes and taxied out to the runway end. As I swung the plane into position for take-off I called to Else: " All set? Have you fixed your safety belt?"

" Yes," she called back. " I am okay."

" Fine," I shouted and reached up to the throttle levers. Reaching up to control the engines stretched the muscles of my back and I bit my lip with the pain of my shoulder. My right hand was useless. To adjust the engines I had to let go of the control column. Again I was conscious of that feeling of emptiness in my stomach. I was a fool to try and fly in the state I was in. But there was no alternative. We had to get out of the Russian Zone.

The plane rocked and juddered as the engines revved. My eyes ran over the dials of the control panel. Everything was okay. I peered through the windshield. It was sheeting with rain now. The spotlights showed a few yards of weed-grown concrete streaming with water and then lost themselves in the steel curtain of the rain.

For a moment I hesitated, unwilling to commit myself to the take-off. Then, quickly, before reason could support my instinctive fear, I released the brakes and the plane began to move forward into the steel rods of the rain. The concrete came at me out of the murk and streamed beneath me, faster and faster. I braced my knees against the control column, steadying it as I adjusted the engines. Then the tail lifted and a moment later my hand was on the control column, pulling it back, pulling the plane up off the ground. Something slid away beneath us—it may have been a tree or the top of one of the ruined airfield buildings. After that I was alone in the lighted cockpit, riding smoothly through the inky blackness of the night, seeing nothing in the windshield but the water washing down it and the image of my own face, white in the glass.

I trimmed the engines and banked slowly on to my course, climbing all the time. At 7,000 feet I levelled out clear of the rain clouds in bright starlight and relaxed in my seat. I checked oil pressure and engine revs. Everything was okay. I felt drained of all energy. My eyelids closed for a second, and then I forced them open. It would be so easy to slip into unconsciousness. I fought off the faintness, holding myself against it as one does when one is tight and refusing to go under. I glanced at my watch. It was a quarter to five. By five o'clock I should be approaching Gatow. I was shivering with cold.

Once Else came through into the cockpit to see if I was all right. She looked tired and her eyes seemed very large in the pallor of her face. She held the gun firmly in her hand and her gaze was concentrated on the door to the fuselage as she spoke to me. " Is Saeton all right?" I asked her.

" Yes."

" Has he tried to move?"

" No. He do not try anything. I think he is dazed by what has happened. Also, he has lost much blood. He is very weak I think." She put her hand on my arm. " Can you land all right, do you think?"

" Yes," I said. " Better get back to your seat. And strap yourself in tight. I'll be going down in a few minutes."

She nodded. " Good luck, Neil!"

I didn't say anything and she went back into the fuselage. Below me I could just see the grey fluffy sea that marked the topside of the rain clouds. It was one thing piloting the plane up here in the clear, starlit night. But I had got to go down through that stuff. Somewhere, only a few minutes ahead of me, I had got to go down and contact a single square mile of ground through the impenetrable murk of the rain. The thought of it made me feel sick and I wished now that I had gone north to Lübeck. Maybe the weather would have been better at Lübeck. But I was committed now. It was no good turning back.

As I sat there in the cockpit, I was conscious of a growing sense of panic. To go on and on—that was all I wanted—to go on into infinity, into unconsciousness. Automatically I kept glancing at my watch. Just as automatically I pressed forward on the control column, as my watch came up to five, pushing the nose of the plane down. It was only years of operational training that enabled me to do that, for it was against all reason, against all the instinctive desire of mind and body. It meant action.

The clouds came up to meet me. From a flat sea of grey they became a tenuous, insubstantial drift of mist. Then the stars were blotted out and nothing was visible beyond the pulsating interior of the cockpit. I watched the altimeter dial— 6,000—5,500—5,000. Through my earphones I was picking up instructions from Gatow Airways to planes reporting over Frohnau: *Okay York 315. Channel A-able and call Controller.* And then another York was in my headphones reporting number and cargo at twenty miles. *York 270. Clear to Beacon.*

I pressed my A button for automatic radio tuning to Gatow Tower. *York 315. Clear to QSY. Channel D-dog and call Gatow director.*

Channel D-dog. That was Ground Control Approach! Things were bad down there. It meant ceiling zero and driving rain. It meant that I should have to do a controlled approach landing. I'd never done one before. I'd never been talked down in my life. We hadn't had those sort of aids when I had been flying on Ops. I cleared my throat and pressed my B button. "Hallo, Gatow Airways!" I called. "Hallo, Gatow Airways!"

Faint through the earphones came the answering voice from Gatow. *"Gatow Airways answering. Give your number and position please. Give your number and position please. Over."*

"Hallo, Gatow. I have no number. This is Saeton's Dakota returning from Hollmind. Fraser piloting. I am now levelling out at Angels Five and will give you my position from Frohnau beacon. Can you direct me in please? Over."

*"Gatow Airways answering. You cannot land at Gatow. I repeat, you cannot land at Gatow. Overshoot and proceed to Wunstorf. Proceed to Wunstorf. Acknowledge please. Over."*

A wave of dizziness caught me and for a moment I thought I was going to black out. Then it had passed. "Fraser answering. I must land at Gatow. I am injured. I must land at Gatow." I started to tell them what had happened to Tubby and how Saeton was wounded, but they cut me short. *"Overshoot and proceed to Wunstorf. I repeat: Overshoot and proceed to Wunstorf."*

"I cannot fly any farther," I cried desperately. "Am coming down. Repeat I am coming down."

There was a pause. Then: *"Okay, Fraser. Give your position, please."*

I looked quickly down at the instrument panel. The plane was fitted with a Sperry automatic pilot. "I am going back now to get M/F bearings on Frohnau and Gatow. Off."

I switched over to the automatic pilot and went back to the navigator's desk. I got the M/F bearings and found that my position was almost directly over Spandau. I moved back to the cockpit and in sliding into the pilot's seat wrenched my arm so that I had to bite back the scream of pain that came to my throat. Half-collapsed over the control column I called Gatow again: "Hallo, Gatow. Fraser calling. Am flying Angels Five directly above Spandau. Please direct me. Please direct me. Course now 085 degress. Please direct me. Over."

*"Hallo, Fraser. Keep flying your present height and course. I will direct you in a few minutes. Give speed and acknowledge. Over."*

" Speed 135," I answered. " I await your directions. Over."

I wiped the sweat from my forehead and disconnected the automatic pilot. Waves of nausea swept over me. My mind seemed a blank, unable to concentrate. Through the earphones came the sound of Gatow calling other planes. From the fuselage behind me I heard Saeton's voice call out, " Fraser! Are you in trouble?"

" No," I said. " No, I'm all right."

" If you want any help . . ."

But I didn't trust him. " I'm all right," I called back. " Don't flap." My throat felt dry. My tongue was like a piece of coarse flannel. I wanted to vomit.

" *Hallo, Fraser. Gatow Airways calling Fraser. Can you hear me? Over.*"

" Fraser answering. I hear you." My voice sounded weak and hoarse. *Oh God!* I breathed. *Let's get this over.*

" *GCA think they have located you. Channel D-dog and call Director.*"

" Roger, Gatow." I pressed my D button, my hand trembling and damp with sweat. " Hallo, Gatow Director. Fraser calling Gatow Director."

A new voice, much clearer, sounded in my earphones. " *Turn 180 degrees, Fraser. Turn 180 degrees.*"

" Roger, Director." I braced myself for the effort and shifted the control column, giving right rudder at the same time. The movement brought the sweat cold on my forehead again. I should never make it. I felt I just couldn't make it. The control column was heavy as lead. To work the rudder brought my shoulder in contact with the back of the seat. Pain seared through my neck and up into my head as I completed the turn and straightened out. God! This was going to be hell.

" *Thank you, Fraser,*" came the voice of the Director of Controlled Approach. " *I have now identified you. New course. Left on to 245 degrees and reduce height to 3,000. Acknowledge.*"

" Roger." I turned the plane on to its new course, my senses strained to catch the director's voice. I felt sick with the strain. If only I had done one of these landings before! A sheet of water lashed against the windshield. The plane bucketed violently, wrenching at my shoulder as I moved to maintain course, the control column thrust forward, my eyes fixed on the altimeter dial and the luminous circle of the compass where the needle hovered at 245.

Else touched my arm. "Are you all right, Neil? Can I do anything?"

"No," I said. "I'm all right. Just watch Saeton, that's all."

She wiped the sweat from my forehead with her handkerchief. "If you want me . . ."

"I'm all right," I almost screamed at her. "Strap yourself in. Go on. Fix your safety belt. We'll be going down in a minute."

She hesitated. Her hand touched mine—a caress, a wish that she could help—and then she was gone and I was alone with the voice of GCA saying, *"Right on to 250 degrees now, Fraser. Right on to 250. Speed should be 120 now. You're doing fine. You'll be into the glide path soon. How are you feeling?"*

"I'm feeling all right," I answered. I wasn't, but there was no point in telling him that my eyes found it difficult to focus on the instruments. The concentration was causing dizziness. *Hallo, York 270. Climb to 3,000 and return to base. Climb to 3,000 and return to base. Emergency landing ahead of you. Acknowledge. Over.* It was the voice of Gatow Director, clearing the way for me and almost immediately 270 acknowledged. Then GCA was calling me again: *"Right on to 252 degrees now, Fraser."* I shifted the rudder slightly and slid on to the new course. *"That's fine, Fraser. You're on the glide path now. Reduce speed to 100. Lower flaps and undercarriage. Two miles to touch-down. You're doing fine. Can you hear me? Over."*

"Yes, I can hear you," I answered.

A new voice came in: *"This is talk down. Don't acknowledge from now on. Check flaps and undercarriage. Reduce height by 500 feet per minute. Fine. Right two degrees. You're one and a half miles from touch-down now. You're fifty feet above the glide path. You're doing fine. Right on the glide path now. One mile to go. . . ."*

I could see nothing through the windshield—just my reflection, that was all. I stared at the instrument panel. The dials were blurred. I seemed conscious of nothing but the voice in my earphones. My whole body was tense, reacting to the GCA Director's instructions. The pain was blinding. My body

seemed one screaming hell of pain. It shot along my nerves
and jangled in my head like a burglar alarm. I could feel the
nerves of my brain stretched taut. And I prayed—*God, don't
let me black out now.*

". . . *Half a mile to go now. You're coming in a little too
steeply. You're below the glide path. Keep up, Fraser! Keep
up!*" I jerked at the control column, cursing blindly to keep
myself from screaming. "*That's fine. You're bang on now.
Left one degree. You're coming in to touch-down now. Start
to level out. You should be able to see the runway lights now.
Level out! Level out! Look ahead and land visual.*"

I jerked at the control column, peering through the streaming
windshield. A light showed—a row of lights. They were
blurred and unreal. I felt the plane sag. I had pulled it up
too hard. It sagged right down on to the lights, dropping on
its belly, heavily, uncontrollably. The wheels hit and I
screamed as the seat slashed up into my shoulder. For a
second we were airborne and instinctively I applied left rudder
and altered the position of the control column. We hit the
deck again. But this time we stayed there. I sagged over the
control column in a blinding sheet of pain and then I reached
for the brakes and applied them. The plane swung—right
rudder—but the wing dipped and suddenly we were pivoting
to a stop and I blacked out.

I couldn't have been out long, for when I came round, Else
was just coming through into the cockpit. "Are you all right,
Neil?"

I sat up slowly, feeling the stillness of the plane, the lack
of motion. Thank God! We were on the ground. I wiped the
cold sweat out of my eyes with the back of my hand. I was on
the floor and outside the plane I heard voices and the sound of
cars and then the roar of a plane landing close by. "Yes," I
said weakly. "I'm all right. What about you?"

"I had my safety belt fixed." She had knelt down beside me
and was loosening my collar. "You were wonderful, Neil.
Saeton said you were crazy to try it. He do not think you will
do it. I do not think he want you to do it. And when you have
done it he ask me . . ." She turned her head at a sound from
the open door of the fuselage. "They are coming now. You
will soon be in hospital and then you will be able to rest."

Figures appeared in the cockpit doorway. The faces were
blurred and I pushed my hand across my eyes. "What's all

this about, Fraser?" It was the Wing Co. Flying. "Because of you two planes have had to overshoot and return to base. You were told to proceed to Wunstorf . . ."

"Please," Else interrupted him. "He is hurt."

"It's his own fault," the wing commander snapped. "If he'd done as he was told——"

"He is hurt with a bullet," Else cut in. "How can he go on to Wunstorf? Now please let the doctor see him. He is very bad I think."

I caught hold of Else's arm with my left hand. "Help me to my feet," I said. She put her hands under my armpits and levered me up. I braced myself against the navigator's table, my eyes closed, fighting to maintain consciousness. The station commander appeared in the doorway. From very far away it seemed I heard him call for a medical orderly. Then he turned back to me. "Before you go off in the ambulance, Fraser, perhaps you'll explain the extraordinary message you gave Airways."

"What was that?" I asked uncertainly.

"Something about Carter having been murdered."

I pushed the sweat out of my eyes again. God! I felt weak. "He *was* murdered," I said. "Saeton killed him because he knew I would try to get him back from the Russian Zone. If I brought Carter back, then you would have to believe what I put in my report." My vision had cleared slightly and behind the station commander I saw the figure of Squadron Leader Pierce. "Do you believe me now?" I asked Pierce.

"Where's Saeton," he asked. "I thought you said you'd brought him back?"

"Why are you piloting the plane I let Saeton borrow?" the wing commander asked.

And then Pierce again: "What have you done with Saeton?"

Questions, questions, questions—why the devil couldn't they leave me alone? "You don't believe what I told you." My voice was shrill. "You don't believe me, do you? All right then." I pushed them out of the way, staggering blindly as I stumbled into the body of the plane. "Pierce," I called, standing over the blanketed figure of Tubby still strapped along the seats. "Take a look at that."

Pierce pulled back the blanket. There was a gasp and a short heavy silence. "So Carter was at your farmhouse at

Hollmind." He slowly put back the blanket. Then he turned to me and gripped my left arm. " I'm sorry, Fraser. I've been rather dense. Now. Where's Saeton?"

I looked round. I couldn't see him and I glanced at Else. " You were in charge of him. Where is he?" I asked.

She shrugged her shoulders. " I do not know. After you land I come straight to the cockpit. I do not trouble myself with him any more."

Pierce strode to the door. " Sergeant! You were the first here. Did anybody leave the plane?"

" Yes, sir," came the answer. " A big, powerful-looking man." There was a hurried exchange of words and then the sergeant added, " He commandeered one of the jeeps. Said he had something urgent to report. He was injured, I think, sir. Leastways, there was a lot of blood on 'im."

Pierce glanced at me. " Did Saeton do that?" He nodded to the figure huddled under the blanket.

" Yes," I said.

" Right. Sergeant! Take my jeep—find the man and arrest him. His name is Saeton." Pierce turned and pushed his way up the fuselage. A moment later I heard him on the R/T to Emergency, ordering them to signal R.A.F. Police to close all exit gates and patrol the standings where aircraft were parked.

Another plane thundered in down the runway. The station commander took my arm. " I'm sorry, Fraser. It seems we've all made a mistake. Now we'll get you to the M.O." He piloted me to the door. An ambulance was waiting. " Ah, there you are, Gentry. Fraser's hurt. Better get him across to the sick bay right away."

Else and the station commander helped me out of the fuse-lage. The rain drove in sheets across the runway lights. We were just moving across to the back of the ambulance when Pierce flung out of the plane shouting for a car. " What is it, Pierce?" the station commander called.

" Saeton," he shouted. " Control have just come through on the R/T. Plane 481—that's Saeton's Tudor—has just passed the tower, taxi-ing towards the runway. They've ordered him to stop, but he doesn't answer. They're calling an R.A.F. Regiment patrol car now."

We halted and our eyes were turned eastwards towards the purple lights of the perimeter track. Faintly through the driving rain the lights of an aircraft showed, swinging on the last turn, moving forward to line up at the runway end. The driving squalls of rain periodically wiped it out, but a moment later we caught the roar of its engines and twin spotlights came hurtling through the murk towards us, went roaring past us and swept up and on into the night, a single white light that dwindled and was lost almost instantly. In the moment of its hissing, thundering passage past us I had recognised Saeton's Tudor—my Tudor—the cause of Tubby's death.

I felt suddenly sick at heart at the thought of Saeton getting away with it. There were the engines, too. They were Tubby's work as much as his. "You must stop him," I said to the station commander. "Stop him!"

"Don't you worry," was the reply. "We'll get him. We'll send fighters up and force him down."

I felt sorry then. I had asked for a man-hunt and it seemed I was going to get it. I shivered violently and the M.O. hustled me into the ambulance. All the way to the sick bay I was thinking about Saeton, alone up there in the cockpit of his plane. He was injured, like I had been. But there was no comforting goal for him, nothing for him to try for. He would eventually black out and then. . . .

"It is best he go like this," Else said quietly.

I nodded. Perhaps it was best. But I couldn't help thinking about it. Where would he try to make for—Russia? One of the satellite countries? He could sell those engines to the Russians. He would be safe behind the Iron Curtain.

Again as though she had read my thoughts, Else said, "You do not have to worry about Saeton. He is gone behind the Iron Curtain. Now I must work to reproduce the engines that we of the West have lost. And you must help, Neil. You are the only person now who know what those engines are like."

I didn't say anything. I was only remembering that Saeton had fought in two wars for his country. He had murdered a man so that those engines would be produced in British factories. Surely he wouldn't barter them with the Russians for his life?

The M.O. wanted to put me straight to bed. But as soon as he had dressed my shoulder I insisted on being taken down to the Operations Room. He tried to make me remain in the sick bay, but somehow I couldn't face the thought of lying there, waiting for news. In the end he agreed to let me go, but before I left he gave me a dry overcoat and a blanket to wrap round me.

The Operations Room seemed crowded. There was the station commander and Pierce, the Wing Co. Flying and the I.O. Somebody tried to stop Else from coming in with me. I told him to go to hell, and then Harry Culyer was coming towards me. "I just been down to the mortuary with Di," he said. "She asked me to tell you how much she appreciated . . ." His voice trailed off. "She was pretty cut up, poor kid."

"What's the news of Saeton?" I asked.

"They've got fighter squadrons up searching for him."

The station commander turned at the sound of my voice. "We'll get him," he said. "The weather's clearing to the west."

"To the west?"

He nodded.

"He's flying westward?" I asked.

"Yes. One of our mobile radar outfits located him a few minutes back just south of Hanover."

"Then he did not go to Russia?" Else exclaimed.

"Of course not," I said.

"But why does he not go to the Soviet Zone? Is he so stupid he does not know he will be safe there? I do not understand."

It was impossible for me to explain to the satisfaction of her logical German mind why Saeton had turned his back on the East, so I let it go. I found a chair and slumped into it. Reports were coming in all the time on an R/T loudspeaker, but I didn't listen. It was squadron-to-base stuff—the fighters reporting back. I didn't want to listen. It was horrible to think of Saeton up there being hounded by a pack of fighters. And he could so easily have turned eastwards.

The minutes dragged slowly by. Five-thirty . . . six . . . six-thirty. Dawn was breaking over the airfield. And then suddenly there was a whoop and somebody's voice was crackling over the radio: "*I've got him now. Flying at 10,000 feet, course slightly north of west. He is now over the Scheldt estuary. Making for England, home and beauty, I should say. What do I do now? Over.*"

"Tell that boy to start heading him off, back into Germany," the station commander ordered. " And get the rest of the squadron up with him."

We followed it all in the R/T messages. In a moment the whole pack of them were buzzing round Saeton, beating him up, diving past his nose, flying just above him, trying to force him down and away from the coast. And I sat there and thought of Saeton alone there in the cockpit of the Tudor, his hand undressed and bleeding, and the fighters hurtling across the perspex so close that he could almost touch them. I could almost feel him wincing at each roar of a machine scraping at the paint of the aircraft. I remembered the pain I had suffered at each movement of the control column. God! It was horrible.

Intermittently the voice of a radio operator kept calling Saeton, ordering him to return to base, to return to Wunstorf. I sat rigid in my seat, expecting all the time to hear Saeton's voice come in. But he didn't answer. And as the minutes dragged by, the Operations Room, with its constant stream of instructions to planes coming in and the group of officers waiting, became unreal. In my mind I was there in the cockpit of the Tudor with Saeton. *He has turned north now. He has turned north. We are diving right across his nose, but we are making no impression. He won't turn back. The bastard won't alter course. What are your instructions please? We cannot fly any closer. Over.* The voice of the leader of the fighter squadron, excited, tensed up with the danger of the thing he was doing.

I didn't hear the reply. I was with Saeton, seeing him hunched over the control column, his face grey, the blood oozing between his fingers and sticky on the wheel. I could see him in my mind so clearly—solid and square, as immovable from his purpose as a bull who has seen the red of the matador's cloak. What was his purpose? What did he plan to do?

And as if in answer to my question the leader of the squadron came back on the air. *He's putting his nose down now. We're over the North Sea.* And then more excited. *He's going into a power dive. He's trying to shake us off. He's going straight down now. My God! No, it's all right. F for Freddie swept right across his nose, but he's clear now. Thought they'd tangle that time. I'm right on his tail now. He's diving on full power. Air speed 320. I'm keeping right on his tail. He's going straight down. We're at 5,000 now. Four—three—two. My God! Isn't he ever going to pull out? I don't think he can pull out. He can't possibly pull out.*

There was a pause then. The fighter was pulling out of his dive. I knew the rest of it before the squadron leader came back on the air. *I've just pulled out and am banking. The Tudor drove straight into the sea. There's a great column of water. It's settling now. Can't see anything of the plane. There's just some slick on the surface of the sea. That's all. He went straight in. Never pulled out of that dive. Went slap in. Am returning to base now. Am returning the squadron to base.*

There was a heavy silence in the Operations Room, broken only by the squadron leader's voice calling his aircraft into formation. In that silence I had a strange feeling of loss. One shouldn't have any sympathy for a man like Saeton—his ambition had outrun the bounds of our social code, he had killed a man. And yet . . . There had been something approaching greatness in him. He was a man who had seen a vision.

I shifted stiffly in my chair and found that Else's hand was gripping mine. Culyer was the first to speak. "Poor devil! He must have blacked out."

But I knew he hadn't blacked out. Else knew it, too, for she said, "He choose the best way." There was a note of admiration in her voice.

"I'm sorry it had to end like that," the station commander murmured. I think he was regretting his order to send fighters up.

I closed my eyes. I was feeling very tired.

"Fraser."

I looked up. Culyer was standing over me.

"You worked on those engines with Saeton, didn't you?" I nodded. I was too tired to speak.

"You know we were arranging for Miss Meyer here to get to work for us and the Rauch Motoren? Well, that's going to take time. Suppose we do a deal with the British? Suppose the two of you work on the project together?"

Still the engines! I wanted to say, "Damn the bloody engines." I wanted to tell him that they'd already cost the lives of two men. And then I looked up and saw Else watching me. There was excitement—a sort of longing in her eyes. And then I knew what the future was.

" All right," I said. " We'll work on it together."

Somehow that seemed to make sense—if we reproduced those engines for the West, then perhaps Saeton and Tubby would not have died for nothing. As soon as I had made the decision the tenseness inside me seemed to ease and I was relaxed for the first time in days. Else was smiling. She was happy. And despite the pain of my shoulder I think I was happy too.

### THE END

# HAMMOND INNES

"His work stands in a class by itself." *V. S. Pritchett*

**Atlantic Fury**
"For sheer physical authenticity and power of sustained and vivid imagery . . . stands almost *sans pareil* in sea-going literature. This powerful, storm-wracked, rock-hard novel demands to be judged by Conradian standards." *Peter Green, Bookman*

**Wreckers Must Breathe**
A tale of espionage, violence and the claustrophobic stress of life under the sea. "Hammond Innes deals magnificently with disaster." *Observer*

**The White South**
"I can still hear the roar of the ice as the great bergs close in upon those stranded men of the whaling fleet." *Daphne du Maurier*

**Maddon's Rock**
"As grim and thrilling as you could wish . . . Hammond Innes certainly knows how to describe storms at sea." *Oxford Mail*

**The Strode Venturer**
"Yes! A rip-roarer!—those action sequences at which he is so brilliant, the equatorial heat, the bubbling sea-bed, an outworn ship and a drunken skipper—Splendid!" *Richard Lister, Evening Standard*

**Dead and Alive**
The disappearance of a girl in the chaos of post-war Europe leads to a dangerous expedition among men who deal in violence and death. "Hammond Innes has an ability to make anything he touches excitingly readable." *Dennis Wheatley*

*All available in Fontana Books*

# HAMMOND INNES

"Hammond Innes is a writer who is a master of his craft —he earns my enjoyment as much as my respect." *John Connell*

## The Angry Mountain
"Begins under the evil shadow of terrorism in Czechoslovakia . . . reaches a magnificent climax on the slopes of Vesuvius in full eruption." *Sunday Times*

## The Land God Gave to Cain
"It is set along and beyond the construction camps of a great railway being driven yard by yard into the wastes of the Labrador . . . A first-class story, a highly authentic background—Hammond Innes scores on both counts." *Richard Lister, Evening Standard*

## Air Bridge
"Hammond Innes is in the forefront of modern writers of the straightforward action story. He achieves a masterly sense of urgency as the story rises to the climax." *Daily Telegraph*

## The Blue Ice
A desperate man searches for precious metals among the desolate mountains of Norway. "The description of the long, lonely ski trek is a masterpiece." *Manchester Evening News*

## The Wreck of the Mary Deare
"The ship and the sea that batters it emerge as dramatis personae in their own right." *Peter Quennell, Daily Mail* "People say people can't write stories any more. Tell that to Hammond Innes!" *John Metcalfe, Sunday Times*

## The Doomed Oasis
A searing story of present-day Arabia. "The writing shines as vivid and sharp as the desert sun." *Gavin Lyall*

*All available in Fontana Books*

# HAMMOND INNES

"A master story-teller." *Daniel George*

## The Strange Land
Morocco . . . stronghold of the turbulent Berbers. "Hammond Innes has a particularly fine feeling for landscapes . . . Really excellent." *Observer*

## The Killer Mine
An old tin mine on the bleak coast of Cornwall is the dramatic setting for Hammond Innes's story of up-to-date smuggling. "The final horrific scenes take some beating." *Sphere*

## The Trojan Horse
The vault of a famous city bank . . . rat-infested London sewers . . the hold of a destroyer—areas of danger, darkness and death. "Hammond Innes is a master of suspense." *Spectator*

## Attack Alarm
A story of the Battle of Britain, written 'under fire' on an aerodrome where the author was a young gunner. "Hammond Innes tightens suspense to the pitch of nightmare." *L. A. G. Strong*

## Campbell's Kingdom
"A fast and expertly-managed story . . . the Rockies, the squalid 'ghost towns' the oil-boring, the dam-building—these are memorably presented." *Sunday Times*

## The Lonely Skier
"From the first page we are gripped by that sense of tension, mystery and urgency that Hammond Innes so well commands." *Elizabeth Bowen*

*All available in Fontana Books*